I'LL GET YOU FOR THIS

. . .

THE PAW IN THE BOTTLE

. . .

JAMES HADLEY CHASE

Introduction by Nicholas Litchfield

STARK HOUSE

Stark House Press • Eureka California

I'LL GET YOU FOR THIS / THE PAW IN THE BOTTLE

Published by Stark House Press
1315 H Street
Eureka, CA 95503, USA
griffinskye3@sbcglobal.net
www.starkhousepress.com

ISBN: 979-8-88601-123-4

Cover design and layout by Mark Shepard, shepgraphics.com
Proofreading by Bill Kelly

First Stark House Press Edition: January 2025

Gore, Vengeance, Greed, and Betrayal, As Told By James Hadley Chase

by Nicholas Litchfield

Though very much a product of England, René Brabazon Raymond (1906–1985), best known by his pseudonym James Hadley Chase, found fame emulating the popular hardboiled crime fiction produced in America in the Thirties. He was thirty-three when his first effort, *No Orchids for Miss Blandish*, was published by Jarrolds in London in 1939. Allegedly written over six weekends in the summer of 1938, the novel would become an immediate bestseller—one of the biggest-selling books of the decade—spawning a well-reviewed stage play in the West End that subsequently ran for seven years on tour and a controversial movie adaptation that broke box office records in Britain (Murphy, 1989). It is said that the novel was "the most popular work of fiction read by the armed forces during World War II," with an estimated four million copies sold worldwide (Silet, 2003).

None of his subsequent books achieved the popularity of *No Orchids for Miss Blandish*, although he did pen numerous internationally bestselling novels. His infamous *Miss Callaghan Comes to Grief*, from 1941, considered a lurid account of the white slave trade, was labeled obscene and banned in Britain. Other notable books (*More Deadly Than the Male, Eve, Just Another Sucker*, and *One Bright Summer Morning*) attained major film treatments, and over thirty of his novels were adapted for French cinema.

Vicious conflict and tough guy talk course through much of his work, the stories "liberally sprinkled with hotcha blondes and lots of shooting" (Manning, 1941). Heroines suffer, blood gets spilled, and death comes in waves. Frequently, the book titles (*Do Me a Favour–Drop Dead, You're Lonely When You're Dead, You've Got It Coming, Hit Them Where it Hurts*) were as punchy as his two-fisted characters, and yet American audiences didn't always embrace his novels, and influential book critics like Anthony Boucher weren't easily won over by the author's mimicking of American speech and customs. "Mr. Chase is an exceedingly prolific and sensational novelist who pretends to the English public that he is a tough American. To the credit of American publishers and readers, most of his sterile and inept ersatz products have failed to appear in this country" (Boucher, 1950).

Apparently, René Raymond was nothing like the unsavory characters that populated his books. "He's got a wispy moustache, a slight stoop when he walks and, with his glasses on, he looks like a college professor," divulged a Pennsylvanian daily (Manning, 1941).

Beyond America, his work sold well, particularly in Europe, Africa, and Asia, and even his espionage novels, especially those featuring the tough, wily Paris-based spy Mark Girland, achieved commercial success. His impressive canon of work comprises ninety books, nearly all of which were translated into many languages (L.A. Times, 1985). The British newspaper *The Star* lauded him as "The most remarkable among British and American thriller writers." However, despite the notoriety his novels drew, there's a sense that his work hasn't endured as well as that of other writers of his era. As crime and mystery pundit Charles L.P. Silet puts it: "For all the controversy his fiction stirred up during his lifetime, the large number of books he wrote, and the successful movie adaptations of them, Raymond is among the least read and least appreciated of postwar British crime writers" (Silet, 2003).

Over the past twelve years, Stark House Press has fronted a revival of Raymond's work, reissuing sixteen of his novels, with this latest twofer showcasing a couple of slick 1940s crime yarns. They are surprisingly dissimilar and highlight the author's keenness to exhibit work that in no way resembled *No Orchids for Miss Blandish*.

The first, *I'll Get You for This*, was originally published under the author's pseudonym James Hadley Chase by Jarrolds of London, England, in 1946 and reprinted in the U.S. by Avon in 1951. In keeping with his other early novels, this, too, was made into a feature film (titled *Lucky Nick Cain*). Actor George Raft played the lead, and William Rose, screenwriter of the excellent *The Ladykillers* and *Guess Who's Coming to Dinner*, co-wrote the screenplay. Though filmed on the Italian Riviera and London, in the book, the setting is Paradise Palms, a fictitious town about seventy miles from Miami. It's an affluent, picturesque place with beaches that are heaving with pretty women. Alas, it turns out that it's also an unsafe place, full of shady politicians, lawbreakers, killers, and racketeers.

The disreputable main protagonist, wiseguy Chester Cain, fits right in, although his naivety paints a big target on his back. Handsome, self-assured, and fearless, he has twenty thousand dollars in life savings and an interest in relocating to the area. Recently out of the army, he's killed five men in the last four months, claiming self-defense, and amassed his fortune working the gambling joints of New York.

When casino owner Don Speratza invites him to his establishment and plies him with copious booze and a beautiful female companion—the curvaceous blonde, Miss Wonderly, with "breasts like Cuban pineapples"—Chester has a right to be suspicious. Lust and greed get the better of him, though, and his cocky arrogance traps him in a tricky situation. John Herrick, an elected politician running for reelection, winds up murdered, and evidence implicates Chester in the crime. Managing to elude the police, he goes on the run but with a plan to uncover the real culprit and exact revenge, hence the book's title.

Written in a breezy style, without literary embellishments or much emphasis on character, the novel becomes a brisk, pulpy tale of vengeance, with entertainingly crafted scenes of violence, gunplay, and savage fistfights. Highly proficient in pounding out novels at lightning speed, you get the feeling that Raymond might actually have typed *I'll Get You for This* in a couple of days rather than six weekends. Despite its derivative plot, a memorable prison breakout and a couple of exciting, if strikingly gory, scenes elevate the novel. Raymond also instills his central character with smart alec humor to good effect. It's the Carter Brown kind, although Raymond wisely uses it more economically.

John Betjeman, noted book reviewer for the *Daily Herald* wrote glowingly: "The plot is cunning and intricate, the atmosphere sustained and terrifying, the characterisation never falters." Although *I'll Get You for This* is one of his more famous books, Betjeman's praise feels more suited to *The Paw in the Bottle,* the second novel in this volume, an underrated drama that the well-known British newspaper *The Observer* deemed "Genuinely tense."

Initially published by Jarrolds in 1949 under another of the author's many pen names, Raymond Marshall, it was reprinted by Hamilton in 1961 under the Chase pseudonym. Set in London in the Forties, it's a deeply absorbing tale of greed and betrayal with some delightful plot twists, impressively layered characters, and brilliant black humor.

When vain, self-seeking, money-driven Julie Holland, a 22-year-old woman living just above the poverty line, catches the eye of Sam Hewart, she's motivated to join a world of seedy, small-time crooks. Sam is the owner of the Bridge Café, a known hangout for gangsters, where robberies are planned and crimes brokered. Julie, though wary of associating with underworld villains and attracting unwanted police attention, is desperate to escape poverty, and the good wages and tips given for circulating messages between thieves secure her services. Alas, her stunning looks entice the dashing, well-dressed ladies' man Harry Gleb, who's part of a gang that are planning a high-risk burglary. Harry is "hard, without scruples, shallow, cocky and selfish," and so he's a fairly good match for the fickle, sly, avaricious Miss Holland.

Though deeply attracted to each other, it's a union destined for failure. Harry wants her to accept a job as a maid working for a ludicrously rich married couple living in the swanky Mayfair district. The homeowner is Howard Wesley, an aircraft designer on the verge of a major aviation breakthrough, and his wife is the once-popular musical comedy actress Blanche Turrell. There is a safe in their home that houses a stunning collection of mink furs worth thirty thousand dollars. Several botched theft attempts have persuaded people to regard the safe as impossible to crack. Harry's gang, considering themselves smarter than other thieves, believes all they need is an inside woman to study the safe and share her findings.

The job feels like a fool's errand, with a bounty that isn't worth the risk, and the woman they lure into their scheme, though smart and crafty, is the inevitable weak link in a poorly planned caper. That said, it turns out there are plenty of weak links among the suckers and sadists, philanderers and phonies loitering throughout the book, wreaking havoc on each other's lives and ultimately sabotaging their own best interests.

In contrast to the furious pace and ugly brutality of *I'll Get You for This*, *The Paw in the Bottle* is a measured, suspenseful, dryly amusing examination of the social classes in England, where sin and wrongdoing are not exclusive to the lower strata, and where some people are too clever for their own good. While both are highly entertaining, enduring tales, they feel like they were written by different authors. Together, they are a testament to the author's extraordinary versatility and capacity to continually find ways to excite, intrigue, shock, and delight his legions of fans.

—November 2024
Rochester, NY

....

Nicholas Litchfield is the founder of the literary magazine *Lowestoft Chronicle* and editor of twelve literary anthologies. His stories, essays, and book reviews appear in various magazines and newspapers, including *BULL*, *Colorado Review*, *Daily Press*, *Pennsylvania Literary Journal*, *Shotgun Honey*, *The Adroit Journal*, *The MacGuffin*, *The Virginian-Pilot*, and *Washington Square Review*. He has written introductions to numerous books, including twenty-one Stark House Press reprints of long-forgotten noir and mystery novels. Formerly a book critic for the *Lancashire Post*, syndicated to twenty-five newspapers across the U.K., he now writes for *Publishers Weekly*. You can find him online at NicholasLitchfield.com or Twitter: @NLitchfield.

Works Cited

Boucher, Anthony, 1950. "Reports on Criminals at Large: Spook Sonata Fruity Import Nero and …" *The New York Times*, October 15: BR21.

Silet, Charles L. P., 2003. "James Hadley Chase (24 December 1906-6 February 1985)." British Mystery and Thriller Writers Since 1960, edited by Gina MacDonald, pp. 81-89. Dictionary of Literary Biography Vol. 276, Detroit : Gale Group, 2003.

Murphy, Robert, 1989. Realism and Tinsel: Cinema and Society in Britain 1939-49, p. 210, London: Routledge, 1989.

L.A. Times, 1985. "James Hadley Chase; Prolific Mystery Writer." L.A. Times, Feb. 7.

Manning, Paul, 1941. "London's Night Life Picks Up." Public Opinion, November 5: p.9.

I'LL GET YOU FOR THIS . . .

JAMES HADLEY CHASE

Chapter One
FALL GUY

1

They had told me that Paradise Palms was a pretty nice spot, but when I saw it, I was knocked for a loop. It was so good I stopped the Buick to gape at it.

The town was built along the semi-circular bay with its miles of golden sand, palm trees and green ocean. The buildings were compact, red roofed with white walls. Tree-lined avenues led into the town from four directions. Flower-beds decorated the sidewalks. Every tropical flower, tree and plant grew in the streets, and the effect was like a dream in Technicolor. The colours hurt my eyes.

After I'd stared at the flowers, I concentrated on the women, driving in big luxury cars or walking along the sidewalks, or even riding bicycles. It was as good as an Earl Carroll show. There wasn't a woman who hadn't stripped down to the bare essentials. My eyes hadn't over-eaten themselves like this in years.

As a curtain-raiser for a vacation, it couldn't have been better. And that's what I was on: a vacation. Four months of working the gambling joints in New York had been a pretty hard grind. When I had acquired a roll of not less than twenty grand I had promised myself a real vacation with all the trimmings. By the time I'd saved fifteen, I nearly threw it up, but, somehow, I kept on, in spite of the bags under my eyes, a couple of bullet wounds and a flock of opposition. You don't win twenty grand without making enemies. I made plenty. It got so bad that I was driving around in an armoured car, putting newspapers on the floor around my bed so no one could get at me without waking me, and toting a gun, even in my bath.

I got my roll and I got a reputation. They said I was the fastest gun-thrower in the country. Maybe I was, but I didn't tell anyone that I practised two hours a day, wet or shine. I killed guys, but it wasn't murder. Even the cops said so, and they should know. Every time I killed a guy I made sure he had the drop on me first, and I had witnesses to prove it. I'd worked it so I could pull a gun and shoot before the other guy could squeeze his trigger. That wanted a lot of doing; it meant hard work, but I stuck at it, and it paid dividends.

I was never even arrested.

I had acquired my roll, bought the Buick, and here I was, ready for a vacation in Paradise Palms.

While I was gaping at the women, a traffic cop came over. He actually saluted me.

"You can't park here, sir," he said, resting his foot on my running board.

Imagine: a cop calling me "sir".

"I've just blown in," I said, starting my engine. "It's taken my breath away. Boy! This certainly looks good."

The cop grinned. "It gets you, don't it?" he said. "I gaped plenty when I first arrived."

"It sure does," I said. "Look at those dames. They make me feel I have X-ray eyes, and that's something I've always wanted. I'm scared to look away in case I miss something."

"You should see 'em on the beach," the cop said wistfully. "They're no more self-conscious than a tree."

"That's the way I like my women."

"So do I," the cop said, shaking his head, "but it doesn't add up to anything here, except a strained eyesight and a stiff neck."

"You mean they're hard to make?"

He whistled. "Takes a piano mover to throw 'em over."

"I'm good at moving pianos," I said, and asked him where I could find Palm Beach Hotel.

"Some joint," he said, sighing. "You'll like it there; even the food's good," and he gave me directions.

I reached the hotel in two or three minutes, and the reception I got would have satisfied Rockefeller himself. A flock of bellhops grabbed my luggage, somebody drove the Buick to the hotel garage, and a couple of pixies, dolled up in blue and gold fancy dress, would have carried me up the steps if I'd let them, and if they'd had the strength.

The reception clerk did everything except go down on his hands and knees and knock his head on the floor.

"We're delighted to have you here, Mr. Cain," he said, handing me the register and a pen. "Your rooms are ready, and if you're not satisfied with the view you have only to let me know."

I wasn't used to this line of treacle, but I made out that I was. I told him I was pretty fussy about views, and the one he'd arranged for me had better be good.

It was good. I had a private balcony, a sitting-room and a bedroom with a bathroom attached that only Cecil B. de Mille could have designed.

I went out on the balcony and looked across the beach, the palms and the ocean. It was terrific. To my left, I could look into some of the other rooms of the hotel. The first one I looked into was as good as a peep-show you sometimes find in a back street in New York; only it had more class. The dame was an eye-stopper. She was wearing a couple of dumbbells in either hand. Maybe she called it exercising in the nude. I caught her eye. Before she ducked out of sight, her smile said: "We could have fun together, big boy."

I told the reception clerk who'd come up with me that the view was swell.

When he had gone, I went back onto the balcony, hoping to see some more of the dumbbells, but I'd seen all there was to see.

I hadn't been out on the balcony more than three minutes before the telephone rang. I answered it, thinking maybe it was a wrong number.

"Mr. Cain?"

I said as far as I knew it was.

"Welcome to Paradise Palms," went on the voice: a rich, fruity baritone with a dago accent. "This is Speratza talking. I manage the Casino Club. I hope you'll come over. We've heard about you."

"You have?" I said, pleased. "That's swell. Sure, I'd like to come over. I'm on vacation, but I still gamble."

"We have a fine place here, Mr. Cain," he said, goodwill oozing from every pore. "You'll like it. How about tonight? Can you make it?"

"Sure. I'll be over."

"Ask for me: Don Speratza. I'll see you're fixed good. You got a girl?"

"Not right now, but there seem to be plenty kicking around."

"But not all of them are obliging, Mr. Cain," he said, laughing. "I'll fix you with one who knows her way around. We want you to have a good time while you're with us. We don't often have such a celebrity. You leave the girl to me. You won't be disappointed."

I said it was pretty nice of him and hung up.

About ten minutes later the telephone rang again. This time it was a bass voice that said it belonged to Ed Killeano. I didn't know any Ed Killeano, but I said I was glad he had called.

"I heard you were in town, Cain," the voice said. "I want you to know we're glad to have you here. Anything I can do to make your stay a pleasant one be sure to let me know. The hotel will tell you where you can find me. Have a good time," and before I could think of anything to say he rang off.

I was human enough to call the desk and ask who Ed Killeano was. They told me in a hushed voice that he was the City Administrator. They made it sound like he was Joe Stalin.

I thanked them and went back to the balcony.

The sun shone on the golden beach, the ocean sparkled, and the palms nodded their heads in the lazy breeze. Paradise Palms still looked wonderful, but I was beginning to wonder if it was too good to be true.

I had a hunch that something was cooking.

2

I drove down Ocean Drive. The traffic was heavy, and I moved slowly, the damp, salt smell of the sea in my nose, the pounding of the surf in my ears.

It was the kind of night you read about in books. The stars looked like diamond dust on blue velvet.

Two blocks further up I came upon a lighted drive that led to a big building with one of those fancy fronts made of marble or glass or porcelain or something—a kind of powder blue with "Casino" in sizable letters on a ledge at the top of the first floor. The whole building was lit by indirect lighting, and the over-all effect was pretty nice.

The Negro doorman's brass buttons gleamed in the light. He pulled open the door of the Buick, and another Negro stepped forward to drive the car to the garage.

I walked in under the blue canopy and found myself in a corridor lined on both sides with discreet private dining-rooms with numbers on the doors. At the other end of the corridor was an arch and beside it was the booth occupied by a blonde hat-check girl.

"Check, Mister?" she asked nasally.

I wolfed her over. She was wearing a tight little bodice in sky blue satin, open all the way down the front and laced together loosely by black silk cords. Apparently she had nothing on under the bodice. It was one of those outfits that keeps everyone warm except the wearer.

I gave her my hat and a friendly leer.

"That's a nice view you have there," I said courteously.

"The night some guy doesn't make that crack I'll drop down dead," she returned, sighing. "It's part of my job to have a nice view."

I paused to light a cigarette. "A view to what?" I asked.

"No dice. That gag's transparent with age."

"Sorry," I said. "I don't often come to a joint like this. I'm a home lover, and one gets kind of old-fashioned in life's little backstreams."

She looked me over and decided I was harmless. "That's all right by me," she said, smiling. "I like variety. The trouble here is that all men seem cast in the same mould."

"But surely some are more mouldy than others?" I said.

She giggled. Three men came up to check their hats, so I drifted on through the arch into as sweet a night club layout as you would wish to see, done in pastel shades with indirect lighting and with a beautiful crescent-shaped bar on one side. It was a terrific room with a place for an orchestra and small dance floor made of some composition that looked like black glass. Out of the floor, out of blue and chromium boxes, grew banana trees with broad green leaves and clusters of green bananas. Vines clung to the trunks of the trees, bearing fragile blossoms; pink, orange, bronze and henna. Half the room had no roof and overhead were stars.

A fat bird came up to me and gave me the teeth, which was supposed to mean he was glad to see me. He wore patent-leather shoes, dark trousers, a Dubonnet-red cummerbund and a white drill coat tailored like a mess jacket.

"Give me Speratza," I said.

He gave me the rest of the teeth, including a couple of gold inlays.

"I am the manager, please," he said. "Is there something I can do?"

"Yeah," I said. "Drum up Speratza. Tell him Chester Cain has blown in."

If I'd said I was King George VIth I couldn't have got a faster double-take.

"A thousand apologies for not recognizing you, Mr. Cain," he said, bowing in half. "Señor Speratza will be enchanted. I will have him informed you have arrived." He swung round and signalled frantically to a dressed-up dummy who was posed by the bar. The dummy shot away like he had a rocket in his pants. It was a pre-arranged, regal routine, and it impressed me as it was meant to impress me.

"Nice place you have here," I said for something to say. I was only giving him half my attention. The other half was reeling under the impact of the women in the joint. They were something to see. Even a horse would look over his shoulder at them. A dark woman in a red dress drifted past as I was about to compliment him further. She stopped me in mid-stride. She had the most provocative walk I had ever seen. Her hips were sheathed in this red silk, pulled so taut that light rippled over the fabric as she moved. They flowed under the dress like heavy and seductive liquid, like molten metal.

"We hope you'll like it here, Mr. Cain," he was saying, as if he'd rushed around and built the place as soon as he'd heard I was coming. "May I introduce myself? Guillermo at your service. Would you care for a drink?"

I tore my eyes away from the woman's hips and said I was glad to know him and a drink would be swell.

We went over to the bar and put our feet on the elegant brass rail. The bar was glistening and spotless but the barman hustled up and wiped it mechanically, his eyes on Guillermo.

"What'll it be?" said Guillermo.

"A little bourbon, I guess," I said.

The barman gave me three inches of the finest bourbon I'd ever encountered. I said as much.

At this moment a tall man with a terrific torso appeared at my side.

"Señor Speratza," Guillermo said, and faded out of the picture.

I turned and looked the newcomer over. He had everything in the way of good looks a man could want. He was as big as a house, his eyes were black and the whites of them like porcelain. His hair was rather long and curled a little over his temples. His skin was cream-rose. He was really handsome in a Latin way.

"Mr. Cain?" he said, offering his hand.

"Sure," I said, and shook hands.

He had a grip like a bear's, but then so have I. We cracked each other's bones and pretended we weren't hurting each other.

He said how pleased he was to meet me, and how he hoped I'd enjoy my stay at Paradise Palms.

I admired his place and told him they had nothing like it in New York. That seemed to please him.

By that time I'd finished my bourbon, and he called the barman.

"Two," he said. "Take a good look at Mr. Cain because I want you to remember him. Whatever he wants is on the house, including his whole party."

The barman nodded and gave me a quick up-and-down, and I could tell there wasn't a chance he would ever mistake me for anybody else.

"All right?" Speratza asked, beaming at me.

"Swell," I said.

"I don't know what your plans are, Mr. Cain," he went on, after we had dipped into the bourbon, "but if you want a little relaxation and a mild gamble, you could do worse than spend some of your time here."

"That's just what I do want," I said. "I'm figuring on a quiet time, and a little company when I feel that way." I fiddled with my glass and then went on, "I don't want to sound ungrateful, but frankly, I'm a little puzzled by all this attention."

He laughed. "You're modest, Mr. Cain," he said, shrugging. "Why even in this little place, far from anywhere, we've heard of you. We're glad to offer hospitality to such a successful gambler."

"I appreciate it," I said, and shot him a hard look. "But I'd like to get this on record for all that. I'm on vacation: that means I'm not working. I wouldn't be interested in any proposition from anyone. I don't suggest that I am going to be propositioned, but this build-up is a little overwhelming. I don't kid myself that I'm all that important. So pass the word around. I'm not in the market for anything except a vacation, and persuasion makes me mad. So if you still want to entertain me, go ahead, but it's all right by me if you want to put up the shutters and send me home."

He laughed silently and easily as if I'd cracked the funniest gag in the world.

"I assure you, Mr. Cain, you won't be propositioned. This town is small but very rich. We're hospitable people. We like distinguished visitors to have a good time. All we want is for you to relax and enjoy yourself."

I thanked him and said I would.

But in spite of his smoothness and his easy laugh, I had a feeling that he was jeering at me.

3

After we had chit-chatted a while, and had worked through some more of the bourbon, Speratza said he guessed I was about set to enjoy myself, and how about a girl?

"Well, how about her?" I said.

"I've asked Miss Wonderly to look after you," he told me, showing his big white teeth in a knowing smile. "I'll have her come over. If she's not quite your type, say so, and I'll introduce you to some of the others. We have a lot of girls working for us, but Miss Wonderly rates high with us."

I said I hoped Miss Wonderly would rate high with me.

"I'll be surprised if she doesn't," he returned, and with another smile of goodwill, he set off across the restaurant.

I looked after him and wondered how much longer it would be before he or whoever it was behind this civic welcome would demand payment. I was as sure as I could be that someone was sweetening me for a shake-down of some description.

A tall, distinguished man with white hair and a dark strong face had been looking at me. He was standing alone at the far end of the bar. He looked like a judge or a doctor or a lawyer, and his tuxedo looked like it had been cut by an angel.

I saw him beckon to the barman and say something to him. The barman gave me a quick look, nodded and turned away. The white-headed man came over to me.

"I understand you are Chester Cain," he said curtly.

"Sure," I said.

He didn't seem friendly so I didn't offer to shake hands.

"I'm John Herrick," he said, looking straight at me. "You haven't heard of me, but I have heard of you. Frankly, Mr. Cain, I'm sorry to see you here. I understand you are on vacation and I only hope it is true. If it is, then I hope you won't stir up trouble here."

I stared at him. "Thank God someone's sorry I've arrived," I said. "I was getting to think my welcome was genuine."

"This town has enough trouble without importing wild gunmen," Herrick returned quietly. "I suppose it would be too much to ask you to give us no cause to complain?"

"You've got me wrong," I said, laughing at him. "I'm not so wild. And listen, so long as I'm left alone, I'm the nicest guy on earth. It's only when people start crowding me that I get nervous, and when I'm nervous maybe I do get a little wild."

He regarded me thoughtfully. "Forgive me for being so blunt, Mr. Cain. I am sure if you were left alone you would behave as well as anyone of us. But I think it might be as well if you changed your mind about staying in Paradise Palms. I have a feeling that someone will crowd you before long."

I looked down at the bourbon.

"I've got the same feeling," I said, "but I'm sticking around for all that."

"I'm sorry to hear that, Mr. Cain," he said. "You may easily regret your decision."

I felt Speratza at my elbow.

Herrick turned abruptly away and walked across the room and out into the lobby.

I looked at Speratza and he looked at me. There was just a flicker of doubt in his eyes that told me he was uneasy.

"That was not one of the Welcome Committee," I said.

"You don't have to worry about him," Speratza said, flashing on his smile. It cost him something, but he did it. "He's running for election next month." He pulled a little face, and added, "On a Reform ticket."

"Seems anxious to keep Paradise Palms a nice clean town," I said dryly.

"All politicians have platforms," Speratza said, shrugging. "No one takes him seriously. He won't get in. Ed Killeano is the people's choice."

"That's nice for Ed Killeano," I said.

We looked at each other again, and then Speratza waved.

A girl came across the room towards us. She was wearing a bolero for a dinner jacket of blue crêpe. Her skirt, split eight inches up the side, was of blue crêpe, too, but her blouse was red. She was a blonde, and I bet every time she passed a graveyard the corpses sat up to whistle after her.

By the time I'd recovered my breath, she was standing at my side. Her perfume was Essence Imperiale Russe (the perfume that quickened the pulse of kings). I can't begin to describe what it did to my pulse. Speratza was looking at me anxiously.

"Miss Wonderly," he said, and raised his eyebrows.

I looked at her and she smiled. She had small glistening teeth as white as orange pith.

"Suppose you let Miss Wonderly and me get acquainted?" I said, turning back to Speratza. "I think we'll get along fine together."

He looked so relieved that I laughed.

"That's fine, Mr. Cain," he said. "Maybe we'll see you in a little while upstairs. We have four roulette tables or we could make up a game of poker for you."

I shook my head.

"Something tells me I won't be gambling tonight," I said, and taking

Miss Wonderly's arm I walked with her over to the bar.

Out of the corner of my eye I saw Speratza go off, and then I gave the whole of my attention to Miss Wonderly. I thought she was terrific. I liked the long wave of her hair, and her curves—particularly her curves. Her breasts were like Cuban pineapples.

"This calls for a drink," I said, beckoning to the barman. "What part of Paradise did you escape from?"

"I didn't escape," she said, laughing, "I'm out on parole, but thought it was just another job. I know different now."

The barman looked at us.

"What'll you have?"

"A green parrot," she said. "It's Toni's special."

"Okay," I said to the barman. "Make it two."

While the barman was fixing the drinks, I said, "So you don't think it's just another job?"

She shook her head. "I read character," she said. "I'm going to have fun with you."

I winked at her. "That's only half of it. What shall we do? I mean, let's map out a programme."

"We'll have a drink, then dinner, then dance, then we'll go to the beach and swim. Then we'll have more drinks and then—"

"Then—what?"

She fluttered her eyelashes.

"Then we'll see."

"That sounds exciting."

She pouted.

"Don't you want to dance with me?"

"Sure," I said.

I had a feeling I wasn't going to move a piano tonight.

The barman put down two large glasses, three-quarters filled with green liquid. I made a move to reach for my roll, but he had already gone.

"I can't get used to this on-the-house business," I said, picking up the glass.

"You will," she said.

I took a long gulp at the drink, and hurriedly put the glass on the counter. I clutched at my throat, coughed and closed my eyes. The stuff seemed to explode in my stomach, but a moment later I felt like I was sitting on a cloud.

"Phew! That stuff kind of sneaks up on you," I said, when I could speak.

"Toni's very proud of it," she said, sipping her drink. "It's wonderful! I feel it going right down to my toes."

By the time we'd finished the green parrots we were behaving like we'd known each other for years.

"Let's eat," she said, sliding off the stool, and taking my arm. "Guillermo has a special dinner for you." She squeezed my arm and smiled up at me. Her eyes were frankly inviting.

Guillermo was there to see us into our seats. Above us were the stars. A warm breeze came in from the sea. The orchestra was playing a dreamy melody, and trumpets rolled muted notes like balls of quicksilver, round and smooth. The food was as incredibly good as the wine that went with it. We didn't have to bother to say what we wanted. The food came, we ate and marvelled at it.

Then we danced. The floor was not overcrowded, and we swept around in wide circles. It was like dancing with Ginger Rogers.

I was thinking that this was the best evening I'd ever spent when I spotted a thick-set man in a green gaberdine suit who was standing near the band. He had a flat, evil-looking puss, and he was watching me with a vicious gleam in his eyes. When he caught my eye, he turned abruptly and ducked out of sight behind a curtained exit.

Miss Wonderly had seen him, too. I felt the muscles in her back stiffen, and she missed step so I nearly stubbed her toes. She broke away from me.

"Let's swim," she said abruptly, and walked towards the lobby, keeping her face averted.

I caught a glimpse of her in a mirror.

She was pale.

4

I drove along the coast road to Dayden Beach, a lonely strip of sand and palms a few miles from the Casino.

Miss Wonderly sat by my side. She was humming a tune under her breath, and she seemed to have shaken off her depression.

We coasted along in the moonlight. It was hot, but the breeze from the ocean came in through the open windows of the Buick.

"We're nearly there," Miss Wonderly said. "Look, you can see it now."

Ahead was a ring of palms close to the surf. There was no sign of life, and it looked good.

I drove the Buick off the road and down on to the sand until it turned too soft, then I stopped, and we got out.

In the far distance I could see the bright lights of Paradise Palms, and could hear the faint sound of music. The night was still, and sounds carried easily.

"Pretty nice," I said. "What shall we do?"

Miss Wonderly had pulled up her skirt to her knees, and began to roll down her stockings. Her legs were slim and muscular. "I'm going in," she said.

I went around to the back of the car, unlocked the boot and took out a couple of towels and my trunks. It took me less than two minutes to shed my clothes. The warm breeze against my skin felt swell. I came around the Buick. Miss Wonderly was waiting for me. She was in her white brassiere and pants.

"That's a hell of a swim suit," I said.

She said I was right, and took them off.

I didn't look at her.

We walked across the strip of sand, hand in hand. The sand was hot, and we sank in up to our ankles. I eyed her as we began to wade through the surf. A sculptor could have cast her in bronze for a perfect thirty-four, and he'd never have to do anything more about it. I was surprised I could take her so calmly.

We swam out to a moored raft. The sea was warm, and when she hoisted herself on to the raft, she looked like a sprite from the ocean bed.

I floated around the raft so I could study her in the moonlight. I've known plenty of women in my day, but she was a picture.

"Don't," she called; "you're making me shy." I came up on to the raft and sat beside her.

"It's all right," I said.

She looked at me over her shoulder, then leaned against me. Her back was warm, but the tiny drops of water on her skin felt cold against me.

"Tell me the story of your life," she said.

"It wouldn't interest you."

"Tell me."

I grinned at her. "Nothing happened much until I went into the Army. I came back from France with a lot of sharp-shooting medals, a beautiful case of shell-shock and an itch to gamble. No one wanted me. I couldn't get a job. One day I got into a poker game. I kept in that poker game for three weeks. We shaved, ate and drank at the table. I made five grand, and then someone got mad. I hit him with a bottle, and he pulled a gun on me. Guns don't scare me. I was in the Ardennes push. Anything that a punk gambler starts after that is kid's stuff. I took the gun away and beat the guy soft with it. We went on playing with him under the table. We used him as a rug."

She crossed her arms over her breasts and kicked the water gently. "Tough guy," she said.

"Uh huh," I said. "I didn't like that gun. It made me think. One of these days, I thought, some guy will pull a gun on me, and he'll know how to use it. So I bought myself a gun. I wanted to be better at gun-play than anyone else. You see, after messing around in the Army you get a kind of pride in doing things better than the next guy. I stuck in a room in a tenth-rate hotel and practised pulling the gun from my belt and pulling the trigger. I did that six hours a day for a week. I guess I got smooth. I haven't met a guy yet who can draw faster than I can. That week's work saved my life five times."

She shivered. "They said you were ruthless, but now I've seen you, I don't believe it."

"I'm not," I said, and put my hand on her thigh. "I'll tell you what happens. A punk comes along who thinks he's a world beater. He thinks there's no one as good as he is. Maybe he's slap-happy or drunk or something. I don't know. But whatever it is, he thinks he's so good that he must prove it to everyone. No one cares whether he's good or not, but the punk doesn't understand that. So what does he do? He looks around for a guy with a reputation, and he calls on the guy and starts trouble. He reasons that when he's licked this guy, he'll stand ace-high. And he usually picks on me." I swirled the water with my feet. "I take everything he gives me, because I know I can beat him any time I want, and I don't care for killing guys. There's no sense in it. So I sit there and let him rib me. Maybe I'm wrong, because it encourages him, and he goes for his gun. Then I have to kill him because I'm fond of myself in my odd way, and I don't want to die. Then people say I'm ruthless, but they're wrong. I've been crowded, and I can't help myself."

She didn't say anything.

"And it's going to happen here," I went on. "Some smart punk in this town thinks he's good, and he's arranged an elaborate set-up to show this town that he can pull a fast one on me. He's getting me into a position so he can crowd me. I don't know who he is or when he's going to start, but I know that's what's going to happen, and something tells me that you are in this too." I smiled at her. "But whether you know what's in the wind, or whether you're just part of the extravagant trimmings, remains to be seen."

She shook her head. "You're crazy," she said. "Nothing's going to happen."

"That still doesn't tell me whether you're for me or against me," I said.

"I'm for you," she said.

I put my arm around her and swung her legs across mine so she was sitting on my lap. She leaned against my chest, her hair, damp and perfumed, against my cheek.

"I knew it would be fun with you," she said.

I took her chin between my finger and thumb and raised her face. She closed her eyes. She looked white, like a beautiful porcelain mask in the moonlight. I looked down at her, then I kissed her. Her lips tasted salty. They were firm and cool and good. We stayed like that while the raft rode the ripples; and I didn't care what was going to happen, even though I was sure that something was going to happen.

She pushed away from me suddenly, slid off my lap and stood up. I looked at her. Her beauty gave me a hell of a buzz. She dived in as I grabbed at her, and swam away from me. I sat there and waited. After a while, she turned and came back. I tilted the raft down into the water so she slid up it on her stomach. She lay close to me, her chin in her hands, flat, her ankles crossed. She had a beautiful little back.

"Now tell me the story of your life," I said.

She shook her head. "There's nothing to tell."

"There must be. How long have you been here?"

"A year."

"Before then?"

"New York."

"A show girl."

"Yes."

"How did you meet Speratza?"

"I met him."

"Do you like him?"

"He's nothing to me."

"You take care of his distinguished visitors?"

"That seems to be the idea."

"Who else beside me have you taken care of?"

"No one."

"So I'm Paradise Palms' first distinguished visitor?"

"You must be."

"Like the job?"

She rolled over on her back. "Yes," she said, and looked at me.

I could see from the expression in her eyes that from now on I'd be wasting time by staying on the raft.

"Come on," I said. "We'll go."

She was the first to hit the water.

5

"I want to show the young lady the view from my balcony," I said to the night clerk, as he gave me my key. I expected him to remind me that this was a respectable hotel, or at least leer, but he didn't.

He bowed. "I'm delighted you find the view worth showing to madam," he said. "Is there anything I can send up for you, Mr. Cain?"

I made sure he wasn't being sarcastic, but he seemed to be falling over himself to give me service.

"Some Scotch would be nice," I said.

"There is a stock of liquor in one of the cupboards in your sitting-room, Mr. Cain," he returned. "Mr. Killeano sent it over with his compliments not an hour ago."

I nodded. "That was a nice thought," I said. I didn't show him that I was surprised.

I walked with Miss Wonderly across the deserted lobby to the elevators.

She looked at me, raising her eyebrows.

"He's just crazy to give me a good time," I said, shrugging. "He's ready to come up and tuck us in."

She giggled.

The house dick passed us. I could tell he was the house dick by the size of his feet. He didn't seem to see us.

The elevator attendant and the bell-hops looked through Miss Wonderly as if she was the invisible woman. All these lackeys certainly had a swell line intact.

The clock over the reception desk showed two-twenty. I wasn't even sleepy.

As we walked along the broad, thickly carpeted corridor to my room, I said, "Do you know this guy Killeano?"

"And I was hoping you were thinking only of me," she said, reproachfully.

"I got a split mind," I said. "I think of two things at once."

I unlocked my door, and she followed me in. I never did get an answer to that question.

When I closed the door I found I didn't have a split mind after all.

Miss Wonderly disengaged herself, but only after I got a buzzing in my ears.

"I came to look at the view—remember?" she said, but I could see by the rise and fall of her chest she wasn't much colder than me.

"It's a swell view," I said, and we went across the room to look at it. As I passed a mirror I saw my mouth had a smear of lipstick on it. I even got a bang out of that.

We stood on the balcony. The moon was like a pumpkin. The traffic had gone to bed, and only a straggler or two roamed along the coast road.

I undid the buttons of her blouse. She'd taken off her bolero coat on her way up. She leaned against me and held my hands.

"I don't want you to think I do this with everyone," she said, in a small voice.

"All right," I said. "This is the night reserved for you and me."

"I know, but I don't want you to think—"

"I don't."

She turned and slid her arms around my neck. We stood like that for a long time. It was pretty nice. Then I carried her into the bedroom and put her on the bed.

"Wait for me," I said.

I undressed in the bathroom, put on a silk dressing-gown and went into the sitting-room. I nosed around in the various cupboards until I found Killeano's gifts. He'd sent me four bottles of Scotch, a bottle of brandy, and Whiterock. I took the brandy and went into the bedroom.

She was in bed. Her hair had dried and it lay like spilt honey on the pillow. She looked up at me and smiled.

I poured two brandies. I gave her one, and sniffed at the other. It had a nice bouquet.

"You and me," I said

"No, just to you," she said.

"All right, and then to you."

I drank.

She put her glass down on the bed-table without touching it. Her eyes were wide and dark.

I looked at her, feeling a chill run down my spine. The liquor grabbed at my stomach.

"I should have thought of that," I said.

The room revolved slowly, then tilted.

"Killeano's gift," I heard myself mumbling. "But not for the bride."

I was staring up at the ceiling The lights were going out the way a movie-house dims its lights. I tried to move, but my muscles wouldn't work. I felt rather than saw Miss Wonderly get out of bed. I wanted to tell her to be careful not to catch cold, but my tongue was like a strip of limp leather.

I heard voices—men's voices. Shadows moved across the wall. Then I rode down a dark shute into darkness.

6

I began to crawl up the dark well towards the tiny pinpoint of light at the top. It looked a tough job, but I kept at it because somewhere close a woman was screaming.

Then quite suddenly I was at the top of the well, and sunlight blinded me. I heard myself groan, and as I tried to sit up, the top of my head seemed to fly off. I grabbed hold of it and rode the pain, cursing. The woman kept on screaming. The sound chilled my blood.

I made the effort. The floor tilted under my feet as I stood up, but I crossed the room. I walked like I was breasting a hundred-mile gale.

I reached the bedroom door, clung on to the doorpost and looked into the sitting-room.

Miss Wonderly was standing pressed against the opposite wall. Her arms were widespread, her hands flat on the egg-blue paint. She was as bare as the back of my hand, and her mouth hung open. As I looked at her, she screamed again.

My head felt as if it was stuffed full of cotton wool, but the scream wormed its way through and jarred all the nerves in my teeth.

I shifted my eyes from her to the floor. John Herrick lay on his back, his arms bent stiffly to the ceiling, his hands clenched. The front of his forehead was shoved in, and black blood stained his white hair and formed a gruesome halo around his head.

Heavy fists beat on the door. Someone shouted.

Miss Wonderly drew in a shuddering breath and screamed again.

I crossed the room and slapped her face. Her eyes rolled back until only the whites showed and she slid down the wall to the floor. She left two damp marks from her shoulders and hips on the egg-blue paint.

The door flew open and half the world burst in.

I faced them. They came so far and then stopped. They looked at me, they looked at Miss Wonderly and they looked at John Herrick. I looked at them.

There was the reception clerk, the house dick, a bell-hop, two ritzy-looking women, three men in white flannels and a fat man in a lounge suit. Right in front of them all was the evil-faced guy in the green gaberdine suit I'd noticed watching me at the Casino.

The two ritzy dames started screaming as soon as they saw Herrick. I didn't blame them. I felt like screaming myself. But it made the man in the gaberdine suit mad.

"Get those bitches outa here!" he snarled. "Go on, get out, all of you."

The reception clerk and the house dick stayed, but the rest of them were shoved out.

When the door closed, the man in the gaberdine suit turned to me.

"What's going on?" he demanded, clenching his fists and shoving out his jaw.

I guessed from that dumb crack he was a copper. He was.

"Search me," I tried to say, but the words wouldn't come. My mouth felt like it was full of rusty three-inch nails.

Moving like he was in church, the big house dick tip-toed across the room, into the bedroom. He came back with a blanket which he self-consciously draped over Miss Wonderly. She lay on her back, her arms and legs grotesquely spread out, her eyes closed.

"Who's this guy?" the man in the gaberdine suit asked, turning to the reception clerk, and pointing at me.

The reception clerk looked like he was going to throw up. His face was pale green.

"Mr. Chester Cain," he said, in a far-away voice.

That seemed to give the ugly guy a buzz.

"Sure?"

The reception clerk nodded.

The guy faced me. His flat puss was loaded with viciousness. "We know all about you," he said. "I'm Flaggerty of the Homicide Bureau. You're in a hell of a jam, Cain."

I knew I had to talk if it killed me.

"You're crazy," I said. "I didn't do it."

"When I find a rat with your reputation locked in with a murdered man I don't have to look all that far to find his killer," Flaggerty sneered. "You're under arrest, and you'd better start talking."

I tried to think, but my mind wasn't working. I felt like hell, and my head throbbed and pounded.

The reception clerk plucked at Flaggerty's sleeve and pulled him away. He started whispering. At first Flaggerty wouldn't listen. Then I caught Killeano's name, and that seemed to hold Flaggerty. He looked at me doubtfully, then he shrugged.

"All right," he said to the reception clerk, "but it's a waste of time."

The reception clerk left the room. He had to force his way through the crowd outside in the corridor, and three or four of them tried to squeeze into the room. Flaggerty slammed the door in their faces. Then he went over to the window and stared out.

The house dick touched my arm. He offered me a glass of whisky.

I took it and drank it. It was just what I needed.

I said I would have some more.

The house dick gave me another shot. He stood smiling stupidly at me, a blend of servility and horror in his eyes.

Then quite suddenly the cotton wool in my head dissolved, the pain went away and I felt as fine as could be expected under the circumstances. I asked the house dick for a cigarette, and he gave me one and lit it for me. His fat hairy hand was trembling.

"Make the punk at home," Flaggerty said from the window. He was watching me now, and he held a snub-nosed automatic in his hand. "Stay where you are, Cain," he went on. "I'm not taking any chances with you."

"Skip it," I said. "I know it looks bad, but she'll tell you what happened as soon as she comes to the surface. I don't know a thing about it."

"They never do," Flaggerty sneered.

"I wouldn't say anything, Mr. Cain," the house dick whispered. "Not until Mr. Killeano comes."

"Is he coming?" I asked.

"Sure. You're a guest here, Mr. Cain. We want to get you out of this mess if we can."

I stared at him. "I guess there's no other hotel in the world with such service," was all I could think to say.

He simpered at me, but avoided my eye.

I looked over at Miss Wonderly. She was still out, and I made a move to go to her.

"Hold it, Cain!" Flaggerty barked. "Stay where you are."

I had a feeling that he'd shoot if I gave him half a chance, so I shrugged and sat down.

"You'd better get that dame out of her faint," I said. "She's got plenty of talking to do."

"See what you can do with her," Flaggerty said to the house dick.

The big man knelt beside her. She seemed to embarrass him, because he just stared and did nothing.

I looked around the room. Cigarette butts filled the ashtrays. Two bottles of Scotch stood empty on the mantelpiece. Another lay on the carpet and a big damp patch showed that it had leaked. There was a stink of spirits in the room. The rugs had been kicked up, a chair overturned. The stage had been set to look like a drunken orgy. It looked like a drunken orgy.

On the floor by the dead man was a heavy Luger pistol. The butt of the pistol had white hair and blood on it. I recognized the pistol. It was mine.

I sat staring at it, and I felt spooked. Unless Miss Wonderly started talking I was in a sweet jam. I hoped she'd start talking soon.

We sat around for half an hour without saying anything. Miss Wonderly moved once or twice and moaned, but she didn't come out of her faint. It was the longest faint on record. Maybe she wanted to earn herself a title.

As I was beginning to lose patience, the door was thrown open and a short, square man, wearing a big black hat, bustled in. He reminded me of Mussolini when Mussolini used to shake his fist from his balcony. He took in the room at a glance, and then came straight to me.

"Cain?" he said, offering his hand. "I'm Killeano. There's nothing to worry about. I'll see you get a straight deal. You're my guest, and I know how to look after my guests."

I didn't shake his hand. I didn't get up.

"Your political rival's dead, Killeano," I said, eyeing him up and down. "So you've got nothing to worry about either."

He lowered his hand hurriedly and looked at Herrick.

"Poor fellow," he said. I swear there were tears in his eyes. "He was a grand, clean fighter; this is a great loss to the Administration."

"Save it for the newspapers," I advised.

We were all posed there like a bunch of dummies when Miss Wonderly sat up and started to scream again.

7

Killeano turned out to be quite a guy for getting things organized.

"We're going to be fair to Cain," he said, thumping his fist on the back of a chair. "I know it looks bad for him, but he's my guest, and I'm going to see he gets a break."

Flaggerty muttered under his breath, but Killeano was the boss.

"So what?" Flaggerty asked, shrugging. "Why waste time? I want this guy down at headquarters for questioning."

"We don't know he's guilty," Killeano barked, "and I won't have him arrested until I am satisfied you've got a case against him. We'll question him here."

"My pal," I said.

He didn't even look in my direction. "Keep that woman quiet," he went on, pointing at Miss Wonderly, who sat alone, weeping into the house dick's handkerchief. "I don't want her shooting off her mouth until we've heard the other witnesses."

I smoked and looked out of the window while Killeano yelled down the telephone and got things organized. Finally he had everything the way he wanted and we started. The reception clerk, the house dick, the elevator boy, Speratza and the barman from the Casino had been collected and lined up in the corridor outside. They were told to wait.

Miss Wonderly was taken into the bedroom in charge of a stout woman in black who'd been rushed up from the local jail to keep an eye on her. They told her to get dressed.

There were two tough-looking cops who stood behind my chair and pretended they weren't going to slug me if I showed any signs of walking out on the assembly. There was Flaggerty, two plain-clothes dicks, a photographer and a doctor. There was a stenographer, a pop-eyed little man, who sat in a corner and scribbled away as if his life, and not mine, depended on him getting it all down straight. Then there was me, and, of course, my pal, Killeano.

"All right," Killeano said. "Now we start."

Flaggerty nearly fell over himself to get his claws into me. He stood in front of me with his jaw thrust out and an ugly look in his beady little eyes. "You're Chester Cain?" he demanded, as if he didn't know.

"Yeah," I said, "and you're Lieutenant Flaggerty, the boy who hadn't any friends to tell him."

Killeano jumped up. "Look, Cain, this is a serious matter for you. Maybe you'd care to cut out the gags?"

"I'm the fall guy," I said, smiling at him. "Why should you worry how I handle this louse?"

"Well, it won't do you any good," Killeano muttered, but he sat down.

Flaggerty was moving about restlessly, and as soon as Killeano had settled, he started in again.

"All right," he said. "You're Chester Cain, and you're a gambler by profession."

"I don't call gambling a profession," I said.

His face went a dusty red. "But you admit you earn your living by gambling?"

"No. I haven't started to earn a living," I told him. "I'm just out of the Army."

"You've been out four months, and during that time you've been gambling?"

I nodded.

"You've made a heap of dough?"

"Fair," I said.

"You call twenty grand just fair?"

"It's not bad."

He hesitated, then decided to let it go. He'd established that I gambled.

"Is it true you murdered five men in four months?" he suddenly shot out.

Killeano jumped to his feet. "Keep that out of the record," he exclaimed, his little eyes wide with indignation. "Cain killed those men in self-defence!"

"He killed them!" Flaggerty shouted back. "Think of it! Five men in four months! What a record! Self-defence or not, it's appalling, and every decent citizen in this country is appalled!"

Killeano sat down, muttering. I guess he wanted to be thought a decent citizen too.

"Come on," Flaggerty snarled, standing over me. "You killed those five men, didn't you?"

"Five punks with the trigger itch tried to shoot me and I defended myself," I said quietly. "If that's what you mean, then I did kill them."

Flaggerty swung around to the stenographer and threw out his arms.

"A self-confessed killer of five innocent men!" he bawled.

That got Killeano on his feet again, but I was getting sick of this.

"Skip it," I said to Killeano. "The facts are on record and the New York D.A.'s given me a clean bill. Who do you think cares what a lousy small-town copper says? Save your breath."

Flaggerty looked like he was going to have a hemorrhage.

"Get on with it," Killeano snapped, sitting down and giving me a hard look.

"We'll see who cares or not," Flaggerty said, clenching his fists. "Now I'll tell you something. You came to Paradise Palms because you knew it was a gold mine, and you planned to clean up at the gambling tables."

"Aw nuts!" I said. "I came here for a vacation."

"And yet you ain't been in town a few hours when you rush around to the Casino," Flaggerty sneered.

"I was invited by Speratza," I said, "and not having anything better to do, I went."

"How long have you known Speratza?"

"I don't know him."

Flaggerty raised his eyebrows. "So you don't know him? Ain't it odd Speratza should invite you over to the Casino when he didn't know you?"

"Most odd," I said, grinning at him.

"Yeah," Flaggerty said. He took a step forward. "Maybe he didn't invite you. Maybe you invited yourself because you wanted to horn in and clean up fast." He was wagging his finger in my face and yelling at the top of his voice.

"Don't do that," I said gently, "unless you want a poke in your pan."

He turned round, crossed the room, opened the door and hauled in Speratza.

Speratza was wearing light blue trousers, very neat, with pleats at the waist; and his coat was a kind of mustard colour and flared out so wide at the shoulders that he looked bigger than a house. The lapels of his coat came out in a peak about eight inches long on each side and in the left one there was a white rosebud. I bet there were some women who'd swoon at the sight of him.

He smiled around, took a look at Herrick's body under the blanket, and switched off the smile. He looked at me, then looked away fast.

I lit another cigarette. In a moment or so, I'd know where I was heading.

I found out quick enough. Speratza said that he hadn't called me. He claimed he didn't even know I was in town until he saw me in the Casino. He went on to say that he'd heard of my reputation, and he was sorry to see me in this place.

Then I knew for sure that I was being taken for a ride. I called Speratza a liar, and he looked hurt. But he had nothing to worry about. It was his word against mine, and mine was a drug on the market.

Flaggerty got rid of Speratza and came back looking like the cat that'd swallowed the canary.

"Lying won't get you anywhere, Cain," he said. "You'd better watch your step."

"Go take a nap under a falling axe," I said, and blew smoke in his face.

"You wait 'til I get you to the station," he snarled.

"You haven't got me there yet," I reminded him.

Killeano told Flaggerty to get on with it.

"You met Herrick at the Casino?" Flaggerty demanded, after he'd choked down his rage.

"That's right."

"He told you to get out of town?"

"He advised me to get out of town," I corrected him.

"Then what did you say?"

"I said I'd stick around."

"You told him to go to hell, and you said if he didn't keep his snout out of your business you'd fix him."

"Moonshine," I said.

Flaggerty called in the Casino barman who said I had threatened Herrick. "He said 'You keep your snout out of my business or I'll push it through the back of your head'," the barman told Flaggerty. He looked shocked and sad.

"How much did they pay you to recite that little piece?" I asked.

"Never mind, Cain," Flaggerty snapped. He turned to the barman. "Okay, that's all. You'll be wanted at the trial."

The barman walked out, still shaking his head.

"Then you returned to the hotel with this woman," Flaggerty went on, pointing to Miss Wonderly, who'd been brought in. She looked out of place in her blue crêpe in the sunshine. She looked unhappy too. I winked at her, but she wouldn't catch my eye. "You two got drunk. She passed out, and you got brooding about Herrick. You figured he might be dangerous, and might upset your plans, and that made you mad. So you called him and asked him to come over, because you thought you could scare him to lay off you."

"Don't be a dope," I said. "I was the sucker who passed out. Ask baby-face over there. She'll tell you. Better still, get that bottle of brandy in the next room; it's full of shut-eye medicine."

"What brandy?" Flaggerty demanded.

One of the cops went into the bedroom. He came back after a moment or so.

"No brandy," he said.

"There wouldn't be," I said, shrugging. "Well, ask her. She'll tell you."

"I don't need to ask her!" Flaggerty roared. "The hotel telephone operator has a record of a call made by you at two o'clock this morning. We've traced that call to Herrick's residence. Ten minutes after the call Herrick arrived here. He brought the reception clerk for your room number, and the bell-hop brought him up to this room. How do you like that?"

"Very cosy," I said.

"You and Herrick talked. You were drunk and vicious. You're a killer, Cain. You don't think twice about killing. You're as mad as a mad dog! Herrick wouldn't scare, so you hit him with your gun. You were so goddamned drunk you forgot all about him the moment you'd done it. And I'll tell you why. You wanted that floozie. She was in bed waiting for you, wasn't she?"

I laughed at him. "Ask her. She's my witness." I looked at Miss Wonderly. "Listen, baby, last night you said you were for me. Well, here's your chance. You're the only one who can bust this frame wide open. I'm relying on you. They've got me in a sweet jam. There's nothing I can do about it. But if you have the guts, you can tell the truth, and that'll put me in the clear. We had a swell time together. We can still have a swell time together. Only you've got to be on my side. Now tell them."

"Wait," Killeano said, starting to his feet. His expression was a nice blend of suspicion and doubtful friendliness. He gave the idea that in spite of wanting to help me, he was gradually being persuaded that I was as guilty as hell. It was a nice act. He crossed the room and stood over Miss Wonderly. "Your word in a court of law hasn't much value. You're in a jam yourself. If Cain didn't kill Herrick, then you must have killed him. I'll tell you why. *The door was locked on the inside!* So don't lie. Maybe Cain was nice to you, but you've got to tell the truth, because you just can't afford to lie."

I saw then that they had taken care of everything. If Miss Wonderly said I had passed out, then they'd hang the murder on her. They wouldn't care so long as they hung it on someone.

"Okay, baby," I said. "Lie if you want to. He's right. They've been a little too smart for us."

"I'm not talking," she said, and began to cry.

That was right up Flaggerty's street. He grabbed hold of her arm and yanked her out of her chair. "You'll talk, you floozie!" he bawled, and shook her so her head snapped back.

I'd left my chair and reached him before the two cops could move.

I spun him around and hit him in the mouth. It was a sweet punch, and I felt my knuckles grate on his teeth. He went over backwards, spitting blood. It did me a power of good.

Then the cops jumped me, and one of them bounced a night-stick across my head.

I came round as Flaggerty was sitting up. I had a bump on my head, but he had lost a couple of teeth.

Killeano sorted us out.

After a while the atmosphere quietened down, but Flaggerty was still too groggy to continue questioning. Killeano took over. He stood in front of Miss Wonderly, his short fat legs astride.

"Unless you tell us what happened you'll be arrested," he said to her.

"What does it matter?" I said, rubbing my head. "Why do it the hard way? Tell 'em you passed out, and know nothing about it. They've got all the witnesses they want."

One of the coppers slapped me across the mouth.

"Shaddap," he said.

"That's going to be too bad for you," I said, and the look in my eyes made him edge away.

Miss Wonderly looked at Killeano and then at me. She was pale, but there was a light in her eyes that gave me hope. "He didn't do it," she said. "It was a frame-up. I don't care what you do to me. He didn't do it! Do you hear? *He didn't do it!*"

Killeano looked at her as if he couldn't believe his ears. His fat face went yellow with rage.

"You bitch!" he said, and slapped her hard across her face.

One of the cops wound his night-stick across my throat and held on. I couldn't move: I couldn't breathe.

Flaggerty and Killeano just stood looking at Miss Wonderly. She held her burning cheek and looked back at them.

"He didn't do it!" she repeated, wildly. "You can keep your rotten money. You can kill me. But I won't go through with it!"

I gave a croaking cheer.

Killeano turned to Flaggerty. "Arrest them," he said, in a thin reedy voice. "We'll get her on an accessory rap. And soften both of them." He looked at Miss Wonderly. "You'll be sorry for this," he said, and crossed the room, opened the door and went out. He closed the door gently behind him.

8

"Get that punk dressed," Flaggerty said, "and watch him."

The two cops and the two plain-clothes dicks convoyed me into the bedroom.

"Are we going to have a swell time with you when we get you to headquarters?" one of the plain-clothes dicks said. He was a massive guy with a red, rubbery face and hard green eyes. His name was Hyams. The other dick was thin and dyspeptic. He had a long red nose and his ears were so big they made him look a taxi-cab with its doors wide open. They called him Solly.

"I hope I have a good time too," I said, smiling at them.

The copper who'd slapped me dug me in the ribs with his night-stick. "Get dressed, wise guy," he said. "I'm one of the boys who'll work over you."

I climbed into my clothes. They went over each garment before handing it to me. They weren't taking any chances.

Solly said, "I hope Flaggerty lets me handle that diz."

"He'll handle her himself," Hyams said. "But, I'd like to be a fly on the wall."

"What a break!" Solly exclaimed, licking his lips. "Fancy taking a toots with her build to pieces."

"Yeah, and legally at that," Hyams said.

They grinned at each other.

I fixed my tie and put on my coat. If I didn't start something soon, it'd be too late. Once they got us down to headquarters, it was going to be just too bad for us. From the look of these thugs, Belsen would be a picnic to what they'd do to us.

"Come on, punk," Hyams said, "and listen, if you start anything, we'll shoot first and apologize after. We don't want to kill you before we've had a chance of working on you, but we will, if you try anything smart."

"I wouldn't dream of it," I said. "I've only read about the third degree. I'd like to experience it."

"You will," Solly said, looking at me out of the corners of his eyes.

We went into the sitting-room.

Flaggerty was pacing up and down. Miss Wonderly sat in a chair, and the stout woman stood behind her.

Flaggerty grinned at me. He looked nasty. There was a gap in his teeth and his lips were swollen.

"Five men in four months," he said, standing in front of me. "A killer, huh? Well, we'll show you what we do to killers. You've got two weeks before you come before a judge. That means two weeks of hell for you, Mr. Killer Cain."

"Don't be dramatic, you big-mouthed pixie," I said.

The big Irish cop, who'd slapped me before, clouted me from behind with his club. I staggered forward and ran into a bang in the jaw from Flaggerty. They were two juicy wallops, and I went down on my hands and knees.

Flaggerty gave me the boots. I got my head out of the way, but his heavy toe-cap sank into the side of my neck.

"We don't want to carry the creep," Hyams said, worried.

Flaggerty drew back. "Get up," he snarled.

I was lying near the blanket-covered body of Herrick, and I pretended to be dazed. I put my hand over my eyes so they couldn't see what I was looking at: peeping out from under the blanket was my Luger. They'd forgotten to pick it up, and when they'd covered Herrick, they'd covered the gun.

Flaggerty was bawling at me. "Get up, you louse, or I'll boot you again!"

"I'm getting up," I said, crawling slowly to one knee. I acted like I was half dead.

The blood-smeared gun butt was six feet from me. I tried to remember if any of the dicks carried guns in their hands. I didn't think they did. They were all too cocky, now they were sure I was unarmed.

Flaggerty booted me.

I flopped over on top of Herrick. It gave me a funny feeling to lie on the body, stiff in death. My hand closed around the gun butt. It was slippery with blood, but I didn't care.

I stood up.

Flaggerty's face turned green when he saw the Luger. The other guys turned into waxworks.

"Hello," I said. "Remember me?"

I didn't point the gun at them. I held it loosely, and I stepped to the wall so I could see everyone in the room.

"Well, come on," I said, smiling at them. "We were going to headquarters for fun and games."

They didn't move or say anything.

I looked over at Miss Wonderly. She was sitting on the edge of her chair, her eyes round with wonder.

"Just a bunch of weak sisters playing at tough guys," I said to her. "You coming with me, baby?"

She got up and came over. Her knees were knocking, and I put my arm around her waist.

"Can you be useful?" I asked, pulling her against me.

"Yes," she said.

"Go into the bedroom and pack some of my stuff in one of the bags. Take the best stuff, and leave the rest, and hurry."

She went past the waxworks without looking at them, and disappeared into the bedroom.

"Any of you guys know how fast I can pull this rod?" I asked cheerfully. "If you're curious, just give me the chance to show you," and I stuck the gun down the waist-band of my trousers.

None of them moved. There were eight of them, and the stout woman. They were too scared even to bat an eyelid.

I lit a cigarette and blew smoke at Flaggerty.

"You boys have had your fun," I said, "and now I'm going to have mine. I came here for a vacation. All I wanted to do was to have a good time and spend my roll. But you thought you'd be smart. You wanted to murder Herrick because he was in your way. You picked me for the fall guy, and you nearly got away with it. If you hadn't been so dumb, you would have got away with it. You killed Herrick, but you haven't killed me, and you'll find I'm a lot harder to kill than Herrick. I'm going to find out why you wanted Herrick out of the way, and then I'm going to complete his job. I'm here until I've taken this town to pieces and found out what makes it tick. I'm here until I've bust your Administration wide open: try to stop me if you can. I don't like being crowded by a bunch of small-town yeggs. It hurts my pride."

Still they didn't say anything.

I beckoned to the Irish cop.

"I want you, brother," I said.

He came towards me like he was treading on egg-shells; his hands above his head.

I let him get to within six feet of me, then I hauled off and busted him in the nose. He staggered back, banged into Flaggerty, and they both sat on the floor.

They remained like that. The cop's nose began to bleed. Miss Wonderly came out of the bedroom, carrying one of my grips.

"Wait by the door, honey," I said.

I walked over to the window, pulled back the curtain, and collected the cigar box I'd hidden behind the pelmet. The box contained eighteen grand: my vacation money.

Although I didn't even bother to watch them, they still didn't flutter a muscle. I guess my reputation stood pretty high in Paradise Palms or else they were plain yellow through to their jaegers.

"We'll go," I said to Miss Wonderly.

She opened the door.

"So long," I said to Flaggerty. "Come after me if you feel like it. I'm itching to be forced into a fight, but I don't shoot first. I don't have to." I winked at him. "I'll be seeing you."

He sat on the floor hating me with his eyes, but he didn't say anything.

I took Miss Wonderly's arm and we crossed to the elevator. The cage doors slid back the second or so after I'd rung.

"Going down, sir?" the attendant said. It was the guy who'd sworn he'd taken Herrick up to my room.

I pulled him out of the cage, and hit him between the eyes. He fell down and lay as quiet as a mouse.

I pushed Miss Wonderly into the cage and stepped in myself.

"Going down," I said, smiling at the attendant, and closed the cage doors.

Chapter Two
THE HEAT

1

"Do they know where you live?" I asked Miss Wonderly, as I shot the Buick out of the hotel garage.

She shook her head.

"Sure?"

"Yes. I changed my apartment a day or so ago. No one knows yet."

"We'll go there and get you some clothes," I said. "Where is it?"

She clutched my arm. "No. Let's get out of town. I'm scared."

"We've got the time," I said. "And you don't have to be scared. They won't get us if we use our heads. Now where is the place?"

"It's at the corner of Essex and Merrivale."

I nodded. "I know. I passed it as I came in."

I pushed the Buick along, and I kept my eye on the mirror. No one was following us—yet.

"You and I have a lot to talk about," I said, casually. "Thank you for being on my side."

She shivered. "Will they catch us?"

"They couldn't catch a train," I said, but I wasn't all that happy. I wondered if they'd taken the number of my car at the hotel, and how soon it would be before the attendant gave it to Flaggerty. I wondered where in hell we were going to hole up, or if it'd be better to get out of town. I didn't want to get too far away because I was determined to go after Killeano. I had to be near at hand if I was going to bust him, and I was going to bust him all right.

"Listen, honey," I said, in my soothing voice, "I want you to use your head. Is there anywhere in town or near at hand where we could stay and be reasonably safe?"

She twisted around. "We're going to get out of here," she said wildly. "You don't know what they'd do to me if they catch me."

I patted her hand and nearly pushed in some guy's fender who had pulled out suddenly from behind a truck. We cursed each other amiably.

"Now take it easy," I said. "No one's going to catch you. But we're bucking the police, and they'll seal up all the highways leading out of town. We can't get far with their two-way radio sets working against us. We'll have to hole up until the heat's cooled off. Then we'll slide out one night, and blow."

"We'd better go now," she said, clenching her fists.

"We'll be all right, but you must think. We want a nice snug hideaway for three or four days. Now think, and keep on thinking."

While I was talking we reached Essex and Merrivale. I whizzed the Buick down Essex Street and nailed her before a shabby looking apartment block.

"Come on," I said, grabbing the cigar box, "let's hustle."

We ran up the wooden steps to the house, and she led me up the stairs into a big bedroom overlooking the front of the house. She packed her things as if the devil was pricking her with his fork. She was so efficient that I just stood back and gave her room. In three minutes flat she had a big grip crammed full of the pick of her cupboard and drawers.

"Swell," I said, grabbing the grip. "Now watch my dust." As I reached the head of the stairs, I paused. She clutched at my arm, looking at me with round eyes.

"What is it?" she whispered.

I motioned her to be quiet and listened. The radio was giving a police message. They were telling Paradise Palms to watch out for us.

"How do you like being called a blonde killer?" I asked, smiling at her.

She pushed past me and scurried downstairs. At the foot of the stairs, she stopped. A thickset man in his shirt sleeves had come out of the front room. He stood gaping at her.

"Hey, you," he said, stepping up to her. "Not so fast. They want you!"

Miss Wonderly gave a startled squeak, spun on her heel and tried to bolt up the stairs, but he reached out and grabbed her.

"They want me too," I said, coming down slowly.

The man let go of Miss Wonderly as if she'd bitten him. He stepped back, his face going a dirty white.

"I don't know anything about anything, mister," he said in a low, hoarse voice.

I smiled at him. "You don't look as if you do," I said, and put Miss Wonderly's bag down. "Where's your telephone, bud?"

He waved his hand to the room from which he had just come. I jerked my head and he went in. I followed him. Miss Wonderly pressed herself against the wall. She didn't look as cute as she had when she'd pressed herself against my hotel wall, but then, she was dressed this time. It makes a difference.

The room was big and untidy. There were shutters up at the windows to keep out the sun.

An old woman was holding the telephone receiver to her ear. When she saw me, she gave a gasp, and dropped the receiver. It fell with a little crash on the table. Then she sat down heavily in a rocking-chair and threw her apron over her face. I thought she looked pretty dumb sitting like that, but it seemed to give her some comfort.

I took hold of the telephone and jerked. The cord came away from the wall, and I tossed the instrument on the floor.

"Now you won't be able to talk to anyone about anything," I said, winking at the man. "That'll be a nice change for you."

He jerked and shook and sweated plenty. I seemed to scare him.

I left them huddled and silent, and collected Miss Wonderly. She seemed scared too. Hell! I was scared myself.

We ran down the steps, and I slung her bag into the car. We bundled in, and I shot out of Essex Street like a cat off a hot stove.

"Have you thought of a place, honey?" I asked, as we bolted along Ocean Drive.

She shook her head. "No."

"Well, concentrate or else we'll be in a jam."

She banged her clenched fists together and started to cry. She was scared all right.

I looked across the Bay. The opalescent waters of the Atlantic and the Gulf were changing hues as clouds moved overhead. Scattered green islands gleamed like emeralds on an azure field. On the distant horizon the Gulf Stream pencilled a line of indigo, with here and there above it a smudge of grey smoke from the funnels of a passing steamer.

"How about those islands?" I said, slowing up. "Know any of them?"

She sat up, and her tears dried like magic. "Of course, the very place," she said. "Cudco Key. It lies to the left of the islands, and it's small. I know a shack there. I found it when I was out there once."

"Fine," I said. "If we can get there, that's where we'll go."

I didn't know where we were, but as we were heading in the same direction as the islands, I didn't worry. We passed Dayden Beach, and I looked at the moored raft. It seemed a long time since we sat on it together. We kept on, and after a while I saw a wharf ahead. That gave me an idea.

"We'll trade this car for a boat," I said.

"I'm glad you're with me," she said. It came from the bottom of her heart.

I patted her knee. It was a nice knee, and she didn't take it away, so I left my hand on it.

We stopped by the wharf and got out. I made sure my gun was handy, and I kept a firm grip on my cigar box. That was one thing I wasn't losing. We looked around. There were a number of U Drive pleasure boats moored along the wharf, but they weren't fast enough for me. I wanted something that'd shake a police boat if it came to shaking police boats.

I found what I was looking for after a while. She was a trim thirty-foot craft; mahogany and steel and glistening brass. She looked very fast.

"That's her," I said to Miss Wonderly.

While we were looking at the boat, a fat little man came out of a house on the waterfront, and hustled down to the boat. He gave us a hard look, then stepped on board.

"Hey!" I said.

He looked up, and climbed off the boat again. His face was burned nearly black by the sun, and his hair was bleached yellow. He didn't look a bad guy in a tough, hard way.

"Want me?" he said, eyeing us over, then he grinned. "By Golly!"

I hunched my shoulders and grinned back.

"Not you—your boat," I said.

"Chester Cain, by Jeese!" he said. He took elaborate precautions to keep his hands still and not to make any move, but he wasn't scared.

"Sure," I said.

"That's okay with me," he said. "The radio hasn't let up for the past half-hour. The whole town knows you're on the run." He eyed Miss Wonderly. She apparently made a hit, because he pursed his mouth in a soundless whistle. "So you want my boat?"

"That's the idea," I said. "I'm in a hurry, but I'm not going to rob you. Take my Buick and a grand?"

His eyes opened.

"Do I get the boat back?"

"Sure, if they don't sink her."

"Sink her? They'll never see her."

His optimism made me feel good.

"She that fast?"

"Fastest boat on the coast. Fate was kind to you, sending you to me."

"I guess so. So you'll trade?"

He grinned. "I don't want to, but I'll trade. I never did like that buzzard Herrick anyway."

"Sure this is your boat?" I asked.

"You bet. Tim Duval's the name. I use her for Tunny fishing and other things. When you're out of this jam, you come on a trip with me. You'll like it." He winked. "I'll be glad to have her back, but keep her as long as you like. She's gassed up and ready to go. She'll take you to Cuba if you're figuring on going that far."

Miss Wonderly came staggering back with the two suitcases. She wasn't scared to make herself useful. She looked kind of cute in her blue crêpe—like she was in a fancy dress, and it showed off her figure. Duval had trouble keeping his eyes off her. I had trouble too.

We dumped the grips on board, and then she ducked down into the cockpit.

"Get into the cabin, sweetheart," I called. "It'll be safer there." I didn't want anyone to see her as I pulled out along the long wharf.

She went into the cabin and shut the door.

"Want me to come along?" Duval asked hopefully.

I shook my head. "No."

He shrugged. "Okay," he said. "I'd sooner travel alone—with her. Nice, eh?"

"Huh uh," I said, and gave him the keys of the Buick.

"You won't have any trouble with that boat. She's sweet to handle," he said, taking the keys. "I'll look after the heap for you."

"Yeah, look after her," I said.

"Sure will."

I went aboard and started the engines.

Duval cast off the lines.

"I think Flaggerty's a buzzard too," he said.

That told me he wasn't going to sell us out as soon as we were out of sight.

"So do I," I said.

I spun the wheel and edged the boat through the narrows to the cut that led to the outer bay.

The swell was long, fairly easy. After a while I rounded the breakwater and we were in the bay.

I looked back.

Duval was waving. I waved back. Then I gunned the engine and the boat leapt forward with a roar, throwing water and cream-white foam.

2

Cudco Key was a tiny island five miles from the chain of islands skirting Palm Bay. It had a dazzling white beach bordered with coconut palms, white orchid trees, covered with pale white flowers delicately veined with green, and the woman's tongue trees with their long slender pods in which seeds rattle monotonously at the slightest breeze. Further along the coast, and inland were mangrove and buttonwood thickets. Spires of smoke hung in the air where mangroves were being burnt for charcoal.

I ran the boat into the heart of the mangrove thickets, and I was fairly sure that no one would spot it from the sea.

We left our grips on board and we struck inland to find the shack.

Miss Wonderly had changed into bottle-green linen slacks, a halter and an orange wrap around to keep her curls in place. She looked cool and cute.

It was hot on the island, and I had stripped down to a singlet and gaberdine slacks, but I sweated plenty.

We kept to the thickets. Miss Wonderly said there were only a couple of dozen Conch fishermen living on the island, but we didn't see any of them.

I got the surprise of my life when we found the shack. It not only commanded a fine view of Palm Bay and Paradise Palms in the distance, but it wasn't a shack at all. It was a hurricane-proof house that had been built as an experiment by the Red Cross some years back in their drive to counteract storm damage.

These hurricane-proof houses are built like small forts. They're made of reinforced concrete and steel; steel rods anchor the house to solid rock. The roof, floors and walls are of concrete, the walls a foot thick. All partitions extend from the roof through the house to bedrock. Window-sashes are of steel, with double-strength glass and double shutters. Wood is used only in the triple-strength cypress doors. Drain-pipes run from the roof to a cistern cut in the bedrock under the house, providing water in emergencies.

This house was on the far side of the island, and because of its exposed position no other dwelling was within two miles of it. It was a successful experiment, but no one lived in it now. I guess the Conchs preferred their wooden shacks or else someone was asking a high rent.

"Your shack, eh?" I said, looking at the place. "Some shack."

Miss Wonderly clasped her hands behind her back, and raised herself on her toes. She admired the house.

"I only caught a glimpse of it from a boat," she said. "I was told no one lived in it. I didn't think it was as good as this."

"Let's try and get in," I said.

It wasn't easy, and in the end I had to shoot off the lock of the front door. The place was dirty and as hot as an oven, but after opening all the windows the air got better.

"We can make this pretty comfortable," I said, "and it's safe. Let's have a look around."

I found a small harbour that had been built while the house was under construction. Mangroves had overgrown it, and it was practically invisible. I only came upon it by nearly falling down the ramp that had been covered with dead foliage.

"This is terrific," I said, after I'd cleared away the undergrowth. "We'll get the boat round here and settle in. Come on, let's go."

As I steered the boat around the island, I came upon the village community dumped down on the east shore. There were three or four ketches moored to the sea wall, a dozen or so wooden shacks and a big wooden building that looked like a store.

"Stay in the cabin," I said to Miss Wonderly. "I'm going in to get some provisions."

There were a bunch of men standing on the sea wall as I edged the boat to a mooring ring. One of them, a big fellow, stripped to the waist and barefooted, shambled forward and caught the rope I tossed him.

The men eyed me over as I climbed on to the sea wall, eyed the boat over and exchanged glances.

"That's Tim's boat," the big fellow said, rubbing his hands on the seat of his dirty white canvas trousers.

"Yeah," I said, and in case they thought I'd stolen it, I added, "I hired it off him. I'm on a fishing vacation."

"Swell boat," the big fellow said.

"That's so," I said.

I made the rope fast, conscious that they hadn't taken their eyes off me for a moment, then I strolled over to the store, hoping that no one would start anything. No one did.

The storekeeper told me his name was Mac. I told him my name was Reilly. He was a wizened little guy with bright eyes of a bird. I liked him. When I started buying, he liked me. I bought a load of stuff.

We roped in some of the loungers, including the big fellow, to cart the stuff down to the boat. Mac came, too, but he didn't carry anything.

"Duval's boat," he said, when he reached the sea wall.

"That guy seems pretty well known around here," I said.

"Sure is," he said, and grinned.

I lit a cigarette and gave him one.

"Kind of quiet here," I said, looking up and down the deserted beach.

"Sure is," Mac said. "No one bothers us. We get along."

"I guess you do," I said.

"Hear there was some excitement over at Paradise Palms," he said, after a pause. "A political killing. The radio's been yelling its head off."

"I heard that too," I said.

"I reckon it's no business of ours."

I wondered if that meant anything.

"You alone?" he went on, looking down into the boat.

"Yeah," I said.

He nodded, then spat into the sea.

"Thought maybe you'd brought your wife along."

"Not married," I said.

"We all can't be."

The big fellow climbed off the boat and came over. He was sweating plenty.

"That's the lot," he said, then added, "the cabin's locked."

"Yeah," I said.

Mac and the big fellow exchanged glances. I guess they were thinking hard.

I gave the big fellow a fin. He took it like it was a C note. He was excited.

"Maybe we'll see you again," Mac said hopefully. "Any friend of Tim's my friend."

"That's good news," I said, and meant it.

"I reckon Duval wouldn't hire his boat to anyone but a right guy," Mac went on.

"I guess not," I said, thinking that Duval rated high around the island. I stepped down into the boat.

"A patrol noses around here every so often," Mac said, sitting on his heels so he was near my ear.

"That so?" I said, looking up at him.

He closed one eye. "We don't tell 'em much."

"Fine," I said.

"Maybe you'd better let her out. It must be plenty hot in that cabin," he went on, looking over my head and admiring the view.

"Huh-uh," I grunted, then added, "Don't be smarter than you can help."

He took out a hunk of chewing tobacco and bit off a lump.

"The cops around here don't rate with me," he said, chewing hard. "That guy Herrick tried to clamp down on our trade. He was a nuisance. I reckon the boys are kind of grateful someone removed him."

I nodded. "I heard he wasn't popular."

I cast off and started the engine.

"I got gas if you ever want it," he called after me.

I waved.

3

A moon that looked like a Camembert cheese hung in the cloudless sky. The nodding palms cast long, spooky shadows. The red glow of the charcoal fire reflected on Miss Wonderly's skin. She lay on her back, her arms crossed behind her head, her knees bent. She wore blue shorts, a red halter and sandals. Her honey-coloured hair hid one side of her face.

I knelt before the fire, grilling a couple of spareribs. They smelt and looked fine.

We were tired, but we had the house ship-shape. I was surprised the way Miss Wonderly put her back into cleaning the joint. We had scrubbed and swept and dusted. We had laid coconut-matting down in two rooms and shifted the boat's bunks into one of them. We'd unscrewed the two small arm-chairs from the cabin and dragged them into the house, and we'd taken the table too. With a couple of good paraffin lamps, the place looked almost like home.

In the cockpit of the boat I had found a Thompson and an automatic rifle and enough ammunition to start a minor war. I brought the automatic rifle to the house, but left the Thompson in the cockpit. I didn't know when we might be cut off suddenly from the house or the boat, and I reckoned a division of weapons wise.

There was a portable radio on the boat, and we brought that up to the house too.

It had been a good day's work in spite of the heat, and now we were ready for something solid to eat.

I divided up the spareribs, the hashed brown potatoes and a couple of Cokes.

"Here we go," I said, dumping the plate on Miss Wonderly's chest. "Eats."

She sat up, after putting the plate on the beach wrap she had spread out so she shouldn't get sand in her hair. In the moonlight and the firelight she looked swell.

"Still scared?" I asked, cutting my meat.

She shook her head. "No."

We'd been so busy that we hadn't even thought about Killeano and the rest of them.

"It doesn't seem like it all happened this morning, does it?" I said. "I guess you've got some talking to do. How do you figure in all this?"

She sat for a while without saying anything. I didn't rush her, but I had to know.

"I was a fool," she said suddenly. "I came out here because I was promised a job, and because I was sick of pushing off men who thought showgirls were easy to make. The job sounded good, but it turned out to be just another masher's build up. He didn't want me to work. He wanted me to give him a good time. It wasn't my idea of a good time, so I found myself stranded here without the means to get back."

"When will you girls learn?" I said.

"Speratza came along. He wanted someone to look after the flowers and decorations at the Casino. I got the job."

"You and flowers go together," I said.

She nodded. "It was all right for eight months. I liked it, and the money was good. Then suddenly Speratza sent for me. He was in his office with Killeano and Flaggerty. They stared me over, and I didn't like the way they whispered to each other. Killeano said that I'd do, and he and Flaggerty went off. Then Speratza told me to sit down and offered me a thousand dollars to entertain you. I didn't know it was you then. He told me you were an important visitor and said, for reasons I needn't know, I was to entertain you, and if I did the job well he'd give me the money and my ticket home."

"And what did you think?"

"I didn't know what to think. It was an awful lot of money, and I wanted to get home, but there was something about the way Speratza talked that warned me not to touch the job. I asked him exactly what I had to do. He said I was to take you around, give you a good time, and then persuade you to take me back to your hotel. He said I was to sleep with you, but you would be doped and you wouldn't bother me. It was important that I should spend the night in your room. I thought it was a divorce frame-up. I didn't like it, and I refused." She gave a little shiver and stared across the moonlit bay. "He tried to persuade me, but the more he talked the surer I was that something was wrong. Then he got up and told me to follow him. We took a trip in his car to the harbour."

She stopped talking and stared down at her hands. I didn't hurry her, and after a while, she went on.

"He took me to a house on the waterfront. As soon as I was inside I knew what it was. I could tell by the awful old woman and the girls that peered over the banisters. It was horrible."

I gave her a cigarette. We smoked in silence for a few minutes.

"He said he'd keep you there if you didn't play. Is that it?" I said.

She nodded. "I was so scared I would have done anything to get out."

"That's all right," I said.

"Well, I said I'd go through with it, and he took me back to the Casino. He said they'd watch everything I did. He and Flaggerty would be with us the whole time, unseen, but watching, and if I warned you, they would kill you and send me to that place."

"Nice guys," I said. "What happened when I passed out?"

"I knew the brandy was drugged. They had to tell me that so I wouldn't drink it myself. After you had passed out, I let them in. Speratza and Flaggerty looked you over and put you into the bed. They told me to get in with you and to stay there until it was daylight. They told me I wasn't to move until then. I was so scared I did what I was told. I knew something horrible would happen. I heard them moving about in the sitting-room, and I know now what they were doing. I stayed awake all night, and then when it got light I went into the sitting-room. Well, you know what happened then."

I shifted closer to her.

"But you sold them out in the end," I said. "Why? Why did you take that risk?"

She looked away. "I wouldn't railroad anyone into murder," she said. "Besides, I said I was on your side, remember?"

"I remember," I said, "but you were in a jam. I wouldn't have blamed you if you had played with them."

"Well, I didn't," she said.

I turned her face so I could see her.

"I could go for you," I said.

She slid her arms round my neck and pulled my head down. "I've gone for you," she said, her lips against my neck. "I don't care. I can't keep it to myself. I wouldn't let them hurt you."

We played around for a while: loving her wasn't hard work.

"Now I wonder what I'm going to do with you?" I said, after the Camembert moon had moved around to our left.

"Do?" She sat up, her eyes scared. "What should you do?"

"Can I leave you here? Can you manage on your own?"

She clutched at my arm. "What are you going to do?"

"Use your nut, baby," I said. "I've got plenty to do. There's Killeano—remember him? That fat little guy who looks like Mussolini?"

"But you're not going back to Paradise Palms?"

"Sure I'm going back, I only came here so you could be safe."

"Oh, you're crazy," she cried. "What can you do against so many?"

"You'll be surprised," I said, smiling at her. "There's a murder rap hanging over us. I'm going to bust that for a start. We're not safe until I find Herrick's killer and persuade him to come clean."

"But you can't go back alone," she said frantically.

"I'm going back alone, and I'm going in a few minutes," I told her. "All I want to be sure about is that you'll be all right while I'm away."

"I won't be all right," she said quickly—too quickly.

I shook my head at her. "Oh yes, you will. Now listen, I'll be back tomorrow night. I'm taking the boat, and you're to stay near the house. You've the rifle and enough food. You keep your ears and eyes open, and you'll be all right. If anyone comes, lock yourself in the house. They won't get at you, if you use your head. But no one will come."

"Suppose you don't come back?" she asked, her lips trembling.

"You'll still be all right," I said. "I'm leaving you seventeen grand.

Go to Mac. He'll get you back to New York somehow. I'll drop in and talk it over with him."

"No," she said, "don't do that. I'd rather no one knows I'm alone."

That made sense.

"But you mustn't leave me." She pressed her face against mine. "I don't want to lose you now I've just found you."

We argued back and forth, but I was going anyway. She got the idea at last, and stopped trying to persuade me. She sat with her hands folded in her lap, looking scared and sad.

"All right," she said.

"Herrick knew something important. It was so important that they killed him," I said. "Can you think what it could have been?"

She shook her head. "I hardly knew him. He used to come to the Casino, but I never spoke to him."

"Did he have a girl?"

She nodded. "He went around with a red-head. She's a singer, and has an apartment on Lancing Avenue, a big chromium and black marble block on the left as you go up."

"Know her?"

"No, but I've heard the other girls talk about her. She's hard, not my type."

"Her name?"

"Lois Spence."

"Okay, maybe she'll know something."

"You will be careful?" she said, putting her hand on my knee.

"Sure," I said. "Now Killeano. Know anything about him?"

"Only that he is important, owns the Casino and is the City Administrator."

"Did you ever ask yourself why Herrick should hang around the Casino? He wasn't a gambling man, was he?"

"No."

"Well, all right," I said, getting up. "Maybe Miss Spence will answer all the questions. I'm going to dress now, honey."

I went into the house and put on a dark blue linen suit, a dark blue shirt and a dark red tie. I went into the sitting-room and found her waiting for me. She was making a brave show, but I could see she was near tears.

I gave her the cigar box.

"Take care of that, sweetheart," I said. "That's all the dough I have in the world, and I sweated earning it."

She clung to me.

"Don't go," she said.

I patted her.

"If anything should happen to you . . ." she said.

"It won't. Come down to the boat."

It was still hot, and mangroves burning in the still air smelt fine. She looked so nice standing in the moonlight I nearly said the hell with it. But I didn't.

I cast off.

"No sleeping-draught for me tomorrow night," I called, as the boat drifted out of the harbour.

She waved, but she didn't say anything. I guess she was crying.

4

Paradise Palms looked if anything nicer by night than by day. I could see the lighted dome of the Casino in the distance as I steered the boat towards the wharf. I wondered if there would be a reception committee with shotguns waiting for me when I landed.

It was just after ten thirty, and the wharf, as far as I could see from this distance, was deserted. I cut the engine, put the Thompson where I could get at it, and drifted in.

When I was within twenty yards of the wharf, I saw a short fat figure rise up out of the shadows and walk to the edge of the wharf. I recognized Tim Duval.

He caught the rope I threw to him and made fast.

"Hello," he said, grinning.

I glanced up and down the wharf.

"Hello," I said.

"They came down here a couple of hours back, but I kept out of sight. The old woman told them I'd gone on a trip. That took care of the boat. They didn't find your heap, and they shoved off after nosing around. There were a lot of them."

I nodded. "Thanks," I said.

He hitched up his dirty grey flannels.

"What now?" he said.

"I've got a little business in town. How's the heat?"

He whistled. "Fierce," he said, "but their description of you is punk. They're calling you handsome."

I laughed. "Well, I'm going in."

"I guess it takes a lot to stop a guy like you. Want me to come along?"

"Why in hell do you want to mix yourself up in this?" I asked.

"Damned if I know," he said, running thick fingers through bleached hair. "Maybe I don't like this town. Maybe I don't like Killeano. Maybe I'm nuts."

"I'll go in alone," I said.

"Okay. Anything I can do?"

"I want a car. Can you lend me one?"

"Sure. It looks a wreck, but it goes."

"Get it."

I smoked while I waited. I could hear the dance music from the distant Casino.

Duval came back after a while, driving a grey Mercury convertible. It looked as if it had been kicked around plenty, but the engine sounded all right.

I got in. "Want me to pay you now?" I asked.

"I got the boat, your heap and a grand, haven't I?" he said. "What more do I want? Except maybe I'd like to horn in on this."

I shook my head. "Not yet, anyway," I said.

He shrugged. I could see he was disappointed.

"Oh well," he said.

I had an idea. "Know any newspaper men around town?"

"Sure. There's Jed Davis of the *Morning Star*. He's often around. We go fishing together."

"Get me some dirt on Killeano. Ask Davis. Dig deep. A guy like Killeano must have plenty of dirt in his life. I want all I can get."

His face brightened. "I'll get it," he said.

"And there's a cat-house somewhere on the waterfront. I want to know who owns it. Speratza of the Casino has access to it. I'd like to tie him in closer than that if I can."

"I know the joint," he said. "Okay, I'll get the stuff."

I started the engine. Then I had another idea.

"Gimme your telephone number," I said.

He gave it to me.

"I may run into trouble," I said, eyeing him. "I might not get back. If that happened, would you do something for me?"

He got it all right.

"Sure, I'll look after her. Do you want to tell where she is?"

I had to trust someone. I thought I could trust him.

"Cudco Key," I said.

He nodded. "Yeah, that's a good place. Mac's there."

"I know, and he's a good guy."

"Hell! we're all good guys. I'll look after her."

"I like that girl," I said slowly. "If anything should happen to her . . ." I gave him the cold eye.

He nodded. "I'll look after her," he said.

I thanked him and drove away.

5

Lancing Avenue was in the better-class district of Paradise Palms. It was a broad avenue lined by Royal Palms that were as straight-cut as a row of skittles.

I found the chromium and black marble apartment block without difficulty. It had a half-circular drive to the entrance and a lot of bright lights. It looked like a Christmas tree out of season.

I drove the Mercury up the drive. Half a block of dark limousine blew me off the road with its horn and went past making a noise like snowflakes on a window. It stopped before the entrance and three dizzy-looking dames, all cigarettes, arched eyebrows and mink coatees got out and went in.

The Mercury made me feel like a poor relation calling on his rich relatives.

I parked behind the limousine and went in too.

The lobby was no smaller than an ice-skating rink, but cosier. There was a reception desk, an enquiry desk, a flower-stall, a cigarette kiosk, and a hall porter's cubby-hole. It was class; the carpet tickled my ankles.

I looked around.

The three dizzy dames had gone over to the elevators. One of them pulled down her girdle with both hands and gave me the eye. She had too much on the ball for me to be more than mildly interested. She was the kind of dame who'd pick out your gold inlays without an anaesthetic.

I took myself over to the hall porter. He was a sad old man dressed up in a bottle-green uniform. He didn't look as if he had much joy in his life.

I draped myself over the counter of his cubby-hole.

"Hi, dad," I said.

He looked up and nodded. "Yes, sir?" he said.

"Miss Spence. Miss Lois Spence. Right?"

He nodded again. "Apartment 466, sir. Take the right-hand elevator."

"She in?"

"Yes, sir."

"That's fine," I said, and lit a cigarette.

He looked at me and wondered, but he was too well bred to ask why I didn't go up and see her. He just waited.

"How are you off for folding money, dad?" I asked casually.

He blinked. "Always do with some, sir," he said.

"Kind of tough here?" I asked, glancing around. "All silk for the customers and crêpe for the staff?"

He nodded. "We're supposed to make it in tips, sir," he said bitterly. "But they're so mean here they wouldn't give a blind beggar the air."

I took out a five spot and folded it carefully. He eyed it the way I eye Dorothy Lamour.

"Miss Spence interests me," I said. "Know anything about her?"

He glanced around uneasily. "Don't flash that money so anyone can see it, sir," he begged. "I wouldn't like to lose my job."

I hid the note in my hand, but I let the end show in case he forgot what it looked like.

"Do you talk or do you talk?" I asked pleasantly.

"Well, I know her, sir," he said. "She's been here three years, and you get to know them after a while." He said it as if he hated her guts.

"Nice to you?"

"Maybe she doesn't mean it, sir," he said, shrugging.

"You mean she doesn't kick you in the face because her leg doesn't stretch that far?"

He nodded.

"'What's her line?" I asked.

His old face sneered. "Tom—he runs the elevator—says she'd flop at the drop of a hat. Perhaps you know what he means. I don't."

"It's a cynical way of saying she's a push-over," I said. "Is she?"

He shook his head. "Maybe the first time, but not after that. She kind of whets a guy's appetite and then holds him off. It comes kind of expensive the second time. I've seen guys climb walls and gnaw their way across the ceiling because they couldn't make the grade."

"She kind of gets in your blood, huh?"

He nodded. "One sap shot himself because of her."

"Tough."

"I guess he was crazy."

"How did Herrick make out with her?"

He eyed me narrowly. "I don't know whether I should talk about him, sir. The boys in blue have been buzzing around here today like wasps."

I showed him the other end of the five spot, hoping it would look more interesting that way.

"Try," I said.

"Well, he was different. He and the Basque."

"The Basque?"

He nodded. "He's up there now."

"She played around with Herrick?"

"Well, they went around together. Herrick had a lot of dough, but I wouldn't say they played, if you mean what I think you mean, sir."

"You wouldn't, eh? How about the Basque?"

He shrugged. "You know what these women are like. They have to have one regular among the many. I guess he's it."

"And not Herrick?"

"He was different. He never stayed nights with her. I guess they were on a different footing. Maybe they were in business or something together."

"You wouldn't swear to that?"

"No, but she didn't take any trouble to hide up the Basque from Herrick. He'd be with her when Herrick called. It seemed to make no difference."

"Who is this Basque, anyway?"

"Name's Juan Gomez. He's a jai alai player. The local champ around here."

"What does he do beside play?"

The old man's eyes rolled. "Get's out of training with Miss Spence, I reckon."

"Did the cops pay her a visit?"

He nodded.

"Hear anything?"

"No, but Gomez was with her." A wintry smile crossed his face. "I bet she had to do some fancy talking to explain what that dago was doing in her room at eight o'clock in the morning."

"Probably said he'd come to fix the refrigerator," I said. "Ever see Killeano in here?"

"No."

"Right," I said, and slid him the five spot. He snapped it up the way a lizard nails a fly.

I was moving away when he leaned forward and whispered, "Here they come now."

I looked over my shoulder and saw them. Being interested in women, I looked first at Miss Spence. She had on a pair of long-waisted, rust-coloured slacks, Bata shoes, a brown and white print shirt and an orange scarf. Apart from being a trifle heavy in the beam, she had a long-limbed languorous figure. Her red hair was as artificial as a lawyer's smile, her mouth was wide, her eyes blue, and the mascara made her eyes look like miniature iron railings. She wore Revlon's "Fatal Apple" make-up (the most tempting new colour since Eve winked at Adam). As she wafted past me on a cloud of No. 5 Chanel, I observed the utterly disdainful expression on her face and the strange sins that lurked in her eyes.

I decided it'd be interesting to have a session with her, providing two strong men were outside the door to rescue me if the going got too tough, and if she left me enough strength to scream for help.

The Basque was a turn on his own. He was tall and broad and unpleasantly strong looking, and as lithe as a jungle cat and twice as dangerous. His brown, lean face was coldly savage, and there was a chilled expression in his eyes that didn't make you feel you wanted to slap him on the back.

Miss Spence handed over the keys to the hall porter as if he was the invisible man, and then strolled across the lobby, with Gomez tailing her.

As she walked, she managed to make her hips quiver, and all the men in the lobby, including me, peeped at them.

Half way across, she paused to ask her boy friend for a cigarette. He was lighting it for her when a loudspeaker extension crackled into life.

"Paradise Palms Police Department," said a tinny voice. The loudspeaker hummed slowly, then spluttered to sound: "Repeat as of nine fifteen on Herrick killing. Wanted: Chester Cain. Description: six foot one—a hundred and ninety pounds—about thirty-five—dark hair—sallow complexion—wearing grey suit, grey soft hat. Probably trying to get out of town . . . don't take any chances—he's dangerous. Anyone recognizing the wanted man should report at once by telephone to the Police Department. No attempt should be made to apprehend this man unless you are armed. That is all."

Miss Spence threw down her cigarette and stamped on it. "Haven't they caught that bastard yet?" she demanded angrily.

6

Jai alai is the fastest and toughest sport in the world. It is played with a *cesta* or basket, strapped to the player's right hand. The curved, three-foot basket has a maximum depth of five inches. A player can wear out three or four baskets during a contest. The hard, rubber-cored ball or *pelota*, slightly smaller than a baseball, is covered with goatskin.

The ball is driven with such speed that it sometimes breaks a leg or arm. The playing court or *cacha* is spacious, its green walls rising to the high-netted skylight of the auditorium. Where the concrete of the *cacha* floor ends in the red foul line and meets the wooden floor of the auditorium, there is a vertical wire screen which protects the tiers of customers.

The server drops the ball, catches it on the rebound, and hurls it with a terrific forehand stroke against the wall. The opposing player has to intercept the ball with his basket and keep it in play. The players move like lightning, their *cesta*-lengthened hands reaching out miraculously to intercept and return bullet-like rallies of the ball. The *pelota* continues in play until it falls in illegal territory, or a contestant fails to make good a return.

There are few ball games calling for greater strength, endurance and skill, and it is said most jai alai players die young. If they're not sooner or later severely injured by the ball, their hearts give out.

I had followed Miss Spence and her boy friend in their Cadillac sedan to a large coral-tinted stucco building, which turned out to be the jai alai headquarters. I had watched Miss Spence leave her boy friend at the player's gate and enter the auditorium. I had tagged along behind her.

Now I was sitting beside her on a plush seat in the front row of the first of the tiers behind the wire screen, looking down into the floodlit *cacha*.

Four energetic young Spaniards were dashing about the floor slamming the almost invisible ball back and forth, and performing acrobatic miracles. The crowd seemed to be getting a big bang out of them, but I was more interested in Miss Spence.

She had spread out on the flat plush top of the balcony wall a program, a pair of binoculars, her hand-bag, a carton of cigarettes and her orange scarf. The heady perfume of No. 5 Chanel brooded over her nick-nacks, herself, and of course, me.

Sitting so close to her—the seats were cut on economical lines—I could feel a subtle warmth from her body, and her perfume had a distinct effect on me. I wondered vaguely what she would do if I enfolded her in a Charles Boyer embrace.

The four Spaniards finished their game and walked off the court to a scattering of applause. They looked jaded and hot. If I'd been in their place I would have been carried off on a stretcher, with a dewy-eyed nurse in attendance packing ice around my temples.

There was an interval, and Miss Spence looked around the auditorium as if she expected the rest of the audience to stand up and sing the National Anthem at the sight of her. They didn't.

She looked to her right, and then to her left. As I was on her left, she looked at me. I gave her a sad, coy leer, and hoped it would unhook the disdainful expression on her face. It didn't exactly do that, but it registered enough for her to study me.

I leaned forward confidentially. "They say the elastic shortage has made woman's position in world affairs less secure than it was four years back," I said briskly.

She didn't say "Huh?", but she wanted to. She looked away instead, the way you look when a drunk speaks to you. Then she looked back and caught my grin. She smiled bleakly.

"Reilly's the name," I said. "I'm a playboy with a lot of dough and a yen for red-heads. You'd better scream for help while there's time. I'm considered to be a fast worker."

She looked me over. No smile now. Eyes medium to hard.

"I could handle you without help," she said in a husky voice that sent chills up and down my spine, "and I don't like playboys."

"My mistake," I said, shaking my head. "I missed out on psychology when I worked my way through college. I'd've thought playboys would have been your strong suit. Let's forget it," and I picked up my program and pretended to study it.

She gave me another bleak stare and concentrated on the court below.

Four men had just walked on. One of them was Gomez. You could tell he was the local champ. Not only did the crowd give him a tremendous hand, but the other three players hung back and let him scoop the limelight. He was full of bounce and arrogance. I watched him wave to the crowd. He certainly had something to be arrogant about. I've never seen such a specimen of a he-man. He looked in our direction and gave Miss Spence a special wave. She ignored him, so I waved for her, just for the hell of it. He didn't seem to appreciate the gesture.

Miss Spence's mouth tightened, but she didn't say anything.

The four men were now in a huddle in the middle of the court, testing the *pelota* which had just been thrown in. Then they broke up and went to their positions.

"Do these guys get paid to play this sissy game?" I asked out of the corner of my mouth.

"What makes you think you're so tough?" she snapped back, before she remembered her dignity.

"Give me a chance and I'll show you," I said.

She leaned forward and looked down at the players. Her eyes brooded sudden death.

Gomez served. I'll say this for him, he could certainly sling a mean *pelota*. The ball whizzed through the air, struck the front wall and shot back, hugging the wall and buzzing like an outsized hornet. One of the other players turned into the side wall and took three quick steps up its perpendicular height, like a man running up a short flight of stairs. He trapped the ball in his *cesta*, dropped back and slammed the ball away. White figures darted about the court, arms reached out, the ball whizzed to and fro. Gomez did all the things you'd expect a champ to do, and did them well. His stamina was terrifying. The score moved quickly. It looked a walk-over for him.

I gave Miss Spence a sidelong look. She was watching the game with a bored disdainful expression on her face as if she knew what was going to happen, and didn't care if and when it did happen.

I remembered what the hall porter had said about her flopping at the drop of a hat. I wondered if it had to be a certain kind of a hat or whether any hat would do. I wished I'd asked for further details.

"Before long that side of beef will be looking for you," I said softly. "Suppose you and me walk out on him? I could show you the moon. If you don't like moons, I'll show you my tattoo marks instead."

Her long, slender, red-tipped fingers tapped on the binocular case.

"I still don't like playboys," she said, and looked away.

Gomez had smashed his *cesta*. Scowling, he signalled time out, and went over to a Negro attendant who strapped a new basket on his hand.

I looked around to make sure no one was paying us any attention. No one was. I made my hand into a fist and slugged Miss Spence just above her hip bone. She rocked, and breath whistled through her nose.

"Maybe you like tough guys better?" I said, smiling at her.

She didn't look at me, but her nose was pinched and her eyes like holes in a mask. She gathered up her junk off the balcony wall and stood up.

"Show me the moon," she said in a brittle hard voice, and pushed past the spectators to the gangway.

I followed her out, accompanied by a storm of cheering. I guessed Gomez had taken the final tanto, and I'd launched Miss Spence just in time.

The dignified doorman signalled for her car as soon as he saw her coming. By the time we had reached the revolving doors the black and chromium Cadillac was lined up, waiting.

The doorman gave me a hard look as he handed Miss Spence into the car. She left the driving seat vacant, and I slid under the wheel. We drifted away with the smoothness of a falling leaf, and with less noise.

I drove fast to Lancing Avenue. She didn't say anything during the drive, and she sat stiff and straight, looking at the road ahead, her big white teeth gnawing her underlip.

I stopped outside the big apartment block, opened the door and got out. She got out too. We walked across the lobby, and as I passed the hall porter I winked at him. He stared back as if he was seeing a mirage.

We rode up to the fourth floor in an automatic elevator, and walked along the broad corridor to apartment 466. We didn't speak or look at each other. The atmosphere was loaded with an off-key excitement.

She unlocked the door and we went into a big room full of apricot and chromium furniture. I shut the door, tossed my hat on a chair and faced her.

She looked at me from the fireplace. Her disdainful expression was still hooked to her face, but her eyes were expectant, bright. "Come here," she said, almost thickly.

I crossed the room and put my hands on her hipbones. I smiled at her.

"Hold me close, you beast," she said.

I put my arms around her loosely at first. Her hair had a harsh feeling against my face. I tightened my arms and pulled her against me. Her mouth felt hard against mine, but after a while her lips opened. She was shivering.

"Tough guy," she said softly, her breath going into my mouth.

"What was Herrick to you?" I asked.

Her body stiffened in my arms and her breath made a harsh sound. Her head pulled back until her eyes, wide open, were staring at me.

"Who are you?" she asked, in a soft dull voice.

"Chester Cain," I said.

Her face fell to pieces. She pushed away, white, her eyes vacant, blank. I let her go.

"Who?"

"Chester Cain."

Slowly she got herself in hand. Her eyes roved around the room, lit on the telephone, lingered, then came back to me. "Sit down," I said. "I want to talk to you."

She wandered towards the telephone. A gentle hissing sound came from between her tightly-locked teeth.

"I don't want to talk to you," she managed to jerk out, in a voice made husky by fear or rage or something.

I let her get to the telephone and then I walked over and grabbed it. She struck at me with her nails. I let go of the telephone and grabbed her wrist, twisting it. She was surprisingly strong. We swayed, and she tried to claw me with her free hand. I ducked my head, and she missed. I expected her to scream, but she didn't, she fought silently, panting a little, her eyes glowing, her mouth working.

We scuffed up the rugs, and did a lot of tramping and shuffling, but I worked her over to the divan and then trapped her ankle and pushed.

She hit the divan and bounced up, but I flung her down again. She kicked me on the shin, gave me a punch in the face and tried to bite my jugular. I cursed her gently and went into a clinch with her. She writhed, twisted and scratched. We were both panting. She butted me in the eye with the top of her head.

I said, "The hell with this," flung her off and stood back. I pulled my gun on her. "Let's skip it," I went on, "or I'll blow a hole in you."

She glared up at me, her eyes savage, but the gun seemed to cool her.

"Stay put, sister," I said, drawing up a chair. I sat down.

She looked me over, and then flopped back on the divan. I'd torn her shirt and a shoulder peeped through. It was a nice shoulder, white and firm.

"You think I killed Herrick," I said, "but I didn't."

She continued to eye me savagely, and said nothing.

"Killeano's mob killed him, and tried to pin it on me," I went on.

"You killed him all right," she said, and added some fancy names. Her language would have turned a stevedore pale.

"Use your head," I said. "I've just arrived here. I never saw Herrick before until I met him in the Casino for a couple of minutes. He asked me to get out of town because he thought I'd cause trouble, and Killeano made that the excuse for killing him and framing me. Can't you see how simple it is? Why should I want to kill Herrick? Think, Toots, work on it. If you were Killeano and you wanted Herrick out of the way, wouldn't you spring the killing when a guy with my reputation blows into town? It was a gift."

She looked doubtful.

"Killeano wanted him out of the way all right," she muttered. "It could be, but I don't believe it."

I told her the story, how Speratza had invited me to the Casino, how Miss Wonderly had been detailed to look after me, how I'd seen Flaggerty watching us, and the whole works. She sat watching me, and the angry bitterness seeped out of her eyes.

"All right," she said, shrugging. "I'm the sucker, so you didn't kill him."

"I didn't kill him," I said. "But I'm in a jam. You can help me out."

She raised her eyebrows. "Why should I?"

"Suppose you tell me," I said, smiling at her. "What was Herrick to you?"

She swung off the divan and went over to the big cocktail cabinet.

"I'm keeping out of this," she said, taking out two glasses and pouring whisky. She came over and handed me one, looked down at me, and smiled coldly. "You're tough, all right," she said. "I feel like I've been fed through a mangle."

I pulled her down on my lap. She was a big armful, but I handled her.

"Let's be friends," I said. "You liked Herrick, didn't you?"

She pushed away from me and stood up.

"Cut that stuff right out," she said. "I'm not quite a sap."

I drank some whisky, lit a cigarette and shrugged.

"I could beat it out of you," I said, giving her the cold eye.

"Try," she said, sitting on the divan.

"I've got a better idea," I said. "I'll have a talk with your pal Gomez. He'll be interested to know you sexed me up to this room."

That threw a scare into her.

"You dare!" she snapped, jumping to her feet.

"Come on, be nice."

"Herrick paid me to play the tables at the Casino," she said, after a moment's hesitation. "I don't know why, so don't ask me. He always took the money I'd won and gave me other notes in exchange."

I stared at her.

"Why did he do that?" I said.

She was just going to say she didn't know, when the door jerked open and Gomez walked in.

Chapter Three
GUNFIRE

1

A police siren wailed in the still night air. Car tyres bit gravel. Doors slammed. Feet pounded on concrete.

I stood in the shadow of the wall facing the rear exit of Miss Spence's apartment block. It wasn't a particularly good place to be in with a flock of buttons buzzing around, but I'd been in worse places.

The alley was narrow and sealed at one end. The other end, opening on to the front drive, was lit by a white-blue overhead lamp.

I held the Luger in my right fist, and edged along the shadows. I came to the dead end, looked up. A couple of feet above me I could see the dark sky and the stars. I looked back down the alley. A flat, capped figure was peering around the corner of the wall. He couldn't see me, but I could see him.

He was very cautious, but I could have drilled him between the eyes without buying myself a truss. He seemed shy of showing me any more of himself. Maybe he thought his head was made of bullet-proof steel. Maybe it was.

I went down on one knee, waited.

He did exactly what I thought he would do. He pulled a flash and sent a long bright beam of light in search of me.

The roar of the Luger rolled around the narrow alley, bounced off the walls. The cop's flash disintegrated; darkness settled down again.

I had about sixty seconds to get moving before he recovered his nerve. I moved.

The top of the wall was gritty under my hands. I was glad I'd learned the trick of rolling over walls instead of sitting astride them. I was dropping into the far-side darkness when the cop opened up with a chopper. Slugs threw up a little cloud of mortar and brick dust six feet above my head. I didn't wait.

Beyond the wall was an expanse of trees, shrubs and darkness. I guessed it was the garden of the apartment block. I melted into the darkness; kept edging to my right, where I knew I'd eventually come out to the main street.

There was much shouting in the front drive. Heads peeped cautiously out of windows. The chopper continued to grind away. No one was taking chances.

I kept on. The Army certainly did a swell job in teaching me how to act like a Red Indian. Sitting Bull had nothing on me. Moving through the shrubs and trees, I made no more noise than a ghost and was a lot less visible.

The night was now full of police sirens, some near, some distant, some almost too faint to hear. There seemed a lot of Law on the move.

I reached the wall surrounding the garden as some bright boy decided to turn on a floodlight. I had just pulled myself up and was lying on top of the wall when the lights came on. I felt like a nudist in a subway on a Friday in the rush-hour.

Enough artillery opened up to slaughter an army. Slugs hummed and buzzed. One of them nicked my sleeve. I dropped into the street faster than a lizard.

A cop from across the street took a pot-shot at me as I zigzagged along the sidewalk. I took a pot-shot at him. He fell on his knees, clasping his wrist. He yelled blue murder.

I got into my stride. Maybe I did touch the ground twice in my sprint for a friendly archway, but I doubt it. The archway led to a big house that loomed white above high white walls, capped with red tiles that reflected the moonlight.

Bullets skipped by me, struck sparks from the road. I reached the archway, ducked under cover. I was breathing like an old man with asthma, sweat running down my face. Keeping close to the protecting wall, I looked into the street. Men moved, darted for cover, edging nearer to me. The street was lousy with cops.

I drew a bead on one of them. The slug passed through his hat, and he fell down, half-dead with fright.

I ducked back as soon as I'd fired. Three choppers opened up, and for the next three minutes death hung in the air. I let them blaze away, sneaked backwards, took the bend of the wall, and did another sprint. I was over another wall into another garden before they had made up their minds that it'd be safe to advance.

I was getting tired of this cat-and-mouse business. Instead of climbing the next wall I turned towards the house. It was a big one with a wide verandah overlooking the garden. No lights showed.

I kicked in a window, entered a room that smelt of cigar smoke and perfume. I crossed the room, opened the door and stepped into a passage.

There was a man and a woman in the passage, standing against the partition wall, out of the way of flying glass and slugs.

"Hello," I said, smiling at them. "How are you liking the circus?"

The man was tall and beefy with a red face and a military moustache. His eyes were hard and stupid, his neck thick. The woman was a dark, nicely moulded trick in an interesting Grecian affair—black crêpe with gold bands crossed high on the bodice and double gold bands around the hem. She was about thirty-five, and there was a wordly look in her slaty eyes that I like to see in women of thirty-five.

The red-faced guy stiffened his backbone after the first shock of seeing me had passed. He growled deep in his throat, started a ponderous swing that a battleship could have dodged.

I let the swing sail over my head and ruin a lot of air in the passage. Then I pushed the Luger into his fat ribs.

"Skip it," I said. "You'd be better at the ballet."

His red face went a waxen white.

I looked at the woman. She hadn't turned a hair. She looked back at me, her eyes interested, unafraid.

"Think of the fun you'll have telling your friends," I went on to the man. "Chester Cain passed this way. You could even put a plaque on the outside of the house."

They didn't say anything, but the man had difficulty in breathing.

"Would you both go into one of these rooms?" I said, jerking my head to a line of doors. "I'm as harmless as a spinster aunt so long as no one crowds me."

I manoeuvred them into a front room, made them sit down. The furniture was as heavy and as dull as the man's face. The woman continued to eye me with interest.

I put my gun away to ease the atmosphere, peered out of the window.

Searchlights roamed the sky, car lights lit up the street, flat caps moved back and forth.

"I'll stick around," I said, sitting down so I could watch the two. "That reception committee still looks like business." I lit a cigarette, then remembered my manners, offered the pack to the woman. She took one, giving me a long, curious stare as she did so.

"Jill!" the man spluttered. "What the hell do you think you're doing?"

"Why shouldn't I smoke?" she asked in a tired voice.

He opened and shut his mouth, then scowled at her.

I struck a match and lit her cigarette. I had an idea at the back of my mind that I might have fun with her.

We sat around while the cops tramped up and down, poked into bushes and scared hell out of each other.

Maybe the red-faced man thought I was harmless without my gun in my hand, maybe his manhood nudged him. He suddenly bounded out of his chair and came at me like a charging rhino.

I had my gun out by the time he arrived, but he was coming so fast he hadn't time to apply his brakes. I cracked him on top of his skull and he stretched out on the carpet.

"I'm sorry," I said to the woman. "But you saw how it was."

She looked down at the mountain of flesh without a great show of interest or distress.

"Have you killed him?" she asked.

She sounded as if she hoped I had.

I shook my head. "No."

"He won the Purple Heart," she said, looking at me. "I wonder if you know what that means? He likes to explain the battle to people."

"You mean he moves the salt cellar and the spoons and the pepper-box, and shows dispositions, manoeuvres and advances?" I said.

"That is the general idea," she said, lifting her elegant shoulders.

I looked down at the red-faced man and thought she couldn't have much fun with him.

"Yeah," I said. "These boys who live in the past are hard to take."

She didn't say anything.

A double knock on the front door brought me to my feet.

"That sounds like the Law," I said, twirling the Luger.

"Are you scared?" she asked, staring at me. "I wouldn't have thought anything would scare you."

"You'd be surprised," I returned, grinning. "Spiders give me goose pimples." I opened the room door. "Come on," I said. "I want you to talk to the Law. You won't throw an ing-bing?"

"No, I won't do that," she said. "I suppose if I tell them you're here, you'll shoot me?"

I shook my head. "I'll have to shoot the coppers, and that'd be a shame," I said.

We went down the passage to the front door. I stood against the wall in the shadows where I could see without being seen.

"You don't want to be told what to say, do you?" I asked.

"I don't think so," she said, opening the door.

There were a couple of cops standing on the front step. When they saw her they saluted.

"Everything okay, Mrs. Whitly?" one of them asked. His voice was loaded with respect.

"Except the noise," she said calmly. "Is it necessary to shoot so much? Surely one man can't be as dangerous as you make him sound."

"He's a killer, ma'am," the cop said, breathing heavily. "The Lieutenant's not risking lives. We shoot first and talk after."

"Very interesting," she said, in a bored voice. "Well, I hope it stops soon and I can go to bed."

"We'll catch him, ma'am," the cop said, sticking out his chest. "But don't worry, we reckon he's some way from here by now."

She closed the door, and we stood in the dim light, listening to the cops as they pounded their way up the street.

She fingered a ruby and gold bracelet, glanced at me.

"Is that Mr. Whitly?" I asked, jerking my thumb in the direction of the room we had just left.

She nodded. "Charles Whitly, the son of John Whitly, the millionaire," she said, in a hard, toneless voice. "We are very respectable people, and even the police salute us. Our friends are very respectable too. We own three motor-cars, six racehorses, a yacht, a private beach, a library of expensive books that no one reads, and lots of other very expensive and useless things. My husband plays polo . . ."

"And he won the Purple Heart," I said, shaking my head. "It sounds wonderful."

Her lip curled. "It does. It was when I married him."

"Yeah," I said. "Well, it isn't my idea of fun."

"It hasn't turned out to be mine either," she said, examining the bracelet.

We could go on like this all night, so I opened the front door.

"I guess I'll be running along," I said. "I enjoyed meeting you, and I'm sorry about the expensive things, and I'm sorry about hitting your husband on the head."

"Don't be sorry about that. It'll give him another topic of conversation," she said, and swayed towards me.

"I'm still sorry," I said.

Our faces were close.

"You don't find life dull, do you?" she asked.

I put my arm around her and kissed her.

We stayed like that for a minute or so, then I pushed her gently away.

"Life's fine," I said, and went down the steps of the house.

I didn't look back.

2

I ran the Mercury convertible into the wooden garage next to Tim Duval's place on the waterfront. I cut the engine and the lights, shut the garage doors and walked over to the house.

Searchlights still waved over Paradise Palms. Maybe they thought I was hiding in the sky. Every now and then a nervous cop would let off his gun. The activity was now a couple of miles away, and right where I was seemed quiet enough.

I rapped on the door of the squat, faded house and waited. There was a long pause, then a woman's voice called from an overhead window, "Who is it?"

"Tim around?" I asked, stepping back and peering at the white blob that looked down at me.

"No."

"This is Cain," I said.

"Wait," the woman said, and a moment or so later the front door opened.

"Where's Tim?" I asked, trying to see the woman in the darkness.

"You'd better come in," she said, standing to one side.

"Who are you?"

"Tim's wife." There was pride in her voice.

I wondered if a bunch of Law was waiting for me in the house. I didn't think so. I entered, followed her along the passage to a room at the back of the house.

The room was square-shaped and lit by a paraffin lamp. A fishing net hung in folds along one of the walls. Slickers, a southwester, rubber boots hung near it. There was a table, three straight-backed chairs, a plush arm-chair and a cupboard. There were other odds and ends. The place was clean. Somehow the room managed to look cosy and like home.

Mrs. Duval was a big woman, long-legged, big-handed, big-hipped, still handsome. She looked a young forty-five, and her red-brown face was strong. Black hair, without a strand of white, capped her head like painted tar.

She eyed me over. Her china-blue eyes, deep-set, were thoughtful.

"Tim said you were all right," she said. "I hope he knows what he is talking about."

I grinned. "He's trusting," I said. "But I'm harmless enough."

She nodded briefly. "You'd better sit," she said, and went over to the stove. "I guessed you'd be out here in a while. I kept something hot for you."

I found I was hungry.

"Swell," I said, sitting down.

She threw a clean white cloth over one end of the table, set a knife and fork and then went back to the stove.

"You men are all alike," she said, without bitterness. "You have your fun, and then come back to be fed."

"That what Tim does?"

"You do it too, don't you?"

I looked at the T-bone steak she had set before me, hitched up my chair.

"I've had a lot of fun tonight," I said, beginning to eat. "Where's Tim?"

"He went over to Cudco Key."

"Take the boat?"

"He rowed. He said you might want the boat."

"That's a long haul."

"He'll make it."

I tapped my plate with my knife. "I appreciate this."

She nodded, then said: "Jed Davis is out the back waiting for you. Do you want to see him?"

I frowned, then I remembered.

"The newspaper guy?"

She nodded.

"Is he okay?"

"He's a friend of Tim's," she said. "Tim picks bums for friends, but he won't bite."

I laughed. "I'll see him," I said.

She went away.

I was half through my steak when the door opened again and a mountain of man came in. His face was round, fat and purple. His eyes small and reckless. He wore a tweed suit that looked as if he hadn't taken it off since he bought it, and that had happened a long time ago. A battered slouch hat, slightly too small for him, rested on the back of his head. He chewed a dead cigar between small, even white teeth.

He stared at me, then came further into the room, closed the door.

"'Lo front page news," he said.

"Hullo yourself," I said, continuing to eat.

He took off his hat and combed his hair with a little ivory comb, grunted, put his hat on again and sat down in the plush arm-chair. It creaked as it took the strain.

"You certainly started something in this burg," he said, taking the cigar from between his teeth and examining it through half-closed eyes. "I feel like a war correspondent again."

"Yeah," I said.

He looked at the table. "Didn't she give you a drink?"

"I didn't miss it," I said.

He climbed laboriously out of the chair. "Must have a drink," he growled. "Hetty's a swell cook, and a good woman, but she just doesn't understand that guys need a drink." He opened a cupboard and produced a black unlabelled bottle. He found two glasses and poured whisky into them. He gave me a glass and went back to the chair with the other. "Clot in your bloodstream," he said, waving the glass at me.

We drank.

"How long do you reckon to keep up this shindig?" he asked.

"Until I've found Herrick's killer."

"So you didn't kill him?"

"No. I was the fall guy. It was a political killing."

He took another drink, rolled the liquor round in his mouth before swallowing it. "Killeano?"

"What do you think?"

"Well, yes; it'd suit him to knock Herrick off."

"Your rag interested one way or the other?"

"The Editor's too fond of life. These boys are tough eggs to monkey with. We stay neutral."

"Mean anything to you personally?"

He looked sleepy. "Well, if some guy came along and bust this Administration wide open, I'd have something to write about, providing the bust was complete. I'd do what I could to get the story, but I'd have to play it close to my chest."

I didn't say anything.

He eyed me narrowly, then went on. "Killeano's a louse. But he's got the town in his pocket, and now Herrick's out of the way, anything could happen. He's well in the saddle, and it'll be a hell of a job to unstick him."

"Depends how it's played," I said, lighting a cigarette. "If I can get the right information, I'll crack Killeano."

He nodded slowly. "What kind of information?"

"Did Herrick work on his own?"

"Practically. He and Frank Brodey. Their organization was small: too small."

"Who's Brodey?"

"Herrick's lawyer. He's at 458 Bradshaw Avenue. He lives with his daughter."

"Will he take over from Herrick?"

Davis shook his head. "Not a chance. He ain't built for a fight with Killeano. No, I guess he'll stay put and let Killeano walk it."

I made a note of the address.

"Ever thought why Herrick went so much to the Casino?" I asked.

"Yeah, but it didn't get me anywhere. He was trying to turn up some dirt, but whether he got it or not I wouldn't know."

"I think he did and that's why he was rubbed," I said. "Ever heard of Lois Spence?"

"Ever heard of Mae West?" he returned, grinning. "Lois is famous around here."

"Killeano know her?"

"Even I know her. She's balanced that light a breath of wind would blow her over."

"So she knew Killeano?"

"Yeah, about two years ago they were like that." He crossed his two fingers. "That was before Killeano took over the town. When he got into power he ditched her. Had to, I guess. You can't run a town and Lois at the same time: both are full-time jobs."

"Herrick went around with her too?"

"Yeah, but there was nothing to that, although some mud- slingers tried to make something out of it. My guess is he was using her to dig up dirt on Killeano, and she strung him along, took his dough and gave him nothing."

"He paid her to play the tables at the Casino."

That surprised him. He stared at me, lifted his hat, combed his hair while he thought. "Why did he do that?" he asked at last, putting the comb away.

"He took the dough she had won and gave her other notes in exchange. Looks like he suspected the Casino of passing dud notes."

Davis brooded. "Well, that's an idea," he said, "but it wouldn't be easy, and no one's complained."

"It might be worth checking. Could you do that?"

He nodded. "I guess I could. I go there off and on. I could sniff around."

"If you knew what you were looking for, it might not be so tough."

"Well, I can dig a little."

"This guy Gomez seems a tough egg."

Davis grinned. "I'll say. You met him? Take my tip and keep out of his way. He's dynamite."

"I've met him," I said, shrugging. "I was with Lois when he blew in. It took my reputation and the Luger to hold him. I thought I'd have to shoot him he was so mad, but Lois grabbed him and I got out. He was the one who started the Law on the move."

"He's a bad guy," Davis said, shaking his head. "He doesn't like anyone hanging around Lois unless it's strictly business. One guy thought he was soft. Gomez shot him. It was fixed to look like suicide, but I know how it happened."

"Kind of jealous, eh?"

"He certainly is, and as hot-blooded as a stove."

"What do you know about a cat-house along the waterfront? Who owns it?"

"Speratza."

"Sure?"

Davis nodded. "It's the only joint of its kind in town. He must have plenty of protection to keep it open, and he makes a good thing out of it."

"Huh-uh," I said, giving myself another drink. I passed the bottle to Davis. "And Flaggerty? Anything on him?"

"He's Killeano's stooge. He puts up a front, of course, but Killeano pulls the strings; he jumps. There's nothing to him. He's just another crooked cop."

"He helped in Herrick's killing."

Davis paused in pouring his drink. "The hell he did?"

"Yeah," I said. "About Herrick. Was he married?"

"No. He lived in an apartment with a guy called Giles who looked after him. Give you the address if you want it."

"Where?"

"Macklin Avenue. It lies off Bradshaw Avenue. But you won't get anything out of Giles. I talked to him. He doesn't know anything."

"Maybe he'll talk to me." I got up. "I guess I'll pay some calls."

"They're still looking for you," Davis reminded me. "And it's getting on for midnight."

"We'll get 'em out of bed."

"We?"

"Sure, I'm going with you. They won't expect me to be with you."

He produced his comb again and ran it through his hair.

"Say, that's not such a hot idea," he said. "I gotta keep in the clear. How'd I look if they spotted you with me?"

I smiled at him. "Come on," I said. "You and I are going on a little trip. First we'll go to Macklin Avenue and then Bradshaw. You got a car?"

He nodded.

"Fine. I'll be tucked up in the back under a rug. That way the cops won't worry us and we'll get places."

"I can always say I didn't know you were there," he said, his face brightening. "Okay, let's go."

3

I lay under the rug on the floor of Davis's battered Ford and sweated.

Davis sweated too, at least, he said he was sweating. "Gawd!" he exclaimed, "the place is lousy with cops. Any second now they'll start shooting."

"That's okay," I said. "They're not likely to hit me. I'm too well protected down here."

"But I'm not," Davis grunted. He braked sharply. "That's torn it. They're signalling to me."

"Keep your shirt on," I said, feeling for my gun. "Maybe they want to ask the time. You know what coppers are."

"Quiet!" he hissed dramatically.

I relaxed, waited.

Voices came out of the night. Feet scraped on the road.

"What the hell are you doing out here?" a voice growled into the car.

"Hello, Macey," Davis said. "I'm just passing through. How's the battle coming? You caught him yet?"

"We will," the voice said. "Where are you going?"

"Home," Davis said. "Think I'll get through?"

"You might, only don't blame me if one of the boys shoots you. The streets aren't healthy."

"You telling me," Davis said. "I've had twenty heart attacks in so many minutes."

The cop laughed. "Well, don't try any speeding. You'll be okay at the top of the road. We've just been through this district. The punk's as good as the invisible man."

"Thanks," Davis said, and eased in his clutch. "Be seeing you."

The car moved on.

"Phew!" Davis said after a while. "I'm shaking like a jelly."

"That shouldn't be hard for you to do," I said. "What's it look like?"

"He's signalled me through. There're cops all along the street glaring at me, but that's all they're doing. If there are any of them up at Herrick's place we'd better skip it."

"Have a drink and calm down," I said, sliding the bottle we'd taken from Tim's place over the back of the seat.

Gurgling sounds followed.

"Leave me some," I said sharply.

"You don't need it like I do," Davis said, but he dropped the bottle back. It hit my head.

"Hey!" I said. "Do you want to brain me?"

"I wouldn't mind," Davis replied, accelerating. "You can come out now. The cops are out of sight."

I threw off the rug, sat up, wiping my face. We were in a narrow street lined on each side by neat villas.

"We're just there," Davis said. "Next street."

As I was looking, a big brown Plymouth sedan shot round the corner, and belted down the street towards us. Davis gave a startled snort and swerved violently to the right. The Plymouth missed us by a couple of inches, and was gone.

"The crazy loon!" Davis exclaimed. "What's his hurry?"

"Maybe he remembered a heavy date," I said. "Don't let a little thing like that disturb you."

We turned the corner, pulled up outside a small villa.

"This is Herrick's place," Davis said. "Want me to come in?"

I shook my head. "You and me had better not be seen together," I said.

"Yeah," he said, reaching over the back of his seat. He found the bottle and patted it lovingly. "I can keep myself amused."

I left him and walked up the path to the house. No lights showed. I thumbed the bell, waited. Somewhere in the house the bell rang, but no one answered. I rang again, thinking the man, Giles, was asleep. But after five minutes of continuous ringing, I decided no one was home.

Davis stuck his head out of the car window. "Bust down the door," he said. He sounded a little tight.

I went round to peer in a window. There was enough moonlight to see something of the room. I found myself staring at a large desk. The drawers were open, papers were scattered on the floor. I looked closer and saw an arm-chair had been ripped to pieces.

"Hey," I called to Davis. "Come here."

Muttering under his breath, he heaved his bulk out of the car and joined me.

He peered through the window, saw what I had seen, stepped back.

"Looks like someone's been going over the joint," he said, producing his little ivory comb. He combed his hair thoughtfully. "That's good liquor of Tim's," he went on. "I think I'll have another shot. My nerves are kind of unsteady."

I tapped, broke a small section of glass near the window catch, opened the window.

"Hey," Davis said, his eyes round. "What do you think you're doing?"

"I'm going in there to take a look," I said.

"I'll stick around and toot on the horn if any buttons show," Davis said, moving towards the car.

"And leave that bottle alone," I said.

I had a look round the room. Someone had gone over it carefully. There wasn't anything in one piece. Even the stuffing in the chairs and settee had been hauled out and sifted through.

I went over the house. Each room had been treated in the same way.

Upstairs in the front bedroom I came upon a man in white pyjamas. He was lying half across the bed, the back of his head had been smashed in. I touched his hand. He was still warm; but he was dead. It looked as if the killer had surprised him in bed, and had bust him before he could raise the alarm.

I went down the stairs, opened the front door, called Davis.

"Come upstairs," I said.

We went up. Davis looked at the man.

"That's Giles," he said, making a little grimace. "Hell! We'd better get out of here."

"He hasn't been dead more than a few minutes," I said, staring down at the dead man. "Think that Plymouth's anything to do with this?"

"I wouldn't know," Davis said, moving to the head of the stairs. "All I know is if Flaggerty finds us here, we're dead pigeons."

"I guess you're right at that."

We went down the stairs and out of the house.

The night was quiet now. The searchlights had ceased to grope in the sky. Gunfire no longer sounded. It was hot and still.

We got in the car.

"You're passing up a good story," I said, looking at Davis with a grin.

"I'll wait until they find him," he said, starting the engine. "I'm not sticking my glass chin out by telling them he's there. They might tie me to it."

He let in the clutch and we shot away from the kerb.

4

"Is this where Brodey hangs out?" I asked, as Davis stopped the car in front of a big house on Macklin Avenue.

"Across the way," Davis said, pointing. "I'm not parking before any more death houses. Jeese! That was a dumb trick. If a copper had seen us come out—"

"Forget it," I said, getting out of the car. "Show me the place, and don't get so excited."

"Excited? For crying out loud! I don't like running into corpses that haven't been turned up by the cops. It's too dangerous."

We crossed the road. Somewhere out of sight a car engine roared. Davis paused in mid-stride.

"Hear that?" he said, clutching my arm.

"Come on," I said, and started forward.

Brodey's house was big, and it stood back from the street. The garden was full of palms and tropical shrubs. It was difficult to see much of the house from where we were.

As we approached the front gates, which stood open, we heard the car coming down the drive. We ducked back into the shadows. The brown Plymouth sedan shot into the street, belted away. It was out of sight before we got over our surprise.

I had caught a glimpse of a man who was driving, but I couldn't see much of him. The car was fitted with curtains which happened to billow out as the car passed me. That was how I saw the man; Davis didn't see him at all.

"Looks bad for Brodey," I said, and began to run up the drive.

Davis panted along behind me. "Think he's been knocked off?" he groaned.

"Looks like it, doesn't it?" I said. "Same car. Same hurry to get away. They're after something pretty important."

A turn in the drive brought us to a big Spanish house that was in darkness.

"If they've killed Brodey, there'll be a hell of a stink," Davis gasped, following me up the steps.

"They're sitting pretty," I said, "so long as they can pin it on me; and that's what they'll do."

"Then what the hell am I doing trailing around with you?" Davis demanded. "If you're the killer, what am I?"

"Ask the judge . . . he'll tell you."

I touched the front door; it swung open.

"Looks bad," I said.

"I'm not coming in," Davis said, backing away. "I'm scared, Cain. This is getting too deep for me."

"Take it easy," I said. "Stick around. Don't run out on me now."

"I'll stick, but I ain't coming in."

"What's the matter with you? This may turn out to be front page news."

"I'd sooner find it without you being around," Davis said, shaking his head. "If they're going to pin it on you, they'll book me as a material witness or something."

I left him arguing with himself, and entered the dark lobby. This time I'd brought a flashlight from the car. I looked into the various rooms that led off the lobby. They were undisturbed, but when I came to the last door at the end of the passage, I found what I expected to find. The room was Brodey's study. It was big and well-furnished and equipped like an office. Here, a search had been made. Papers were strewn on the floor, desk drawers were open. The search had not been as thorough as in Herrick's place. The chairs hadn't been ripped open, nor had the pictures been taken off the walls.

There was no one in the room, and I stood looking round, wondering what to do next. It was a big house to go over; I didn't know how many servants were sleeping upstairs: but I had to know if Brodey was dead.

As I turned to the door I heard or sensed something which made me feel I wasn't alone. I snapped off the flashlight and stood motionless, listening. I heard nothing. The room was as black as tar. I eased the Luger out, and held it down by my side. Still no sound. I crept cautiously to the door, reached it. Nothing happened. I stood listening. No developments. I touched the door, peeped into the passage. It was dark out there and silent. I kept still, listened, and tried to see through the darkness. I stayed there a long minute, listening. There wasn't a sound in the house, nor in the street outside, yet I was sure I wasn't alone. I could sense the presence of someone, and that someone wasn't far off.

I waited, hoping whoever it was out there had weaker nerves than I had. It was a nasty business standing half in and half out of the room in darkness and silence, waiting for someone's nerve to crack.

Then I heard something. It was an almost soundless sound, and at first I couldn't place it. After listening carefully I realized it was someone breathing near me. It gave me a spooked feeling.

Slowly I raised my flash until it was pointing in the direction of the breathing. Then I pressed the button, ready to jump if someone opened up with a gun.

The harsh beam of the flashlight lit up the passage. There was a choked gasp of terror which made the hair on the back of my neck bristle. I found myself staring at a girl crouched against the passage wall. She was slight, young, about eighteen, pretty in an immature way; chestnut hair, brown eyes. She was wearing a black and gold kimono and the trousers of her pyjamas were dark blue silk.

She stayed motionless, her eyes empty with terror, her mouth formed in a soundless scream.

I guessed she was Brodey's daughter.

"Miss Brodey," I said sharply. "It's all right. I'm sorry if I scared you. I'm looking for your father."

She shivered and her eyes rolled up. Before I could move she had slipped to the floor. I bent over her. She was out cold.

I slipped the Luger back into its holster and picked her up. She was thin and light, and I could feel her ribs under the silk kimono. I carried her into the study and put her on the settee.

Silence brooded over the house. I wondered if there was anyone else in the place.

I went to the front door, but Davis wasn't in sight. I found him by the car, his head back and the bottle to his mouth. I moved silently up to him and tapped him on the shoulder.

"Got you!" I said in a gruff voice.

Davis didn't jump more than a couple of feet, and hollered, "Yow-ee!" He nearly swallowed the bottle. I took it away from him with one hand, thumped him on his beefy back with the other. After a while he recovered from his choking fit.

"You loon," he gasped. "You scared me silly."

"Come on," I said. "I want you."

"Don't tell me you've dug up another corpse?" he asked, alarmed.

"Not yet, but Brodey's daughter has thrown an ing-bing. She's nice, and she's got on a kimono."

"Japanese style, eh?" he said, interested. "Well, maybe I'd better come at that."

Miss Brodey was lying where I had left her. She looked small and pathetic.

"The idea is to put her head between her knees and a key on the back of her neck," Davis said, combing his hair.

"That's for nose bleed, you dope," I said. "At least, the key part of it is."

"Well, give her some Scotch," he advised. "I bet Brodey's got a bottle somewhere around."

He found it after a short, intensive search, took a long swig himself.

"Not bad," he said, shaking his head at the bottle. "Lawyers always do themselves well."

I sampled the Scotch too. He was right.

"Well, come on," Davis said. "This is no time for boozing. Let's get this kid on her feet. Scraggy little thing, ain't she?"

"She'll ripen," I said, and lifted the girl's head. I forced whisky between her clenched teeth. It brought her round after a while, and her eyes fluttered at me.

"Bet she asks where she is," Davis muttered. "They always do."

But she didn't. She took one look at me and dived off the settee to the wall. She gave us the fright of our lives.

"Now take it easy," I said.

"Let me handle this," Davis said. "She knows me." He advanced towards the girl with a kindly leer on his fat face. "Hi, Miss Brodey, remember me? Jed Davis of the *Morning Star?* We heard there was trouble up here and blew in. What's wrong, baby?"

She stared at him, tried to speak.

"Now don't get upset," he went on gently. "Come and sit down and tell me all about it."

"He's taken him away," she blurted out in a thin, hysterical voice. "He made him go with him."

Davis led her back to the settee. "All right, kid," he said. "We'll fix it. Just sit down and tell us about it."

She gave me a scared look. I stood behind her so she couldn't see me. Davis was patting her hand, clucking over her. I was surprised at his technique.

He got the story out of her inch by inch. She told us she'd been asleep, and voices coming from her father's study had woken her. She'd gone down. The study door was ajar and she peeped in. Brodey was up against the wall with his hands in the air. A man in a brown suit was threatening him with a gun. She heard the brown man say: "Okay, if that's the way you want to play it. Come on, we'll go for a ride." She wanted to get help, but she was too scared to move. The brown man hustled Brodey out of the room. It was dark in the passage and neither of them saw her. They went out the front door, and a moment or so later she heard a car drive away. Then I showed up.

Davis and I exchanged glances.

"Seen this guy before?" Davis asked.

She shook her head. She was shivering with shock and looked as if she'd pass out any moment.

Davis tried to make her take another drink, but she wouldn't; she kept saying: "You must get him back. Please. Don't sit there. Get him back."

"We'll get him back," Davis assured her, "but we must know who took him. What was this guy like?"

"Short and thickset," she said, putting her hands over her eyes. "He was horrible—like an ape."

"Did he have a scar down the side of his face?" Davis asked, stiffening.

She nodded.

"Know him?" I asked.

"I guess so," Davis said, his eyes popping. "Sounds like Bat Thompson, Killeano's strong man. He's one of the tough boys from Detroit, and make no mistake, brother, he's tough."

"Know where we can find him?"

"I know where he hangs out," Davis said. "But we don't want to find him. He's a guy best left alone."

"Where does he hang out?"

"Sam Sansotta's gambling joint."

"Okay. Let's see how tough he is."

Davis sighed. "I knew you were going to say that. You're a nice reckless sort of a punk for me to fall in with."

"Get the police," Miss Brodey said, crying.

"We'll get everybody," Davis said, patting her shoulder. "Now go to bed and wait. We'll get your poppa back for you."

We left her sitting on the settee, her eyes like great holes in a sheet.

"Listen, Cain," Davis said, when we reached the car. "You ain't really going to call on Bat, are you?"

"Why not? We want Brodey, don't we?"

"Listen, Bat'll tear your ears off. He's a bad hombre. You're not going to scare him."

"I can try," I said, getting into the car.

"My pal," Davis said, but he got in too.

5

Sansotta's gambling joint was at the far end of the coast road, leading out of Paradise Palms. It was a squat building, three storeys high; a broad verandah, on which stood tables and chairs, circled the building. Beyond, two large glass doors gave on to the main hall.

Although it was after one o'clock, the place was still lit up. A number of people sat on the verandah, and dancing was going on in the hall.

Davis parked his car on the opposite side of the road, reached for the bottle, swished it round, drained it. He threw the bottle at the sandy beach.

"My need's greater than yours, pal," he said.

I was studying the layout of the place.

"You don't think you're going to walk in there and bring Brodey out, do you?" Davis went on, mopping his face with a not over-clean handkerchief.

"That's the general idea," I said.

"Superman stuff, eh?"

"That's it."

"Well, count me out. I'm too big a target to take Bat on. He's a killer."

"So am I," I reminded him.

He looked at me. "Well, brother, I'll be sitting out here admiring the view. I'll write you a nice obituary when they carry you out. What flowers would you like?"

"You're coming in. I'm a stranger seeing Paradise Palms for the first time, and you're showing me around. Somehow you're going to get me upstairs because that's where Brodey is."

"Oh no," Davis said emphatically. "Not me. I'm staying right here, keeping my nose clean. I'm not easily scared, but that guy Bat sure makes my flesh creep."

I stuck my Luger into his fat ribs. "You're going in," I said, giving him the hard eye, "or I'll make holes in you."

He looked at me, saw I meant business, sighed.

"Well, maybe I'll go buy a drink," he said. "No harm in that, is there?"

He opened the car door and we walked across the road, up the steps into the brightly-lit hall.

No one took any notice of us. We went to the bar. The barman nodded to Davis and set up a bottle. He seemed to know Davis.

We had a couple of snorts before a thin little man with polished black hair, polished black eyes and a paper-thin mouth came out from behind a curtain and joined us.

"'Lo, Sansotta," Davis said, tipping his hat. "Here's a pal of mine who's blown in looking for a good time. George, this is Sansotta, I was telling you about."

I nodded to the little man, thinking he looked a tough egg in spite of his size.

"Hi yah," I said. "Glad to know you."

He nodded. His puss didn't reveal anything.

"Nice town you have here," I said, like I thought he owned the burg.

"Fair," he said, looking around the room. His eyes were continually on the move.

I trod on Davis's foot.

He grunted, then said, "Any poker going on tonight? My pal's anxious to lose his roll."

Sansotta looked me over, and then looked at Davis. He raised his eyebrows.

Davis nodded. "He's okay."

"He can go up. They're playing in Room 5."

"Thanks," I said, finishing my drink. "Coming?" I said to Davis.

He shook his head. "I'll stick around for a drink or two, then beat it. You can get a taxi back."

"Okay," I said, and started up the stairs.

Half-way up, I glanced back, paused.

Flaggerty appeared in the main doorway. He was still wearing his green gaberdine suit, and a cigar burned unevenly between his teeth. He was scowling as he joined Davis at the bar.

I shot up the stairs and out of sight, glancing back after I'd rounded the corner to make sure he hadn't seen me. He hadn't. Davis was combing his hair, a fixed grin on his face. Flaggerty was buying himself a drink.

I walked along the passage to Room 5, listened to the hum of voices from inside and then moved on. There were three other doors in the passage, but I didn't bother with them. I headed for the second lot of stairs.

Half-way up I heard someone coming along the lower passage; I took the remaining stairs three at a time. I found myself in a dimly lit passage with two doors facing me.

Footsteps went along the lower passage, a door opened and then shut.

I stepped over to the first door facing me and listened. Silence. I moved along to the next door, listened. A voice was speaking, but the words were lost. I stood there, my ear to the panel, waited. Then I heard a muffled groan that set my teeth on edge. I was sure Brodey was in there.

Any moment Sansotta might discover I wasn't in Room 5 playing poker. As soon as he'd found that out, he'd be looking for me. If I was going to do anything, I'd have to do it now and fast.

I turned the handle. The door wasn't locked; it gave as I pushed.

I walked in.

On a bed in the corner of the room was a bald-headed man in a grey lounge suit. There was blood on his face and shirt front. One eye was closed and bruised, and a patch of broken skin showed by his right ear where he had been punched. His wrists and ankles were roped to the bed, and he was gagged.

Standing over him was a short, thickset man in a baggy brown suit. He was bow-legged and his battered, apish face was moronic and cruel. He was raising his great hairy fist as I walked in.

"Grab some cloud, Bat," I said.

He stiffened, then without moving his body he looked over his shoulder. His small pig eyes hardened when he saw me. His right hand moved, but I showed him the Luger.

"I shouldn't, Bat," I said gently. "I'm Cain."

That held him. Slowly he raised his hands to shoulder height. He grinned at me. His teeth were black and broken.

"Hello, bub," he said.

"Get over to the wall," I said, watching him, "and face it."

"You're my meat, bub," he went on, grinning at me. "Not now, but later. I'm as good with a rod as you."

"We'll try it sometime," I said. "Get over to the wall."

Still grinning, he sidled over to the wall.

"Turn," I said.

He turned.

I stepped up to him and belted him over his head with the gun barrel. I hit him as hard as I could. He slumped down on his hands and knees, but he wasn't out. He had the hardest head in the world. He squirmed round, grabbed at my legs. He nearly had me over. I kicked him off, hit him again with the butt of the gun. I hit him so hard the gun jumped out of my hand. He stretched out flat.

I cut the ropes that tied Brodey to the bed and sat him up. He fell off the bed before I could catch him. He was out.

As I stooped to pick him up, the door jerked open and Sansotta walked in. He stopped, gaped at me, at Bat; then his hand flashed to his hip pocket.

I let go of Brodey, flung myself at Sansotta's legs. We went down in a squirming heap. He clubbed at my head with his fist, but I wriggled away, caught him a bang under his right eye. His head snapped back, but he was on his feet before I was on mine. He was as fast and as tricky as a lizard.

The Luger had vanished under the bed. Bat was stirring, trying to sit up. Brodey was lying like a dead man a few feet from me. Sansotta jumped me. I caught him round his waist, dragged him down, belted him about the body.

He tried to fight me off, but my weight was too much for him. He gave a strangled yell, but I had him by the throat. I squeezed.

Green gaberdine trousers came into the room. I threw myself sideways, but I was too late.

Something that felt like the Empire State Building descended on my head.

6

I opened my eyes. Bat grinned at me.

"Hullo, bub," he said. "How you feel?"

I fingered a tender lump on the back of my head, grimaced.

"Lousy," I said.

He nodded, looked pleased. "I guessed it," he said. "But it ain't nothing to what's coming to you."

I grunted, and looked around the room. It was fair sized, windowless and contained a bed on which I was lying, and a chair on which Bat was sitting. High up in the ceiling was a naked electric light bulb. The room wasn't clean.

"How long have I been out?" I asked.

Bat grinned again. "Three-four hours," he said, leaning back in his chair. He seemed to regard the whole business as the best joke in the world. "You ain't so tough," he added as an afterthought. His short, greasy hair was matted with blood where I had hit him, but he didn't seem to worry about it.

"Where's Brodey?" I asked.

"Him? They put him somewhere. That guy's nuts. He don't know what's good for him," Bat returned, fishing out a package of cigarettes and lighting one. He tossed the package and a box of matches to me. "Have a smoke, bub, you ain't got so long to live."

I lit a cigarette. "What's cooking?" I asked.

He shrugged. "They'll be along to see you when they're through with Brodey," he told me. "You'll know soon enough."

I wondered what had become of Jed Davis. I hoped he'd ducked out in time.

"Well, well," I said, trying to blow a smoke ring. It didn't come off. "I'm not curious. I'll wait."

He grinned some more. "Don't start anything smart," he said. "I'm as fast with a rod as you are—faster."

I laughed at him. "You've kept it quiet then," I said.

A tiny spark of rage burnt in his pig eyes. "Whatja mean?" he demanded, leaning forward.

"Bat Thompson doesn't mean anything to me," I said. "But Chester Cain means plenty to you. Work it out for yourself."

"Yeah?" he said, his face a dusty red. "Listen, I could take you any time with a rod, see?"

"That's what you say."

"Watch, punk," he said, getting to his feet.

He crouched. There was a blur of white as his hand moved; a .38 sprang into sight. It was a fast, smooth draw. It surprised me.

"How's that?" he asked, twiddling the gun around on his thick finger.

"Do that standing in front of me when I'm heeled, and you'd be a dead pigeon," I said.

"You're a liar," he said, putting the gun away, but there was a look of doubt in his eyes.

"All right, I'm a liar, but I can beat you to the draw easy. I'll tell you why. You waste time. You don't co-ordinate your movements."

"Don't what?" His eyes opened a trifle.

"You're all wrong. Show me again."

He stared at me, his curiosity battling with his rage. Then he set himself, the gun jumped into his hand. It was fast and smooth. I knew I'd have to be extra good to beat him.

"Yeah," I said, "the holster's in the wrong position. I thought that was the trouble. It's too high. You want to sling it lower. You waste time catching at the butt. When you get the rod out you have to lower the barrel before you fire. See? Wastes time."

"Got it all worked out, ain't you?" he said, staring at the gun. I could see he was impressed. He put the gun back into the holster, adjusted the strap to bring the gun in a slightly lower position. "That right?" he asked.

"I'd make it lower," I said, "but then you're not as tall as I am."

He hesitated, then let the strap out another notch. The way he had it now was the way I wanted him to have it if I could lay my hands on a gun. The holster was now loose enough to go with the gun when he pulled it, and that'd mean a time lag before he could free the gun.

"Yeah," he said, looking at the way the gun was hanging. "That's okay." He grinned at me. "You ain't so smart, are you, bub?"

"What the hell?" I said, shrugging. "I still got confidence. I don't murder guys. I give 'em a chance."

He stared at me. "You ain't murdering me," he said, showing his teeth. "I know I'm good."

"To me you're just a tough egg from Detroit, but not tough enough to stay in Detroit."

He was sliding across the room, his great fist set to belt me, when the door opened and Killeano and Flaggerty came in.

Bat paused, dropped his hand to his side.

"Hi, boss," he said to Killeano.

Killeano ignored him. He stood at the foot of the bed, looked at me.

"Hullo," I said, stubbing out my cigarette.

Flaggerty stood by the door. His face was set.

"Where's the Wonderly girl?" Killeano snapped.

"How do I know?" I said. "Think I carry her around in my pocket?"

"You'd better talk, Cain," he said. "We want that girl, and we're going to get her."

"You don't expect me to help, do you?" I said, lighting another cigarette. "I wouldn't tell you if I knew. We parted company last night after I'd given her enough dough to get out of town."

"She hasn't left town," Killeano said, stroking the bedrail with his small white hands. "There wasn't time before we closed the roads."

"Then she must still be in town," I said, shrugging. "Why don't you look for her?"

Bat threw a punch at me, but I saw it coming. I rolled off the bed on to the floor, grabbed him around the ankles. He came down on top of me. Flaggerty jumped us, and after a little squirming around and thumping, I felt a gun barrel against my ear. I relaxed.

Bat's moronic face was close to mine.

"Take it easy," he said, "or I'll blow your lid off."

"I'm easy," I said.

They stood away. I got up.

"Look," I said, dusting myself down, "this won't get us anywhere." I sat on the bed, and reached for another cigarette. "Let me do a little talking. Maybe we'll find out where we stand."

Bat folded his fist, but Killeano stopped him.

"Let him talk," he said, sat down on the chair.

Bat and Flaggerty stood behind the bed ready to jump me if I looked like starting trouble.

"I'm making a lot of guesses," I said, looking at Killeano, "but this is the way I see it. You're the top shot in town. The only guy who might have been dangerous to you was Herrick. You own the Casino, which is a swell place for getting rid of dud currency which you're printing. You didn't think I knew that, did you? It didn't take me long to figure that one out. You have the Bank and the police in your pocket, and no doubt you're paying the boys to keep their mouths shut. The dud money circulates in the town. But if the visitors take it out of town, you've made sure it's good enough to fox anyone until it's too late to trace it back to you. But what happens? Herrick suspects that you're passing dud notes, and he begins an investigation. He can't go to the police because they're playing with you. He has to work on his own. He gets some of your dud notes and he is ready to spring the surprise on the Governor of the State. But you get wise, and knock him off." I flicked my cigarette away and grinned at Killeano. "How am I going?"

His square-shaped face was expressionless. "Go on," he said.

"Herrick is an important citizen and is running for election. He's not the guy you can knock off regardless. You hear I'm coming to town. It doesn't take you long to figure I'm the boy who's to be blamed for the killing. You fix it, and you make a swell job of it, and I'm the fall guy. Okay. But you slip up on a couple of points. You forgot that Brodey was wise and had evidence too, and you misjudged the girl who was to lead me into this mess. She ratted on you, and you know she can blow the lid right off your racket. Without her, you're sunk, even if you have made Brodey spill what he knows."

Killeano took a cigar from his vest pocket, bit off the end, spat. He lit the cigar carefully and blew out a cloud of smoke. "Finished?" he asked.

"Yeah," I said.

He looked over at Flaggerty. "He knows too much," he said. "We'll have to alter our ideas. It wouldn't do to bring him before a jury now. They might cotton on."

"Killed while resisting arrest?" Flaggerty said, raising his eyebrows.

"That's it," Killeano said. "You'd better do it quick. This guy's a tricky customer."

"I'll say I am," I said, winking at Bat.

"With him out of the way, we can concentrate on finding the girl. She can't get away," Killeano went on.

"It wouldn't be a bad idea to get rid of both of them," Flaggerty said.

Killeano shook his head. "We've got to put on a show," he pointed out. "We'll fix her so she won't talk when it comes to the trial. Girls are easy." He looked across at Bat, who leered at him. "Could you handle her?"

"I could sort of try," Bat said, showing his teeth.

Killeano got up. "Get rid of him," he said to Flaggerty.

"So long, Fatso," I said. "Don't think you're safe. You're not. It'll catch up with you in the end."

He took no notice and went out, closing the door sharply behind him.

Bat looked at Flaggerty.

"Do it now?" he said hopefully.

"Not here," Flaggerty said. "We'll take him for a ride."

"Give it to me quick," I said to Bat, "and shoot straight."

"Sure, bub," he said, patting my arm. "It won't hurt."

7

Flaggerty drove; Bat and I sat in the back.

"How's it feel to take your last ride?" Bat asked, looking at me with simple curiosity.

"All right," I said. "I got good nerves."

"You have, at that, bub," he said admiringly. "But don't think you're going to skip out on this. You ain't."

"Doesn't look as if we'll find out who's the better man, does it, Bat?" I said after a while.

"I don't have to find out; I know," Bat said, grinning. "I can take you any time."

"Not you," I said. "I'd rather meet you in a gun fight than a paralysed old lady in mittens."

He clouted me in the face with his fist.

"Shaddap," he snarled. "I could take you blindfolded."

"You haven't the nerve to try, have you?" I said.

"He ain't going to," Flaggerty broke in. "We're not taking chances with a snake like you."

"See?" I said to Bat. "Even your pal thinks I'm better than you. Hear him?"

Bat breathed heavily.

"You ain't so good," he said, struggling with his fury. "I could take you. To hell with that lousy flatfoot. I could take you with a guy hanging on each of my arms."

"Pipe dreams," I said, and jerked my head out of the way as he slammed a punch at me. His fist hit the rear window of the car and smashed the glass.

Flaggerty cursed him.

"Cut it out, will you?" he snarled. "You're going to plug this rat the way I tell you."

"The tough egg from Detroit taking orders from a small-time cop!" I jeered, digging Bat in the ribs.

Flaggerty slowed down and stopped.

We had arrived at a lonely stretch of beach. The lights of Paradise Palms were fading in the light of the dawn. It still looked a nice spot, but to me, it looked a long way away.

"Come on out," Flaggerty said. He sounded worried.

We got out.

Bat's face was purple in the yellow light.

"I'm going to show him," he snarled to Flaggerty. "I'm faster than he is, and I'll make the punk admit it!"

"You'll do what I tell you!" Flaggerty bawled.

"Tell him to jump into a lake," I said to Bat. "He thinks you're a sissy."

Flaggerty's hand whipped inside his coat, but Bat grabbed his wrist.

"Make a move like that and I'll blast you too," he raved. "I don't like coppers, see? I'm going to prove it to this punk, and a yellow shamus like you ain't stopping me."

"You're crazy," Flaggerty spluttered. "Suppose he beats you? He'll kill us both."

Bat grinned. "No, he won't," he said. "I ain't as nutty as that." He took Flaggerty's gun and broke it open. Cartridges spilled on the sand. "See?" he went on, leering at Flaggerty. "He has an empty rod. I have a loaded one. He still gets it even if he beats me to the draw, but he won't."

"Get it?" He looked over at me. "Suit you, bub?"

"Sure," I said. "I'll go happy showing you a turn of speed."

Flaggerty backed away. He didn't like it, but there was nothing he could do about it.

"Well, get on with it," he said angrily.

Bat tossed me the gun. It was a blue Colt .45. It balanced sweetly in my hand.

"How's that, bub?" he asked, grinning at me.

"Swell," I said, and stuck the gun in the waist-band of my trousers.

"Okay," Bat said, squaring up. "You ready?"

"Don't rush it," I said. "Like to make a bet on it?"

"Haw! Haw!" Bat doubled up with laughter. "You'll kill me, bub. How you gonna pay after I creased you?"

"Cut this out," Flaggerty stormed. "Get on with it. Kill the punk."

"Yeah," Bat said, suddenly scowling. "Well, bub, this is curtains for you." He crouched, shuffled his feet in the sand. I watched him, but even though he knew my gun was empty, he still hesitated.

"I'll give you time to go for your gun, Bat," I said, smiling at him. "A guy always has the drop on me before I kill him."

He snarled at me. "Only this time, I'll do the killing," he rasped.

Then he went for his gun.

If he hadn't loosened his holster, he'd have got me. But his gun stuck for just a fraction of a second, and it gave me time to yank out the Colt. I had it out by the time his hand was tugging at his gun butt.

"Beat you," I said, and flung the Colt in his face. I put everything I had into that throw. The Colt whizzed through the air, hit him a hell of a belt between the eyes. He went over backwards with a startled curse.

I jumped him, grabbed his gun, twisted away as Flaggerty threw himself at me. I kicked Flaggerty in the face, turned and hit Bat behind his ear with the Colt as he floundered to his knees.

Both of them stretched out flat in the sand, their arms flung wide and their faces turned to the morning sky.

That's the way I left them.

8

Strong sunlight was trying to force its way through the wooden shutter as I woke to find Hetty Duval standing over me. I sat up in the bed, blinked at her.

"I guess I must have slept," I said, running my fingers though my hair, exploring the lump on my head tenderly.

"I've brought you some coffee," she said. "Davis is waiting to see you. Shall I send him up?"

"Sure," I said, sniffing at the tray she had put on the bamboo table at my side. "What time is it?"

"Twelve," she said, and went out of the room.

I yawned, poured coffee, reached for a cigarette. I was lighting it when Davis lumbered in.

"Hi," I said, grinning at him.

"For crying out loud!" he said, staring at me. "I didn't expect to see you again."

"Nor did I," I said, waving him to the only chair in the little room. "Got any whisky on you?"

He produced a half-pint bottle from his hip pocket and handed it over.

"I was sure worried," he said, sitting down and mopping his face. "I'm getting cast-iron arteries through you."

I poured a couple of inches of the Scotch into my coffee and gave him back the bottle. He took a swig, sighed, shoved the bottle back into his pocket.

"Well, come on," he said impatiently. "Give. You ought to be dead." I told him.

"I'll be damned for a Red Indian," he exclaimed when I was through. "What happened to you?" I asked.

He puffed out his cheeks. "Brother, I thought it was all up with me. It certainly did me no good when Flaggerty blew in."

I laughed. "I saw you," I said. "You looked like a fugitive from a nightmare."

"You telling me," Davis said, shaking his head. "What a moment! Flaggerty and Sansotta got together, and Sansotta mentioned you. He said I'd brought in a guy who was a stranger to him. Flaggerty was on me like lightning. He wanted to know where I'd picked you up. I acted like I thought he was crazy, and told him I'd found you in a bar, and that you wanted a poker game. I swore that was all there was to it, and I had no idea who you were, and it was phoney enough to sound true. Flaggerty wanted to know what you looked like, and Sansotta supplied a detailed description. That tore it. 'It's Cain!' Flaggerty bawled, and you should see the way the crowd gaped. I acted surprised, but I needn't have bothered. They'd forgotten about me, and they made a dive for the stairs. I drifted. There seemed no sense in hanging around. I wrote you off as a funeral debt."

"Are you in the clear with them?"

He nodded. "Yeah, it looks all right. I've talked with Flaggerty this morning. He was half out of his mind with rage because you got away, and as for Bat—" He broke off to whistle.

"Why did you see Flaggerty?"

"They've pinned Giles' murder on you," Davis said, taking out his comb and running it through his hair. "I've just written a piece about you. Like to see it?"

I shook my head. "Any news of Brodey?"

"Only that he's missing. They hint you're at the bottom of that, too."

I lolled back on the pillow. "We've got to get organized," I said thoughtfully. "These boys are good, but there's one way to lick them."

"Yeah? What's that?"

"Play one against the other," I said. "It'll need a little thought and planning, but it can be done. I won't be out of this jam until I've cleaned up the whole mob and that includes Killeano, Speratza, Flaggerty and Bat. If I can get them out of the way for good, I guess their organization will fold."

"I guess it will," Davis said, scratching his nose. "How are you going to do it?"

"I'll find a way," I said.

"What do you want me to do?" he asked, after a pause.

"You still with me?"

He grinned. "Sure," he said. "Keep me under cover if you can, but if you can't, the hell with it. I'll stick whichever way it jumps. I like your style."

"Swell," I said, and meant it. "I hit the dud currency angle right on the nose," I went on. "I could tell by the way Killeano flinched that I'd guessed right. We've got to get hold of some of those notes, and we've got to find out where he makes them. A forgery plant isn't easy to hide. Can you take care of that angle?"

He nodded. "I'll try."

"Then there's Brodey. I'm thinking about the little girl. We promised to find the old guy. Maybe you'd try to get a line on him."

"I reckon he's dead," Davis said.

"I guess so, too. They wouldn't let him loose if he knows anything. Anyway, see what you can find out."

"What are you going to do?"

"I'm going to see Tim."

"Where's he got to?"

"He's looking after the Wonderly girl."

Davis grinned. "Well, I'll be damned. I ought to have thought of that. You watch that girl. Flaggerty wants her bad."

"He won't get her," I said grimly. "Now beat it, and see what you can dig up."

When he had gone, I dressed and went downstairs.

Hetty Duval was scrubbing the kitchen floor. She looked over her broad shoulder at me, paused.

"I'm going to see Tim," I said. "Any message?"

"Tell him to come home when he can. I kind of miss him," she said, and blushed like a schoolgirl.

"I'll tell him," I said, and peered out of the window.

Tim's boat rode at anchor. No one seemed around.

"Like to go out and see if it's all clear?" I asked.

She went. After a few minutes, she returned. "It's all right," she said.

I thanked her and walked down to the boat. I went hell for leather towards the islands. I suddenly wanted to see Miss Wonderly again. I was surprised how much I wanted to see her.

Three-quarters of the way across, I spotted a rowing boat. The guy who was pulling the oars acted like he was in a hurry. He waved to me, and then went on pulling.

I swung the boat off course and headed towards him.

It was Tim. His face was running with sweat and the wild look in his eyes turned me cold.

He tried to speak, but he was so breathless he couldn't make it. He raised his fists and shook them at the sky.

I hauled him on to the boat, grabbed him by the shoulders. I knew what he was going to say.

He said it. "They've got her!"

Chapter Four
CYCLONE SHOT

1

There were a half a dozen Bobby-soxers sitting up on stools at the drug-store counter when I came in. They didn't pay any attention to me. They were too busy telling each other how much they loved Frank Sinatra. I didn't pay any attention to them. I had too much on my mind.

I shut myself in a telephone booth, called Killeano's private residence. They told me he was at the City Hall, and gave me the number. I dropped in another nickel and put through a call to the City Hall.

A girl wanted to know who was calling.

"He'll tell you if he wants you to know," I said. "Put me through and step on it."

There was a delay, then Killeano's oily voice came over the wire.

"This is Cain," I said, speaking rapidly. "Turn that Wonderly girl loose right away, or I'll start something in this town that'll go down in its historical records. I'm not bluffing. I've taken all I'm going to take from you and your small-time outfit. Now I mean business."

"You do, eh?" Killeano snarled. "Well, so do I. Wonderly's confessed to the Herrick killing and she's signed a statement implicating you. How do you like that? We've got an open and shut case, and by God, I'm coming after you. I've given orders you're to be brought in dead or alive . . ."

"Okay, Killeano," I said. "From now on, it's gloves off. I'll get you for this. Make no mistake about it, and no one'll stop me."

I slammed down the receiver, joined Tim Duval, who was waiting outside in the Mercury convertible.

"She's in jail," I said, getting in beside him and slamming the door. "He says she's confessed."

He gave me an uneasy glance. "What are you going to do?" he

asked, engaging gear.

"We'll go back to your place. We've got to make plans," I said, lighting a cigarette and trying to control my trembling hands. I was cold with rage. "I'll get her out of there. I don't care how tough it is. I'll get her out."

"You'll never do it," Tim said. "They'll guess that's what you'll try to do, and they'll be ready for you."

"You don't think I'm going to leave that kid in their hands, do you?" I said, glaring at him. "I've got to get her out."

He nodded. "I can see that," he said, "but I don't figure how you're going to do it."

I snapped my fingers. "Know a good lawyer?"

"Jed would know."

"She's got to be represented. They can't keep a lawyer out. I'll call Jed when we get back. Step on it for God's sake."

I put a call through to Davis as soon as I reached Tim's place. Tim and Hetty hung around waiting.

Davis came on the line.

"They've got her," I told him. "They were tipped off by one of the rats who helped provision the boat. There's a reward for her and he sold her out. They've worked on her, and she's signed a statement. I want a lawyer to represent her. Can you fix it?"

"Sure," Davis said. "Coppinger will handle it. He hasn't any time for Killeano. I'll get after him. Where is she?"

"In the jail. And listen, money's no object. Tell this guy to get down there right away. Then when you've fixed him, come over here fast. I want to talk to you."

"I'll be along," he said, and hung up.

I dropped the receiver on its hook and pushed back my chair.

Tim was eyeing me. "Can he do it?"

I nodded. "He's coming over as soon as he's fixed the mouthpiece," I said, and walked to the window.

I didn't know what the hell was the matter with me. I'd never felt like this before. I was cold; my muscles flicked the way a horse flicks its muscles to get rid of flies. My mouth was dry and I felt sick. I wanted to go down to the jail and start shooting. I didn't care what happened to me so long as I could kill some of those rats who'd got that kid in their hands.

"Give me a drink," I said, without looking round.

Tim gave me a whisky.

I faced him. "You better keep out of this," I said abruptly. "I'm going to start a massacre in this town if I don't get her out. It's Killeano or me, and I'm stopping at nothing."

"Sit down," Tim said quietly.

"To hell with that!" I said. "I didn't realize what she meant to me until they grabbed her. I'm going to take the lid off now, and anyone who gets in my way will get hurt."

"Take it easy," Tim said, pushing me into a chair. "I know how you feel, but it won't get you anywhere to jump off the deep end. There's only one way to tackle this. You've got to use your head. If you get wild and jump in with both feet, you'll be playing into Killeano's hands."

I drew a deep breath, tried to grin. "You're right, Tim," I said. "I'm mad right now, but as you say, there's no sense in rushing into trouble. Somehow we've got to get her out and quick. But it needs planning. I guess I'll go look that jail over."

"You'd better wait for Jed," Tim advised. "He knows the jail. You can't afford to be picked up."

"Right again," I said. "We'll wait for Jed."

We had to wait a couple of hours. They were the longest hours I've ever lived through, and I wouldn't like to live through them again.

Davis came around three o'clock. The afternoon sun was sizzling hot and he was sweating. He stood in the doorway and looked at us.

"I fixed Coppinger," he said. "He's gone down to see her, and he'll be over here when he's through."

"Sit down," I said, waving to a chair. "Is it true she's signed a statement?"

He nodded. "They've given it to the press. It'll be in the evening papers." He took out his comb and fiddled with it. "They've had six hours to work on her before we knew they'd got her," he went on. "That's plenty of time to make a girl talk . . ."

Tim nudged him. "Shut up," he said.

"That's all right," I said, but I knew my face had gone white. "I'm not kidding myself what those heels have done to her. Well, they'll pay for it." I lit a cigarette while the other two exchanged glances. "Any ideas how we can get her out?" I asked suddenly, looking at Davis.

He gaped at me. "Get her out?" he repeated. "It can't be done. There just isn't any way of getting her out. That jail's like a fort, and Flaggerty has about twenty guards around the outside. I went down there with Coppinger and they wouldn't let me in. They're reckoning you'll try to get her out. They've got a couple of searchlights rigged on the roof, and every guard has a Thompson. They've even got dogs patrolling. Not a chance."

I suddenly felt better. I grinned at him.

"I'm getting her out of that jail," I said.

"I'd like to know how you're going to do it," Davis said, his eyes opening.

"Is this place on the main road?"

He nodded. "It stands back a quarter of a mile from State Highway Four. You can see it from the road as you leave town."

"I'll go out and look it over," I said. "When do you reckon Coppinger will be along?"

"About an hour," Davis said. "I'll drive you over to the jail and pick up Coppinger on his way out. You can travel the way you travelled last night."

"Okay," I said, and took out Bat's .38 Police Special. It was a good gun, but I wished I had my Luger. I checked it over, then shoved it down the waist-band of my trousers.

"Still want to be mixed up in this?" I asked Davis.

He looked surprised. "Why, sure," he said.

"I'm asking you because from now on there'll be no backing out. It'll be a fight to the finish."

He scratched his head, then shrugged. "I'll stick."

I looked across at Tim.

"And you?"

He nodded.

"That's fine," I said, and meant it.

I went to the door. Davis followed me.

2

Coppinger was a little guy, about forty years old, with a leathery face and a black moustache. His eyes were blue, sharp and cold. He looked sleepy, but there was something about him that told me he knew more than most guys awake.

"She's in a spot," he said, when he finally got seated. "I don't know what they've done to her, but they've done plenty." He shook his head, and took out a bag of Bull Durham smoking tobacco and a packet of brown papers. He rolled himself a cigarette. "She acts like she's already dead."

The hair on the back of my neck bristled. "What did she say?"

He lit the limp cigarette, let it dangle out of the side of his mouth.

"She said she killed Herrick," he told me in a flat voice. "That's all she did say. Although I was alone with her, although I kept telling her I was working for you, she just wouldn't bite. 'I killed him,' she kept saying. 'Leave me alone. I killed him, and there's nothing you can do about it.'" He shook his head again. "She's a goner, Cain. There's nothing I can do for her. We can plead not guilty, but we can't make a fight of it."

"Okay," I said, "stick around. See her as much as you can, and keep working on her. I wanted to be sure we couldn't beat the rap. Now, I know what to do."

He looked at me thoughtfully.

"I've heard about you," he said. "You've got a reputation. It won't get that girl anywhere if you try violence. They're going to bring her to trial. If she looks like she is sliding through their fingers, she'll meet with an accident. I know Killeano and Flaggerty. Those boys won't stop at anything, and I mean anything. The election's too close. They've got to clean up Herrick's murder before then. So be careful how you step."

I nodded. "I'll be careful."

"Thinking of getting her out?" he asked, after a pause.

I looked at Jed Davis, who was sitting across the room.

He nodded.

"That's the idea," I said. "I went out there this afternoon and had a look. It'll be tough."

"You won't get her out alive," Coppinger said, "if you get her out at all."

"But that's our only chance."

"I know." He stroked his nose, stared down at his feet. "Even if you got inside help, it'd be impossible."

I eyed him. "What inside help?"

He lifted his narrow shoulders. "There's a guard I know . . ." he began, then shrugged. "What's the good? It couldn't be done."

I slammed my fist on the table. "It's got to be done!" I exploded. "What about the guard?"

"A fellow named Tom Mitchell. Flaggerty's fooling around with his wife. Mitchell knows, but he can't do anything. He'd like to get even if he could. You might talk to him."

"I have to be careful whom I talk to," I said.

Coppinger nodded. "Mitchell's safe. He's aching to put one over Flaggerty. But I don't think he could be much use except to give you the layout of the jail. I wouldn't let him know too much."

I turned to Davis.

"See this guy, and bring him down to the wharf when it's dark. I'll talk to him."

Davis nodded, got up and went out.

I slid two hundred-dollar bills over to Coppinger. "There's more to come," I said. "Keep with that kid."

He pushed them back. "I'm doing this for fun," he said. "I've been hoping someone smart and tough enough would blow into town and crack Killeano. I'm not taking payment for having a front row seat. Something tells me you'll crack him."

"I think I will," I said, and shook hands.

After he had gone, I sat down and stared out of the window and watched the Conch fishermen preparing their boats for the night's fishing. I thought about Miss Wonderly, and the more I thought about her, the worse I felt. I remembered the way she looked sitting on the raft at Dayden Beach. I remembered how she looked lying in the sand when I was grilling the spareribs. It all seemed a long time ago. Then I remembered Bat's moronic face, and Killeano saying, "Do you think you could handle her?" And Bat saying, "I guess I could sort of try." I felt bad, all right.

The next three hours dragged away, and by the time it was dark I was lower than a snake's belly.

Tim looked in about eight o'clock, gave me an evening paper. The Herrick killing was smeared over the front page. There was a picture of Miss Wonderly. She looked cute. They called her the Blonde Killer.

They had the confession in full, and I read it. It was cockeyed enough to sound true. Miss Wonderly said she and I had returned to Palm Beach Hotel, and had had a lot of drinks. I was sore because Herrick wanted me to leave town. I said I'd show him he couldn't talk that way to me, and Miss Wonderly admitted she goaded me to call him, thinking I was bluffing. I called Herrick and asked him over. He came. I was drunk by then. We were supposed to have quarrelled and Herrick got angry. We fought, and Miss Wonderly hit Herrick on the head with my gun. Herrick fell down and bust his head open on the fire curb. We passed out, and woke the next morning to find Herrick dead.

That was the story, and it was signed. The signature was shaky and indistinct. I felt like hell looking at it.

Tim came back after a while to say Davis was waiting for me at the end of the wharf. He had Mitchell with him.

I went down.

It was dark, and the stars reflected on the still water of the harbour. There was no one around. At the end of the wharf I found Davis with a big, beefy man who had copper written all over him.

"This is Mitchell," Davis said.

I stepped up to the man, peered at him. I couldn't see much of him in the dim light, but he didn't look as if he would give me any trouble. He peered right back at me.

I didn't beat about the bush. "I'm Cain," I said. "How do you like that?"

He gulped, looked at Davis, then back at me.

"How am I supposed to like it?" he asked, in a thick voice.

"You love it," I said.

He raised his hands shoulder high. "Okay," he said.

"Relax," I told him. "You don't have to be scared of me. But if you start something, you won't have time to be scared. Get it?"

He said he understood. I could see he was looking reproachfully at Davis.

"You don't have to feel sore," Davis said irritably. "We're going to do you a bit of good."

"How'd you like to get even with Flaggerty and pick up five C's as well?" I asked.

Mitchell peered at me. "Doing what?" he asked, interest in his voice.

"Answering a few questions."

"Sure would."

"Where do you live?"

He told me.

I looked at Davis. "Is it far?"

"About five minutes."

"We'll go there, and mind, Mitchell, don't start anything funny."

"I won't."

We piled into Davis's car, drove over to Mitchell's place. He took us into the front room. It was plainly but comfortably furnished.

"You alone?" I asked.

"Yeah," he said, flinching.

"You mean your wife's giving Flaggerty a work out?" I said.

He clenched his fists; his face went yellow.

"Skip it," I said. "We know what's going on; so do you. The idea is to even things up, isn't it? Well, that's why I'm here."

He turned away, brought out a bottle of Scotch. He set up three glasses. We all sat down round the table.

Mitchell was about forty-five. His big, simple face was fleshy and carried a lot of freckles. He wasn't a bad-looking guy, but he had that look of gloom husbands get when their wives are two-timing.

"What's your job in the jail?" I asked, as soon as we'd settled.

"I look after floor D."

"On what floor is Miss Wonderly?"

He blinked, looked at Davis who didn't meet his eye, looked back at me.

"Didn't you say something about five Cs?" he asked cautiously.

"I did," I said, and shot him a hundred. "That's to sweeten you. You'll get the rest when you've told me what I want to know."

He fingered the hundred, nodded.

"She's on A floor."

"Where's that?"

"Top floor."

"Get paper and pencil and show me the layout of the jail."

He got paper and pencil and began to draw. We sat around drinking and smoking until he'd finished.

"This is it," he said. "Here's where you go in. There're two sets of gates. Each has a different key and guard. You book your prisoner in here. Women are booked in on the left. You take your prisoner along—"

"Wait," I said. "I'm only interested in the women's side. Concentrate on the women."

He nodded. "Okay," he said. "Well, the women go in through this door and are booked. They're taken along this passage—"

"What's that square there you've drawn?"

"That's the guards' office. That next to it is the police surgeon's office. That's the mortuary behind it and the P.M. room. We keep them all together because Flaggerty likes to make the jail his headquarters."

"Okay. Where's A floor?"

"You reach it by this elevator. The women are not allowed to use the stairs because the stairs give off to the other floors."

"How many women prisoners have you got in there?"

"Four—no, three. One of 'em died this morning."

"Where's Miss Wonderly's cell?"

He showed me the cell on the map he'd drawn. I made him mark it with a cross.

"How many guards have you up there?"

"There are three women guards. One goes around the cells every hour."

"How about the men guards?"

"They don't go to A floor, but they're around on the other floors every hour. Two to each floor."

"How many in the building?"

"Ten guards on duty, ten off. Since the girl came, Flaggerty has brought down another twenty from Station Headquarters to guard the outside of the jail. It has plenty of protection right now."

I studied the map for several minutes, then sat back and stared at Mitchell.

"If you wanted to get someone out of that jail," I said, "how would you set about it?"

He shook his head. "I wouldn't," he said. "It ain't possible."

I handed him the four Cs, and after he'd fingered them and put them away in his pocket, I took out a thousand-dollar bill.

"Ever seen one of these?" I asked him.

He gaped at it, his eyes round.

"I'd give this to the guy who could tell me how to get that girl out," I said.

He hesitated, then shrugged. "I wish I could, but it just ain't possible." He edged his chair forward. "I'll tell you why. You've got to get in. That's the first step. They've got dogs, searchlights and guards. Maybe you've seen the place? There ain't a scrap of cover around the jail for five hundred yards . . . just sand. The searchlights light up the whole of the expanse of sand, and there ain't a chance of you getting to the gate without being seen."

"Okay," I said. "Let's suppose we do get up to the gate. What next?"

"But you won't get to the gate," he said impatiently.

"Just suppose we do. Go on from there."

He shrugged. "The guard at the gate checks your credentials. No one except the doctor or a police official is allowed near the place now they've got her. They know you're smart and they're taking no chances. Coppinger had a hell of a time getting in."

"Well, okay. Let's imagine the doctor goes there. He gets in. Then what happens?"

"The guard hands him over to another guard who unlocks the second door, and the doc is escorted to his office. He can't go anywhere else in the prison, unless someone's ill. When that dame died this morning, he was escorted to her cell by a guard and the Head Wardress."

"I thought you said the male guards didn't go to the women's quarters?" I said sharply.

"They don't unless a male visitor has business in the quarters. Coppinger, for instance, was escorted by two guards."

I drummed on the table. "So it can't be done?" I said.

He sighed regretfully. "I'd tell you if it could be," he said. "I could use that grand, but I know it's hopeless. Believe me, no one can get into that jail and no one can get out. They could try, but they'd be dead meat before they got properly started. I tell you: Flaggerty is expecting you to try. He's got everything sewn up tight, and when that rat sews up anything tight, it stays tight."

I got up. "Okay, Mitchell," I said. "Keep your trap shut about this. I'll think it over. You might still be able to earn that grand. When do you go on duty?"

"Tomorrow morning at seven."

"What's your first job?"

"Inspect the cells, then I've got the job of cleaning up after the P.M."

"What P.M.?"

"They're trying to find out why this dame died. The P.M. is for nine-thirty tomorrow morning."

"Right," I said. "I'll be seeing you."

Out in the hot darkness, Davis said, gloomily, "What the hell are we going to do now?"

"Get that girl out," I said grimly.

"Talk sense. You heard what the man said."

"Sure I heard," I said. "I tell you what I'll do. I'll bet you ten bucks I have her out by tomorrow night."

He stared at me in disgust. "Aw, you're nuts," he said, getting into the car, "but I'll take your money."

"I'm not nuts," I said, climbing in beside him. "I have an idea."

3

A half an hour later I was in the car again with Davis, driving, and Tim Duval in the back.

"This is it," Tim said, peering out of the window.

Davis swung to the kerb and stopped before a sober-looking building. Above the shop-front was a sign: "Maxison's Funeral Parlour."

"I hope you know what you're doing," Davis said.

"Quit beefing," Tim said, before I could speak. "I'm having the time of my life. Why should you care what he does so long as he does something and takes you with him?"

"Just because you're an irresponsible citizen without a job to lose, don't think there aren't people who have to consider their futures," Davis snorted. "I'm one of them. This guy's got the bit in his teeth, and I want to know into what kind of hell he's dragging me."

"You'll know," I said. "I have one chance to get into that jail, and I'm taking it. That's why we've come here."

"You'll come here after you've been to the jail," Davis pointed out. "Maxison will give you a swell funeral."

"Quiet!" I said, then turned to look at Tim. "Maxison live over the premises?"

"Yep," Tim said. "He's lived there for years."

"Come on," Davis pleaded. "Don't be mysterious. Tell me. I want to know."

"This is a long chance," I said, fishing out a packet of cigarettes and lighting one. I offered them round. The others lit up. "You heard what Mitchell said. No one can get near the jail unless he's an official. He also told us a woman prisoner died this morning, and she's to be posted tomorrow morning. Then she'll be buried. Tim tells me Maxison is the only mortician in town. He does all the official burials, and that includes prison burials. I'm going to be his assistant. In that way I hope to get into the jail."

Davis's mouth fell open.

"For crying out loud!" he gasped. "Now that's what I call a damn smart idea. How did you think of it?"

"I thought of it," I said.

He took out his comb, lifted his hat, combed his hair.

"Wait a minute," he said. "What makes you think Maxison will play, and suppose they recognize you at the jail?"

"Maxison will play," I said quietly. "Tim tells me he has a daughter. I don't want to do this, but I have to. We're going to hold his daughter as hostage. If he tries to double-cross me, we'll threaten to knock the girl off."

Davis's small eyes popped.

"We're gangsters now, eh?" he said. "Jeeze! I don't think I like this much."

"You can duck out whenever you like," I said, shrugging. "Hetty will look after the girl. It's just a threat. I must have some hold on him."

"Don't be a sissy," Tim said to Davis. "You've always looked like a gangster. It's time you acted like one."

Davis grunted. "Well, okay," he said. "Kidnapping carries the death sentence now. Who cares?"

I opened the car, got out.

"Hey," he went on, leaning out of the car. "Suppose they recognize you in the jail? What happens then?"

"Let's wait and see," I said. "You stay with the heap. Tim and I'll handle this. If a copper shows, sound your horn and beat it. We don't want them to get a line on you just yet."

He wrinkled his fat nose. "We don't want them ever to get a line on me," he pointed out. "Well, go ahead, I'll sit here and pray. I'm good at that."

Tim and I went to the side door near the display window. I rang the bell. We waited.

There was a short delay, then we heard someone coming along the passage. The door opened and a thin, narrow-shouldered girl stood in the doorway.

I tipped my hat.

"I wanted to see Mr. Maxison," I said.

She stared at me, then at Tim. "It's very late," she said. "Couldn't you see him tomorrow?"

"Well, no," I said. "It's something I would like him to handle and it's urgent."

She hesitated, then nodded.

"If you'll wait," she said, and turned away. She got halfway down the passage, then came back. "What is the name, please?"

"He wouldn't know my name," I said.

"Oh," she said, looking at me again, and went away.

"That's Laura Maxison," Tim said. "Maxison thinks a lot of her.

Odd little thing, ain't she?"

I shrugged. "I guess if you had a daughter you'd think a lot of her whichever way she looked."

"I guess you're right," he said.

The door opened again, and a lean, elderly man with a stoop peered at us.

"Good evening," he said. "Was there something?"

"Yeah," I said, eyeing him over. He was bald, with a great dome of a forehead, and his eyes were small and close set. He looked what he was, and foxy as well. "Can we come in?"

"I suppose so," he said doubtfully, standing to one side. "It's very late for business."

"Better late than never," Tim said for something to say.

We entered the passage and followed Maxison into the green-carpeted reception-room. The air in there smelt musty. There was also an odour of floor polish and embalming fluid, aromatic, sweet and sickening.

Maxison turned on a few more lights, and took up his stand by a large glass showcase full of miniature coffins.

"Now, gentlemen," he said, pulling nervously at his faded purple and white tie. "What can I do for you?"

"I'm Chester Cain," I said.

He took an abrupt step back, his hand jumped to his mouth. Fear made him look old and stupid. His thin, almost skull-like face turned the colour of ripe cheese.

"You don't have to worry," I said, watching him closely. "I'm here on profitable business . . . profitable business to you."

His teeth began to chatter. "Please," he stuttered, "you mustn't stay here. I can't do business with you . . ."

I jerked a straight-back chair towards him. "Sit down," I said.

He seemed glad to.

"You and I are doing business whether you like it or not," I told him. "I'm going to ask you some questions, and if you know what's good for you, you'll answer them. You're burying a woman prisoner at the jail tomorrow?"

He cracked his finger-joints, his limbs trembled, but he obstinately shook his head. "I can't talk to you," he mumbled. "I hold an official position at the jail, and it'd be a breach of faith."

"You'll talk," I said, standing over him, "or I'll take you for a ride." Jerking out the .38, I rammed it into his chest. For a moment I thought he was going to faint, but he managed to control himself.

"Don't . . ." he began, in a husky whisper.

"You talking?"

He nodded wildly.

I put the .38 away.

"Okay. We'll try again. This time get your answers out quick."

He nodded again. His breathing had a rattle in it that added to the spooky atmosphere of the room.

"You're burying a woman prisoner at the jail tomorrow morning," I repeated. "Right?"

"Yes," he said.

"What time?"

"Ten o'clock."

"What time will you arrive at the prison?"

"Nine-fifty."

"What's the procedure?"

He blinked, hesitated, then blurted out, "I and my assistant will prepare the body after the post-mortem, put it in the coffin and bring it back here for the relatives to claim."

"You load the body into the coffin in the P.M. room or the woman's cell?"

"In the P.M. room."

I grimaced. That was what I had expected, but not what I had hoped to hear. It meant I should have to get Miss Wonderly from her cell down to the P.M. room. That wasn't going to be easy.

"The coffin ready?"

He nodded.

"Show me."

As he got to his feet, a bell tinkled faintly somewhere in the house. The sound took me like a flash to the door.

"Watch him," I said to Tim, and shoved the .38 into his hand. I darted out into the passage.

As I moved towards a door at the far end of the passage, I heard a telephone dial whirring. I ran on tip-toe to the door, jerked it open and went in.

The thin, narrow-shouldered Laura was feverishly dialling at the telephone. She looked up with a gasp as I entered. I crossed the room, gently took the receiver out of her hand, hung up.

"I'd forgotten about you," I said, smiling at her. "Calling the police?"

She jumped back against the wall, her pale, plain little face terrified.

She clasped her hands to her flat chest and shaped her mouth for a scream.

"Don't do that," I said, "I want to talk to you."

Her mouth trembled, hesitated, closed. She stayed where she was and stared at me; fear lurked in her eyes.

"You know who I am, don't you?" I asked.

Her throat tightened, but she managed to nod.

"I wouldn't hurt you, and I want you to help me. Don't be scared of me. I'm in trouble and I want help."

She looked puzzled, blinked her eyes, but she didn't say anything.

"Look at me," I said. "I don't look dangerous, do I?"

She looked. I could see the fear leaving her eyes, and she straightened up.

"No," she said, in a voice that wouldn't have scared a mouse.

"I'm not," I assured her. "You've read about me in the newspapers, haven't you?"

She nodded.

"You know they've arrested Miss Wonderly, and they've charged her with murder, don't you?"

She nodded again. Interest had replaced fear.

I took out the newspaper photograph of Miss Wonderly and showed it to her.

"Do you think she looks like a killer?" I asked.

She studied the photograph. There was a wistful look on her face when she handed it back.

"No," she said.

"She didn't kill Herrick, nor did I. It was a political killing, and they've pinned it on me because I happened to come to this town with a bad reputation."

She looked down at her hands. There was a faint flush on her face.

I stared moodily at her.

"Have you ever been in love, Laura?" I asked abruptly.

She flinched.

"You have?" I went on, when she didn't speak. "It didn't work out?"

"My father . . ." She stopped.

"All right," I said. "It's not my business. But if you have been in love, you'll know how I feel. I'm in love with that girl. I'm crazy about her, and I'm going to get her out of that jail if it costs me my life. I want you to help me."

She began to breathe quickly. "But how can I help?" she said, without looking at me.

"By not making a fuss. I'll tell you what I have to do. I don't want to do it, but I have to do it. My girl's life is at stake, and I'll do anything to get her out of the mess she's in. I'm going to take you away from here, and keep you until she's free. That's the only way I can make your father work with me. I give you my word you won't come to any harm, and you'll be returned here in a day or so."

She started up.

"Oh no," she said. "Please don't take me away."

I walked over to her and lifted her chin.

"Still scared of me?" I asked.

She looked at me.

"No."

"Swell," I said. "Come on, I want to talk to your father. I thought you'd help me."

We returned to the reception-room. Maxison was sitting glaring at Tim, who was trying to look like a Chicago gangster. He didn't do it very well.

"Your daughter's got a lot of guts," I said to Maxison. "Now show me that coffin."

He took us into a back room. It was large with bare walls. Coffins stood on the uncarpeted floor.

Maxison pointed to an imitation ebony coffin with ornate silver handles.

"That's it," he said.

I went over, lifted the lid. It was well finished inside, complete with a lead shell and a thick mattress.

"That's an expensive box for a jail-bird," I said, looking at Maxison. "Who's paying for it?"

"Her husband," he said, cracking his finger-joints and looking at Laura in a puzzled way out of the corners of his eyes.

I took out the mattress, fiddled around trying to get out the lead shell. I spotted the screws, and went over to the tool rack and brought back a long screw-driver. I took out the lead shell. Without the mattress and the lead shell there was an additional twelve inches from the bottom of the coffin to the top.

I did a little measuring and stood back, frowning.

"Could you put a false bottom to this?" I asked Maxison.

He gaped at me. "Yes, but what—"

"Skip it," I said, and turned to Laura, who was watching me with large eyes. "Will you do something for me, kitten?" I said. I patted the coffin. "Get in here."

"Oh no," she said, with a shudder. "I—I couldn't do that."

"Please," I said.

Maxison started forward but Tim raised the gun, bringing the old man to an abrupt stop.

"Stay where you are, Laura," Maxison grated.

She hesitated, looked at me and then stepped to the coffin. I lifted her up and lowered her in. She sat in the thing, her eyes dark, her mouth working. She looked like something out of the *Grand Guignol*.

"Lie down," I said.

Shuddering, she lay down. I took more measurements.

"Fine," I said, and pulled her up. "Out you come." When she was out, I turned to Maxison. "I wanted to see if this coffin was big enough to hold two bodies. It is. You and I are putting your dead woman in and Miss Wonderly goes in under her. You're to fit a false bottom to this box. That's how I plan to get Miss Wonderly out of jail."

4

I arrived at Maxison's place at nine o'clock the next morning. There was a sedate, old-fashioned motor hearse parked outside.

I gave it a quick glance, then pushed open the glass door of the showroom and walked in.

Maxison was waiting for me. He was dolled up in a long black coat with silk lapels and a high hat. His face looked ghastly in the hard sunlight, his mouth twitched.

"Is she all right?" he asked anxiously, as soon as he saw me.

"Sure," I said. "So long as you play ball with me, you don't have to worry about Laura. She isn't worrying, and she has a woman to look after her." I tapped him on his bony chest. "But one false move from you, Maxison, she won't be all right."

He flinched, looked away. I felt sorry for the old geezer, but there was nothing else I could have done. I knew I couldn't trust him, and I had to have a hold on him.

"Did you get rid of your assistant like I said?" I asked.

Maxison nodded. "He's been wanting to do a trip with his wife to Miami for a long time. I told him he could go."

"Okay," I said. "We're almost set?"

"Yes."

"Let's go into the back room," I said, and pushed past him.

The coffin was standing on trestles. I raised the lid, examined the false bottom and the air-holes. Maxison had made a swell job. I told him so.

"We'd better have a couple more air-holes by the handles," I said. "It's going to be a tight fit, and I don't want her to have a bad journey. Will you fix that?"

While he was doing this I unpacked a grip I'd brought with me. Neither Davis, Tim, nor I had ceased to work on our plans during the night, and none of us had had any sleep, but I was now satisfied that everything had been covered satisfactorily. We had seen Mitchell again, and I had bought his co-operation for a grand. He was to play an important part in the jail break. He knew it would cost him his job, but he didn't care. He was sick of Paradise Palms and Flaggerty, and was ready to pull out as soon as he'd done his job for me.

I changed into a prison-guard's uniform that Mitchell had obtained for me. It wasn't a bad fit; I studied myself for a moment in the long mirror on the wall.

Maxison watched me furtively, but he didn't say anything. I took out a long black coat like his and put it on. It was high-necked and successfully hid the guard's uniform. Then I slipped into my mouth two little rubber pads Tim had borrowed from an actor friend. The effect of the pads was remarkable. They completely changed my appearance, making me look plump and rabbit-toothed. A pair of horn-rimmed glasses completed a simple, but excellent disguise.

"How do you like your new assistant?" I asked, turning so Maxison could see me,

He gaped. "I wouldn't have known you," he said, and he sounded as if he meant it.

"I hope not," I returned. "Flaggerty knows me a little too well. This has got to fool him."

Maxison had refitted the false bottom to the coffin and was now ready to go.

"Right," I said, going over to him. "We're not going to fail. Things may get sticky, but whatever happens, you must keep your head. I'm George Mason, your new assistant. Your other assistant is on vacation. I come from Arizona, and I'm the son of an old friend of yours, I don't suppose they'll check up, but if they do, you must give them the answers without batting an eyelid. If I'm caught, it's going to be just too bad for Laura. Understand?"

He licked his lips, looked sick, said he did.

"Okay," I said, putting on a stove-pipe hat like his. "Let's go."

I drove the hearse. Although it looked old-fashioned, there was nothing wrong with its eight-cylinder engine. It had a lot of speed, and I let it out on the coast road. A mile or so from the jail I eased up on the accelerator; we drove along at a sedate twenty miles an hour.

As the roof of the jail appeared above the sand-dunes, I saw two policemen standing in the road. They had Thompsons slung over their shoulders; they looked bored, and waved to us to stop.

"You do the talking," I said to Maxison, out of the corner of my mouth. "This is only a rehearsal for the real thing. These boys won't worry us."

The two cops stood each side of the hearse, peered at us.

"Where are you going?" one of them asked Maxison.

"The jail," he said curtly, and produced a burial certificate and the court order for the release of the body.

The two cops read the papers and handed them back. I could see by the blank looks on their faces they couldn't make head nor tail of the legal jargon, but they weren't suspicious.

"Okay, seems in order," one of them said importantly. He took a yellow sticker from his pocket and pasted it on the fender of the hearse. "That'll get you to the gates. No speeding, and stop if you're signalled."

"And that means stop," the other cop said, grinning. "The boys up there are sure itching to use their rods."

Maxison thanked them, and I released the clutch. We continued up the road.

"They're certainly taking no chances," I said.

Maxison gave me a surly look, grunted. "What did you expect?" he said.

On the other side of the sand-hills, I spotted four cops sitting round a machine-gun on a three-legged stand, covering the road. One of the cops was equipped with a portable radio, and he was tuning-in as I crawled by. They eyed the yellow sticker and then waved us on. It began to dawn on me that Mitchell had been right about it being impossible to get into the jail in the ordinary way.

Four hundred yards from the side road that led through the sand-dunes to the jail was a barricade made out of a big tree-trunk on wheels.

I stopped.

Three cops in their shirt sleeves appeared from behind the barricade, and swarmed round us.

One of them, a big, red-faced guy with sandy hair, nodded to Maxison.

"Hey, Max," he said, grinning. "Howja like the war conditions? Ain't it hell? That punk Flaggerty sure has the breeze up. We've been camped out here all night, and now we're being skinned by the sun. You going to the jail?"

"Yes," Maxison said.

The cop looked me over.

"Ain't seen him before," he said to Maxison. "Who's he?"

"George Mason," Maxison said calmly enough. "My new assistant. O'Neil's on vacation."

"He would be, the lazy rat," the cop said, spitting in the sand. "He's always on vacation." He looked at me. "Glad to know you, Mason. I'm Clancy. Howja like the new job?"

"Pretty good," I said, shaking his sweaty paw. "The beauty of this job is our customers can't answer back."

He bellowed with laughter.

"Say! That's a funny one," he exploded, slapping his thigh. "Did you hear what the guy said, fellas?" he went on to the other two cops who stood around, grinning.

"We heard," they said.

"Pretty funny," Clancy declared. "I didn't think guys in your trade had a sense of humour."

"That's all we have got," I said. "What goes on? I've never seen a jail guarded as tight as this one."

Clancy wiped sweat from his fat face with his forearm. "Aw, the hell with it," he said in disgust. "We got that Wonderly dame locked up, and our Chief thinks Cain's going to get her out. He's nuts, but there's no one with enough guts to tell him. I bet Cain's out of the State by now. Why the hell should he bother with a dame he picked up for the night?"

"She's a nice looker," one of the other cops said. "I'd trade her for my wife."

"I'd trade her for mine too," Clancy said, "but I wouldn't risk my neck for her."

"This guy Cain must be a tough egg if Flaggerty thinks all you boys are necessary to keep him out," I said, grinning.

"I tell you Flaggerty's nuts," Clancy snorted. "Mind you, if that dame did escape, he'd lose his job. I heard Ed Killeano tell him."

"Pretty soft for him," I returned. "I bet he's sitting some place cool, while you boys sweat it out in the sun."

"You bet he is, the monkey-faced punk," Clancy said, scowling. "He's got a swell office with air-conditioning on the top floor so he can keep an eye on hard-working stooges like me." He kicked sand, shaking his head. "I don't know what's come over this jail. A dame died yesterday, and damn me if another ain't gone cuckoo this morning. Dived off the deep end as I came on duty. Brother, she gave me a turn. You'll hear her screaming and laughing when you get inside. It gives me the heebies to listen to her."

"They'll take her away, won't they?" I said curiously.

"Yeah, in a day or so, but she's in the cell next to the Wonderly dame, and Flaggerty reckons it'll soften the poor little judy to have someone like that peering through the bars at her."

I gripped the wheel tightly, and I felt my face turn white, but Clancy didn't notice.

"They didn't oughta keep a dame like that in the jail," he went on. "She's making the other prisoners restless. She's dangerous too. She was in for sticking a knife into her old man. I'm keeping clear of A floor."

"Let us through, Clancy," Maxison said, glancing at me. "We have a job to do at ten."

"Sure," he said. "These boys are okay," he said to the other cops. "Let 'em through."

As I drove the hearse slowly past the barricade, Clancy bawled after me, "If you see that punk Cain, tell him we're expecting him, and not to disappoint us."

"I'll tell him to pick his box first," I called back, "and pick it from us."

They laughed like a bunch of hyenas.

"How are you making out?" I asked Maxison.

He was wiping his face with a handkerchief, and he looked hot and uncomfortable.

"I'm all right," he said shortly.

"Did you hear what that cop said?" I asked, through tight lips. "About that crazy dame being next to my girl? Did you hear it? Did you think what it means?"

"Yes," he said sullenly.

"Oh no, you didn't," I snarled at him. "But put Laura in my girl's shoes and then ask yourself how you'd like it."

I saw his face stiffen; he didn't say anything.

The drab stone building of the jail reared above us. Sunlight baked the granite walls. It was a lost, forlorn place, and it chilled me to look at it.

I stopped before the two large oak and iron gates. On the right of the gates was a small lodge. Two cops came out carrying automatic rifles.

"Hello, Maxison," one of them said. "We've been expecting you."

"Can we go in, Franklin?" Maxison said. "These new regulations are confusing me."

"It's all hooey," Franklin said, scowling. "Sure, you can go in. I'll open the gate for you."

As he moved to the gates he caught sight of me. He turned back.

"Who's this guy?" he demanded. He had a flat squashed face, and eyes like a Chinaman.

Maxison explained I was his new assistant, and where O'Neil, the other assistant, had got to.

Franklin scratched his head. "Well, I dunno," he said. "I got instructions to let in only those people I know by sight. I've never seen this guy before. I guess I'd better call the sergeant."

"Skip it," one of the other cops said. "The sergeant's at breakfast. You don't want to make him mad for the rest of the day."

"Will you hurry?" Maxison asked, trying to stop his teeth from chattering. "I have a job to do. I'm late already."

Franklin stared at me with a worried frown. I leaned out of the car window, jerked my head at him. He came closer.

"Can't you rustle up a crap game?" I asked, keeping my voice low. "The old man can do the work. I got money to lose."

He grinned suddenly, the frown went away. "To hell with that for an idea," he said. "Here, get out of the buggy."

I pulled the .38 from my waist-band as I pretended to fumble at the door. I shoved the gun to Maxison, who sat on it, his face turning a faint green.

I dropped on to the hot sandy road.

"Better make sure you're not heeled," Franklin said, but he was grinning all the time. "Then you can go in."

He ran his hands over my body. If he had told me to undo my overcoat I'd have been sunk, because he'd have seen the guard's uniform. But he didn't.

"Okay, hop in, and beat it," he said, stepping back.

I got into the hearse and slammed the door. My left hand reached under Maxison and retrieved the .38. I slipped it into my pocket. I felt a lot better with that gun within reach.

We drove through the gate into a courtyard. I saw the dogs then. They were massive brutes that strained at their chains when they saw us, snarling and showing their teeth. None of them barked. Their silent snarling made them look like wolves. I was glad to get past them.

We stopped outside a steel grill. Four or five guards paced up and down on the other side of the grill. Each carried a rifle. One of them opened up for us.

"Okay, Maxison," he said. "Go ahead. The doc's just finished."

I released the clutch and drove past the guard. I didn't look at him. We were in.

5

The white-tiled post-mortem room was clean and cool. A strong smell of antiseptics hung in the air. The body of a woman lay on the porcelain table, partially covered by a coarse bleached sheet. Her shaved head rested in the hollow of a small wooden block. She didn't look human, but like a realistic waxwork in an exhibition of horrors.

The doctor, a small, pudgy man, clear-skinned and tanned, was washing his hands in the deep sink. Steam from the hot water dimmed his glasses.

"She's all yours," he said, glancing round. "The poor devil killed herself by swallowing powdered glass. I'd like to know where she got it from."

Somewhere in the jail a woman began to utter clear, high-pitched peals of mirthless laughter as though she were being tortured by having her feet tickled. The sound set my teeth on edge; it was shrill, like a pencil squeaking on a slate.

The doctor scowled, came towards us drying his hands. "I'm going to report that woman," he said, irritably. "She shouldn't be here."

Neither Maxison nor I said anything. We stood around, looking at the doctor, then at the dead woman. I felt spooked.

"It's time Edna Robbins was kicked out of here," the doctor went on. "She's a sadist. I'm not saying she drove that woman crazy, but she couldn't have helped her."

He was addressing me, so I said, "Who's Edna Robbins?"

"The Head Wardress," he said, tossing the towel into a white enamelled receptacle. "You're new here, aren't you?" He shook his head. "She's a bad lot. Well, I can't stay gossiping," he went on. "I'll let you have the death certificate. You can pick it up at my office on your way back."

Maxison said he'd do that.

The doctor was crossing the room when the door opened and a woman came in. She was small, square-shouldered, and her blonde hair shone like brass. It was swept up to the top of her head, a tiny blue velvet bow holding it in place. She wore a black, smartly tailored dress relieved by white collars and cuffs.

"Finished?" she said to the doctor. Her voice made me think of shiny steel rods.

He grunted, went away without looking at her.

She stared after him, chewing her thin under-lip, then nodded to Maxison.

"Get that body out as quickly as you can," she said. "I want Mitchell to clean up here."

"All right, Miss Robbins," Maxison said, giving her a scared look.

He hoisted the coffin on to the trestles he had already set up.

The woman sauntered over to the body on the table and stared down at it. There was something about her small, sharp face that gave me goose pimples. Her nose was small, her mouth almost lipless, and her eyes ice-blue. Her straight eyebrows shot up to her high forehead and gave her a devilish look.

She lifted the sheet and examined the doctor's large stitches with interest. I couldn't take my eyes off her, and she looked up abruptly. Her eyes probed me. It was an odd feeling, as if she could see beyond my clothes.

"You're new here, aren't you?" she asked abruptly.

I nodded, "Sure," I said, and went on unpacking Maxison's bag. I took out his tool kit, took it over to him.

"What's the matter with your mouth?" she said suddenly. "It looks swollen."

My tongue automatically touched the rubber pads, and I had a bad moment.

"A bee kissed me," I said, turning away from her. "I didn't think it showed."

I felt her eyes on me, then she walked across the room to the door.

"Make haste," she said to Maxison and went out.

I had been watching her as she crossed the room. She had narrow hips, and her legs were good. When the door closed behind her I straightened up, wiped off my face with my handkerchief.

"A nice little thing," I said, under my breath. "She knows how to use her eyes."

Maxison was also sweating. "She's dangerous," he said.

"I'll say," I agreed, and stepped over to the door. I opened it, peered into the passage. There was no one about. "Well, here goes," I went on, closing the door. I took off the long black overcoat and shoved it in the receptacle under the towel the doctor had used. I took off my spectacles and removed the rubber pads in my mouth. "You know what to do," I said to Maxison. "Get the false bottom out and hide it under the box. Take your time about preparing the body, but be ready to finish quick when I get back."

He nodded, his eyes popping.

"Watch your step, Maxison," I went on. "No funny business."

The mad woman upstairs began to laugh again, hysterical and unhurried. The sound gave me a chill down my spine.

I went to the door and peered into the passage again.

Mitchell was out there, waiting. He nodded to me.

"Okay?" I said.

"So far," he returned. His eyes were bright with excitement and fright. "For Gawd's sake be careful."

"I'll be careful," I said.

"The stairs are around the corner. The morning inspection's through. You've got a clear hour before they go around again. Look out for Robbins. She's the one to watch."

I nodded. "I'll watch her. You know what to do?"

"Yeah; but I hope I don't have to do it."

"So do I," I said, and walked quickly down the passage.

At the corner I paused, looked round. No one was about. Voices came from a room nearby, but I kept on, crossed the passage to the stairs, went up them.

The stairs were broad and led directly to the upper floor. I walked on, passed the steel grill that guarded the circular gallery housing the cells, and mounted to the second floor. Half-way up I had to pass a convict who was on hands and knees, scrubbing the stairs. He shifted as he saw me so I could pass. I felt his eyes on me and I guessed he was wondering who I was. I kept on until I reached the top floor.

I knew then that I was only a few yards from Miss Wonderly. The thought gave me a queer feeling of panic and exhilaration. As I reached the top of the stairs, I saw the grill gate facing me. That didn't worry me. Mitchell had supplied me with a duplicate pass-key.

As I crossed the passage and reached the grill, the mad woman suddenly gave a high-pitched scream. It rose, swelled, and hung in the air like a shriek of a damned soul. It was so loud, so close, so unexpected, that it froze me. For a moment I was ready to run blindly down the stairs, but I recovered my nerve, started forward again. As I was about to take the pass-key from my pocket, I paused.

I felt someone watching me. I turned.

Edna Robbins was standing in a doorway half-way down the passage. Her hard little face was expressionless, her slim, square-shouldered body without movement.

I felt my heart lurch, but I kept still. We stood there for a long moment looking at each other. She was suspicious, but she wasn't alarmed. The guard's uniform reassured her, but I knew I couldn't give her time to think. I walked slowly towards her.

She waited, her eyes searching my face.

"Any trouble up here?" I asked, when I was within six feet of her.

Her face remained expressionless. "What makes you think there is?" she asked.

"I heard that scream. I was on the next floor, so I came up," I said, looking her over.

"A real conscientious screw," she sneered, but I could see my look had registered. "You've no business up here. Beat it!"

"Okay," I said, shrugging. "You don't have to be mad at me." I let my eyes drift up and down her body. "I wouldn't like anything to happen to a cute trick like you."

"Wouldn't you?" she said. "Come inside and tell me why."

I hesitated, then walked past her into a small room fitted as an office. It was as hard and clean and masculine as she was.

She leaned her hips against the edge of the desk and folded her arms.

"Haven't seen you before," she said.

"I'm one of the new guards from Station Headquarters," I explained, and sat on the edge of the desk beside her. We were close; my shoulder touched her shoulder. She had to turn her head to look at me.

"I've seen you somewhere before," she said, a puzzled, curious look in her eyes.

"I saw you yesterday," I lied glibly, "I was manning the barricade when you passed."

Her eyes narrowed. "You look like that new mortician in the P.M. room," she said.

I grinned. "He's my brother. We're often mistaken for each other. He's fatter in the face than I am, and he hasn't a way with women."

"You have?" The sneer in her voice was pronounced.

I winked at her "I go for women in a big way. They go for me, too."

"Maybe that's why you came sneaking up to the women's quarters," she said.

"The dame's scream scared me. I thought she'd got hold of you."

A thin wolfish expression lit her face. "They don't get hold of me," she said quietly. "They know better."

"Tough, eh?" I said, admiring her. I leaned closer to her. "I could go for you in a big way."

She stood up and walked to the door. "Dust," she said, "and don't come up here again. If you hear any more screams forget it. There's nothing on this floor I can't handle."

"I can believe it," I said, walking to the door. "Well, so long, lady; if there's anything I can do for you, you'll find me on the next floor."

"Scram," she said impatiently.

She came to the head of the stairs to watch me go. I went down and along the passage of B floor. I waited a moment, listening. I heard her go back to her office. The door clicked shut.

I gave her a moment, then moving quickly, I ran up the stairs again, crossed the landing, whipped out the pass-key and unlocked the grill. I moved with urgent haste. My mouth was dry, my heart pounded. I slid back the grill. It moved easily, without sound.

I stepped through and slid the grill into place, locked it. Then I walked down the narrow gallery towards Miss Wonderly's cell.

6

The first three cells were empty. There was a smell of disinfectant and unwashed bodies in the air. I made no sound on the rubber flooring, but I walked on my toes down the narrow gangway, one side of which was the row of cells, and on the other side the high wire screen guarding the sheer drop into the main hall of the prison below. The mesh of the wire screen was so fine that it was not possible to see through it into the lower galleries.

There was movement in the fourth cell. I paused, peered in. A fat old woman, raddled, decaying, grinned toothlessly at me.

"Hello, pretty boy," she said, waddling to the bars. She grasped the bars with raw hands. "Ain't seen a man for ten years. Coming to see me, precious?"

My face was stiff with fright. I shook my head, edged past her, my back scraping along the wire screen.

"After the young 'un, are you?" she leered. "You'll like her. But watch Bugsey. She's in the next cell. She hates screws."

I edged on, staring at the old woman fascinated. As I came to the sixth cell an arm shot through the bars, a thin, sinewy hand gripped my wrist.

I started back, trying to drag myself free. The grip bit into my flesh. The bloodless fingers were terribly strong.

My face was damp with sweat. Butterflies fluttered in my stomach.

I allowed the hand to pull me to the bars so that my face was against the cold steel of the door. I found myself face to face with a young blonde whose mad burning eyes glared ferociously at me. She hissed at me through clenched teeth. Little flecks of foam bubbled on her lips. My hair moved on the back of my neck, my heart skipped a beat. Her other hand whipped through the bars and caught my coat collar.

My heart began to pound again. I was scared.

"Hello, copper," she said. "I've been waiting for you." She closed one eyelid in a gruesome wink. "I'm going to kill you," she went on, in a stage whisper.

"No, you're not," I said, bracing my feet against the bars. "I'm going to get you out of here."

She sounded off with her crazy, high-pitched laugh. It sent spiders' legs up and down my back.

"They won't let me out," she said. Her smile was sad and cunning. "They know what I'll do to them. I'm going to do it to you." Her face tightened, her eyes narrowed. "I'm going to tear your throat out."

I got my feet against the bars, and suddenly heaved backwards. I broke her hold and I fell against the wire screen, slid to the floor.

She glared at me, beating her hands against the bars. As I struggled to sit up, she flopped down on her knees, grabbed my ankle. I kicked at her with my free foot, but I couldn't reach her because of the bars.

She held my ankle between her two hands and hauled. I choked back a yell of fright as I felt myself sliding across the rubber floor. I grabbed at the wire screen, but she jerked, breaking my hold. She hauled me towards her like a landed fish.

I kicked and twisted, but I couldn't get my leg free. The raddled old woman was watching, giggling with excitement. "She'll cut your heart out," she whispered to me.

Sweat ran down my face, and I struggled and writhed in blind panic. There was something about the mad woman's face and the way she laughed and muttered to herself that scared me silly.

I was now against the bars. She released my leg and grabbed my coat again. Our faces were close. I could smell her sour breath. She turned me sick with horror.

"What's the matter with you?" I panted. "I'm going to get you out of here. You and the kid next door."

"You're not touching her," she snarled. "They've done enough to her. I'll stop you and I'll stop them touching her again. Come closer, copper. I want to get my hands on your dirty neck."

I tried to pull away, but she dragged me closer, her hooked fingers moving in little jerks up to my neck. She was so intent watching my face that she didn't see that I'd drawn back my leg. I placed my foot gently on her chest, then kicked out with all my strength.

She shot over backwards, the breath rushing out of her body. Released, I staggered to my feet, reeled against the wire screen. I was trembling, and could scarcely stand.

"That gave you a fright," Edna Robbins sneered.

I went cold, turned.

Edna was standing just inside the grill. She was watching me. Her small, sharp nose looked pinched, her eyes dangerous.

The raddled old woman had disappeared to the back of her cell. The mad woman lay on the floor, gasping and wheezing for breath.

I straightened my torn jacket, ran my fingers through my hair. I felt like hell.

Edna came down the gallery.

"I told you to scram, didn't I?" she said bitingly. "All right, wise guy, you're going before the Warden."

I backed away, my eyes darting to the cell next to the mad woman's. I could see a woman lying on the cot; a woman with honey-coloured hair. My heart lurched. I knew who that was.

"Don't get mad," I said in a croaking voice. "I didn't mean any harm. I wanted to see what this cuckoo looked like."

Edna smiled spitefully. "Well, you've seen her. I've a mind to stick you in with her and let her work on you. Come on, you rat, you're finished here. The Warden will fire you out."

I knew then it was Edna or me. I eyed her small body over. She looked capable, but I was sure I could handle her. I had to get my hands on her throat before she could raise the alarm.

I slouched towards her, looking crestfallen, sullen.

"You might give a guy a break," I muttered, as I reached her.

"You'll get no break from me . . ." she began.

I shot out my hands, seeking her throat. Then I got the surprise of my life. Moving like a lizard, she caught my wrists, pulled me towards her, bent. The next second I was flying through the air. I thudded against steel bars, bounced to the floor. I lay there, stunned.

"I told you I could handle anything on this floor," she said, standing over me. "And that includes you." She drew back her foot and kicked me in the face. "Get up, and come quietly, or I'll break your goddamn neck."

Gritting my teeth, cold with rage, I rolled towards her, grabbed at her legs. I heaved. I heard her quick gasp as she lost her balance, but she was smart enough to throw herself forward, breaking her fall on me.

I clutched at her body, hard as steel under my fingers. I tried to jab her in the face with my head.

She hit me in the eye with bony knuckles, rammed her knee in my chest and caught hold of my wrist with both hands. She was strong and full of jiu-jitsu tricks. She was getting a lock on my arm which threatened to break it. Pain crawled into my brain.

"I'll teach you to fight me," she panted, heaving down on my arm.

Somehow I rolled over, taking her with me. She clung to my arm like a bulldog as I threw her about. Each heave I gave sent fresh waves of pain up my arm. My sinews cracked.

I caught a glimpse of her blonde head and I slammed a punch at it. My fist caught her in the neck. She let go of my arm, flopped on the floor.

I got slowly to my knees, my right arm useless. There was no keeping her off. She raised up, swearing softly, her blonde hair down to her shoulders. She came back at me. I was ready for her, and socked her in the ribs with a left that travelled about three inches.

She went over, completed a somersault and was on her feet before

I could get to mine. She scared me. She was as tough and as dangerous as any man.

This time she didn't rush me, but spun on her heel and ran towards the grill gate. I was after her in a lurching run. Whatever happened she mustn't give the alarm.

I grabbed her as her finger was reaching for the red button of the alarm bell. I tried to close with her.

She clutched me to her, fell straight back, her feet in my stomach. I shot over her head, crashed against the grill. By the time I sorted myself out, she was climbing over me to get at the bell. I got my hands around her waist and pulled her down. She bit, punched and scratched. We rolled over. I pounded her body. At first she hit back, but after three or four of my punches she tried to keep them out with her elbows. They were hurting her as I meant them to hurt. She was panting and sobbing with rage. I caught hold of her throat, but she dug her thumbs in my eyes. I let go. I heaved away from her, my eyes streaming. She staggered to her feet, came at me again, wobbly, but out to finish me. I set myself and hit her with a long, raking left in her throat.

Her mouth opened, and she gave a thin wail as she fell against the door of the mad woman's cell.

There was a moment's pause. I, on my knees, she, with her shoulders against the bars, her knees buckling; then two greedy, claw-like hands shot between the bars and closed round her throat. She gave a wild scream as she felt the hands touch her. Her scream was throttled back into her throat almost before it sounded.

The mad woman, yammering with excitement, pulled backwards. The bars were a shade too narrow for Edna's head to pass through. She couldn't scream, because the mad woman's hands were squeezing her windpipe. She kicked and twisted. One of her shoes flew off and hit me in the face. Her knees burst through her stockings. I couldn't move. I stood against the grill, shivering, staring.

The mad woman continued to pull, bracing hard with her feet. Edna tried to reach inside the cell, but her arms weren't long enough. She looked at me, her eyes starting out of her head, her tongue swelling in her mouth. The mad woman gave a sudden jerk. A horrible muffled sound came from Edna's throat as her head passed through the bars, leaving skin behind. One side of her face was a mass of blood.

"I've got her," the mad woman whispered to me. "Thinks she can handle anything up here, does she? We'll see."

She sat on the floor, her arms raised, her hands round Edna's throat.

The raddled old woman tried to see what was going on, but she couldn't. She hammered on the door with her hands, cursing in a rasping voice.

Edna was arched backwards, her heels digging into the rubber flooring, her head through the bars. Her hands clutched at the bars for support and to relieve her weight from her head. Blood from her face ran down on to the floor, dripped on to her Nylon hose.

The mad woman, grinning at me, not looking at Edna, began to take in and let out slow, long breaths. Her shoulders seemed to grow lumpy, sweat appeared on her face.

I hooked my fingers into the wire mesh of the screen, and watched.

The raddled old woman, her face against the bars, suddenly stood still, listening.

Edna's face, where it wasn't blood-stained, was liver-coloured. Her eyes stood out, blind. Her tongue came out blue between bluish lips. Her slender body writhed. One of her hands began to beat on the bars, mechanically, without force.

The mad woman nodded to me, closed her eyes and strained. Edna's hand stopped beating on the bars. There was a muffled crack, almost immediately, a sharper one. Edna did not writhe now. She sagged, her head still trapped between the bars.

Sick with horror, I stepped past her dragging feet towards the next cell.

The mad woman let go of Edna's throat, sprang to the bars and reached for me. I pulled my gun and beat down her hands with it.

She jumped back, howling.

Even with that horror so close to me, I could now only think of Miss Wonderly.

She was in there. She lay flat on the cot, her eyes closed, her hair like spilt honey on the coarse pillow.

I unlocked the cell, stepped in.

The mad woman's fingers grabbed my arm. Half-crazy with fear, revolted, I struck her between the eyes with my gun butt. Her eyes rolled back and she dropped.

Shuddering, I snatched up Miss Wonderly and blundered from the cell.

The raddled old woman began to scream.

7

I slid back the door of the elevator, peered into the passage. Mitchell, wide-eyed, hopping with excitement, was standing at the far end. He waved to me.

Up on A floor the old woman continued to scream.

I ducked back into the elevator, scooped up Miss Wonderly's limp form in my arms and stepped into the passage. As I did so, Mitchell waved me back, then turned and bolted up the stairs.

Warned, I laid Miss Wonderly on the floor, reached for my gun.

A prison guard, automatic rifle wedged into his hip, came running around the corner. I didn't give him a chance. My .38 cracked once. The guard stumbled, curled up on the floor. His automatic rifle fell out of his hands, exploded. The slug brought plaster down from the ceiling on my head.

I turned, snatched up Miss Wonderly, tossed her over my shoulder. She moved feebly, but I gripped her tight. I ran.

Somewhere in the building an alarm bell began to ring. Its jangling note mingled with the cries of the prisoners, a great rattling of steel doors, and the old woman's screams upstairs.

Half-way down the passage a door flew open, two guards spilled out. I shot one of them in the leg, the other ducked back into the room, kicked the door shut. I sent a slug through the door, heard the guard yell.

I kept on, moving more slowly, turning to look back at every step. I was fighting mad, not going to be beaten now I'd got so far.

I heard heavy feet pounding down the stairs, and I broke into a run. The P.M. room was too far away. I knew I couldn't make it in time. I pushed open the first door I came to, stepped into a small, coldly furnished office. Again I put Miss Wonderly on the floor. She opened her eyes, struggled to sit up, but I pushed her back.

"Stay still, honey," I said. "I'm going to get you out of here."

It gave me a hell of a bang to see the expression in her eyes when she recognized me. She caught her breath, but she lay still, watched me.

I jumped to the door, knelt and peered into the passage. Four guards, one with a Thompson, were staring down at the bodies in the passage. I picked off the guy with the Thompson. The others made a frantic dash for the stairs, disappeared.

I grabbed Miss Wonderly, kissed her, and whizzed down the passage with her. I reached the bend as someone opened up with a chopper. One of the slugs nicked the heel of my shoe. I stumbled, made an effort, rounded the bend.

I burst into the P.M. room, closed the door.

Maxison was crouched against the wall, his face livid with fright. He gave a gulping gasp when he saw me, but he didn't or couldn't move.

I ran over to the coffin, swung Miss Wonderly off my shoulder and into the box in one movement. She sat up, her face stiff, her eyes bewildered.

"Lie down, and don't make a sound," I panted.

She looked at the coffin, and her mouth opened to scream. I put my hand over her mouth, but she struggled, frantic with fear.

I hated doing it, but there was no other way out. I half closed my fist and hit her on the side of her jaw. Her head snapped back, she passed out cold.

Feverishly I straightened her out in the box, whipped in the false bottom and turned the screws. Then I grabbed the long, black overcoat, struggled into it. I put on my glasses, put the pads into my mouth. I stepped across to Maxison and dragged him to the porcelain table.

"Get that body in," I snarled at him, and grabbed the stiff, cold shoulders.

Somehow he managed to pull himself together, and taking the woman's feet, he helped me across the room with her, and together we lowered the body into the coffin. It only just fitted, and I knew the lid would have to be forced down. I snatched up the lid, had it on the coffin as the door was flung open.

Flaggerty and three prison guards stood in the doorway.

I acted like I was scared, backing away and throwing up my hands. Maxison didn't have to act. He thought his last hour had come.

Flaggerty, sweating, white with rage, gave us a quick glance, then looked around the room.

"Anyone been in here?" he grated, glaring at Maxison.

Maxison shook his head. He couldn't speak he was so scared.

"Come on," Flaggerty snarled to the guards, and turned, then he turned back, walked to the coffin and threw off the lid. He stared down at the dead woman, his eyes narrowed, his lips grimacing. He made a gesture of rage, stamped out.

The door slammed.

I wiped my face, tried to recover my breath.

"Take it easy," I said to Maxison. "This is only the half of it."

I grabbed a screw-driver and screwed down the lid of the coffin. I had just finished when the door opened again and Clancy, the guard, came in. His face was red with suppressed excitement.

"Whatja know, fellas?" he said. "That guy Cain's gatecrashed the jail. He's snatched his floozie."

"You don't say," I returned, wiping my face and hands on a towel. "Got him yet?"

Clancy shook his head. "He can't get away. Flaggerty's out of his mind. He's going through the jail with a tooth comb." He gaped at me. "What the hell's happened to your face?"

"One of the guards thought I was Cain," I said. "He pushed me around before Flaggerty stopped him."

"They're sure crazy," Clancy said. "I've never seen so many nuts under one roof. Well, they'll catch Cain. He can't get out."

"Sure of that?" I said.

"I guess so. How can he?"

"How did he get in?"

"Yeah," Clancy said, shaking his head. "I hand it to that guy. He's smart, and he's got guts."

"How soon can we move?" I asked. "I don't want much more of this shooting."

"You stick around. No one's allowed to leave until they've found him," Clancy told me.

I shrugged, lit a cigarette. I wondered how long Miss Wonderly would remain out, and if she'd start to scream when she came round. I sweated to think about it.

We sat around for ten minutes or so, then shooting began again.

Clancy went to the door, peered out. "Sounds like they've cornered him," he said. "Trouble on B floor."

The alarm bell began to ring.

"Now what's up?" Clancy demanded, frowning. "What do they want to ring the bell for?"

Mitchell appeared suddenly. "Come on, mug!" he bawled to Clancy. "We gotta jail break on our hands. The prisoners are loose."

Clancy snatched up his rifle.

"Who let 'em loose?" he asked, rushing to the door.

"Cain, I guess," Mitchell said, pushing Clancy ahead of him.

He looked back at me, winked. "Come on, everyone's to go to B floor. Orders."

They went running down the passage.

I grinned at Maxison.

"Mitchell let 'em loose. I hope he'll be all right," I said. "Come on, we're going."

Between us we hoisted the coffin on our shoulders and made for the exit. The coffin weighed a ton, and we were staggering by the time we'd reached the gate of the prison block.

The lone guard stared at us, lifted his rifle.

We stopped.

"It's okay," I gasped. "I've got a permit to leave. Lemme get this coffin on board and I'll give it to you."

He hesitated, and I went on past him into the courtyard, where the hearse was waiting. He followed us.

Maxison and I shoved the coffin into the hearse, slammed the door.

The guard still threatened us with his gun. His round, red face was puzzled.

"Flaggerty said no one was to leave," he grumbled. "You can't go, so don't you think you can."

"I tell you Flaggerty's given us a permit," I said angrily. "Give it to him," I went on to Maxison. "You got it in your pocket."

With a dazed expression on his face, Maxison put his hand in his inside pocket. The guard swung the gun away from me, covering Maxison, suspicion in his eyes.

I jumped, hit the guard on the jaw, snatched his rifle from him as he fell I belted him over the head with the butt.

"Come on," I said to Maxison, and bundled him into the hearse. I drove across the courtyard, through the first gate which was open, and stopped outside the outer gate which was closed

Franklin came out of the lodge. He eyed us over.

"Getting out while the going's good?" he asked, grinning.

"Sure," I said. "We gave the permit to the guard at the main block. They've got a prison break on their hands now."

He shrugged. "I'm keeping out of it. I'm a man of peace."

He walked to the gate and opened it. "So long, fellas."

I nodded and drove on.

There was only one more obstacle, the barricade. I kept my gun by my side, drove steadily down the sandy track. I could see no guards. The barricade blocked my exit, but no one was there to guard it.

The sounds of shooting and yells came to us from the jail. I guess everyone was too busy to bother about guarding a tree.

Maxison and I got down, rolled the barricade aside; then we got back into the hearse.

We'd done it.

Chapter Five
POINT COUNTER POINT

1

The Martello Hotel, Key West, overlooked the Atlantic Ocean. From our private balcony, shaded by a green and white awning, we could look down at the Roosevelt Boulevard, which was almost deserted; houses were shuttered and dogs slept on the sidewalks. It was noon, and the heat was fierce. Away to our right we could see low emerald islands in a shimmering, painted sea beneath high-piled lavender clouds. Steamers and other craft worked their way through the old Nor'west Channel, a chartered course taken for centuries.

Wearing trunks, sun-glasses and sandals, I lolled in a wicker armchair. A highball, clinking with ice, stood on the chair arm. I relaxed in the heat, stared with narrowed, impatient eyes out to sea.

Miss Wonderly sat by my side. She had on a white swim-suit that clung to her curves like a nervous mountaineer rounding Devil's Corner. A straw hat, the size of a cartwheel, shaded her face. A magazine lay on her lap.

Minutes went past. I moved slightly to reach my cigarettes. She patted my hand as I picked up my lighter. I smiled at her.

"Pretty nice, isn't it?" I said.

She nodded, sighed, took off her hat. Her soft, honey-coloured hair fell about her shoulders. She looked pretty nice herself.

We had been at the hotel for five days. The jail break was a distant nightmare. We didn't talk about it. For the first two or three days, Miss Wonderly had been in a bad shape. She had bad nights, bad dreams. She was scared to leave the hotel, scared if someone came into the room. Hetty and I hadn't left her for a moment. Hetty had been wonderful. She was with us now.

We had taken Miss Wonderly from the jail straight to Tim's boat. Hetty, Tim and I had gone with her, and we had somehow managed to slip through the cordon Killeano had flung round the coast and reached Key West. Tim had gone back to Paradise Palms the following morning with the boat.

Key West, with its sponge and fish docks, its turtle crawls and markets, its leisure and friendliness, was a good spot for convalescing. Miss Wonderly had picked up faster than I had hoped. Now she was almost normal.

"All right, kid?" I asked, smiling at her.

"Yes," she said, stretching. "And you?"

"Sure, this is much more like the vacation I was hoping to find in Paradise Palms."

"How long shall we stay here?" she asked, suddenly, abruptly.

I glanced at her. "There's no hurry," I said. "I want to get you well. We can stay here as long as you like."

She turned on her side so she could watch me.

"What's going to happen to us?" she asked, giving me her hand.

I frowned. "Happen? What should happen?"

"Darling, perhaps I haven't the right to ask, but is it going on between you and me?" Her face flushed.

"Do you want it to go on?" I asked, smiling at her. "I'm not much of a guy to go places with."

"I could stand it if you could," she said seriously.

"I'm crazy about you," I told her, "but I don't know how you would fit in with my kind of life. You see, I haven't learned to settle down. I can't imagine myself settling down. It wouldn't be much of a life for you."

She looked down at our hands, joined together.

"You're going back there, aren't you?" she said.

"Back where?" I asked sharply.

"Please, darling," she said, gripping my hands. "Don't be like that. You are going back there."

"You mustn't worry," I said, smiling at her. "I don't know what I'm going to do."

"But you will, when Tim comes. You're waiting for Tim, aren't you?"

"Well, yes," I said, looking out to sea. "I'm waiting for Tim."

"And when he comes, you'll go back with him?"

"I might."

"You will."

"I might," I repeated. "I don't know. It depends what's happened."

She gripped my hand hard.

"Darling, please don't go back. I didn't think we would get away. When I was in that awful jail I thought I should never see you again. I thought they would catch you and you'd be hurt. But we did get away, and I have you with me. It would be wicked to put all this in danger again, wouldn't it?"

"Don't worry," I said. "I have a job to finish. I like to dot my i's and cross my t's. It's the way I'm made."

"No, it isn't," she said. "No one's made like that."

"I am."

"Darling—don't do this." Her hands trembled in mine. "Let it go—please—this time . . ."

I shook my head slightly.

She took her hands away, "You and your pride," she said, her voice suddenly hard, angry. "You don't care about this. You don't care about us." She drew in a deep breath, burst out, "You've seen too many gangster pictures—that's what's wrong with you."

"It's not like that," I said.

"Yes, it is," she said. Her voice was now elaborately controlled. "You want revenge. You think Killeano has crowded you, and you have to shake your reputation in his face. You can't resist doing that. You like long chances. You think it's big and smart to go back alone against that mob who stop at nothing. Just because Bogart and Cagney do it for a living, you have to do it too."

I took a pull at my highball, shook my head.

"It wasn't as if they beat you, burnt you with cigarettes, took off your clothes and paraded you before a crowd of grinning prison guards," she went on, her voice low. "They didn't come into your cell at night, did they? You didn't have a crazy woman whispering through the bars at you—awful, filthy whispering . . ."

"Honey . . ."

"Well, did you? I'm the one who suffered, not you. I don't want revenge. I want you. I don't want anything or anyone but you. I'm out of it. I'm glad to be out of it. God! I'm glad to be out of it. But you want to go back. You want to fight them. You want to avenge me. But I don't want to be avenged." Her voice broke suddenly. "Darling— can't you think of me a little—can't you let this one thing go—for me? For us?"

I patted her arm, stood up.

There was a long silence, then I heard her get up. She came and stood by my side, slipped her arm through mine.

"Was that what you meant when you said I wouldn't fit in with your kind of life?" she asked.

I looked down at her, put my arm round her, pulled her to me. "Yeah," I said. "I'm not made to be pushed around. I'm sorry, kid, but I'm going back. I said I'd fix Killeano, and I'm going to fix him. I feel a heel doing this to you, but I have to live with myself, and I'd never forgive myself if I let that rat slip through my hands."

"All right, darling," she said. "I see how it is. I'm sorry I didn't understand before. Forgive me?"

I kissed her.

"Darling," she said after a while, "do you want me to wait for you?"

I stared at her. "You're certainly going to wait for me," I said.

She shook her head. "Not certainly," she said. "I'll wait, on one condition. Otherwise I won't be here when you come back. I mean it."

"And the condition?"

"You're not to kill Killeano. Up to now you have defended yourself. If you kill Killeano it will be murder. That mustn't be. Will you promise?"

"Now, I can't promise that," I said. "He might get me in a spot—"

"That's different. I mean you're not to go gunning for him. If he attacks you, then that's different. But you're not to hunt him down and shoot him as you have been planning to do."

"Okay," I said. "I promise."

I held her close, then suddenly I felt her back stiffen. I looked over my shoulder.

Tim's boat was not more than a mile out to sea. He was coming fast.

2

Davis, Tim and I sat around the table in Tim's sitting-room, a bottle of Scotch within reach, full glasses in our hands.

Davis had just come in. It was early evening, and Tim and I hadn't been back long from Key West.

"I've been busy," Davis said, grinning at me, "but before I sound off, how's the kid?"

"She's all right," I said. "They gave her hell in that jail, but she didn't lie down under it. She's fine now."

Davis looked across at Tim, who shrugged.

"Of course, she didn't want me to come back," I said, rubbing my jaw, "but she'll get over that too."

"Well, so long as she's okay," Davis said, combing his hair and looking puzzled, "that's swell."

Tim said, "The trouble with this guy is he won't leave trouble alone. There was a sweet scene when Hetty heard he was coming back—"

"All right," I interrupted curtly. "Let's skip the domestic details. What's new?"

"Plenty," Davis said, lighting a cigarette. "Flaggerty's dead for a start. Howja like that? He was killed by one of the convicts: cracked his skull with an axe."

"That's one less for me to bother about," I said.

"Yeah. And here's a juicy morsel. Killeano's taken over Flaggerty's job. He won't release the jail break to the press. I guess it's too close to the election for bad news to be told to the trusting public."

"What happened to Mitchell?"

"He skipped out. I saw him before he went, and he gave me the whole story. I hand it to you, pal. It was a pretty smooth effort. I wrote it up, but the editor killed it after consulting Killeano. The public doesn't know a thing about it."

"And Maxison?"

"He managed to keep his nose clean, but only just. Laura supported his story, and after sweating him, Killeano turned him loose. He's back at work now, but, I must say, he looks like a fugitive from the Lost Horizon. There's one thing you ought to know. They've turned up Brodey's body."

"He's dead?" I said sharply.

"Yeah. He was found at Dayden Beach. Your Luger by his side. Guess who killed him?"

"I know," I said, clenching my fists. "So I'm wanted for three murders now?"

"You sure are," Davis said, looking smug.

"Too bad," I said, took a drink and eyed him over. "What else?"

"That's all the topical news," he said, reached inside his pocket and took out a five-dollar bill. He tossed it over to me. "Picked that up at the Casino a couple of nights back."

I turned the note over, held it up to the light. It looked all right to me.

"So what?"

"It's a dud."

I stared at the note again. It still looked fine to me.

"Sure?"

"Yeah. I had it checked by my bank. They say it's a first-class job, but it's a dud all right."

"I'll say it's a first-class job," I said. "You got it from the Casino?"

He nodded. "It was with two other fives I won. They were all right; this a phoney."

"Well, that's something," I said, and slipped the note into my pocket.

"Hey, I want a good one in return," Davis said, alarmed. "And while we are on the important subject of money, you also owe me a hundred bucks."

"I do?"

"Yeah. I've been spending your money. Guess what. I've hired a private dick to dig up dirt on your pals. Howja like that?"

"You did? That's a smart idea. Did he find anything?"

"Did he—hell!" Davis rubbed his hands gleefully. "It wasn't such a dumb idea. One thing he did find out was that cat-house you're interested in burns five times the electricity it did two years ago. That anything?"

"Only if it means there's been some electrical equipment installed."

"That's the way I figured it. It'd be a swell hide-out for a coining plant, wouldn't it?"

"All right," I said. "What else?"

"Don't rush us," Davis said, grinning. "This dick ain't been on the job a couple of days. He's turned up something on Gomez if he interests you."

"Gomez?" I said, frowning. "I don't know where I can fit him in."

"Well, let's skip Gomez then."

"What did he find out?"

"Gomez runs human freight into Cuba."

I studied my fingernails. "Go on," I said.

"That's it. He does it in a big way. He has three boats, a bunch of boys working for him, and he gets a thousand dollars a head."

"Who's he carrying?"

"The revolution boys. There's a lot of traffic going on between this coast and Cuba. He's smuggling in guns as well. From what I hear there'll be another bust-up in Cuba before long."

"Too bad for him if Killeano pinched one of his boats," I said, thoughtfully.

"He ain't likely to," Davis said. "He must be giving Gomez plenty of protection."

"But suppose Killeano in a fit of zeal pinched Gomez's boat, what do you think Gomez would do?"

"I know damn well what he'd do. He'd take a crack at Killeano," Davis said, eyeing me doubtfully. "Why should Killeano have a fit of zeal?"

"He's just taken over the police department; the election is close. It'd be a good publicity stunt to make a sudden clean-up on that racket—especially if the press gave him a spread."

Davis's fat face creased. "Now what the hell are you cooking up?"

"Where does Gomez keep his boats?"

"Search me," Davis returned, looking at Tim and then at me. "This dick—Clairbold's his name (hell of a name, ain't it?)—fell over the dirt accidentally. He wasn't looking for it. He was sniffing around in Lois's apartment trying to find any letters Killeano might have written to Lois. It was my idea. I reckoned we could crucify Killeano if we could get hold of some of his mushy letters and print them. Clairbold was digging around in Lois's bedroom when Gomez and another guy marched into the outer room. Clairbold ducks behind a curtain and hears Gomez planning to run a bunch of nationals over to Cuba tonight, and to bring another bunch back the night after."

I nodded. "Nice work," I said. "Did he find any letters?"

"No. He skipped out as soon as Gomez quit. He didn't think it was too healthy to hang around."

"This might develop, Jed," I said. "It's worth going after. Can you get hold of the dick?"

"Yeah. Can get him now if you want him."

"Do that. Tell him to hook himself on to Gomez and follow him wherever he goes. I want to find out where Gomez keeps his boats, and where he'll land those Cubans tonight. Tell him to call back here. We'll wait."

Davis nodded, went over to the telephone.

Tim eyed me thoughtfully. "Can't see where this is getting you," he said.

I moved impatiently. "I'm getting soft," I said. "Know what that kid of mine made me promise?"

He shook his head.

"I wouldn't kill Killeano. Imagine. She thought I was going straight into his office and was going to fill him full of lead. Can you beat that?"

"Well, weren't you?" Tim asked, a sly grin in his eyes.

"That was the general idea," I said, scowling, "but how was I to know she'd know?"

"So you're not going to fix Killeano?" Tim said, surprised. "Then why come back here?"

"I promised I wouldn't kill him, but that doesn't mean I'm not going to fix him," I said grimly. "I have to work it differently now. It'll take longer, but it'll work out the same way. I have to find someone else to do it for me: Gomez, for instance."

Davis came back from the telephone.

"Clairbold says Gomez is at the jai alai court right now. He reckons Gomez will make the trip after the game."

"Okay," I said.

"He'll come over here after he's seen Gomez off," Davis said. "You'll like this guy. He's good."

I put my feet on the table. "Stick around," I said. "We may be busy in a little while."

"Not me," Davis said hurriedly. "I know when you're planning to start something. I smell it in the air. Me—I'm going home."

I laughed. "Suit yourself," I said, handing him a hundred-dollar note and a five spot. "You'll have a fine spread for your front page in a day or so."

"Don't tell me," Davis said with an exaggerated shudder. "Let it come as a surprise."

3

Clairbold was a young blond man in a brown suit and a cocoa-coloured straw hat with a brown and blue tropical band. He followed Tim into the sitting-room, and looked at me the way a morbid sightseer looks at a messy street accident.

I eyed him over. He was very young. His face was pink and plump, and the blond beard on his chin was carelessly shaved. His eyes were inquisitive and a little scared. His teeth projected, giving him a look of a young, amiable rabbit. He didn't look a shamus; that, of course, was in his favour.

"Park your fanny," I said, waving to a chair, "and have a drink."

He edged into the chair as if it was a bear-trap. Then he took off his hat, held it on his knees. His blond hair was slicked down, parted in the middle.

"How do you like working for me?" I asked, pushing the bottle of Scotch and a glass towards him.

"I like it fine, Mr. Cain," he said nervously; shook his head at the bottle. "No, thank you. I don't use it."

"You mean you don't drink?"

"Not in my profession," he returned seriously. "Alcohol dulls one's powers of observation."

I nodded gravely. "So it does," I said. "How long have you been in this racket?"

"You mean how long have I been a private investigator?" he asked, blushing. "Well, not long." He looked at me earnestly. "As a matter of fact, Mr. Cain, I—this is my first big job."

"Well, you're doing fine," I said. "It doesn't worry you to work for me?" I grinned to soften the blow, added, "I'm wanted for three murders."

He stared at his hat, twisted it, put it on the table. "My view of the matter, Mr. Cain, is you've been unjustly accused by an unscrupulous person," he said.

I blinked. "You really think that?" I said, glancing at Tim whose mouth had fallen open.

"Oh yes," Clairbold said. "I've studied the facts very closely. You see, I have my reputation to consider. It wouldn't do for me to work for anyone guilty of murder. I have satisfied myself that you are an innocent party to the murders."

"Pity there aren't more like you around," I said. "Well, you have something to tell me, haven't you?"

"Yes. I have a full report here," he said, drawing a sheaf of papers from his pocket.

I hurriedly waved them away. "Just tell me," I said. "Reading isn't my strong suit."

He squared his shoulders and fixing his eyes on the wall behind my head, he said, "At nine-thirty p.m. this evening, I received instructions from Mr. Davis to shadow Juan Gomez, a jai alai player, suspected of running Cuban nationals between this coast and Havana."

I ran my fingers through my hair, looked at Tim, shook my head.

Clairbold went straight on. "I took up a convenient position where I could observe Gomez without being seen. He was playing on the jai alai court at the time. At the end of the game, I waited in my car at the players' entrance. Gomez eventually appeared with a red-headed

woman I identified as Lois Spence. They drove away in a Cadillac."
He paused to look at his report.

"Never mind the licence number," I said, guessing what he was looking for. "Where did they go?"

He put his report away regretfully. "They took the coast road, and I had no difficulty in following them. The traffic was heavy and I kept two cars behind them. Three miles beyond Dayden Beach there's a branch road that goes down to the sea. They took this road, and I thought it unwise to follow. My headlights would have revealed my presence. I left my car and followed on foot. At the end of the road I found the Cadillac had been parked, and I observed Gomez and Miss Spence walking along the beach in an easterly direction. There was no cover, and it was impossible to go after them without being seen. Fortunately, they did not go far, and I was able to watch them from behind the Cadillac. They waited for several minutes, then a boat, out at sea, began signalling. Gomez returned the signals with a flash-light, and the boat came in. She was a thirty-footer, painted dark green. She wasn't equipped with outriggers and had no mast. One of the windshields on the pilot house was broken." He cleared his throat, holding his hand before his mouth. "I then observed a concrete ramp, cleverly concealed in the sand, had been built out to sea, allowing the boat to come practically up to the beach. The boat tied up to the ramp. Gomez and Miss Spence went aboard." He paused here, blushed slightly. "My instructions were to find out where the boat was going to. From where I was it was impossible to hear anything. I decided to crawl to the boat, although the risk of detection was considerable. However, I succeeded."

I stared at him, imagining him crawling over the white moonlit sand towards a bunch of cut-throats who'd've rubbed him out without a thought. My estimation of him went up sharply.

"That was a nervy thing to have done," I said, and meant it.

The blush turned to a deep scarlet. "Well, I don't know," he said, rubbing his cheek with his hand. "You see, I've had a thorough training." He hesitated, then blurted out: "Although the Ohio School of Detection teaches through the mail, it doesn't leave anything to chance. They impressed on me that the art of stalking was a pretty useful thing to learn. I'd practised it quite a bit in my room."

Tim choked, coughed, looked away. I scowled at him.

"Go on," I said.

"I succeeded in reaching the concrete ramp, and hid behind it,"

Clairbold continued, as if it was just another daily task set by the Ohio School of Detection. "After a while Gomez and Miss Spence came on deck, and I heard what they said. He told her he would leave Havana at nine o'clock tomorrow night, drop his cargo at Pigeon Key, and come back here. She arranged to meet him, and then she left the boat. She drove away in the Cadillac. After further delay, another car arrived and four men, obviously Cubans, went on board."

"What were you doing all this time?" I asked, staring at him.

"I had dug myself a kind of fox-hole in the sand," he explained, "and buried myself. I kept a newspaper I had with me over my face so I could breathe, see and hear. It was an idea I got from the chapter in my course on watching suspected people in sandy districts." He brooded for a moment, said: "It's a very satisfactory course. I—I recommend it."

I blew out my cheeks. "It certainly thinks of everything," I said.

"The boat pulled away from the ramp and headed for Havana. I gave it time to clear and then I came back here to report," he concluded.

"Well, I'll be damned," I said.

He looked up. "I—I hope you're satisfied, Mr. Cain," he said anxiously.

"I'll say I am," I told him. "Now look, young fellow, you ought to be more careful. This is a tough mob, and you're taking too many risks. You've done a swell job, but I don't want to lose you."

He smiled. "Oh, I can take care of myself, Mr. Cain," he assured me. "I have learned boxing, and I can shoot."

I looked him over and wondered where he had left his muscles. Probably at home, I thought. He certainly hadn't brought them with him. "Did you learn boxing and shooting through the mail too?" I asked gently.

He blushed. "Well, yes. I haven't had a chance yet to try any of it out, but I understand the theory pretty well."

This time I didn't dare look at Tim. I took out my wallet, pushed over two hundred-dollar bills. "That's for being a smart guy," I said. "Stick around, and I'll have something more for you before long."

His eyes lit up and he picked up the notes eagerly.

"I'm glad you're satisfied, Mr. Cain," he said. "This means a lot to me." He hesitated, plunged on: "If it's all right with you, I thought I might investigate this—er—house of ill-fame. Of course, I don't like going to such a place, but it's part of my job, isn't it?" He eyed me hopefully, seriously.

"It is," I said gravely.

"Then you think I might investigate there?"

"I think it's a good idea," I said, nodding. "Only be careful some hussie doesn't make a play for you."

He blushed. "I'm not susceptible to women," he said earnestly. "It's part of my training to resist temptation."

I pulled at my nose. "Is there a chapter on that too?" I asked blankly.

"Oh yes," he said. "They go very fully into that subject in a chapter called 'Sex and the Self-controlled Man'."

I whistled. "I'd like to read that," I said. "Maybe I'd get something out of it too."

He said he'd be glad to lend it to me any time, got to his feet and prepared to duck out.

"Just a second," I said, pointing to his cocoa-coloured hat. "Don't think I'm being critical, but is it wise to wear a lid like that? There's nothing wrong with the hat itself. It's a pretty snappy effort, but if you're following anyone, isn't it a little conspicuous? You can see it a mile off."

He positively beamed.

"That's the idea, Mr. Cain," he said. "This is a special line that goes with the course. Actually, it's a trick hat." He took the cocoa-coloured atrocity off his head, whipped off the band, gave the hat a shake and it turned inside out. He reversed the band. He now had a fawn hat with a red and yellow striped band. "Smart, isn't it?" he said. "You see, it keeps people guessing. I personally think the hat is worth the money I paid for the whole course. It's included in the charge."

When he had gone, Tim said, "For crying out loud!" He reached for the Scotch and gave himself a generous shot. He shoved the bottle over to me. "Here, buck yourself up with this."

I waved the bottle away. "Not for me," I said. "I gotta watch my powers of observation."

4

Early the next morning, Tim and I took a trip to Miami, some seventy miles from Paradise Palms. We went in Tim's Mercury convertible, and the trip didn't take us more than ninety minutes.

I called in on the Federal Field Office, leaving Tim in the car outside.

The Federal Agent was named Jack Hoskiss. He was a big, beefy guy, with a shock of blue-black hair, a big fleshy face and humorous eyes. He stood up behind his desk, offered a moist hand.

I didn't beat about the bush. "I'm Chester Cain," I said.

He nodded, said he recognized me, and what could he do?

I stared at him. "I'm supposed to have killed three guys," I reminded him. "Don't you want to make anything of it?"

He shook his head. "When Paradise Palms Police Department call us in, we'll do something about it," he said, offering me a cigar. "Right now, it's off our beat."

I eyed him over. "Your job is to hold me anyway," I said.

"Don't make it hard for yourself," he returned, grinning. "You don't have to tell me my job. We have an idea what you're after." He glanced out of the window, smiled to himself. "We might be after the same thing."

I grinned. "That guy Killeano is nobody's love child."

"It beats me why he hasn't yet made a false move," Hoskiss said. "We've been watching him for months, but so far, he's been smart. I'd like to get something on him."

"So would I," I said, and slid the five-dollar bill Davis had given me across the desk. "That might interest you."

He looked at it without picking it up, looked at me, raised his eyebrows.

"What's the idea?"

"Look at it. It won't bite."

He picked it up, examined it. Then he sat up, bringing his chair straight with a crash. He was interested all right. "Where did you get this?" he snapped.

"Found it," I said. "There're a lot floating around Paradise Palms."

"Yeah," he said savagely. He opened a drawer, took out a box and produced a bunch of notes. He compared the one I'd given him, grunted, put it in the box with the others. "They're good, aren't they?" he said grudgingly. "We've been after that gang for months. But up to now we haven't a lead. No idea where it came from?"

"I might make a guess," I said.

He waited, but I didn't enlarge on it.

"Where?" he asked, when he was sure I'd need persuasion.

I drew on the cigar, blew smoke on to the desk. "I have a proposition to discuss with you."

A thin smile played on his lips. "I thought you might have," he said, nodding. "Shoot."

I told him the story from the time I had hit Paradise Palms. I left Mitchell out of it and where Miss Wonderly was, the rest of it I gave him straight.

He sat huddled in his chair, a blank look in his eyes, and listened. When I was through, he whistled soundlessly.

"Why didn't that fool Herrick come to us?" he said bitterly. "We'd've given him all the protection he needed, and helped him clean up. I love these smart guys who hope to surprise us with a completed case."

"He didn't come to you, but I have," I reminded him gently.

He looked me over. "Well, what now?"

"I'm tired of being the fall guy," I said, flicking ash on the floor. "I'm going to bust Paradise Palms wide open." I pointed a finger at him. "That's why I've come to you."

He raised his eyebrows. "Go on," he said.

"Two things, both of them Federal business: smuggling aliens into the country and counterfeiting."

"Where'll that get you with Killeano?"

I smiled. "That's my end of it. I'm not giving you all the work to do; just part of it."

"Go on."

"Tonight a boat will unload a parcel of Cubans at Pigeon Key. They'll be leaving Havana around nine o'clock. The boat's a thirty-footer, painted dark green, no mast, no outriggers, broken windshield in the pilot house. I'll be glad if you'd take care of it."

"Sure?"

"Sure, I'm sure. It's a hot tip."

"Okay, I'll take care of it."

"Another thing. I want Killeano to get the credit for the tip-off. Davis will handle the publicity. Okay with you?"

He frowned. "What's the idea?"

"Just part of the little plot," I said. "Is it worth your while playing along with me if I turn over the counterfeiting plant and the boys who work it?"

"It might be," he said cautiously. "You seem to know a hell of a lot about this business, Cain. Suppose you open up. And don't think you can use this office to further your own interests, because you can't."

"Now you sound just like a cop," I returned. "Look, I'm giving you a boat full of undesirable Cubans, and I'm going to show you where this dud money comes from. Where's your gratitude?"

He grinned. "Well, okay," he said, "but don't start anything we can't finish."

"I wouldn't do that," I said. "Come to Paradise Palms on Thursday night. Meet me at 46 Waterside at eleven o'clock and come prepared for trouble. If you can arrange to have some of your boys within reach, so much the better, but they are not to show until trouble starts."

He stared. "What's the idea? That joint's a brothel. Why there?"

I winked at him. "Don't you ever relax, brother?" I asked him as I made for the door.

5

Six o'clock the following morning, Davis came bursting into my bedroom. I woke with a start, grabbed my gun from under my pillow, saw who it was, sank back.

"That's the way guys meet with accidents," I said crossly, rubbing my eyes. "What time is it?"

"I like that," Davis snorted. "I've been slaving all through the night and come over here to show you how bright I am, and you talk of accidents."

I yawned, lit a cigarette, sat up in bed.

"All right," I said, "Shoot."

He handed me a copy of the *Morning Star*.

"It's all there," he said proudly. "Careful how you handle it, the print ain't dry yet. Howja like it?" He sat on the foot of the bed, breathing heavily, his eyes alight with excitement. "Gawd knows what Killeano will do to the editor when he sees it. Gawd knows what the editor will do to me if he ever finds out Killeano never said a word of what I've said he said. But this is the way you wanted it, and you've got it that way."

"My pal," I said, and read the banner headlines:

CITY ADMINISTRATOR SWOOPS

NEW POLICE CHIEF'S LIGHTNING ATTACK ON ALIEN
SMUGGLERS

Mysterious Motor-Launch Sunk by Gunfire

Late last night, Ed Killeano, Paradise Palms' City Administrator, in his new capacity of Chief of Police, struck a crippling blow at the Alien smuggling racket.

Too long has this notorious scandal openly flourished along the coast of our fair city. We, representing the citizens of Paradise Palms, are proud to be one of the first to congratulate the new Chief of Police for tackling this racket so courageously and with such speed. It should be remembered that the former Chief of Police made no attempt to suppress the smuggling racket, and it is all the more to Ed Killeano's credit that he has taken such prompt action when only being in office a few hours.

In an exclusive interview with the *Morning Star*, Killeano said that he was determined to clean up Paradise Palms once and for all. "Now I have taken over the job of Chief of Police," he said, "I am showing no mercy to the racketeers hiding in our City. I am going to smoke them out. Let them be warned. I appeal to my supporters to return me to Office so that I can complete the task I have already begun. This is only a beginning."

Acting on information from a secret source, the new Chief of Police ordered Coast Guards to seize a mysterious motor-launch operating off Pigeon Key. A desperate battle ensued, and the motor-launch was sunk, but not before some twelve Cuban nationals lost their lives....

There was a lot more in this vein, photographs of the boat half in and half out of the water, of Killeano and the Coast Guards. It was a nice piece of work, and I told Davis so.

"But wait until Killeano sees it," he said, scratching his head vigorously. "When he realizes how he's been committed, he'll have the shock of his life."

"I guess he will," I said, jumping out of bed. "And there isn't a thing he can do about it. This is terrific propaganda for his election campaign. He daren't deny he sold Gomez out: not even to Gomez. And if he did, Gomez wouldn't believe him."

I scrambled into my clothes.

"Where are you going at this ungodly hour?" Davis demanded. "I've never seen such an energetic guy. Me—I'm dead on my feet."

"Hop into bed, then," I said. "After that write-up I wouldn't deny you anything. I have a date with Gomez."

"Yeah?" Davis said, kicking off his shoes. "Where do you think you'll find him at this hour?"

"With Lois Spence," I said, making for the door. "If he isn't there, I can always look at the dame. She interests me."

He took off his coat and stretched out on the bed. "She interests me too," he said with a sigh. "But not with that Gomez thug hanging around. He cools my ardour."

I took Tim's Mercury convertible, drove out to Lexington Avenue. The night staff were still on duty, and I walked over to the hall porter's cubby-hole.

"Hello, dad," I said, smiling at the old boy. "Remember me?"

He remembered me all right. There's nothing like a little folding money to impress your personality on anyone.

"Yes, sir," he said, brightening up. "I remember you very well, sir."

"I thought you would," I said, and looked round to make sure no one was watching us. I produced a fifty-dollar bill, folded it slowly, giving him ample time to see it, then hid it in my hand.

His eyes started out of his head like organ stops.

"Gomez with Miss Spence?" I asked casually.

He nodded. There was nothing casual about his nod.

"Both tucked up together with nothing between them but their dreams?" I went on.

"I wouldn't know about their dreams, sir," he said, shaking his head. "I don't think I should want to know about them. But they're up there all right."

"That's fine. I'd like to drop in and see them. Kind of surprise them," I said, eyeing him "Would there be a pass-key to their room within reach?"

He stiffened. "I couldn't do that, sir," he said, shocked. "I'd lose my job."

I looked at the row of keys hanging on hooks behind him.

"Now I wonder which it would be," I said. "I'd pay fifty bucks for that information, providing you took a short walk after you've told me."

He struggled with his finer feelings, but the fifty bucks made short work of them.

He turned, lifted a key from a hook, put it down on the counter.

"I'm sorry, sir," he said. "I couldn't do it. I have my job to consider."

I slid him the fifty bucks.

"Okay, but you'd better stick to this," I told him. "If you and I work together much longer, you'll be buying your own apartment block."

He snapped up the note, eased his collar, came out of his office.

"If you'll pardon me," he said, "I have to check on the mail deliveries." He hurried across the lobby without looking back.

It didn't take me longer than it'd take you to blink to pick up the pass-key. I walked over to the elevator, rode up to the fourth floor.

Apartment 466 was silent and in semi-darkness. I pulled my .38, held it in my fist. I had no intention of being jumped by Gomez.

I crossed the sitting-room, wandered into the bedroom.

Gomez and Lois Spence were in bed. He lay on his back; she on her side. Neither of them snored. Neither of them looked particularly attractive.

I sat on the edge of the bed, pinched Lois's toes. She muttered in her sleep, turned, flung out a white arm, hit Gomez on his beaky nose. He cursed, threw her arm off, sat up. His eyes took me in, and he snapped awake. He didn't move. The .38 must have looked pretty menacing from where he lay.

"Hello, sportsman," I said, smiling at him. "How did you like your swim?"

He drew in a deep breath, relaxed back on his pillow. His eyes had that ferocious glare reserved for caged tigers, otherwise he kept surprisingly calm.

"You'll do this once too often, Cain," he said, not moving his lips. "What's the idea?"

"No idea," I said. "I blew in because I was curious to know how you liked your little dip last night."

He studied me for a long moment. "I didn't like it," he said, at last.

"Something told me you wouldn't," I said, grinning. "I must be getting clairvoyant. Well, brother, what are you going to do about it?" Without taking my eyes off him, I pulled out the copy of the *Morning Star* and handed it to him. "Take a gander at that. Our Ed has cut himself a nice slice of publicity at your expense, hasn't he?"

One look at the headlines brought Gomez up on his elbow. He was wearing mauve and white pyjamas. They didn't suit his sallow complexion. What with one thing and another, he looked like hell. I bet he felt that way too.

His sudden move uncovered Lois. She didn't seem to have anything on. She grabbed the sheet back, muttered under her breath, turned over.

Not wishing her to miss the fun, I pinched her toes again.

"Cut that out!" she snapped angrily, opened her eyes. She looked at me, stiffened, clutched Gomez. He threw her off, and went on reading the newspaper.

"Hi, Toots," I said, smiling at her. "Don't froth up your cold cream. Me and Juan are in conference."

She sat up, remembered there were gentlemen present, dived under the bedclothes again.

"What the hell goes on?" she demanded in a voice thick with rage and fright.

"Shut up," Gomez snarled, and went on reading.

"Chivalry in the twentieth century," I said sadly. "Never mind. Relax, beautiful, and wait until the great man has read his paper."

Lois lay back regarding Gomez with glittering, furious eyes. He got through reading the newspaper, slung it down.

"The rat!" he said, clenching his fists, then remembering I was still with him, went on, "What do you want?"

"Ed and I don't get along either," I said. "I thought you might feel like doing something about it."

He stared at me for a moment, then lay back. "Such as what?"

"Are you crazy?" Lois demanded furiously. "Why do you let this heel sit on our bed like this? Hit him! Do something!"

Gomez, snarling, slapped her face, got out of bed. "Come into the other room where we can talk," he said. "Women drive me nuts."

I looked at the telephone by the bed, shook my head. "This blue-eyed twist might get ideas," I said. "I'll keep you both where I can watch you."

Gomez jerked the extension plug from the wall, picked up the telephone and walked across the room.

"I want to talk," he said. "She wants to fight. We'll get nowhere if she's in on the conversation."

"I'll make you pay for this!" Lois stormed. "You can't talk to me like this, you—you gigolo!"

He stepped to the bed.

"Shut up!" he snarled.

"Well, come on," I said impatiently. "If you want to talk, let's talk."

He glared at Lois for a moment, then joined me at the door. Lois started warming up the room with some fancy cursing, but we shut the door and left her to it.

Gomez sat down in an easy chair in the outer room. He ran his fingers through his long oily hair, eyed me the way a snake eyes its first meal after hibernation, said, "Just where do you figure in all this?"

"Killeano's coming after you, buddy," I said, lighting a cigarette. "He knows the only way he can get re-elected is to show the electors that he can handle boys like you. Flaggerty getting knocked off was a break for him. It's given him a chance to show his power. He's sold you out. He'll sell all the other bright boys out too. But you can stop him, if you want to."

"I can stop him all right," Gomez said, clenching his fists. "And I don't want any help or suggestions from you."

"You boys always work the same way," I said, shrugging. "You figure you'll lay for Ed, and fill him full of hot metal. But you won't get near him. He knows you'll come gunning for him, and he'll take precautions. I bet you don't set eyes on him until after the election; then it'll be too late."

Gomez chewed his under-lip, frowning.

"Well, what's your idea, then?"

"An easy way to fix Killeano would be to call at 46 Waterside between eleven-thirty and twelve tonight," I said. "Maybe you didn't know Ed relaxed in that joint. He has a private room in the basement, and his mob goes with him. I don't suppose they'll worry you much, will they?"

He brooded, then stood up. "If that's all you can suggest," he said, "you can beat it. And the next time you snoop into this apartment without being invited, you'll be carried out feet first."

"I'm scared," I said, went to the door, opened it, paused. "If you did find Killeano in that cat-house, it'd look good in the press, wouldn't it? Jed Davis would print all the dirt you gave him so long as you gave him proof. I can't see Ed being re-elected if that kind of news broke on the morning of the election, can you?"

"Get out," he said.

I went.

6

On the outskirts of Paradise Palms a few tumbled-down huts, side by side, sprawled into the darkness. Further along, standing alone, was the only building of importance.

Over its arched doorway, a sign flickered against the night sky. Forty-six.

I had parked the Mercury convertible in a vacant lot some way back, and I approached the building cautiously, keeping in the shadows. Through the open doorway I could hear dance music. The shuttered windows revealed chinks of light.

A man moved out of the shadows, came towards me. I stopped, waited, my hand on my gun butt.

It was Hoskiss.

"Hi, G-man," I said. "Seen this morning's *Morning Star?*"

"Oh, it's you," he said, peering at me. "Yeah, I saw it all right. I bet Killeano's doing a little thinking."

"I bet you are too," I said. "All ready for some relaxation?"

"I'm ready to go in," he said, eyeing the building dubiously. "But I'd like to know what's cooking."

"You will," I said, "only don't rush me. How many boys did you bring?"

"Six. That enough?"

"I hope so. Tell 'em to keep out of sight. We may not need them, but if we do, they'll have plenty on their hands. While they're waiting they can make themselves useful. I want the telephone in this joint cut off. Can they fix the outside lines?"

"I guess so," he said. "What's the idea?"

"I don't want anyone to tip the cops if trouble starts. We'd have enough on our hands without a load of corrupt Law busting in on us."

"I hope you know what you're doing," Hoskiss said. He sounded worried.

"After the way I handed you those Cubans I think you might exercise a little faith," I said.

"You'd make a swell salesman," Hoskiss said, resigned. "I'll tell them."

I waited. After a while he came back.

"They'll fix it," he said. "Do we go in?"

"We go in," I said. "You got a gun?"

"Yeah," he returned. "I hope you have a permit."

I grinned, walked to the open door, went in.

Inside, under dim lights, was a bar and a dance floor. In a corner, on a yellow and red carpet, an orchestra of four played: a pianist with kinky hair, a sallow-faced fiddler, a black drummer and a blond saxophonist. Behind the bar stood a Cuban.

Several couples moved listlessly around the dance floor. The men looked the type you'd expect to find in a joint like this; the girls danced in their underwear. Each had on a brassiere, silk panties, silk stockings and high-heeled slippers. There was a line of flesh on each girl from breast to hip and from one-third down their thighs to their knees. Some of the girls were quite pretty.

The air in the room was torrid, heavy, humid; a combination of human sweat, dime-a-squirt perfume, gin breath. Paper streamers hung from the ceiling like Spanish moss.

We handed our hats to a Chinese boy, and paused to get our bearings.

I glanced at my wrist-watch. It was ten minutes past eleven. "For the next twenty minutes, you can relax. At eleven-thirty we start work."

"Look at those dames," Hoskiss said, gaping. "So this is what the vice-squad calls work. Say, I might even enjoy myself." He eyed a tall blonde in sheer black silk underwear, who was leaning against the bar, a bored expression on her face. "I don't suppose I can come to much harm in twenty minutes. Let's buy a drink."

'That's the worst of bringing a repressed type like you to a joint like this," I said, grinning. "You're likely to make a meal of it."

"I'm not blasé," he said, heading for the bar.

The blonde watched us come. Her wide, painted mouth smiled. She had good teeth, but when I was close to her, I noticed she had pimples on her back.

"Hello, honey," she said to Hoskiss as he sailed up.

"Hello yourself, juicy fruit," he said, draping himself over the bar. "How about rinsing our tonsils together?" He winked at me. "Blondes go for me. It's my powerful personality."

"You want to be careful with this guy," I said to the blonde. "He eats grape-nuts for breakfast every day. You'd be surprised what it does to him."

The blonde was a little pop-eyed. I guess she thought we were drunk.

The Cuban wiped the counter mechanically, asked us what we would have.

"Let's start a famine in whisky," Hoskiss said. "Three triple whiskies, and keep your thumb out of mine."

The blonde continued to eye us. She couldn't make up her mind which of us to concentrate on.

"Well, sugarplum," Hoskiss said, "that's a nice face and body you're wearing, but I'd hate to share you with anyone. Isn't there some frill who'd take care of my boy friend so we can be alone together?"

"Isn't he big enough to find his own frill?" she asked in a drawling voice. "The joint's lousy with girls."

"There you are," Hoskiss said to me. "Don't horn in on my discovery. Take a look around. Peach blossom says the girls' joints are lousy."

I gaped at him. He was certainly relaxing.

The Cuban shoved the whiskies at us, asked twice their worth. Hoskiss waved to me.

"This is your party," he said. He nodded to the Cuban. "My friend will pay. That's the only reason why I go around with him."

I slid five bucks to the Cuban. The blonde leaned against me, smiled. The five spot had decided for her who she was going to be nice to. Hoskiss regarded her sadly.

"You leaning against the wrong man, or did you know?" he said.

"Go bowl a hoop," she said.

He looked quite cut-up.

"And I thought you cared for me for myself," he said, shaking his head at her.

She looked at me. "Tell him to go bowl a hoop," she said. "We don't want him in our party, do we?"

"The lady wants you to bowl a hoop," I said to Hoskiss. "Can you oblige her?"

He finished his whisky, sighed.

"Not immediately," he said, "but don't let that interfere with your fun. She isn't the only blonde who's dipped her head in peroxide. I see a red-head steering my way."

A red-haired girl came up. She was a trifle plump and her face was heavily powdered and rouged. She had on yellow silk panties.

"Want any help?" she asked the blonde.

"Take this crumb off our hands," the blonde said, waving languidly at Hoskiss. "He eats grape-nuts and hasn't any dough."

The red-head sniffed. "Haven't you really any dough, darling?" she asked Hoskiss.

"You bet," he said. "But I only spend it on red-heads. You've arrived at the crucial moment. Have a drink?"

The blonde said to me, "Want to dance?"

"Go on and dance," Hoskiss said. "I have my new-found friend to keep me warm."

I sank my whisky, took the blonde on to the floor. My right hand rested on a bulge of warm flesh above her hip. She turned out to be a good dancer, once I got it into her head that I wanted to dance and not wrestle.

After we'd completed a couple of circuits of the floor, I said, "Who runs this joint?"

Under their heavy coating of blue-black mascara her eyes were surprised.

"What's it to you?"

"Look, girlie," I said patiently. "Never mind the cross-talk. I asked who ran this joint. Do you have to make a mystery of it?"

"I guess not," she said. Her eyes went glassy, blank. I decided she didn't find me particularly interesting. "Madam runs it. Is that what you want to know?"

"Madam who?"

She sighed. "Durelli. Satisfied?"

"I don't need to take anything from you," I said gently. "If you can't work up a little enthusiasm, I'll ditch you."

Her eyes flashed, but she managed to control her temper. "Don't get sore, honey," she said. "I want you to have a good time."

"That makes two of us," I said, manoeuvring her so we passed close to Hoskiss. He eyed us over, said in a loud voice to the redhead: "Extraordinary types you get in here. That fellow would look more at home in a cage." He seemed to be enjoying himself; the red-head too.

"Let's go upstairs," the blonde said, suddenly, impatiently. "It's too hot to dance."

"Sure," I said, and we danced over to the door.

I caught Hoskiss's eye. He looked reproachful.

I winked, waved and followed the blonde out of the room. She ran up a steep flight of stairs, along a passage.

I followed her into a small room furnished with a divan, a cupboard and a carpet.

She stood by the divan, eyed me expectantly.

"You're not going to be mean, are you, honey?" she said.

I reached inside my pocket, produced three five-dollar bills, dangled them before her.

Her eyes lit up and she smiled. The bored, resigned expression vanished.

"Run along and tell Madam Durelli I want to see her," I said.

She stared. "What's the idea?" she demanded, her voice hardening. "Don't you like me or something?"

"Can't you earn yourself a little dough without sounding off? I'm offering it you the easy way. Take this and get Madam. Go on, beat it."

She snatched the money, slipped it into the top of her stocking, went to the door.

"I thought you were a queer fish the moment I saw you," she said. "Stick around. I'll get her."

I sat on the edge of the divan, lit a cigarette, waited.

Minutes dragged by, then I heard a step outside. The door opened and a big, middle-aged woman came in. Her lean face was hard, her eyes jet-beads, and her blonde frizzy hair brittle through constant bleaching. She closed the door, leaned against it, raked me with her eyes.

"What's on your mind?" she asked. Her voice was harsh and flat.

I glanced at my wrist-watch. It was twenty-five minutes past eleven.

"Last night," I said, "the new Chief of Police knocked off a boat belonging to Juan Gomez. Maybe you read about it in the *Morning Star?*"

An alert, suspicious expression jumped into her eyes. "Who are you?" she demanded.

"Never mind who I am," I said. "I'm tipping you off. That makes me your pal. How do you like me as a pal?"

She continued to stare at me. "Keep talking," she said.

"You look smart," I said, flicking ash on the worn carpet. "I don't have to draw you a map. Gomez is mad because Killeano knocked off his boat. He's on his way out here to start trouble."

She stiffened. "How do you know?"

"I got a fleet of midgets who keep me informed about such things," I said.

"I think I'll get someone to talk to you," she said, a snap in her voice. She turned to the door.

I reached out, grabbed her wrist, jerked her round. Her flesh felt soft, puffy. I didn't fancy touching her.

"No, you won't," I said. "I'm dealing with you. If you can't take a friendly tip, then the hell with it. You haven't much time. Gomez will be here any moment now. You'd better get rid of your clients and the girls. He's bringing his mob."

She studied me for a moment. "Wait," she said, went out.

I sneaked to the door, listened, then stepped into the passage.

She was disappearing into a room at the end of the passage as I came out. I went after her, peered into a well-furnished office. She was trying to get some action from the telephone. It didn't take her long to realize it wasn't working. Her face gave her away. She was scared.

"Get organized," I said from the door, "and make it snappy."

She pushed past me, almost ran from the room.

I heard her on the stairs, followed her. I was only three steps behind her when she reached a door to the right of the foot of the stairs.

She turned.

"Get out of here," she snarled, breathing hard. "Go in there and amuse yourself; scram, but don't follow me around."

I nodded.

"Just so long as you know what to do," I said, turned and walked back to the main hall. As I passed the open front door, I paused.

Two big closed cars were drawing up by the tumbledown huts. Men spilled from them.

I thought I might as well launch the balloon. I drew my gun and fired three times above the heads of the running men. Then I slammed the front door, shot home the bolts, put my gun back in its holster, and walked into the dance hall.

7

Hoskiss and I sat under the bar counter. We had the red-headed girl with us, but we had kicked the Cuban out, considering him poor company.

Hoskiss was telling the red-head about his adventures in the Army. He made them sound very exciting and dangerous. The red-head didn't seem to be listening. She sat huddled up, her hands clasping her knees, a look of strained terror on her face.

Bullets sang through the air; gunfire crackled.

"It reminds me of the time when I was cut off from the rest of the boys after crossing the Rhine," Hoskiss said reminiscently. "I was bottled up in a fox-hole, and the Jerries started to mortar my position. I didn't have any whisky to fortify me, and I was scared."

"Not you," I said. "Not a big guy like you."

He anchored his mouth to a bottle of Scotch, took a long pull.

"You don't have to be sarcastic," he said. "I bet there was a time when you were scared too."

I took the bottle away from him, gave myself a stiff shot.

Someone quite close started firing an automatic rifle. The noise was considerable. The red-head screamed, flung her arms round Hoskiss's neck, clung to him.

"I'm glad you invited me to this party," he said to me. "This baby has lost her repressions. She's almost a woman again." He held the red-head tightly, winked at me over her head.

"I hope this counter is bulletproof," I said, pressing the partition with my fingers. It seemed solid enough.

"So long as they can't see me, I feel safe," Hoskiss said. "Don't undermine my confidence."

"I want to go home," the red-head wailed. They were the first words she had uttered since the shooting had begun.

"I should wait if I were you, baby," Hoskiss said kindly. "The air outside is awfully unhealthy. I'd hate to see holes in those pretty pants of yours. Besides, what should I do without you?"

I worked my way to the end of the counter, cautiously peered round. The dance floor was deserted. I could make out the four members of the band sheltering under the piano. The Negro's face was grey; his eyes were closed; he held his drum sticks tightly clenched in his right hand. He was more exposed than the other three, and he kept trying to wriggle further under cover, but they wouldn't let him.

Two of the girls had overturned a table and were crouching behind it. I could see their silk clad legs, no more. Over the other side of the room, a man and girl sat against the wall. The girl looked terrified. The man was smoking. His red, mottled face was slack. He kept saying in a loud voice, "Aw, the hell with it."

All the other men and girls had gone. They were probably hiding in the rooms at the back of the building.

Desultory gunfire kept the night alive. Apart from the automatic rifle, there seemed no organized opposition from within.

"These lads are slow off the mark," I said to Hoskiss.

"Well, we have lots of time," he returned, giving himself another drink. "Do you expect me to join in or something?"

"Not just yet," I said. "You better ease off on the Scotch. When you do go into action, you'll need calm and courage."

"I'm always calm," he returned, grinning, "and I'm stocking up in courage."

I wanted to locate the automatic rifle. It kept banging off nearby, but from where I lay, I couldn't see who was using it. I lay flat, wriggled further out, until my head and shoulders were clear of the protecting counter.

"That's how guys won the Purple Heart," Hoskiss said to the red-head. "It's also a good way to qualify for a funeral."

I looked around, spotted the sportsman with the rifle. He was kneeling against the front of the counter, and every so often he'd fire blindly at the shuttered windows. He was middle-aged, going bald. Thick glasses sat uneasily on his short fat nose.

"How are you making out, bud?" I asked him. "Think you're hitting anyone?"

He jumped round with a snarl of fright, swung the gun in my direction. I didn't wait, but pulled back so fast the red-head squealed with terror.

"Someone say 'Boo!' to you?" Hoskiss asked, grinning.

I sat up, wiped my face, shook my head.

"There's a middle-aged sportsman out there on his own," I explained. "He's banging away without even sighting. Maybe I'd better go out and get things organized. This is no way to wage war."

"Don't be so bloodthirsty," Hoskiss said, frowning. "Me and the girl friend find it exciting, don't we, Toots?"

The red-head said it was too exciting. The language in which she expressed this opinion startled us.

"I can't imagine where you girls pick up such talk," Hoskiss said, pained. "When I was your age—"

The red-head told him to go boil his head, and she added a couple of other suggestions in case the first one didn't appeal to him.

It was funny to see a tough guy like Hoskiss turn pink.

Without warning a machine-gun began firing. Bullets smashed through the wooden shutters. A row of bottles above our heads flew into pieces. Liquor and glass showered down on us. The red-head was soused with gin. Whisky poured over Hoskiss's trouser ends. A piece of flying glass cut my cheek, but I kept dry.

"She'll taste interesting now if you kiss her," I said to Hoskiss.

"I can't stomach gin," he said, regarding the girl crossly. "Why couldn't it've been Scotch?"

"Well, you can always chew your trousers. You might start a new craze."

The red-head had collapsed into Hoskiss's arms, wailing with fright. He shoved her off.

"I don't love you anymore. You smell like hell."

The sportsman with the automatic rifle began blazing away again. I peeped out.

The Negro drummer rolled his eyes at me. The two pairs of silk clad legs behind the table were still as death. The red-faced man over the other side of the room was glaring angrily at the torn shutters. He suddenly got to his feet, lurched across the room. He was very drunk. As he reached the shutters, the machine-gun started up. He was swept backwards by the hail of bullets. Everyone in the room heard the slugs socking into his body. He landed up on his back, blood ran out of him on to the polished dance floor.

"Real bullets," I said, wriggling back under cover. "They've just killed a drunk."

"Shocking waste of good liquor," Hoskiss said, unmoved. He joined me at the end of the counter, looked at the dead man, shook his head. "I feel like letting off my gun now. Childish, isn't it?"

The door to the dance hall suddenly pushed open and three men came in on their hands and knees. They all carried automatic rifles, all looked business-like.

"Shock troops," Hoskiss said, beaming. "Now something ought to happen."

I pulled back as I spotted Don Speratza in the doorway. He didn't come into the room, but directed the men to take up positions by the window. He was careful not to expose himself more than necessary. I was glad to see him.

The men crawled across the dance floor, crept to the windows and began pouring lead into the night. A sudden yell outside proved they knew their job.

"We might take a little walk before long," I said. "I'm getting tired of staying one place."

"Ready when you are," Hoskiss said, pulling a Mauser pistol from his hip pocket. He thumbed down the safety catch.

The red-head squeaked, "Don't leave me," grabbed at him. He threw her arms off impatiently.

"Lay off," he said roughly. "I got work to do now, Toots."

Speratza had vanished. I could hear shooting going on at the back of the building. There were yells. It sounded like a break-in.

"Think your boys will take any action?" I whispered.

"They're on the job now," Hoskiss said, cocking an ear. "I recognize the sound of a Mauser any place. Hark."

We could hear a lot of shooting going on outside.

"That's fine," I said. "In your official capacity I guess you wouldn't hesitate to shoot if anyone looked troublesome?"

"You bet I'd shoot," he said.

"In that case, brother, you'd better go first. I'll cover your rear."

"If you want to lead, go ahead," he said hastily. "I'll take full responsibility for any deaths you cause."

Put like that I hadn't the heart to refuse. I dived for the door, passed into the main hall.

A dim shape standing by the front door twisted round, fired. I felt the wind from the slug fan my face. I shot the dim shape through the head.

"You see how it is," I said apologetically to Hoskiss. "People just naturally shoot at me."

"Don't let it grieve you," Hoskiss said, peering round the hall. "You go ahead. You're faster with a gun than I am. I want to come out of this alive."

There didn't seem any further opposition in the hall. I made for the door at the foot of the stairs.

"This way, pal," I said. "Be ready for action."

I pushed open the door, faced a flight of stairs leading down into a dimly lit basement.

I walked down the stairs, making no more noise than a breath of wind. Hoskiss kept at my heels.

We reached the bottom of the stairs, moved along a passage. I pointed to a thick electric cable running along the wall near the ceiling. Hoskiss nodded, grinned.

At the end of the passage was a door. I paused outside, listened. I couldn't hear anything.

"Shall we go in?" I whispered in Hoskiss's ear.

"I suppose so," he said. "G-men always go in."

I turned the handle, pushed.

The room was big; elaborately equipped with printing presses. Green shaded lights illuminated the stacks of banknotes piled neatly on benches.

A dead man lay on the floor near the printing press. He had been shot. A small blue-red hole showed in the exact centre of his forehead.

Ed Killeano knelt on the floor against the far wall. His fat face was yellow and glistening with fear. His pudgy hands were shoulder high, and his eyes started from his head like long stalked toadstools. Clairbold, the intrepid private investigator, complete with his cocoa-coloured trick hat, stood over him, a Colt .45 in his small hand.

"Take him away," Killeano screamed at us as we came in. "Make him put that gun down."

Hoskiss and I walked over.

"Hello, Fatso," I said. "Don't you like our young friend?" I touched Clairbold on his shoulder. "What are you doing here, bright eyes?"

"Call him off!" Killeano shrieked. "Get that gun away!"

Clairbold lowered the gun, cleared his throat apologetically. "I'm glad you've come, Mr. Cain," he said. "I was wondering what I should do with this—er—man."

Hoskiss ran his fingers through his hair. "Who's this guy?" he asked blankly.

"The greatest private dick since Philo Vance," I said.

Killeano made a sudden dive across the desk, reached for a sheet of paper. Hoskiss flung him back.

"Take it easy," he said. "Park your truss until I can get around to you."

Killeano snarled at him, wrung his hands.

Clairbold picked up the sheet of paper, blushed, shuffled his feet.

"I have a statement here," he said, handing me the paper. "It completely clears you, Mr. Cain. This man admits that Bat Thompson killed Herrick, Giles and Brodey, acting on his orders. They knew about the forgery plant. Killeano also admits he is responsible for issuing forged currency. I think you'll find it in order."

Dazed, I read the statement. It was a beautifully worded confession. Silently I handed it to Hoskiss who read it, said, "For God's sake!"

"I deny every word of it," Killeano babbled. "He was going to shoot me!"

"How did you persuade him to write this?" I asked Clairbold.

He fingered his tie nervously.

"I really don't understand it myself, Mr. Cain," he said, puzzled. "I think perhaps he was frightened my gun wasn't safe." He shook his head. "He could be right because it went off unexpectedly when that man rushed in." He waved his hand at the body by the printing plant. "Killeano thought I might shoot him accidentally. He was quite mistaken, of course, but when I suggested he might care to make a statement he seemed most anxious to do so."

I looked at Hoskiss, who burst out laughing.

"Look," I said to Clairbold, "you don't kid me. You're not half as dumb as you act. Son, you have a great future before you."

He blushed. "Well, Mr. Cain, it's nice of you to say so. I've been trained to appear rather simple. The Ohio School of Detection has taught me that criminals underrate people who act dumb."

I dug Hoskiss in the ribs. "You might get somewhere if you took that course," I said. "Look what it's done for this lad." Then I nodded at Killeano. "Your prisoner, buddy, and it's your job to get him out of here."

"Forget it," Speratza snarled from the door. "Stick up your hands or I'll blast the lot of you."

We turned.

Speratza was covering us from the door with a Thompson. His face was white, his eyes vicious.

I had laid my .38 on the desk as I read Killeano's statement. I calculated the distance, decided it was too far.

Killeano made another rush, tried to grab the statement, but Hoskiss flung him off.

A gun exploded at my side. Speratza dropped the Thompson, swayed. A blue-red hole appeared in the centre of his forehead. He crashed to the floor.

"I don't believe this gun is safe," Clairbold muttered, staring at the smoking Colt, but there was a satisfied gleam in his eyes that told me he was kidding.

I fell into Hoskiss's arms.

"For the love of Mike," I babbled hysterically, "he learned to shoot like that through the mail."

8

On the face of it, it looked as if the show was over. I left the tidying up to Hoskiss. I wish now I had done it myself because they let Bat Thompson slide through their fingers. They threw a drag-net around Paradise Palms, but when they hauled it in, everyone who mattered was in it except Bat.

It worried me at first, but after thinking it over I decided that Bat by himself wasn't a danger. He hadn't the brains to think up trouble, and he was as near moronic as made no difference. But I would have liked to have seen him behind bars. The Feds were pretty sure that he had got away. It spoilt their case, since he was the guy who had bumped off Herrick, Giles and Brodey.

Killeano got twenty-five years. Speratza and Flaggerty were dead. Juan Gomez had been killed by one of the Federal officers in the fight outside 46 Waterside.

Once I was sure that Bat wasn't in town, I asked Tim to fetch Miss Wonderly from Key West.

We were now in Palm Beach Hotel, trying to decide our future.

I sat on the balcony and looked at the green ocean. Only this time I didn't have any presentiment of trouble. She sat on the balustrade.

"All right," I said, after I had heard her argument. "I'll get a job. I'll go respectable if that's what you really want."

Her eyes were full of questions.

"But I want you to be happy too," she said. "If you don't think you could settle down . . ."

"I can try, can't I?" I said. "The thing to do is for you and me to get married. Then I'll have to settle down."

And that's how we fixed it.

Four days later we were married. Hetty, Tim, Jed Davis, Clairbold (the boy wonder), and Hoskiss turned up at the wedding. It was quite an affair.

We decided to spend our honeymoon at Paradise Palms because the others didn't want us to go elsewhere. They were pretty good to us, but at the end of the week I decided, if I was going to get a job, I'd better start looking for one. We packed our bags and arranged air passage to New York.

On our last night at Paradise Palms we threw a party that the staff of the hotel still talk about. Hoskiss brought with him six of his hard-drinking G-men. He announced at the beginning of dinner that Clairbold had entered the Federal Service. Clairbold finished up under the table. I guess he was getting beyond his Ohio School of Detection course by now.

After our guests had gone, we went up to our bedroom. It was around two o'clock in the morning. We were undressing in the bedroom when the telephone rang.

I told Clair—she wasn't Miss Wonderly any more—I'd answer it.

I went into the sitting-room, took off the receiver.

The line crackled, hummed. A woman's voice said, "Chester Cain?"

I said it was, wondering where I had heard the voice before. "This is Lois Spence," the woman said.

"Hello," I said, wondering what she wanted. I had forgotten about her.

There was a lot of noise on the line. It crackled, popped and buzzed.

"Listen, you heel," she said, her voice indistinct, far away. "You tricked Juan, and it was through you he was killed. Don't think you're going to get away with it. I pay off old debts, so does Bat. Remember him? He's right by my side. We're coming after you, Cain. We'll find you wherever you are. You and your floozie, and we'll fix you both."

The line went dead. I replaced the receiver, frowned. Spiders' legs ran down my neck.

"Who was it?" Clair called.

"A wrong number," I said, and went back to the bedroom.

Chapter Six
PAY OFF

1

A Packard sedan swished to a standstill before one of the air towers. I glanced through the office window to satisfy myself that Bones, the Negro help, was on the job. He was there all right. I watched him fussing around the car, gave him full marks for his enthusiasm, returned to work.

I still got a big bang out of seeing a customer arrive although I had now been running the service station for three months. It was a good buy, and after spending money on it, I had already doubled the business the previous owner had got out of it.

Clair had been startled when I had told her I intended to buy a service station. She thought I was planning to get a job with a big company in New York. So I was, but after that 'phone call from Lois Spence I had changed my mind.

I guessed Lois had found out that I had reservations for an air passage to New York, and would follow me there. I decided to duck out of sight. If I had been on my own I'd have waited for them, but Clair complicated things. I couldn't be with her every minute of the day, and they wouldn't have had much difficulty in handling her if they ever caught up with her.

So I cancelled the air passage, told Clair I wanted to go into the motor business, and pulled out of Paradise Palms in the Buick for a long haul to California.

I found what I was looking for on the Carmel-San Simeon Highway, within easy reach of San Francisco and Los Angeles. It was a small, bright well-kept station, and the owner was only giving up through ill-health.

It had four pumps, ten thousand gallons of storage, oil Tube tanks, two air and water towers, and a good bit of wasteland for extra buildings. The thing that really decided us was the house that went with the business. It was only a few yards from the service station, and it had a nice little garden. The house itself was cute, and Clair fell for it the moment she saw it. I fell for it too because she would be close to me all the time, and until I was sure we had lost Lois and Bat that was the way I wanted it.

I began to make alterations to the service station as soon as we moved in. I had it painted red and white. Even the pavements of the driveways were divided into red and white squares. I had a big sign hoisted on the roof which read: THE SQUARE SERVICE STATION.

Clair nearly died laughing when she saw the sign, but I knew it was the kind of thing that pulled in suckers.

I added two more air and water towers. Mechanics put in a new type of hydraulic hoist and a complete high-pressure greasing outfit. Near the rest-room building, startling under its new coat of paint and shining inside with added luxuries, was erected a steel shed to house car-washing and polishing equipment.

I hired Bones and a couple of youths to help, and business went ahead with a bang.

One of the youths, Bradley, was a pretty smart mechanic, and I knew most things about the inside of a car. We didn't reckon to take on any big repair jobs, but we could handle the day-to-day adjustments that came in; but once we did handle three cars that got involved in a smash.

All day long cars kept coming in, and I was on the jump from six in the morning to seven at night. I fixed up a night shift as I found I was turning away business by closing down at seven. I got an old man and a youth to handle the night trade, which wasn't heavy, but kept coming, three or four cars an hour.

I had just finished checking the accounts and I found I'd cleared nine hundred dollars after three months' work. I ran over to the house to let Clair know we weren't broke yet.

I found her in the kitchen, a cook-book in her hand, a puzzled expression in her eyes.

She found the job of being a housewife tougher than I found my new job. She had started off with little or no knowledge of how to run a house, how to cook, but she wouldn't hire any help. She said she wanted to learn to be useful, and it was time she knew how to cook anyway. I didn't dissuade her, reckoning that after a while she'd get tired of it and throw in her hand. But she didn't. For the first two or three weeks we ate some pretty awful meals. I have a cast-iron stomach so I didn't complain, and after a while the meals got better; now they were pretty good, and improving all the time.

She kept the house like a new pin, and I finally persuaded her to let one of the youths do the rough work, but the rest of it she continued to do herself.

"Hi, honey," I said, breezing into the kitchen. "I've just audited the books. We're nine hundred bucks to the good: that's clear profit, and we don't owe a cent."

She turned, laid down the cook-book, laughed at me.

"I believe you're really crazy about your old gas station," she said. "And after all those threats about not settling down."

I put my arm round her. "I've been too busy to realize that this is settling down. I've never worked so hard in my life. I had the idea that when a guy settled down, he parked his fanny, and let moss grow over him. I guess I was wrong."

"Don't say fanny," she reproved. "It's vulgar."

I grinned at her. "Let's run into San Francisco tonight, and paint the town red," I said. "It's time you and I stepped out. We've been working now three months without a break. How about it?"

Her eyes lit up. "Yes, let's do that," she said, throwing her arms round my neck. "Can you get off early?"

"If we leave just before seven it'll be time enough. Going to put on your glad rags?"

"Of course, and so are you. It's time I saw you in something better than those awful old overalls."

The station buzzer sounded. That told me Bones had someone out front whom he couldn't handle.

"A little trouble," I said, kissing Clair. "See how important I am? The moment I turn my back."

She pushed me out of the kitchen.

"Run away," she said, "or you won't have any lunch."

I beat it back to the station.

There was trouble all right. A big Cadillac had hit the concrete wall of the driveway. Its fender had been pushed in and the bumper was buckled. It was a swell-looking car, and it hurt me to see the damage.

Bones was standing by. His usually smiling face was shiny and dismayed. He rolled his eyes at me as I came up.

"It wasn't my fault, boss," he said hurriedly. "The lady got into the wrong gear."

"Don't tell such bloody lies, you rotten nigger," a shrill, hard voice exploded from inside the car. "You waved me on. I thought I had plenty of room."

I signalled to Bones to scram, then walked up to the car, looked in.

A typical lovely young product of Hollywood sat at the wheel. She was dark, expensively dressed, pretty according to the standard hardness of the movie colony. She was also very angry, and under her rouge her skin was white as marble.

"See what your blasted nigger's done to my car," she stormed as soon as she saw me. "Fetch the manager. I'm going to raise holy hell about this!"

"Start raising it now," I said quietly. "I'm the owner, manager and office boy all rolled into one. I'm sorry to see such a grand car busted like this."

She eyed me up and down. "So you're sorry, are you? What am I supposed to do? Smile and drive away? Let me tell you that you haven't started to be sorry yet!"

I would have liked to have slapped her, but remembering that customers are always right, I said I'd have the fender fixed for her immediately.

"What?" she snapped. "I wouldn't let you touch it." She drummed on the steering wheel. "I must have been crazy to have turned into a hick joint like this. Well, it'll certainly be a lesson to me. No more hick joints for me."

I felt my temper rising, so I walked to the front of the car, inspected the damage. It certainly was pretty bad, and it seemed to me she must have rammed the wall with considerable force.

"Just to get the record straight," I said, coming back, "just how did this happen?"

"I was reversing . . . I mean I was coming forward—"

"You were reversing, you mean," I said. "You couldn't have come forward from this angle. But you made a mistake in the gears and your car jumped forward." I glanced inside the car. "If you look, you'll see your gear is still in bottom."

She opened the car door, her eyes flashing.

"Are you suggesting I can't drive a car?" she asked, getting out of the car, facing me.

"It looks that way," I said, sick of her.

Her mouth tightened, and she swung a slap at my face. I picked it off in mid-air, held her wrist, grinned at her. We were close, and I caught the smell of gin on her breath. I looked at her sharply. She was drunk all right. I wondered I hadn't noticed it before.

"What goes on?" a flat voice demanded.

I looked around, saw a State Highway cop frowning at me. I let go of the girl's wrist.

"Arrest that man!" the girl stormed. "He was trying to assault me."

"Bad for business," the cop said, eyeing me over.

"Very," I said.

Clair appeared from nowhere.

I winked at her.

"The lady's charging me with assault," I said, and laughed. Clair took my arm, said nothing. We looked at the cop. The ball seemed to be in his court.

"Why did you try to hit him?" the cop asked the girl. "I saw you do that."

"Look what he's done to my car," she stormed. "Call this a Service Station! My God! I'll sue this crummy bastard out of business."

The cop eyed her disapprovingly, walked to the Cadillac, looked at it.

"Tsk, tsk." He clicked with his tongue, glanced inside the car, spotted the gear lever, gave me an old-fashioned look. "What have you gotta say about this, pal?" he asked.

"My man saw what happened," I said. "I just tried to smooth things over." I turned, waved to Bones, who was watching with enormous eyes in the background. "Tell the officer what happened," I said as he shuffled up.

"If you're going to take that lousy nigger's word against mine, I'll have the coat off your back!" the girl stormed.

"Will you?" the cop said, raising his eyebrows. "You and who else? Come on," he went on to Bones, "spill it."

Bones told how the Cadillac had driven into the driveway very fast, and had pulled up dead, narrowly missing the air tower. He had asked the girl to reverse back to the gas pump as she had wanted gas, and she had promptly driven slap into the wall.

"Yeah, I guess that's about how it did happen," the cop said. He eyed the girl over. "What's your name, sister?"

I thought she was going to explode.

"My good man," she said, after a tense pause. "I am Lydia Hamilton, the Goldfield Production star."

I had never heard of her, but then I seldom went to the movies. Bones apparently had, because he sucked his teeth and goggled at her.

"I don't care if you're George Washington's grandmother or even Abe Lincoln's aunt, you're pinched," the cop said. "The charge, if it interests you, is being drunk while in charge of a car. Now come on, we'll all take a trip to the station."

I thought the girl was going to strike the cop; so did he, because he took a quick step back. But she controlled herself, said, "You'll be sorry you started this," walked to the Cadillac.

"Hey, you ain't fit to drive," the cop said. He looked at me. "Take her over to the station, pal. You'll be wanted as a witness, anyway. Better send the dinge over too."

I didn't want to go, but there was nothing else I could do. I told Clair I'd be right back, asked Bradley to keep an eye on the station, and went over to the Cadillac.

"I'm not having that rat drive me," the girl said.

"Look, sister," the cop said in a bored voice, "I'll send for the wagon if you like. You're under arrest, and you can come to the station any way you like, but you'll come."

She hesitated, then got into the Cadillac. She threw the ignition keys at me, hitting me in the face. I picked them off the floor, got in beside her, shifted the gear lever from bottom to neutral, trod on the starter.

She began cursing me as soon as we had driven out into the highway. She kept on without a pause for a mile or so, then I got tired of it, told her to shut up.

"I'm not shutting up, you cheap grease monkey," she said. "I'll ruin you for this. You and your prissy mouth floozie. When I'm through with you, you'll be sorry you were born."

"Someone who doesn't mind touching you ought to apply a hairbrush to your tail," I said.

She gave a squeal of fury, flung herself at me and wrenched the wheel to the right. The car, travelling at forty miles an hour, slowed across the road. I stamped on the foot brake, lugged back the parking brake. The car stopped dead, and she was thrown forward. Her head slammed against the dash-board. She passed out.

The cop had skidded to a standstill. He got off his motorcycle, walked over to me.

"For the love of Mike," he said crossly. "Can't you drive, either?"

I told him what had happened, and he looked at the unconscious girl.

"Crazy as a bug," he said. "I've heard tales about her. These movie stars give me a pain. This dame is always in a jam, but she buys her way out. This little outing's going to cost her something. Well, come on, I ain't got all day."

We continued on our way to the station.

2

It was our first visit to San Francisco, and neither of us knew where to find the kind of place we were looking for. We took a traffic cop into our confidence and told him we wanted a good meal and some fun. Where did he suggest?

He put his foot on the running board, pushed his hat to the back of his head, and regarded us with a kindly eye. At least, he regarded Clair with a kindly eye. I don't think he even noticed me.

"Well, miss, if you want a night out you couldn't do better than Joe's. It's the nicest joint in town, and that's saying a lot."

"Listen, brother," I said, leaning over Clair so he could see my tuxedo. "We want class with our fun tonight. Nothing's too good for us. I'm burning to spend dough, and low dives are off the agenda."

He gave me a fishy look. "I still say Joe's," he said. "It has plenty of class, and you have a good time as well. If you don't want Joe's, you can go drive into the harbour. Why should I worry my head?"

It seemed as if it had to be Joe's. We thanked him, asked him the way.

He told us. In fact, he did everything except draw a map. "Tell Joe I sent you," he said, winking. "Patrolman O'Brien. Tell him, and you'll get special treatment."

After we had driven a block, I said: "Now, we'll ask someone else. I bet that flatfoot is just a talent scout for Joe's."

Clair said she would like to go to Joe's.

"If it's no good, we can always go somewhere else," she argued.

We found Joe's down a side street. There was nothing gaudy nor de luxe about the place; no doorman to help you out of your car, no one to tell you where to park, no awning, no carpet. It was just a door in the wall with a neon sign: J O E ' S.

"Well, here we are, sweetheart," I said. "Do I leave the car here or do we take it inside?"

"You knock on the door and ask," Clair said severely. "The way you behave you'd imagine you'd never been to a joint before."

"Not in a tuxedo I haven't," I said, getting out of the car. "It makes me kind of shy." I rapped on the door, waited. The door was opened by a thickset man with a tin ear, and a broken nose. He had squashed himself into a boiled shirt, and he looked no more comfortable in it than if he'd been wearing a hair shirt.

"Good evening," I said. "We have come to eat. Patrolman O'Brien recommended this place. How about it?"

"That jerk always recommends us," the thickset man said, spat past me into the street. "As if we want his lousy recommendations. Well, now you're here, you'd better come in."

"What do I do with the car?" I asked, a little startled.

He stared at the Buick, shrugged.

"I wouldn't know," he said. "Maybe you can trade it in for a fur coat, if you want a fur coat."

I tapped him on his chest. "Listen, my fine friend," I said, "I've taken bigger guys than you and made tomato juice out of them."

He looked interested, surprised.

"Who, for instance?"

Clair joined us.

"How are you going?" she asked me.

"Fine," I said. "I was just about to smack this punk's ears down. His manners come out of a zoo."

The thickset man regarded Clair with goggling eyes. He simpered at her.

"Would you please let us in?" she said, smiling at him. "I've heard so much about Joe's."

"Sure," he said, standing aside, "come right in." He caught my eye, said: "Put the heap down that alley. If a cop spots it here he'll have you for obstruction."

"Wait," I said to Clair, drove the Buick down the alley, walked back.

Together we mounted stairs.

The thickset man stared after us.

Clair whispered that he was looking at her ankles, and wasn't he a lamb!

I said if I thought he could see more than her ankles I'd turn him into mutton.

A check girl in peach-bloom Chinese pyjamas came over to take my hat. She gave me a faint leer when Clair wasn't looking. I leered back.

The lobby looked like a high-budget musical: a lot of light and glitter. The walls reached a long way up to a dark ceiling ornamented with stars that really sparkled. At the back of the lobby was a stairway with a chromium and white enamel gangway going up in wide shallow scarlet-carpeted steps. At the entrance to the dining-room a sleek captain of waiters stood with a bunch of gold-plated menus under his arm. He had the sort of face women would wish to smack.

The bar entrance was to the right. It was luxurious under beautiful indirect lighting, and a barman officiated, moth-like, behind a faint glitter of piled glassware.

"This is really something," I said, speaking out of the corner of my mouth. "I don't think there'll be much of our nine hundred bucks profit left by the time this joint's through with us."

"You can always order a glass of milk and tell them you belong to an obscure religious order," Clair murmured, and drifted away to the ladies' room.

I stood around, tried to look as if I spent my whole life in this kind of atmosphere, didn't succeed very well.

A cigarette girl came down the gangway. She wore an ostrich feather in her hair, and a G-string and two gold saucepan lids where they were most needed. One of her beautiful legs was silver and one was gold. She gave me a disdainful glance of a dame who knows all the answers and isn't interested anymore.

As she passed me, I said quietly, "Don't go sitting on a cane-bottomed chair."

Her long slinky stride faltered, but she kept on. I tried not to peep at her naked back, but I peeped just the same. I decided I was going to like this place.

Clair came out of the ladies' room. Her dress looked like seawater sifted over with gold dust.

"Hello," she said.

"Hello," I said, leering at her. "My wife's left me. Shall we go off together and have fun?"

"Wouldn't she mind?" Clair asked gravely.

"She'd be wild," I returned, "but I'm infatuated with your dress.

Let's go and neck in my car."

She slipped her arm through mine. "Don't let's pretend I'm not your wife," she said. "I like being your wife."

"I'm glad and proud about that, Mrs. Cain," I said, and meant it. "Shall we talk to that important-looking gentleman with the menus and see what he would like us to eat?"

She nodded.

We presented ourselves to the captain of waiters. He bowed to Clair, bowed to me.

"This is our first visit," I explained. "We want a good time. Can we leave it to you?"

"Certainly, monsieur," he returned, his voice was as dry as sand. "Perhaps you would care to decide what you will eat first, and then perhaps you would like to visit our cocktail bar? The cabaret begins at eleven. I will arrange a table near the floor for you."

I wasn't kidding myself he was making a fuss of me. He was making a fuss of Clair.

We decided, after some thought and discussion, to have antipasto, steaks broiled over charcoal, hashed brown potatoes in cream, combination salads and a bottle of Liebfraumilch.

The captain of waiters wrote the order in a little gold-covered note-book, bowed, said it would be ready for us in half an hour. He personally conducted us to the cocktail bar, signalled to the barman, left us.

"Royal stuff," I said to Clair. "I believe they've all fallen in love with you."

She shook her head. "It's your determined chin and blue eyes."

I knew she was wrong.

The barman waited, admiring Clair without attempting to conceal the fact. He glanced at me; there was respectful envy in his eyes.

I ordered two large, very dry martinis.

We went over to a sofa seat, sat down, lit cigarettes. People looked at us, but we didn't worry. We were happy enough in our own company. After a while, the barman brought the drinks. I paid him, tipped him, and he went away silently, as if drawn along on wheels.

We sipped the martinis. They were very good.

There was something about the hard standard of prettiness of the women at the bar that reminded me of Lydia Hamilton. I said as much to Clair.

"Don't let's talk about her," Clair said. "She was ghastly. I was so sorry for Bones. She hurt him terribly."

"Not half as much as the judge hurt her," I said with a grin. "Bones is a good lad. I think I'll give him a raise. Do you think it'd be an idea to give him a uniform as well; a red and white check overall or something? I think all the boys might wear a uniform. It'd give the joint tone."

She laughed. "Darling, I'm so glad you like your old gas station. There was a time—"

"Forget it," I said, taking her hand. "It's fun, but it wouldn't be fun without you."

"Honest?"

I nodded. "If it wasn't for you, I'd be still kicking around as a bum."

"I have an idea," she said, looking at me out of the corners of her eyes. "Now, don't say no until I've explained. How would it be if we opened a restaurant? We could use the waste ground by the house. It needn't be an elaborate building. We could serve meals out of doors. Barbecue cooking: chicken, steaks, spareribs, the way we know how to cook them, salad and things. I'd love to organize it all if you'd let me."

I stared at her. "It's a terrific idea," I exclaimed. "However did you think of it?"

Her face brightened. "Oh, I wanted to help. I know I run the house, but I'd rather make some money. Shall we?"

"We'll find out how much it'll cost to put up a suitable building first thing tomorrow," I said, and we forgot our surroundings in the discussion that followed.

After a while, I noticed Clair wasn't concentrating. I looked at her, saw she was flushed, said: "What's on your mind, honey? Got an attack of grippe?"

She didn't smile, shook her head, looked away. "Promise you won't make a scene?" she whispered.

"I never make scenes," I said. "What's wrong?"

"There's a man over the way who hasn't taken his eyes off me since he came in," she said. "He's making me uncomfortable. Now, please . . ."

I looked across the room, located a man in a white dinner-jacket sitting on his own. He had grey hair. There was nothing unusual about his heavy handsome face except a small puckered scar on his left check that had almost the effect of a dimple.

I gave him the hard eye, and he immediately looked away.

"Well, anyway," I said, putting down my empty glass, "it's time we had something to eat. If he really bothers you I'll talk to him."

"You're not to," she said, walking across the bar at my side. "Those days are over."

The barman bowed to her as we left. She gave him a nice smile. I was very proud of her.

The captain of waiters personally conducted us to our seats. The table he had reserved for us was on the edge of the dance floor. I noticed a number of the men diners looked at Clair. She was worth looking at.

We sat down. The antipasto was fine. There were salty anchovies bedded on a firm slice of tomato; scarlet peppers soaked in white vinegar; thin bologna sausages; fat white shrimps; transparent slices of ham, and celery stuffed with cottage cheese. We had two large dry martinis to go with it.

Half-way through the meal, the man in the white dinner-jacket wandered in. He seemed to be known. People nodded to him as he stalked between the tables. He passed close to us, and gave Clair a long penetrating stare. She avoided his eyes. I scowled at him, but he didn't notice. He sat a couple of tables away from us, waved to the waiter, ordered a Rye straight. He lit a cigarette, settled down to stare at Clair.

"I think I'll drop over and talk to that masher," I said, suddenly very angry.

Clair gripped my arm. "No, darling, don't. It'll spoil everything, and I'm having a lovely time. Please, let's forget him. I don't mind."

She began talking about the restaurant idea, but neither of us had much heart for it now. She was worried, and I was getting madder every moment.

Then suddenly I saw her stiffen. I followed the direction of her eyes. Lydia Hamilton had just entered. She swept down the aisle between the tables before the captain of waiters could escort her, arrived at the table occupied by the man in the white dinner-jacket, sat down. He glanced at her in a bored way, waved to the waiter.

"Now, perhaps we'll have rest from that guy," I said. "I'm sorry to see that dame here, but she won't spoil my dinner."

The waiter served the broiled steak. It looked very good. For a while we ate. Then I looked up suddenly. The masher was at it again. His half-closed eyes were probing Clair—X-ray eyes.

I looked at Lydia Hamilton. She was on to him. Her face was hard, furious.

"We're going to have some trouble," I said to Clair in an undertone. "That dame's crazy enough to start anything." I thought it best to warn her.

The words were scarcely out of my mouth when Lydia smacked the man in the white dinner-jacket across his face. He wasn't expecting anything like that, and he nearly fell off his chair. The sound of the smack cracked through the big dining-room. There was a sudden hush, then Lydia's strident voice shrilled, "Take your eyes off that whore."

I found myself on my feet. Clair hung on to my sleeve.

The grey-haired man cursed Lydia in a loud clear voice, calling her about six names that are not usually mentioned by handsome men in white dinner-jackets. Then he drew back his fist, punched her in the face.

Lydia fell out of her chair, blood from her nose ran down her chin. People stood up, craned their necks. A woman screamed. The captain of waiters began a slow, cautious walk towards the scene.

The man in the white dinner-jacket stood over Lydia. He continued to curse her; then he drew back his foot to kick her. I jerked my sleeve free from Clair's clutch, jumped towards him.

There was a sharp crack of gunfire. A spurt of flame came from Lydia's hand. The man in the white dinner-jacket coughed once, twice, folded at the knees. He went down. I grabbed the toy gun out of Lydia's hand. She clawed me down the face with her free hand. I pushed her away, stood back. She stared up at me, her eyes becoming sane again.

"Hello, Hick," she said. "Why couldn't you keep your cheap floozie where she belongs?"

I turned from her, looked down at the man lying on the floor. I decided she wouldn't be able to buy herself out of this jam.

3

Believe me, when a Hollywood movie actress takes it into her head to shoot her boy friend in a swank night club, all hell starts popping.

As soon as it was discovered that the man in the white dinner-jacket was dead, everyone made a dive for the doors. But the captain of waiters was one jump ahead of them. The doors were closed, and the thickset man from downstairs stood with his back against them.

He grinned evilly at the crowd, flexed his muscles, invited anyone to try to pass him. The crowd decided that after all they weren't in a hurry to leave.

"Will you all please take your seats?" the captain of waiters said smoothly. "The police are on the way, and no one may leave without permission."

People went back to their tables, leaving Lydia alone with her dead. She stood over the body, a serviette held to her bleeding nose. She was still drunk enough not to realize that the man in the white dinner-jacket was dead. She kept stirring him with her foot, saying, "Get up, you swine. You can't scare me," but she was beginning to sense the jam she was in, and her voice was going off-key.

It took the police six minutes by my watch to arrive. They came in: three plain-clothes men, four in uniform, a doctor, a photographer and the D.A.'s man.

They went to work in the usual efficient way policemen go to work. It was only when the doctor signed to a couple of the uniformed men to cover the body with a table-cloth that the nickle dropped in Lydia's befuddled mind. As they draped the cloth over the body, she let out a screech that set everyone's teeth on edge.

"Okay, sister," the Homicide man said, tapping her arm. "Take it easy. It won't get you anywhere."

She looked wildly around the room: saw me.

"It's all your fault, you—!" she screamed. "It was you who spoilt my lovely car."

People stood on chairs to look at me. The Homicide man gave me a hard stare. I sat there, looked back. There was nothing else I could do. It was a pretty nasty moment.

Lydia suddenly made a dive at me, but the cops grabbed her.

"Get her out of here," the Homicide man said as she began to curse. Even his face registered disgust.

Things quieted down when she had gone. The Homicide man came over to me, asked where I figured in this.

"She's crazy drunk," I said. "I don't figure in it at all. I only grabbed her gun."

"What's this about her car?"

"We had a little accident this morning. There was nothing to it."

He took out his note-book, asked me my name. I told him Jack Cain. My middle name was Jack, anyway. I gave him my address, went into details about the Cadillac, said nothing about the man in the white dinner-jacket trying to mash Clair. I guessed it would come out at the trial, but I wasn't going to help unnecessarily.

"Any idea why she shot the guy?" the Homicide man demanded.

I shook my head. "I wasn't watching them," I lied. "He suddenly punched her, began kicking her. I went to her aid; before I could reach the guy, she shot him."

"Okay," he said, eyeing me over. I could see he wasn't entirely satisfied, but he had a lot on his mind. "We'll be needing you again."

I said all right, and could we go now?

He sent a cop out to check the licence tag on the Buick. The cop came back, nodded.

"Okay, you can go," the Homicide man said. "Stick close."

We made our way out of the dining-room. Eyes followed us. It was nice to get into the lobby. The captain of waiters had Clair's wrap ready. He dropped it over her shoulders, said he was sorry our evening was spoilt. He sounded as if he was really sorry.

The cigarette girl was standing on a chair, trying to see into the dining-room. Her nakedness had lost its charm for me. She eyed me curiously.

Clair was white and silent. She stood waiting while the check girl found my hat. The peach-bloom pyjamas seemed tawdry, out of place in the tense atmosphere. I cursed Patrolman O'Brien. I decided I must have been crazy to have taken a recommendation from a cop.

"Just a second, sweetheart," I said to Clair, took her chiffon scarf, put it around her head, fixed it so it all but hid her face.

She regarded me with scared eyes. "I don't—"

"Yes, you do," I said. "The press are lurking outside."

I took her arm and we went down the stairs. It was only days after that I remembered I'd forgotten to ask for a check. The captain of waiters either forgot too or else he felt he couldn't ask payment for such an unsatisfactory evening.

As we stepped into the street, four men came hurrying towards us. I grabbed Clair's arm, rushed her to the alley. The men hesitated, stopped, stared after us.

"Get in," I said, jerking open the Buick door.

A flash-light exploded in our faces. I shoved Clair into the car, turned.

A little guy was standing near me, a press camera in his hand. "You're the guy who grabbed the gun?" he asked. "Jack Cain, ain't it?"

"Not me," I said, edging towards him. "Cain's still in there." I grabbed his camera before he could guess what I was at, whipped out the plate, dropped it on the sidewalk, trod on it.

I handed him back the camera.

"You punk!" he exclaimed. "You can't do this to me." He set himself for a swing, but I gave him a quick push, sent him staggering, got into the Buick.

I shot out of the alley.

Clair wanted to know why I had said I wasn't Jack Cain; why I had smashed the photographer's plate. She sounded very scared.

There was no point in keeping it from her any longer. I told her about Lois Spence telephoning me on the night before we left Paradise Palms. I gave her an idea what Lois had said.

"I'm not kidding myself," I said, watching the road unreel beneath the head-lights. "Those two are dangerous, vicious. That's why I ducked out of sight. Maybe I was a fool. I should have put you somewhere safe and gone after them. Now we're stuck. This case is going to get a hell of a lot of publicity. We'll be in the papers. As soon as Lois knows where we are, she and Bat will start something or my guess is all wrong. That's why I gave a wrong name and smashed that plate. It'll give us a little time to make up our minds what to do."

"I know what I'm going to do," she said in a steady voice, "I'm not giving up our home for them. I'm not scared as long as you're with me."

It was what I hoped she would say, but for all that, I had an uneasy feeling that our spell of peace was coming to an end.

4

We read in the morning's newspaper that Clem Kuntz, the shrewdest criminal lawyer on the Pacific Coast, was handling Lydia Hamilton's defence. I expected he'd call on us. He did.

He arrived as I was going off duty. I thought he was a customer when I saw the big Lincoln roll up the driveway, but I soon found out different.

"I want to talk to you," he said, getting out of the car. "I'm Kuntz. Maybe you've heard of me."

I had heard of him all right, even before he had taken charge of the Gray Howard Slaying, as the newspapers called it. Gray Howard was the name of the man in the white dinner-jacket. He turned out to be a big-shot movie director.

I eyed Kuntz over. He was a squat square man with a mulberry-coloured face. He had the hardest eyes I'd ever seen in a man's face, and he gave me the full benefit of them. I stared right back at him, said: "Go ahead. I can give you a couple of minutes, then I want my supper."

He shook his head. "A couple of minutes won't do," he said. "Let's go somewhere where we can talk. You'd better play with me, Cain. I could put you in a hell of a spot if I felt that way."

I hesitated, decided that maybe he could put me in a spot, jerked my head to the house.

"Then you'd better come in."

We went into the house, and I showed him into the front room. He looked round, grunted, took up a position by the window. I sat in the easy chair, yawned, pulled my nose, said, "Shoot."

"You married?" he asked abruptly.

I nodded. "What of it?"

"I'd like to meet your wife."

I shook my head. "Not before you tell me what's on your mind," I said. "I'm particular whom she meets."

His eyes snapped. "Scared to let me see her?" he barked.

I laughed at him. "You're wasting time," I said; "come off your high horse."

The door opened and Clair came in. She was wearing a cute frilly apron over a simple little frock in sky blue. She looked a kid, and a pretty one at that.

"Oh, I'm sorry . . ." she said, backing out.

"Come in," I said. "This is Mr. Clem Kuntz. The Mr. Kuntz." I looked at the mulberry-colored face. "This is my wife. Satisfied?"

He was looking narrowly at Clair. There was an expression of startled dismay in his eyes.

I suddenly got what he was driving at. I grinned.

"Not what you expected?" I said. "I bet your client told you she was hard, brassy, and on the make."

He drew in a deep breath, bowed to Clair.

"I merely wanted to know, Mrs. Cain, if you spoke to Gray Howard on the night of his death," he said, clinging to the shreds of his dignity.

She looked at me, shook her head.

"Look, Mr. Kuntz," I said, "I know what you hope to establish. It's to your client's advantage if you can prove that Clair was trying to make Howard. She wasn't, and I don't think, however hard you try, you'd ever convince a jury she was. Howard was propositioning her. I wanted to fix him, but Clair didn't want a scene. We had been working hard for three months, and it was our first night out together. It was our hard luck that we should run into Howard. Clair didn't encourage him. Your client was sore because Howard couldn't keep his eyes to himself. But that didn't cause the murder. It touched it off, but it had been coming to a head for some time. A guy doesn't punch a woman in the face unless he's sick to death of her. It was the punch that killed Howard . . . not Clair."

Kuntz cleared his throat, grunted.

"I wonder if you always look like that," he said to Clair, speaking his thoughts out aloud.

"She'll look like that at the trial, if you decide to call her," I said. "And she'll hurt your client's case if you try to make out she's a vamp."

He passed his fat hand over his bald head, frowned. He knew when he was licked.

"I don't think I'll call her," he said. "All right, Cain, I guess I'm wasting time. I thought your wife would be a different type." He looked wistfully at Clair, shook his head, went.

We breathed again. Maybe it was going to work out all right. Maybe we weren't going to get any publicity.

The District Attorney's man was the next to call. He had a report from the State Highway cop who had arrested Lydia on the drunk while driving charge. As soon as he learned that Lydia had tried to wreck the Cadillac with me in it, he hot-footed over to see me. He said it was just the kind of evidence he wanted. It proved that Lydia was a dangerous drunk, and it'd carry a lot of weight with the jury. I tried to talk him out of it, but he was too burned up with the idea.

The next morning the press had the story.

They began arriving before we had breakfast, and they crawled all over us. The little guy who had tried to photograph us on the night of the murder was well in the forefront. He snarled at me, and there was nothing I could do about it.

"Hello, wise guy," he said. "So you don't like publicity? My editor will sure fix you for smashing that plate."

Flash-lights exploded around us for the next hour. We tried to duck out of sight, but it was like a siege. When they had gone, I went upstairs, hunted out Bat's .38. I sat on the bed, cleaned, oiled and loaded it. It seemed odd to have a gun banging against my side again. I didn't like the feel of it anymore. I was worried too that I was so much slower on the draw than I used to be. It was nearly four months since I pulled a gun, and I knew I'd have to get in some practice if I was going to match Bat.

Clair found me practising.

I pulled her down on the bed beside me.

"I think I'll send you away," I said. "If Bat's going to start anything, he'll get at me through you. We'll have to think where you can go."

She shook her head. "It's no use running away, darling," she said. "They may never come after us, and we'd be separated for months, waiting. Besides, they want me at the trial and things could happen then if they're going to happen at all. Let's stick together. I'd never have a moment's peace without you." She flung her arms around my neck. "I don't care what you say. I'm not going to leave you."

I thought for a moment, decided she was right.

"We'll wait for them," I said.

I was expecting something pretty bad from the newspapers, but nothing as bad as the front page of the *Clarion*, the paper my friend the photographer worked on. They had dug up the whole story of Paradise Palms and had smeared it all over the front page with photographs of myself, Clair, the service station, Killeano and even Clairbold, the boy wonder.

I took one look, cursed.

5

As the weeks went by and nothing happened, we gradually relaxed. But we still took precautions. I carried a gun, I continued to practice, and I regained my speed. We had a couple of fierce police dogs around the house, but no one can continue to be keyed up all the time waiting for trouble if trouble doesn't come.

At first, we both had the jitters, catching each other listening to any unusual sound, breaking off our conversation at an approaching step, looking uneasily at each other whenever the telephone rang. But that kind of tension doesn't last. After the fourth week we were almost back to normal, although I took care never to approach any car that came into the station unless I could see the driver. If I couldn't see who was driving, I sent Bones. I never did a night shift either.

Lydia Hamilton's trial was a three-day sensation. Kuntz knew she hadn't a chance to beat the rap so he pleaded her guilty, but insane. The D.A. was after her blood, and he didn't call me, as my evidence would have helped establish the fact that she was insane.

Kuntz got his verdict after a terrific battle, and after the usual ballyhoo from the press the story died a natural death.

A week after the trial, and five weeks after the newspapers had first discovered me, Lois Spence showed her hand.

I had finished for the night, and had handed over to Ben, the old guy who handled the night shift, when the telephone in the office rang.

"I'll answer it," I said to Ben as a car came up the driveway.

I returned to the office, lifted the receiver.

"Cain?" a woman's voice asked.

I knew at once who it was. I felt my lips lift off my teeth in a mirthless smile. So it had come at last.

"Hello, Lois," I said. "I was expecting you to call."

"Like the wait?" she asked, a jeer in her voice.

"All right. It gave me time to prepare for you. Coming to see me?"

"You bet I am," she said, "but it'll have to be a surprise. Don't be embarrassed, we won't expect you to dress."

I laughed, although I didn't feel like laughing.

"How's Bat?" I asked.

"He's fine, I shouldn't laugh, Cain. You won't like it when we do come."

"Why don't you grow up?" I said. "You always were a dumb red-head. Do you think I care what you do? I can handle Bat and you. Tell him. And don't forget, Lois, if you slip up, you'll have a nice stretch in jail ahead of you. Bat's wanted for murder and that makes you an accessory after the fact. Thought of that?"

"Listen, you heel," she said, losing her smooth tone. "I've waited too long to even things up with you. It's been fun making you sweat, but I'm through with waiting now."

"Watch your elastic, sister," I said. "There's no need to get excited. Tell me, what do you plan to do, or is that a secret?"

"What do you think? We'll get that girl of yours, and then we'll invite you to call and see her. Bat still wants to match his skill against yours."

"With an empty gun, of course," I said.

"Not this time," Lois returned. "He's been getting ready for you. He's wise to that loose holster trick now. You won't pull another gag like that. Well, so long, Cain. We'll be around, so make hay while there's a sun." She hung up.

I stood thinking, then I went out, climbed into the Buick. "Tell Mrs. Cain I won't be twenty minutes," I said to Ben, drove on to the highway.

I paid a visit to the police-station, asked to see Lieutenant Mallory.

Mallory and I knew each other well. He was always passing the service station, and he knew where he could get iced beer with a smile from Clair whenever he wanted it.

"What's on your mind, Cain?" he asked, offering me a cigarette.

I took it. We lit up. "I want protection," I said.

He gaped at me, burst into a roar of laughter. "That's rich," he said. "You want protection. I don't believe it. Why you're the original tough egg."

"I know," I said, "but this is different. My shooting days are over. Take a pew, Lieutenant, I want to tell you a story."

I gave him the story, told him Bat was after us, and that Lois had just called me.

"You're not scared of a punk like Thompson, are you?" he asked, blankly.

"I didn't say I was scared of anyone," I said patiently. "I'm respectable now. My wild days are over. I own a wife and a service station. I'm not risking being sent to jail or the chair because you boys can't do your job."

He eyed me thoughtfully. "Well, we'll keep an eye on your place," he said. "Will that do?"

"That's what I want, and suppose Bat turns up when your eye isn't on the place. What then?"

"You deal with him. You'd be within your rights."

I shook my head. "I've killed about six men now and pleaded self-defence. That plea is wearing a little thin. A bright lawyer might sway a jury and railroad me to the chair. I'm through with that stuff. Have me made a deputy sheriff. I haven't even a permit for this rod."

"Don't show me," he said, hurriedly closing his eyes. "I don't want to know about it. I can't make you a deputy sheriff. Maybe the D.A. might play."

I had an idea. "Say, Bat's wanted by the Federal Office. Maybe . . ."

"Try them," Mallory said. "In the meantime I'll detail a patrolman to keep an eye on your place."

I thanked him, drove over to the Federal Bureau, asked to see someone in charge.

It took me an hour, but I came out with a gun permit, and a piece of paper which stated that I was temporarily attached to the Federal Office as special investigator. A long-distance call to Hoskiss had got me that.

I was late back for supper, and Clair was worried, but as soon as she saw the light in my eye, she brightened.

"Where have you been?" she asked, leading me into the dining-room where supper was waiting.

I told her about Lois; showed her the gun permit and my authority.

"I'm a G-man now," I said. "How do you like that?"

She looked a little scared, but tried to hide it.

"I like it fine," she said. "There's a cop in the kitchen eating apple pie. He said he had been detailed to keep an eye on me until you returned."

I laughed. "Swell idea," I said. "Well, I'm ready for Bat now. I don't think they'll come after you, honey. Lois wouldn't have told me if that was their idea."

Three days went by, and still nothing happened. Every three hours a patrolman would look in, wink at Clair, say "No trouble?" shrug and go on his way.

I didn't relax this time. I was sure something would happen before long, and if I didn't keep on my toes, I'd be surprised.

It happened the following night.

We had gone to bed about eleven. I had locked the bedroom door, bolted it. I had fixed the mesh-wire screen over the open window. No one could get in our room without waking us.

It was a clear moonlight night, and the night air was hot. Ben had been busy up to ten-thirty, and now trade had slackened off.

Clair and I lay side by side in the big double bed. I was half asleep when I heard a car drive up. I thought nothing of it, relaxed, began to drift off. Then suddenly I was wide awake, listening. Clair also sat up, looked at me in the dim light, whispered, "What is it?"

I shook my head. "I don't know. Did you hear anything?"

"I thought I did," she said. "But I'm not sure."

We listened. Silence.

"A car came in a minute or so ago," I whispered. "It hasn't gone." I swung my feet to the floor. "I don't hear Ben around!"

I went to the window. A big Plymouth sedan stood on the driveway. There was no sign of Ben or the driver.

I waited, frowning.

Footsteps sounded on the concrete below, feet scraped, paused, came on. A woman's shadow came into my vision. I couldn't see the woman unless I moved the screen and leaned out of the window. I wasn't going to do that. I studied the shadow.

A sudden electric thrill ran down my back. I thought I recognized the shape.

I turned quickly, grabbed my trousers, slipped them on, dragged on socks, shoes, snatched up my gun.

"Have they come?" Clair asked in a small voice.

"I think so," I said grimly. "There's a woman down there. I think it's Lois. Stay here. I'm going to have a look." She whipped out of bed, clung to me.

"No, don't," she said. "Please, darling. Let's call the police. They want you to go out there. They'll be waiting for you."

I patted her arm. "Okay, we'll call for the police," I said. "You better get some clothes on."

I slipped out of the room, crept down the stairs. It was dark. I moved cautiously, silently, I suddenly remembered what Clairbold had once said about the art of stalking. It occurred to me that I might have put in a little practice in my room the way he had. It wasn't such a dumb idea after all.

I reached the lobby, crossed to the front room where the telephone was. We had drawn the curtains before going to bed, but I didn't risk putting the light on. I wanted them to think we hadn't heard them.

I groped around, trying to find the telephone, found it, lifted the receiver. There was no humming sound on the line. I rattled the cradle once, twice, smiled grimly, hung up. They had cut the wires.

I crossed to the window, lifted the curtain an inch, looked out. The Plymouth still stood deserted on the runway. I couldn't see the woman, but after peering round I saw a dark shape lying by the office building. It could have been Ben, or it might have been one of the dogs.

I went back to the lobby, stood listening.

Clair came to the head of the stairs; she had a flash-light in her hand.

"Keep that light off the curtains," I said softly.

"Are the police coming?" she asked,

"The line's cut," I returned. "Wait here. I'm going to look out the back."

"Don't go out," she said breathlessly. "I know that's what they expect you to do. They're watching the doors."

I thought she was probably right.

"I won't," I said, moved along the short passage to the kitchen.

Here, the blinds weren't drawn. I crawled on hands and knees across the room, raised myself, looked out of the window.

Lois Spence was out there, I saw her distinctly. She was wearing dark slacks and coat. She was looking up at the upper window. I could have shot her easily enough, but I hadn't the stomach to shoot a woman.

Clair joined me. We squatted on our heels, side by side, watching Lois, who continued to stare up at the upper windows. The moonlight was bright enough for me to see she still favoured Fatal Apple make-up. She looked as coldly disdainful as she had always looked.

"I'd like to give her a fright," I said, "but as long as Bat keeps out of sight, we'll play possum."

"Where is he?" she whispered, her hand on my arm. I was surprised it was so steady.

"I haven't seen him yet," I said. "When I do I'm going to make a little hole in his hide. I'm taking no risks with Bat."

Lois suddenly turned, walked away, heading for the front of the house.

Faintly we could hear through the closed window a clink of metal against metal.

"What's that?" Clair asked, stiffening.

I listened. Something metal dropped on the concrete, out of sight. It came from the gas-pump section of the station.

"I don't know," I said uneasily. "I wish I knew what has happened to Ben. It's not his fight. If they've hurt him . . ."

Clair's grip on my arm tightened. "Please don't do anything rash—"

"I won't, but I'm getting tired of letting these two roam around as if this is their home," I said. "I'm going into the front room. Maybe we'll see something from there."

She went with me. As we reached the lobby, a wild scream rang out. The sound came from the front of the house. I darted forward, but Clair hung on to me.

"It's a trap," she said. "Wait . . . listen . . ."

I paused.

A car engine suddenly roared into life, gears clashed, tyres screeched on the driveway.

I darted into the sitting-room, lifted the curtains, peered out.

The Plymouth sedan was roaring down the driveway. It turned as it reached the highway, belted away into the night.

Lois Spence was lying on the concrete by the air towers.

I jumped to the front door.

"Wait," I said to Clair, threw off her restraining hand, opened the door.

"No!" she cried. "Don't!"

I slipped out, waved her back, reached Lois as she struggled to rise.

Her face was ghastly with terror. A red-blue mark showed on her face where she had been struck.

"He's lit a fuse to the gas dump," she mouthed at me. "Get me out of here! My God! We'll be blown to hell! The stinking rat double-crossed me! Get me out of here."

She grabbed at my pyjama jacket. I wrenched free, leaving a strip of material in her hand.

"Clair!" I yelled frantically. "Quick! Come to me! Clair!"

I dashed towards the house, saw Clair in the doorway, yelled to her again.

The whole sky seemed suddenly to split open; a long tongue of orange flame rushed up into the night, and I was conscious of a tremendous noise.

I saw Clair, her hands before her face, her eyes wide with terror. I couldn't run anymore. I was crouching, my hands over my ears when a blast of suffocating air struck me down.

I struggled up on my knees, saw the house sway, crumble, tried to yell, then the ground kicked up, trembled, and another tremendous explosion ripped open the shattered night sky. The blast picked me up and threw me away as the house came down like a pack of cards.

6

The nurse beckoned. I stood up, braced myself, crossed the corridor.

"You can go in now," she said. "You'll keep her quiet, won't you? She's still suffering from shock."

I tried to say something, but words stuck in my throat. I nodded, went past her through the open doorway.

Clair was lying in the small bed facing me. Her head was a helmet of white bandages; her right hand was bandaged too.

We looked at each other. Her eyes smiled. I went over, stood beside her.

"Hello," she said. "We made it, darling."

"We made it all right," I said, pulling up a chair. "It was a close call, Clair. Too close. I thought I wasn't going to see you again." I sat down, took her left hand.

"I'm tough," she said. "Did they say if I—I—"

"It'll be all right," I assured her. "You're more scorched than burned. You'll look as lovely as ever when they're through with you."

"I wasn't worrying for myself," she said. "I didn't want you to have an ugly wife . . ."

"Who said I had a pretty one?" I said, kissing her hand. "Someone's been kidding you."

She fondled my hand, stared at me.

"There's not much left of our home, is there?" she asked in a small voice.

I shook my head. "It's all gone," I said, ran my fingers through my hair, smiled at her. "It was a lovely blaze while it lasted."

Her eyes darkened. "What are you going to do, darling? You won't get unsettled?"

I patted her hand. "No. I'm going to build again. As soon as you're better we'll talk it over. I have ideas. We can build that restaurant of yours. The joint's well insured. There won't be any trouble about money. It'll take a little time, but maybe it'll turn out to be a good thing in the long run. I never did like the position of the station. I'll rebuild it facing the road."

"What happened to them?" she asked, gripping my hand.

I knew that question had been on her mind ever since she had recovered consciousness.

"Lois is here," I said. "She was pretty badly burned. The Doc doesn't think she'll get over it."

She shivered. "You mean she's going to die?"

I nodded.

"And Bat?"

"Yeah . . . Bat. Well, they got him. He ran into a police car. There's nothing to worry about, darling. He's fixed."

I bent down, pretended to fiddle with my shoe-lace. I knew if she looked at me now I wouldn't have been able to have met her eyes, and then she'd have known I was lying. Lois was in the hospital, but Bat was still loose. I wasn't going to tell her that.

"You mean our troubles are really over?" she asked.

"You bet they are," I said, straightening. "As soon as you're well enough to leave here, we'll start right in again. You'll like that, won't you? You'll be able to have your restaurant, and we'll make a pile of dough."

She closed her eyes, relaxed.

"I did so hope you would say that, darling," she said.

The nurse looked in, beckoned.

"Well, here's the tyrant again," I said, getting up. "I'll be back tomorrow. Take it easy. We have a lot to look forward to." I kissed her lightly, touched her hand, went out.

There was another nurse waiting in the corridor.

"Miss Spence is asking for you," she said.

"Okay," I returned, looked at her. "How's she making out?"

The nurse shook her head. "She was dreadfully burned," she said. "I don't think it will be long now."

I followed her along the corridor to Lois's room. A cop paced up and down outside. He nodded to me as I went in.

Lois was lying flat. Her face hadn't been touched. They had told me that hot oil had flowed over her chest. She looked practically done.

I stood over her, waited.

She looked up, her eyes, dark with pain, searched my face. "Hello, gambler," she said. "You had all the luck."

I didn't say anything.

She chewed her lip, frowned. "I want to talk to you."

I pulled up a chair, sat down.

"You'd better take it easy," I said. "You'll need all your strength. You're pretty ill, Lois."

"I know it," she said, her mouth twisting. "I'm through. But I wanted to see you before . . ."

"Okay, go ahead," I said, waited.

"Men have been my bad luck," she said, staring at the ceiling. "They all let me down except Juan. I was fond of Juan, Cain. I kind of went crazy when I lost him. But I should have left you alone. Evening things up isn't my strong suit—not against you, anyway. You're too lucky, Cain."

"You haven't done so badly," I said. "You blew my home and business to hell. What more do you want?"

She sneered. "But you're still here, and your girl. Juan isn't, and I'm finished too."

"Let's skip it," I said. "This won't get us anywhere."

"Bat double-crossed me," she said, spitefully.

"What did you expect? The snake would double-cross his own mother."

"My fault again," she said. "I wanted to use him to even things with you, but he thought I'd fallen for him. I ought to have played with him until this was over, but I gave him hell. How could I fall for a filthy brute like him? I told him so, and he fixed me." She moved her legs restlessly. "They swear they've filled me full of dope, but it hurts—it hurts like hell."

I didn't say anything.

"I taught Bat how to explode the gas dump, rehearsed him for weeks. God! He was dumb. He couldn't have done it without me. He wanted to shoot you, but I had to be smart. You see, it didn't work out. I wanted to see you and your girl go up in flames along with your smug little home."

I looked away. It was no use hating her; she was dying and she'd paid for what she had done.

"You're not letting Bat get away?" she asked abruptly.

I shook my head. "Where is he?"

"What'll you do to him?"

"Shoot or arrest him," I said. "I don't care which. One or the other."

She grimaced, sweat was running down her face. "I wish he could suffer the way I'm suffering," she said.

"Where is he?"

"He'll have cleared out of my apartment by now," she said, frowning. "He'll go to Little Louis. I think you'll find him there. He won't know where to hide. You'd've caught him long ago if it hadn't been for me. He hasn't any brains."

"Where's Little Louis?" I asked impatiently.

She gave me a downtown address in San Francisco.

"Who is he?"

"Just one of the boys," she said indifferently. "He holes up anyone on the run. Watch your step, Cain. I want you to catch Bat."

"I'll catch him," I said, standing up.

She closed her eyes.

"Well, I don't look awful," she said, "that's something, I guess. I'd hate to die ugly."

I couldn't stand the atmosphere any longer.

"So long," I said.

"Kill him for me, Cain," she said.

I went.

Waiting for me in the corridor was Tim Duval. At first, I couldn't believe my eyes.

"What did you expect?" he said, shaking hands. "As soon as we read about it, I flew up. All the boys pooled the fare. They wanted to come too, but they couldn't get away."

"Am I glad to see you," I said, slapping him on the back.

"So you should be," he said, grinning. "Hetty'll be along soon. She's coming by train. How's the kid?"

"Not so bad," I said. "She'll be all right in a month or so. It was a close call, Tim." I scowled at him, added, "I have a job for you."

He nodded. "I knew it," he said. "That's why I came. Bat, eh?"

"Sure," I said, "only you're camping outside Clair's door. So long as I know she's safe I can get to work. Now don't argue," I went on hurriedly as he began to speak. "Bat's dangerous. He might come here to finish the job. Stick around, Tim. I know Clair will be safe if you're here. I have things to do."

"Well, I'll be damned," he said. "And I was planning to get in on a man-hunt."

I punched him lightly on his chest.

"You watch Clair," I said. "This man-hunt is going to be between Bat and me." I led him to Clair's door. "Not a word about Bat. I've told her he's in jail. Go in and see her for a minute, then get a chair and park outside. I don't expect to be long."

I left him before he could protest.

7

The taxi driver slowed, stopped.

"This is as far as I can take you, Bud," he said. "The joint you want is down that alley, if it is the joint you want."

I got out of the cab, peered down a narrow alley, blocked by two iron posts.

"I guess it is," I said, gave him half a buck.

"Want me to stick around?" he asked. "It don't look like your home."

"It isn't, but don't wait," I said, and walked towards the alley.

It was dark; mist from the sea softened the gaunt outlines of the buildings. The single street lamp made a yellow pool of light on the slimy sidewalk. Not far away a ship's siren hooted. The sound of moving water against the harbour walls was distinct.

I lit a cigarette, moved on. Little Louis had selected a lonely spot for a home, I thought. The buildings I passed were warehouses, most of them in disuse. The property, the taxi driver had told me, had been condemned and was going to be pulled down. It should have been pulled down long ago.

A half-starved black cat appeared out of the shadows, twisted itself around my legs. I stooped, scratched its head, went on. The cat followed me.

Little Louis's place was the last building in a row of battered wooden ruins. I flipped my cigarette into a puddle, stood back, looked up at the house. The cat moved delicately towards the puddle, sniffed at the cigarette, howled dismally.

"Some joint, puss," I said.

The building was a three-storey job; no lights showed, most of the windows had rotten planks nailed across them. It was a proper dump, the kind of building Hollywood favours when creating a chiller atmosphere.

I tried to get round the back of the building, but found it looked on to a kind of reservoir. The stillness and blackness of the water was deceptive. It looked solid.

I went back to the front of the building, tried the front door. It was locked. I prowled around, found a lower window, tried to move it, but it wouldn't budge. I went to the next window, heaved. It creaked loudly. I cursed the plank, took out my gun, forced the barrel backwards and forwards until the plank broke away from its rusty nails. I made less noise than I expected. I hoped no one had heard the first creak, which had been something.

I worked on the next plank, got rid of it, and was ready to squeeze through. I looked into the room beyond, saw nothing but darkness, heard nothing. I fished out an electric torch from my hip pocket, turned the beam into the room. It was unfurnished, dirty; a rat scurried away from the light.

With my gun in my right fist, I stepped over the sill, down into the room.

The cat jumped up on the sill, peered at me. I shooed it away. It seemed reluctant to leave me, but it went eventually, jumping down into the darkness outside. A full minute of breathless listening got me nowhere. Holding my gun-arm tight against my side, I began exploring the room. There were footprints in the dust on the floor; a hand-print by the door. The place smelt of decay, bad drains.

I reached the door, turned the handle, pulled the door gently towards me. I peeped into a dingy passage, lit by a naked gas-jet. I listened. Nothing. Sliding my torch back into my pocket, I edged out of the room into the passage. Another door faced me. To my right was the front door; to my left a flight of stairs. They looked rotten and broken, and there were no banisters. It was some hide-out.

I crept across the passage to the opposite door, put my ear against the panel, listened. After a moment or so I heard feet scrape on the wooden floor.

I wondered if Bat was behind the door. My heart was beating steadily; I wasn't excited. I had come to kill Bat, and I was going to kill him.

My hand slid over the brass door-knob. I squeezed it, turned slowly. It made no sound as it turned. When it wouldn't turn any further, I pushed.

I looked into a narrow, dimly lit room full of wooden packing-cases stacked up along the unpapered walls. In the centre of the room was a table and chair. Near the rusty stove stood a truckle bed, covered with a grimy blanket.

Little Louis sat at the table. He had a deck of greasy playing-cards in his hand, and he was laying out a complicated patience game. He raised his head as I stepped into the room.

Little Louis was a hunchback. The complexion of his dried-up face looked as if it had been sand-blasted. His hard little eyes glinted under thick black eyebrows. His shapeless mouth, like a pale pink sausage split in two, hung open.

He stared at me, his right hand, hairy and dirty, edged off the table to his lap.

"Hold it," I said, lifted the .38.

His mouth tightened, snarled, but his hand crept back on to the table again.

I moved further into the room, closed the door with my heel, advanced.

He watched me, puzzled, suspicious.

"What do you want?" he asked. His voice was high-pitched,

effeminate.

"Get away from the table," I said, pausing within a few feet of him.

He hesitated, pushed back the wooden box on which he was sitting, stood up. Something fell to the floor off his lap. I glanced down. A broad, squat knife lay at his feet. It looked very sharp, deadly.

"Get back to the wall," I said, advancing on him.

He retreated, his hands raised to his shoulders. There was no shock of fear in his eyes. As I passed the knife I picked it up, dropped it into my pocket.

"Where's Bat Thompson? " I asked.

His eyes narrowed. "Who wants him?"

"You'd better talk," I said. "I'm in a hurry."

He grinned evilly. "You've made a mistake," he said. "I don't know any Bat Thompson."

I edged towards him. "You'd better talk," I said.

"Who are you? You're new to the racket, ain't you? Guys don't threaten me. I'm everyone's pal."

"Not mine," I said, smacked him across his face with the barrel of my gun.

His head jerked back. A red weal appeared on his harsh skin. His eyes glinted murderously.

"Where's Bat?" I repeated.

He snarled at me so I hit him again.

"I can keep this up all night," I told him pleasantly, grinned. "Where's Bat?"

He pointed to the ceiling. "Top floor; the door facing the stairs." He began to curse me softly, a mumbling flow of obscenity.

"Alone?" I said, lifting my hand, threatening him.

"Yeah," he said.

I studied him. He was too dangerous to leave. I decided to provoke him into a fight. It turned out to be a dumb idea.

I nodded, shoved the .38 down the waist-band of my trousers. "Why couldn't you have said so before?" I asked. "It'd've saved you a lot of grief."

Two terrifying long arms shot out towards me; arms that seemed to stretch like elastic. I thought I was well out of his reach, and was waiting for him to jump me, but the arms came as a surprise. Two hands clamped on my wrists. They felt as if they had been welded to my flesh. He jerked me towards him.

He had twice my strength and the jerk nearly snapped my neck. I cannoned against him, felt his hands whip up to my throat. He was a shade too slow. I got my chin down, so he gripped that; before he could dig his claws into my neck, I sank a punch into his belly with all my weight behind it. He doubled up, snarling, and as I rushed him, he swung his fist, clouted me on the side of the head. It was like being hit with a hammer. I found myself lying on my side, bells ringing in my ears. I twisted over, saw through a red mist the misshapen legs moving towards the door. I grabbed at them, hung on, pulled him down. He fell close, squirmed around and uncorked another sledge-hammer blow. I ducked under it, felt it whizz past my head. My right hand yanked out the .38; holding it in my fist, I punched him in the face with it.

He gibbered with pain, got close, his evil-smelling head under my chin. He clawed at my body with steel fingers. I continued to hit him about his face and head with the gun butt. I couldn't get much steam into the blows because he was lying on top of me, but I succeeded in making a mess of his face.

He got sick of it before I did, scrambled away, opened his mouth to yell. I rammed the gun barrel into his open mouth.

"Make a sound and I'll blow your top," I said.

The cold gun barrel in his mouth terrified him. He gagged, tried to wriggle away, but I forced the barrel further down his throat. He grabbed my wrists, yanked. The barrel shot out of his mouth, but the gunsight caught his front teeth; they shot out too. He yammered in his throat, flung me off, raised himself up, half-crazy with rage and pain, slammed down at me with both fists. If they had landed he would have flattened me, but I rolled against him, stabbed him in his belly with the gun barrel.

He gave a croaking howl, fell back, holding on to himself. Blood oozed between his fingers.

I knelt over him, panting, belted him between the eyes. He passed out.

Getting to my feet I fought to recover my breath. My legs felt weak, my heart thumped furiously. We had only fought for a couple of minutes, but it had been an experience. He had been as strong as an ape.

I left him, made for the stairs. I started up, my hand on the wall, treading cautiously. The stairs were in a bad way, gave under my weight. I kept on, mounted to the first floor, listened.

From one room I heard voices. A woman cursed in a shrill hard tone. A man yelled to her to shut up. I walked along the passage, made for the next flight of stairs.

The door behind me jerked open. I glanced around. A thin, miserable-looking woman half fell into the passage. She wore a dirty kimono, and her hair hung loose.

"Save me, mister," she gasped, crouching against the wall.

A big, red-faced man, in shirt sleeves, stepped into the passage, grabbed the woman by her hair, dragged her into the room again. The door slammed. The woman began to squeal.

Ignoring her, I mounted the next flight of stairs. I was sweating, uneasy. This was a hell of a joint, I decided.

A naked gas-jet burned at the head of the stairs. It hissed and flickered in the draught. I paused as I reached the landing, looked back. Nothing moved. No one showed.

If Little Louis had been telling the truth I was now facing Bat's door. I stepped across the passage, put my ear against the door, listened.

A woman said: "God! I'm sick of this. I was crazy to throw in with a mean jerk like you."

I frowned, slipped back the safety catch of the .38, put my hand on the door handle.

Bat said: "Aw, the hell with you! I'm sick of you too." His harsh Brooklyn accent was unmistakable.

I opened the door, went in.

8

A girl, wearing black lace underwear, had her back to me as I entered. Her legs and feet were bare, her blonde hair piled untidily to the top of her head. A cheap imitation tortoise-shell comb failed to capture the straggling ends of hair from her neck. She was standing by a table on which was the remains of a meal and several bottles of whisky.

She turned swiftly as she heard the door open, stared at me. All I could see of Bat was his foot and leg. The girl stood directly in front of him. She was sharp-featured and she stared at me with sultry eyes, one of which was puffed and the other had been socked several days ago. She also had a bruise on her throat and her hand held a tall cool glass of amber fluid.

"Beat it," she said to me. "You've picked the wrong room."

"I want Bat," I said between my teeth. "Get out of the way."

She saw the gun, screamed, dropped the glass.

Bat recognized my voice, grabbed the girl around her waist, crushed her to him. He peered over her shoulder at me, grinned.

"Hello, bub," he said. His brutal face was the colour of mutton fat.

"Let go of the frail," I said. "What's the matter with you, Bat? Milky?"

The girl struggled frantically to get away, but Bat easily held her. I could see his thick fingers sinking into the loose flesh above her hips.

"Shaddap, you," he snarled in her ear, "or I'll break your goddamn back."

She stopped struggling, faced me, her eyes wide with terror, staring at the gun like an idiot child at a moving shadow.

It puzzled me why Bat didn't go for his gun. I saw his pig eyes glaring, followed the direction. A Luger lay on the mantelpiece, out of his reach.

I laughed. "For God's sake," I said, "getting careless, aren't you, Bat?" I jumped across the room to the gun. It was my own Luger.

Bat shuttled round, still holding the girl in front of him. He cursed softly, vilely, backed.

I had left the door unguarded by my move to the gun. Bat jerked it open, stepped into the passage, dragging the screaming girl with him. The door slammed.

I snatched up the Luger, shoved the .38 into my pocket, ran to the door. The passage outside was in darkness.

A door opened at the end of the passage, a man's head appeared. I fired above it. The head jerked back, the door slammed. Voices sounded below. A man bawled up to know what was going on. At the head of the stairs the blonde screamed wildly for help. Her scream was throttled back into her throat.

If Bat had been on his own I'd have nailed him then, but I couldn't see, and I didn't want to kill the girl. I swore softly, moved out into the passage.

Bat suddenly yelled: "Gimme a gun, Mike. Quick!"

I ran towards the sound of his voice. I could just see him with the girl held in front of him, crouching against the wall at the head of the stairs.

"Come out of it, you yellow rat," I said, caught hold of the girl's arm.

She kicked out, screamed like a train whistle.

Bat made himself small behind her, cursed me, hung on.

"Let go of her," I panted, dodging her kicks. One of them caught me in the stomach, winded me for a moment.

I heard footsteps pounding up the stairs, turned.

The red-faced man from the next landing was rushing up, a gun in his hand. He fired wildly at me. The bullet slapped into the wall above my head. I shot him between the eyes. He went down like a pole-axed bull.

I heard a grunt from Bat, spun around. I hadn't a chance to get out of the way. Bat had caught up the girl, held her above his head. He flung her at me as I tried to dodge. Screaming frantically, she sailed through the air like a shell. She hit me chest high. I went over, heard her wail, then crash through the rotten banisters and thud to the landing below.

Bat rushed down the stairs, missed his step, jumped. He landed with a crash as I fired after him.

I waited, listened.

A ghastly sobbing sound from the girl drifted up the wall of the staircase.

I peered over the rotten rail into darkness.

A spurt of flame lit the landing below. A slug cut through my coat sleeve, slicing a piece out of my arm. For blind shooting, it was impressive. I fired back, flung myself down as Bat opened up. He fired three times, stopped.

I crawled towards the stairs, began to go down them head first, flat, pulling myself forward with my hands.

"You there, bub?" Bat called. "You won't get away this time."

The girl began to scream again.

"Oh, my back!" she gasped. "Bat! Help me. My back—it's broken. Help me, Bat."

I heard Bat curse her. I crawled on, the hair on the back of my neck bristling at the whimpering screams from the girl.

"Shaddap," Bat hissed at her. "I can't hear him with all this racket. Shaddap!"

"It's my back," she sobbed, screamed again.

Half-way down I crawled into the body of the man I had shot. I paused, touched him, tried to satisfy myself that he was dead. He didn't move as I pawed him over in the sticky darkness. I decided to crawl over him.

Bat said to the girl, "I'll finish you if you don't shaddap."

I was nearly on him now. He couldn't hear me because of the noise the girl was making.

I heard him curse. The girl suddenly stopped screaming.

"What are you doing?" she moaned. "Take that gun away. Bat!" Her voice shot up in a shrill note of terror.

A single crack of gunfire exploded close to me. There was silence.

I caught a glimpse of Bat as he moved, lifted my gun, fired. He must have seen my movement for he fired at the same time. His bullet ploughed a weal along my cheek. I watched him. He rose up, tottered back, his gun slipping out of his hand. I fired again. The slug socked into him, throwing him back. He fell down, stretched out.

I pulled out my electric torch. The beam lit up a nightmare scene. The girl lay on her side, bent back, half her face was shattered by the heavy bullet from Bat's gun. Bat lay near her, his hand touched her naked foot. Blood seeped out of him like water from over-boiled cabbage.

I turned him over. He moved, blinked his eyes, snarled at me.

"So long, Bat," I said, put the gun to his ear. Before I could squeeze the trigger, his eyes rolled back, fixed. I stood up.

My arm ached. Blood dripped down from my fingers, from my face on to my collar. My side hurt. I didn't care. It was over—finished. I could go back to Clair now and start afresh.

I walked to the front door, slid back the bolts, stepped into the night.

I was still holding the Luger. I looked at it, wondering if I should get rid of it. Maybe I wouldn't need it again. Maybe I would. It was hard to believe that I was going to settle down. I had tried it for a few months and it hadn't worked. Well, I was going to try it again, but I was going to be prepared. Some wise guy might try to crowd me again, and I would be ready for him. I didn't know. I didn't care. Right now, I wanted to get back to Clair. The future, I decided, as I set off in the darkness, could take care of itself.

THE END

THE PAW IN THE BOTTLE

. . .

JAMES HADLEY CHASE

CHAPTER ONE

I

Rain pounded down on the pavements, and water, inches deep, ran in the gutters as Harry Gleb came up the escalator of New Bond Street underground. He paused at the station exit and surveyed the night sky, heavy with sullen black clouds in dismayed disgust.

"My infernal luck," he thought angrily. "Not a hope of a taxi. Damn and blast it! I'll have to walk. The old mare'll be livid if I'm late." He shot his cuff to look at his gold wrist-watch. "If this perisher's right, I'm late already."

After hesitating for a few minutes, he turned up his coat collar and, still swearing under his breath, set off quickly along the wet, greasy pavement, his head bent against the driving rain.

"This about rounds off a mucking awful day," he told himself as he hurried along, rain dripping from the brim of his hat and splashing against his legs. "Cigarette deal falls through, blasted dog comes in fourth, forty quid down the drain, and now this mucking rain."

From habit he walked in the shadows and avoided the street lights. Half-way down New Bond Street he spotted the faint gleam of steel buttons. Automatically he crossed the road.

"West End's lousy with bogies," he thought, hunching his broad shoulders as if he expected a heavy hand to fall on them. "That fella's as big and strong as an ox. Doing nothing except making a nuisance of himself. He'd be a lot more useful down a mine."

He recrossed the road when he had put a hundred yards or so between the policeman and himself and turned down Mayfair Street. After he had walked a few yards, he looked over his shoulder. Satisfied there was no one to see where he was going, he stepped into a doorway next to an antique book seller's shop and entered a dimly lit lobby.

A blonde woman in a leather jacket and flannel slacks, an umbrella under her arm, was coming down the stone stairs. She paused when she saw him and her hard, painted face brightened.

"Why, hello, *chéri*, were you coming to see me?"

"Not on your life," Harry said shortly. "I've a lot better things to waste my money on than you." Seeing the bitter twist of her lips, he went on in a kinder tone: "And listen, Fan, you might just as well put up the shutters. You won't find any suckers on the streets to-night. It's raining like hell, and there's no one around except the bogies."

"There's you," the woman said, and smiled invitingly.

Harry felt sorry for her. He was on friendly terms with most of the tarts in the West End, and he knew Fan was having a thin time. She was getting too old for the game and competition was cut-throat.

"Sorry, Fan, but I'm busy to-night." He shook the rain from his hat, asked: "Anyone gone up yet?"

"Bernstein and that stinker, Theo. The little swine offered me half a dollar."

Harry hid a grin.

"Don't worry about Theo. No one does. He's got a dirty sense of humour."

The woman's eyes gleamed angrily.

"I'll fix him one day. I've met some dirty rats in my time, but the things that little beast says to me turns my stomach."

"The look of him turns mine," Harry said carelessly. "Well, so long, Fan."

"Come and see me when you've finished," she urged. "I'll give you a good time, Harry. I will—honest."

Harry suppressed a shudder.

"One of these days, but not to-night. I'm taking Dana home. Here, get your little paws on this." He held out a couple of pound notes. "Buy yourself a keepsake."

"Thanks, Harry." The woman took the money eagerly. "You're a nice boy."

"I know I am," he returned, grinned, and went on up the stairs. "Poor mare," he thought. "She's getting fat and old. Give me a good time—ugh!"

At the head of the stairs he paused outside a door on which was the inscription:

Mrs. French
Domestic Agency
Enquiries

He waited a moment, then tip-toed to the banisters and looked into the lobby below. The blonde woman was standing in the doorway, staring up at the falling rain. As he watched, she put up her umbrella and moved into the street. He shook his head, shrugged, and rapped on the door.

A light flashed on inside the room and the shadow of a girl appeared on the frosted panel of the door, a key turned in the lock and the door opened.

"Hello it's me," he said cheerfully. "Last to arrive as usual."

"Come on in, Harry. They're waiting for you."

"Let them wait." He pulled the girl to him and kissed her. Her lips felt warm and yielding against his. "You're looking swell. How do you do it, and after last night, too?"

"Don't talk about last night." She smiled up at him. "I had an awful head this morning."

"As hard and as beautiful as a diamond," he thought, "and as expensive."

"Come on, Harry, they're waiting. You know what Mother is." She touched his face with slender caressing fingers.

He put his arm round her.

"What's she want? I haven't seen her for weeks, and I'm damned if I want to see her now. Every time I see her there's trouble."

"Don't be silly, Harry. Do come on, and don't do that! You're getting too free with your hands."

He grinned as he followed her across the small office into an inner room, lit by a desk lamp, its bright beam focused on a white blotting pad on the big desk. The room was full of cigarette smoke and dark shadows.

Mrs. French sat at the desk. Sydney Bernstein and Theo sat facing her. They all looked up as Harry came in.

"You're ten minutes late," Mrs. French said sharply. She was a bulky woman with a sallow complexion and sharp, bright eyes. She wore jet ear-rings that bobbed and flashed in the lamplight.

"Couldn't help it," Harry said airily. "It's raining cats and dogs. Hark at it. No taxis. Had to walk." He stripped off his overcoat, tossed it on a chair. "Hello, Syd, boy; how's things? Blimey! Is that young Pimples biting his nails in the dark? How are the spots and boils, Theo, my beauty?"

"Get stuffed," Theo snarled from out of the darkness.

Harry laughed good naturedly.

"What a lovely boy!" He rested his big hands on the desk and beamed at Mrs. French. "Well, here I am; better late than never. What's cooking?"

"Yes, let's get it over, Mother," Dana said impatiently. "I want to go to bed."

"Sit down, Harry." Mrs. French waved to a chair near her. "It's time we did another job together."

Harry sat down.

"Is it? Well, I don't know." He took out a packet of Players, lit one and tossed the packet to Bernstein. "The bogies are getting a bit hot, Ma. Look at the way they picked up Parry last night. The poor mutt hadn't left the house before they nabbed him. They're right on their toes just now. That mucker who shot Rawson's done it. Start shooting coppers and there's trouble. I don't know if this is the right time for a job."

Mrs. French made an impatient gesture.

"Parry's a fool. He just wanders around looking for an open window. This is a good job, Harry; a planned job. There's no risk to it."

Harry snatched up his cigarettes as Theo's dirty hand reached for them.

"No, you don't!" he snapped. "You buy your own damned fags."

Theo cursed him under his breath.

"Shut up!" Mrs. French barked. "I'm talking."

"Sorry, Ma; go ahead," Harry said with an apologetic grin. "What have you got in mind?"

"How would you like to take a crack at the Wesley furs?"

Harry stiffened. His breath whistled down his nostrils. "Hey! Now, wait a minute. Are you trying to get me put away for five years? I'm not all that wet, you know."

"That's what I say," Bernstein broke in vehemently. He was a little man with a face as brown and as wrinkled as a monkey's. His hands were covered with fine black hairs, and hair grew in coarse tufts on his wrists and showed above his shirt collar. "Be reasonable. It's no use running your head against a brick wall. The Wesley furs! It's madness!"

"But you'll take them if we get them?" Mrs. French asked, her eyes hardening.

He nodded.

"Yes; but you haven't a hope of getting them. Why don't you be reasonable?"

"Are you serious?" This from Harry. "You know what we'd be up against?"

"I know." Mrs. French tapped ash from her cigarette on to the floor. Her mouth was a hard line. "It won't be easy, but it can be done."

"I say not!" Bernstein said and thumped his small, hairy fist on the desk. "Four have tried it. Look what happened to them. It's too dangerous."

"He's right, you know," Harry said, pulling a face. "But it would be a sweet job if we could pull it off. Still, I don't fancy our chances, Ma."

"You're talking like a fool," Mrs. French said angrily. "You don't know anything about the job; only what you've heard. All right, four fools have tried to get the furs. None of them took the trouble to find out how the safe operates. They didn't use their brains because they hadn't any brains to use."

"You're wrong," Bernstein said, shifting forward on his chair. "Frank took a lot of trouble. He spent four months casing the place, but he was nabbed before he even opened the safe. What do you say to that?"

"We can learn from the mistakes of others. It means there's an alarm on the safe that rings if the safe is touched. We're going to find out about that. That's the first thing we're going to do."

"And how are we going to do that?" Harry inquired.

"Mrs. Wesley wants a maid. She's tried all the other agencies, and now she's come to me. I've been waiting a long time for this chance."

"And we put in a plant?" Harry looked interested. "That's an idea, Ma. It might even work."

"It will work. If we can get a girl in there who'll keep her eyes open she might find out how the safe operates. If she does, will you take on the job?"

"I might." Harry scratched his head. He thought of Parry. Only the night before last they had played snooker together. Now Parry was in a cell. A job as big as the Wesley furs would carry a five-year stretch. He flinched at the thought. "It'll be some job, Ma. I'd like to know more about it first. Is Theo coming in?"

Theo stopped biting his nails to say, "Course I am. I ain't windy if you are."

"One of these days I'm going to flatten those pimples of yours, you little ape," Harry said amiably, "and I'll flatten your face with them."

"We can't do anything without the girl," Mrs. French broke in. "Know anyone who'd do the job, Harry?"

"Well, I know a lot of girls," Harry said, and looked out of the corners of his eyes at Dana. "Depends on what kind of girl you want."

"I want someone smart and young with good appearance and who wants to pick up some quick money," Mrs. French said promptly. "I'll take care of the references."

Harry tilted back his chair and stared up at the ceiling. "Well, there is a girl," he said, after a pause. "She's a smart kid. Her name's Julie Holland. She works for Sam Hewart at the Bridge Café. Syd's seen her. Think she'd do, Syd?"

Bernstein shrugged. A scowl darkened his wrinkled face. "I don't know. She might, but she'd have to watch her temper. She's a bad-tempered little bitch."

Harry laughed.

"He's prejudiced, Ma. He pinched her bottom the other night and she caught him a slap in his puss. Laugh! I nearly bust my truss. Don't listen to him. I think she'd do. She's got the looks and she's nobody's fool. Hewart thinks a lot of her and you know how careful he has to be."

"Do the police know her?" Mrs. French asked.

"No, nothing like that. She's kept clear of trouble, but I know she's after big money. She's told me a bit about herself. She's ambitious and fed up with scraping along on a few quid a week. I think she's reckless enough to take a chance if the money's good enough."

"We can't tell her anything. It's too risky. And when the job's done, we'd have to be sure she keeps her mouth shut. The police will guess it's an inside job and they'll pick on her. We'd have to make very sure she won't talk if things went wrong."

Theo leaned forward so the light fell on his face.

"Let him find the bride. I'll see she doesn't talk," he said.

Theo was a short, stocky youth with long, dark hair that fell in lank, greasy strands over his ears and on to his coat collar. His round, pasty face was inflamed with blockheads and pimples, and his green eyes were close-set and cruel. He wore a shiny blue serge suit, baggy and shapeless, and his wreck of a hat, resting far back on his head, looked like a dead, furry animal that had been left in the gutter. There was something horribly vicious and spiteful in his expression and they looked at him, startled. There was a sudden uneasy tension in the room.

"No violence," Bernstein said quickly, "I don't stand for violence."

"Get stuffed," Theo said, and withdrew into the darkness again.

"And that goes for me, too," Harry said sharply. "You're a bit too keen on bashing girls, Pimples. One of these days you'll get a bash yourself, right in your ugly snout."

"Cut it out!" Mrs. French snapped. "We must have the girl or we can't do the job. Does she like you, Harry?"

Harry grinned.

"Well, she doesn't exactly hate me. It's a rum thing, but girls do go soft on me. Don't ask me why." He hastily moved his leg as Dana kicked out at him. "Present company excepted, of course," he went on, winking. "But this kid goes all dewy eyed when she sees me, if that means anything."

"Work on her," Mrs. French said. "She won't talk if you handle her right; not if she's soft on you."

"You and your damned women," Dana said angrily. "Why don't you grow up?"

"I'm getting along fine as I am," Harry said, patting her hand. "They mean nothing to me. You know that."

"Why don't you two go somewhere and have a nice cry together? You make me spew," Theo sneered.

"I'll bash this fat ape in a moment," Harry said wrathfully.

"Work on this girl, Harry," Mrs. French said, scowling at Theo. "We can't do anything until we've got her. I'll want her in about a week. Can you manage it by then?"

"Now, wait a minute. I didn't say I was going to do the job. What's in it for me? It's got to be convincing or I'm not interested."

Mrs. French was expecting this. She picked up a pencil and pulled a pad of paper towards her.

"The furs are insured for thirty thousand. Suppose we say we'll get seventeen for them?" She looked inquiringly at Bernstein.

"It's no good looking at me," Bernstein said sharply. "I don't know what they're worth until I've seen them. But seventeen's too much, anyway. More like ten if they're as good as you say they are. But I want to see the stuff before I talk prices."

"Then there's the jewellery," Mrs. French went on, deciding to ignore Bernstein. She began scribbling on the paper while the others watched her, "Your cut, Harry, shouldn't be less than eight thousand. It might be more."

"Cripes!" Harry exclaimed, his eyes lighting up. "Now you're talking. For eight thousand . . ."

"This is crazy!" Bernstein cried. His hands fluttered over the desk like two frightened bats. "You can't make such promises. You want me to take the stuff, don't you? Well then, I make the price. You can't say they'll be worth this and that. I must see the stuff first."

"If you can't talk figures, Syd, someone else will," Mrs. French said mildly. "You're not the only fence who'd like to handle the Wesley's furs."

Theo nudged Bernstein.

"Stuff that up your vest and see how it fits," he said, and laughed.

Rain splashed against the windows and ran in gurgling little rivers in the gutters. The lone policeman, walking down Mayfair Street, snug in his rainproof cape, had no idea that robbery was being planned within a few yards of him. He wasn't interested in robberies. He was thinking of the spring cabbages he had planted that afternoon. The rain, he reckoned, would give them a fine start.

II

If you happen to look for them, you will find an odd assortment of cafés, restaurants and clubs that somehow manage to conceal themselves in the jungle of brick, stone and dirty windows along King's Street, Fulham Palace Road and Hammersmith Bridge Road. You may wonder how such derelict-looking places keep open; who amongst the teeming crowd of shoppers and loafers converging from Hammersmith Broadway are likely to go to such places for a meal. But it is only at night, and in the small hours of the morning, that these particular cafés and restaurants come to life. If you happened to be in the district after eleven o'clock, you would find them crowded with a rather sinister-looking collection of men and women who sit over their tea or coffee talking in low tones, and who glance up suspiciously whenever the door opens and relax when the newcomer is recognized.

It is to such places that the Service deserters, tired of remaining in their rat-holes, come for a quick coffee and a look round before going to the West End; where the small gangs meet to check the final details of a new haul, and where the filthiest of all the scrapings of London's gutters—the painted youths in sandals and bright sweaters—eat before beginning their nightly prowl.

The king among these cafés and restaurants was the Bridge Café, owned by Sam Hewart, a dumpy, hard-faced man of indeterminable age. He had taken over the café during the height of the London blitz, and had got it cheap. Hewart believed in looking ahead, and he knew sooner or later there would be a need for such a plate in such a district: a place for the wide boys to meet, to leave messages that they knew would be delivered, to get information, to be told who was in Town and who wasn't, and who was paying the best prices at the moment for silk stockings, cigarettes, and even mink coats.

Six months ago a girl had come to Hewart's office. Her name was Julie Holland, and she worked at a nearby two-penny library. She had heard, she told him, there was a vacancy on his staff.

"I could be useful," she had said quietly. "I'm not fussy what I do."

Hewart had been impressed. He liked the way her dark, shiny tresses fell in natural waves each side of her small, rather pale face. He liked her alert grey eyes, and he particularly liked her figure, which, he thought in his loose-minded way, would be sensational without clothes. He couldn't understand how it was he hadn't seen her before. If, as she said, she worked in the library he should have seen her. He was annoyed with himself because he hadn't seen her. It made him feel old. He wouldn't have missed her five years ago, he told himself. He spent nearly all his waking hours thinking about girls. They dwelt in his mind consciously and subconsciously the way death sometimes dwells in the minds of the timid; although lately he hadn't been as preoccupied with these thoughts as he used to be, and when he was conscious of this it worried him. It was, he told himself bitterly, a sign of age.

This girl who now stood before him aroused in him an almost forgotten feeling of desire. She wore a sweater that showed off her breasts and her skirt was tight and short. There was scarcely a line of her body that he couldn't see. Her lipstick was vivid and put on to make her mouth look square, and her lips had a soft, yielding look that made Hewart feel short of breath.

He would have been startled and annoyed had he known she had deliberately dressed herself in this way to appeal to his ageing sense of lust. An amiable young spiv had given her the tip that Hewart wanted a smart girl who could keep her mouth shut. Hewart was all right, the spiv had told her, if she didn't mind being pawed occasionally.

"He's getting old," the spiv had said, with a cynicism that appealed to Julie. "You know what old men are like. It's all handy-pandy stuff; nothing you couldn't handle."

As for the café well, she didn't have to be told what some of the cafés were like in that district, and the Bridge Café was no exception, but the money Hewart paid was good. That was the point. The money was excellent. "He'll pay six quid; maybe more, and if you let him pinch your leg occasionally, you might screw him up to seven."

Seven pounds a week! At that time such a sum was the pinnacle of Julie's ambition. She made up her mind to get the job. What did she care if Hewart were tiresome? She was used to that sort of thing by now. Seven pounds a week! It was a fortune.

Julie was twenty-two years of age. Twenty of these years had been milestones of bitter poverty, of pinching and scraping and making do. Her parents had been miserably poor, her home squalid and dirty, and she had been continually hungry. As long as she could remember she had had a desperate, trapped feeling that life was slipping away from her, and she was missing all the good things that would have been hers had she the money to buy them. It was hunger that formed her character. It was hunger that sharpened her wits, and made her sly and cunning. Hunger and envy; for envy tormented her, making her a morose and unsociable child, and later a shrewd, hard, calculating young woman.

As soon as she was old enough to discriminate between those who have and those who have not, envy had laid hold of her. She envied people with clean homes, good clothes, cars, and the blind beggar who stood at the corner of her street when people gave him money. She envied the other children at school if they were better dressed than she. She pestered her parents for more to eat, for pocket money, for better clothes until, exasperated by his inability to give her what she wanted, her father flogged her to silence. But the flogging didn't cure her of envy. She was determined to have the good things of life, and since her parents failed to provide them, she began to help herself. At first she took only small things: a bar of chocolate from a classmate; a bun, sneaked off the baker's counter; a hair ribbon from her sister; a wooden peg-top from the boy next door. She took with cunning and no one suspected her. But the more she took, the more she wanted, and to celebrate her twelfth birthday she raided the jewellery counter in Woolworth's. But this time she wasn't dealing with children, and she was caught.

The magistrate had been lenient. He understood children, and when he had read the report on Julie's home life, he called her to him. She was too frightened to remember all he said to her, but she did remember the fable of the monkey and the bottle he had selected as the corner stone for his sermon.

"Have you ever heard how they catch monkeys in Brazil, Julie?" he had asked, to her surprise. "Let me tell you. They put a nut in a bottle, and tie the bottle to a tree. The monkey grasps the nut, but the neck of the bottle is too narrow for the monkey to withdraw its paw and the nut. You would think the monkey would let go of the nut and escape, wouldn't you? But it never does. It is so greedy it never releases the nut and is always captured. Remember that story, Julie. Greed is a dangerous thing. If you give way to it, sooner or later you will be caught."

He had sent her home, and she hadn't stolen again.

But as she grew up her envy of riches increased and her mind was obsessed with the longing for money. When her parents were killed in an air raid and she set up on her own in a dingy bed-sitting-room, the unexpected freedom of supervision led to the discovery of a hitherto unsuspected means to get what she wanted. She learned, now that she could stay out at all hours of the night, that there was something about her that attracted men. She had been vaguely aware of this power for some time, and at first she had resented the way men, at the slightest opportunity, put their hands on her. She was irritated when bus conductors helped her off the bus, when old gentlemen took her arm and insisted on seeing her across the road, or when a heavily-breathing man ran his hand down her leg in a cinema while he pretended to hunt for a dropped article in the darkness. But, after a while, she became used to these attentions, and now she had freedom she wondered if she couldn't capitalize this power.

The war and the coming of the American troops gave her the opportunity, and she joined the vast army of other young girls who came from the East End to have a good time with the Yanks.

Although only seventeen at that time, Julie quickly acquired a sophistication that distinguished her from the other giggling chits who hung about at street corners ogling the G.I.s as they loafed along Piccadilly. She mixed exclusively with the officer ranks, and her dingy bed-sitting-room scarcely ever saw her at night. Before long she acquired a veneer that a steam hammer couldn't crack, a wardrobe of flashy clothes, an intimate knowledge of the physical desires of men and fifty pounds in the Post Office Savings Bank. For a time she lived well, but the war ended and the Americans went home. Then followed the lean years, and life became a wangle. She had to wangle to avoid being sent to a factory. She had to wangle to get clothing coupons, food and money. She was lucky to get the job at the two-penny library, although it only paid two pounds ten a week. It was all a wangle now, and she began to realize that those who didn't take risks these days were in for a thin time. It seemed now that you were either honest and went short or you were dishonest and had a good time. There seemed to be no happy medium. She knew the Bridge Café had an unsavoury reputation and was a meeting place of crooks, but the money was good, and that was all that mattered. She was sick of making do on fifty shillings a week.

"If you work for Hewart you'll meet all the wide boys," the young spiv had told her. "Play your cards right and you won't be short of anything. A girl with your looks should be having fun. You don't call this library fun, do you?"

Seven pounds a week! That decided her. What did it matter if the café was shady? She could look after herself. If Hewart would have her, she was ready to work for him.

As soon as Hewart saw her he knew she was the right type for the job.

"There's two jobs going here," he told her. "One of them is for the day shift and pays three quid a week. There's not much to it. A bit of cleaning, preparing sandwiches for the night trade. Not much of a job . . . but a job."

"And the other?" Julie asked, knowing well enough that the second job was the one she was going to take.

"Ah," and Hewart winked. "The other's a good job. A job for an ambitious girl who can keep her mouth shut. Might suit you."

"And what does that pay?"

"Seven quid a week. You'd look after the cash desk and take messages. It's night work—from seven to two in the morning. But you'd have to keep your mouth shut, and when I say shut, I mean shut, see?"

"I don't talk," Julie said steadily.

"It doesn't pay to; anyway, not in this neighbourhood. I remember a girl, not much older than you, and as pretty, who heard something that didn't concern her, and she talked. You know how it is: girls like to talk; second nature to 'em. They found her in a back alley. Made a mess of her looks. No, it doesn't do to talk."

"You don't scare me," Julie said sharply. "I wasn't born yesterday."

"That's right," Hewart grinned at her. "You're smart. The moment I saw you I knew you'd do. Now, listen, we give our customers service, see? Taking messages is an important part of the service. You'll have to be smart about that. Nothing must be written down. You'll have to pass the messages quick. There may be as many as twenty a night. For instance, you may get a 'phone call for Jack Smith, see? You'll have to know who he is and whether he's in the place or not. If he isn't, you say so and take the message. It's your job to see Smith gets it as soon as he comes in, and no one else must know about it. You'll have to be smart all the time. But you can do it. There're no flies on you." Seeing her hesitate, Hewart went on: "You won't know anything, see? What you don't know about you can't get into trouble about, can you? This is a chance to pick up a little easy money. Some of the boys will slip you a quid, maybe two, for giving them a message. I've seen it done. And listen, I like you. I'll make it eight quid if you'll take the job. Can't be fairer than that, can I? The boys'll be crazy about you. You're smart; pretty, too. I know a good thing when I see it. Think: eight beautiful pound notes every Friday. Think of the silk stockings you can buy."

But Julie wanted to know more about the job before being rushed into it. She said so.

"That's where you're wrong," Hewart said. "You don't want to know anything—like me. I just run this place, see? The boys and girls come here. They leave messages; sometimes a parcel or two, and I give 'em food and a little service, but I don't ask questions. Sometimes the bogies look in. They want to know this and that. I don't know anything so I can't tell 'em lies, can I? They may talk to you, but if you don't know anything what can you tell 'em? That's what I call being smart."

"The police come here?" Julie asked, startled. "I don't think I'd like that."

Hewart waved his hand impatiently.

"You know as well as I do the police poke their noses in everywhere. It's their job. It doesn't matter where you work, the police'll look in sooner or later. Who cares? We're not doing anything shady: we're giving service. It's not our funeral if our customers get up to tricks, is it? And besides, why do you think I'm offering eight quid? The job's worth fifty bob. I could get dozens of girls for fifty bob: hundreds of 'em. But I'm paying eight quid because the bogies might ask questions. I don't say they will, but they might; and I know a girl doesn't like being mixed up with the police. No one does, so I pay a little more."

Put like that it seemed reasonable enough, and the money, of course, was marvellous. If she let this chance slip through her fingers she might never get another.

"All right," she said, "I'll take it."

She was surprised how easy the work turned out to be. The café didn't get busy until after eleven o'clock. Then the regular customers began to drift in and soon the place was full of cigarette smoke and the murmur of voices. It was like having a front row in the stalls, Julie thought. Sitting in the glass-screened cash desk, she didn't feel she was part of the room, but rather an unseen observer looking through a secret window at an odd, exciting play. Hewart, cigar between his teeth, a big diamond ring flashing on his little finger, had stayed with her on her first night. He kept up a muttered commentary on the people in the room.

"The bloke over there in the fawn coat is Syd Bernstein," his voice droned in Julie's ears. "Remember him. He's got a big fur store in Gideon Road: expect you've seen it. If you ever want a cheap fur go to Syd. He'll fix you up if you mention my name. The fella he's talking to is the Duke. They call him that because of his beautiful manners. You watch him. You'll never catch *him* drinking out of his saucer. Never mind what he does for a living. The less you know . . . That's Pugsey over there. The fella in the grey suit; big dog-racing man. Knows more about doping dogs . . ." Hewart caught himself up, cleared his throat: "Well, never mind that. He's Pugsey; just remember who he is and forget the rest. The bloke lighting a cigarette is Goldsack. Now there's a smart 'un for you. When I met him—couldn't be more than a couple of years ago—he wasn't worth thirty bob. That's straight. Now he can write a cheque for ten thou and thinks nothing of it. He's one of the big betting boys."

Julie got to know Bernstein and Pugsey and the rest. She overheard things. For instance, she overheard a few scattered words from Pugsey as he and the Duke passed her.

"I won't split them," Pugsey was saying. "Twenty-five thousand or nothing. You can handle them all right. What's worrying you?"

"That's a big number for me," the Duke returned doubtfully. "Most of 'em are Players, you say?"

"That's right." Pugsey glanced up, caught Julie's eye, and winked.

"Twenty-five thousand Players," Julie thought "How much would they make out of that deal?" She saw in the next morning's newspaper that twenty-five thousand cigarettes had been stolen from a Houndsditch warehouse. It wasn't difficult to put two and two together.

Life in the café was full of variety and excitement. The telephone kept her busy. The messages she received meant nothing to her. "Tell

Pugsey greyhound looks good. Got it? Greyhound looks good." Ask Mr. Goldstack to call me. Boy Blue at twelve." Message for Mr. Bernstein. Usual time; usual place, C.O.D." And so on, code messages that puzzled and intrigued her; that meant money to the men who received them. Pugsey, Goldsack and the others were making themselves rich by these messages because they were wide and in the know. She envied them, although she knew she shouldn't grumble, for by the end of her third week she was earning twelve pounds a week: eight from Hewart and four from tips. But the more she earned the more she wanted. Her expenses had gone up. She had taken a small furnished flat in the Fulham Palace Road that cost four pounds a week. She had bought clothes; and she spent money on cinemas and useless junk she picked up in the big stores. It was nice not to work during the day; nice, but lonely. She hadn't any friends. That was the snag of working a night-shift. You never had the chance of meeting anyone during the day: they were all at work.

She needed male companionship, and sighed for the days when she could have had her pick of escorts by hanging about outside one of the Officers' Clubs. Going to the cinema on your own wasn't much fun. She wanted a man who would say nice things to her, buy her presents, and on whom she could bestow favours if she felt so inclined.

The men she met in the café were too busy making money to bother with her. She could have had Hewart easily enough but he was too old. At first he was tiresome, but she quickly learned how to handle him. Enclosed in the glass cash-desk all the evening, he didn't get much chance of pawing her. The time to watch out was when she arrived and when she left, and she took care to arrive and leave with the other members of the staff. To keep him happy, she allowed him a few liberties, and as the spiv had said, he was easily satisfied. She wanted a companion of her own age, who could share her interests and wouldn't be pawing her all the time.

She had been working at the café for over three months when Harry Gleb breezed in. She was interested in him the moment she saw him, for Harry had a terrific personality. His wide grin made you want to grin too. His laugh was infectious, his confidence in himself enormous. He was a dashing, colourful figure, and well dressed; his hand-painted tie made Julie gasp. He had a great deal of dark wavy hair, a fine pencil-line moustache, greenish eyes that twinkled with an expression of bawdy good humour. Although he was hard, without scruples, shallow, cocky and selfish, you couldn't help liking him. He was always smiling, always ready to crack a joke, to lend you a quid, to get a tenner on the toss of a coin or drink you under the table. He knew most of the waiters in the swagger West End restaurants by their Christian names. He knew most of the West End tarts, the playboys and the gold diggers, and they liked him. He was a typical London spiv, and he didn't care who knew it.

He seemed to Julie to be someone right out of a motion picture. Comparing him to other men who frequented the café was like comparing Clark Gable to the fat old man who sat next to her in the underground.

But she was too fly to let him know the impression he had made on her. She was confident of her powers of attraction, and she was sure, sooner or later, he would make the first overtures.

At this time Harry was doing a deal with Syd Bernstein. He didn't like the Bridge Café, nor did he like Hewart, but as Bernstein always went there Harry began going there, too.

He was quick to spot Julie as she sat in the cash-desk, and, as any pretty girl mildly interested him, he took a mild interest in her. It wasn't until one evening when Julie left the enclosed cash-desk to give a message to the Duke, that Harry had the opportunity of seeing her figure, and immediately he gave a long, low whistle.

"That's a nice bit of crackling," he said to Bernstein, and jerked his thumb towards Julie. "Where did Sam find her?" Bernstein had no idea, and after he had gone Harry wandered over to the cash-desk and began to flirt with Julie.

She had been waiting patiently for this opportunity, but she didn't let him see her eagerness. She was cool to him, laughed at his flattery, and snubbed him when he became familiar.

Women were attracted to Harry as pins to a magnet. Julie's behaviour surprised him. Women were a lot of soppy mares, he had always considered, but they were fun. If you had nothing better to do. But this girl was different. He could tell that. She was friendly enough, but there was a jeering expression in her eyes that irritated him. It showed plainly that she knew what he was up to, and was certainly not going to take him seriously. He could be as nice and flattering as he liked, but it wouldn't get him anywhere.

This attitude intrigued him, as Julie intended it to intrigue him, and he was continually popping in to have a word with her, to bring her a pair of silk stockings or a box of chocolates, and to try to break down the jeering barrier she had erected to keep him at safe limits. He had asked her time and again to go out with him, but Julie refused. She wasn't going to risk being dropped. She had had a lot of experience with men, and she knew the longer she kept him dangling on a string the more ardent he would be when she did give in.

When Mrs. French asked him if he knew of a girl who'd help them, he immediately thought of Julie. She wanted money, had brains, and was sufficiently reckless to take a chance. But he was a little worried by her persistent refusal to become friendly. Somehow he had to rush her defences, and the best way, he decided, was for her to lose her job at the café before he put the proposition to her. So long as she had a job and some regular money coming in she was independent, and if she had scruples she might turn him down. Harry had a horror of independent women. It was Julie's independence that kept them apart now. He was sure of that.

The first thing, then, was to get her the sack. But how was he going to do that? He racked his brains to no purpose. She was in solid with Hewart, and there seemed no reason why she should ever leave the café.

"Well, something will turn up," he consoled himself. "It always does."

And it did, but not in quite the way he expected.

III

Two evenings after the meeting in Mrs. French's office, the telephone on Julie's desk rang, and a woman's voice, breathless and urgent, asked: "Is Mr. Harry Gleb there, please?"

Julie felt a tingle run up her spine. She hadn't seen Harry for three days. She was beginning to wonder if she had handled him a little too roughly, and had driven him to some other woman.

"I'm afraid he isn't," she said, wondering who the woman could be.

"Are you sure? It's very urgent. He said he'd be there. Will you please make sure?"

There was a hysterical note in the voice that startled Julie.

Hewart, coming from his office and seeing Julie looking round the café, trying to penetrate the thick screen of tobacco smoke, came over.

"What's up?"

"A woman asking for Mr. Gleb. She sounds worried."

"All Gleb's women are worried," Hewart said, and smiled sourly. "It's the natural state of their health, the damn fools. He's not here."

"I'm sorry, but we haven't seen him to-night," Julie said into the mouthpiece.

There was a pause on the line which crackled and hummed, then the woman said, "He'll be in. Will you ask him to call me at once? Take the number, please."

Julie memorized the number, said she would tell him the moment he came in, and hung up.

Hewart scowled.

"I wish that fella would keep away from here," he growled "He's no good to anyone."

A few minutes later Harry breezed in. Julie waved to him.

"Hello," he said, coming over to her, "Don't tell me you're pleased to see me for once."

"There was a 'phone message for you a few minutes ago. A woman wants you to call her. She says it's urgent. Riverside 58845."

His smile faded and his greenish eyes hardened. "Can I borrow the blower?"

She liked him like this. He was no longer flippant, and seeing him now she thought he looked hard and dangerous. She watched him dial the number, and noticed his hand was unsteady.

"Dana?" No one else in the room except Julie could heal what he was saying. "This is Harry. What's up?" He listened, and Julie saw his hand tighten on the telephone. "How long ago? Right. Keep your chimmy on. All right. No, stop flapping. It'll be all right. Yeah, yeah; so long." He hung up.

"Someone found you out?" Julie asked, watching him intently.

"Yes." He studied her for a moment. "Like to do me a favour?" He locked quickly over his shoulder, then slipped a small package done up in white tissue paper into her lap. "Hang on to this until to-morrow, will you? Keep it out of sight. And if anyone asks you, if I've given you anything—not a word. O.K.?"

"I wouldn't do it for anyone else, but I'll do it for you," Julie said, and smiled.

"Good kid. How about coming out with me to-morrow? I'll buy you a lunch."

"Not to-morrow. I'm pretty booked up." Which wasn't true. "The day after, perhaps. You'll be in to-morrow night?"

"You bet. Keep that safe for me. 'Bye now," and he went quickly to the door. As he opened it he came to an abrupt stop and took a step back.

Two men came in: big men in slouch hats and raincoats. With a sudden sinking feeling Julie recognized them. Police! She might have guessed that was why Harry had been so anxious to get rid of the package.

Harry was talking to the two police officers. He was smilingly at ease. The rest of the men and women in the café watched, not moving, silent and effacing. Detective Inspector Dawson, whom Julie knew by sight, jerked his head in the direction of Hewart's office. Harry shrugged and walked back down the gangway. He passed Julie without looking at her.

The moment they were out of sight the men and women in the café made a quick scramble for the exit. In a few seconds the café was empty.

Frightened, Julie grabbed up her bag and was about to put the package in it when she changed her mind. That was the first place they'd look, she told herself. She glanced quickly round the empty café, then pulled up her skirt and pushed the package down the top of her girdle.

The police officers weren't in Hewart's office for long. They came out with Harry, followed by Hewart, who was pale with rage.

The younger police officer walked down the gangway with Harry. They went out together.

Hewart and Dawson stood talking for a few moments, then wandered over to Julie.

Dawson raised his hat. He belonged to the old school and believed politeness paid.

"Good evening, miss. Do you know that young fellow Gleb?"

She looked at him insolently.

"I don't, and even if I did, I don't see what it has to do with you."

"Wasn't he talking to you just now?"

"He was buying cigarettes."

Dawson stared at her until she had to look away.

"Was he? He didn't have a packet on him when I searched him. How do you account for that?"

Julie changed colour. That was a slip and a bad one. She didn't say anything.

"He didn't give you anything to look after, did he?"

She felt a cold little shiver run up her spine, but she forced herself to meet his inquiring eyes.

"He didn't."

"Would you let me examine your bag?"

"You haven't any right to look in my bag," she flared, "but if it'll satisfy you, you can." She pushed the bag towards him, but he didn't touch it.

"That's all right, miss. I won't bother." He glanced at Hewart. "Well, so long, Sam. See you again one of these days." His eyes travelled around the empty café and he concealed a smile. "Sorry to have spoilt your trade. Your customers are a little sensitive it seems."

"So long," Hewart said, his eyes hard.

Dawson raised his hat to Julie.

"I don't know any other fellow who could get a girl into trouble faster than Gleb," he said. "There may be others, but I doubt it. Good night."

When he had gone, Hewart gave Julie an ugly look.

"What's the idea?" he demanded roughly. "What the devil are you playing at?"

Julie raised her eyebrows.

"I don't know what you mean, I'm sure."

"I'll have a word with you when we've shut," Hewart said, and walked into his office, slamming the door behind him.

Julie was putting on her hat before the chipped mirror that hung on the store-room wall when Hewart came in. They were now alone in the café, the rest of the staff had gone.

"What did Gleb give you?" Hewart demanded, coming to the point with his usual bluntness.

Hewart's aggressive tone and cold searching eyes warned Julie to be cautious.

"You heard what I told Dawson, didn't you?" she snapped. "He didn't give me anything."

Hewart said, "I heard what you told Dawson all right." He came close to her. "If you can't lie better than that you'd better keep your mouth shut. Dawson knew you were up to something. If he didn't guess Gleb had given you the rings, he knew something was on between you two."

Rings? Julie felt herself go white under her make-up. "I—I don't know what you're talking about."

"Now, look, kid," Hewart said, seeing the frightened expression in her eyes and softening towards her. He was fond of Julie, and didn't want any trouble with her. "So far you've been a damned smart girl; but you're not being smart now. Gleb works outside our circle. We don't do things for him, and he doesn't do things for us, see? You didn't know that. I should have given you the tip. All right, I'm not blaming you, don't think that. He's too smooth. No one ever gets anything out of his deals."

"I tell you he didn't give me anything," Julie said, her heart beating rapidly. If she once admitted she had received stolen rings from Harry, she would be at Hewart's mercy. What a fool she had been to have taken the package. She might have guessed it was stolen property. She was furious with herself for being so green.

Hewart studied her. His hatchet face was hardened.

"Listen, this evening a society woman left three diamond rings worth a thousand quid on her dressing-table for a couple of seconds, no more, and they vanished. A couple of seconds, see? That's Gleb: split-second timing and specializes in bedrooms. That's his line. Dawson knows all about him; so do I. He came here directly after the robbery, and it's my guess the woman who 'phoned tipped him the police were after him and he dumped the loot on to you. That's another of his pet tricks. Never mind if he gets anyone into trouble so long as he saves his own dirty hide. Now, look, Julie, Gleb is rank poison. I don't like a fella who brings the cops here. I have no time for him, and I want those rings."

Julie snatched up her hat and coat and moved quickly to the door, but Hewart stepped in front of her.

"Now, wait a minute," he said, an ugly glint in his eyes.

"I don't know anything about the rings. Would you please mind out of the way, Mr. Hewart? I want to go home."

"Not just yet. I'm being patient with you, Julie, because I like you. But you're making a damn fool of yourself over this fella. I don't miss much that goes on here. I've seen you talking to him and putting on airs. You're trying to hook him, aren't you? You watch out. Gleb knows all about women; he specializes in them. You leave him alone. You can get plenty of other fellas without taking on a rat like Gleb. He never did any girl any good."

"Oh!" Julie exclaimed furiously. "How—how dare you talk to me like that! Get out of my way."

"I'm warning you," Hewart said, losing patience. "You're not leaving here unless you hand over those rings, and if I have to take 'em from you, you'll get the sack."

"You're not having them, and I don't want your rotten job! I can always get another! I'm not scared of you, you old bully!"

Seeing her white, furious little face, her determined attitude and her clenched fists, Hewart was struck with admiration. He burst out laughing.

"Come on, Julie, don't be a little fool. You've got a lot of nerve, and you and me can get on well together. Hand over those rings, and we'll forget the whole business."

"I tell you I don't know what you're talking about. I haven't the rings, and if I had I wouldn't give them to you!" Julie snapped, and darted past him.

Hewart caught hold of her, and holding her wrists in one hand he ran his other hand over her body.

"How dare you!" Julie stormed, struggling to break his hold. "Let me go or I'll scream the place down."

"Scream away," Hewart panted. His face was congested. "If the bogies come I'll tell 'em Gleb gave you the rings and you'll be for it. Stand still and stop struggling. You've got 'em on you—I know." His questing fingers felt the little bulge of the package. "Ah! Here they are. Now stop fighting. It won't get you anywhere."

But Julie struggled and kicked. Her toeless shoes made no impression on Hewart's thick legs and she couldn't get her hands free. As he began to pull up her skirt, she let out a squeal of outraged fury.

"Well, I am surprised at you, Sam," Harry said as he pushed open the door. "You could get six months for half what you're doing."

Hewart released Julie as if she had suddenly become red hot. Harry leaned against the doorway, his hat cocked rakishly over one eye, his hands in his pockets, a hard, cynical expression in his eyes.

"How did you get in here?" Hewart asked feebly. He was frightened, not liking the look Harry gave him. There was a half-concealed threat in the clenched fists hidden in the pockets.

Julie staggered away from Hewart; her face was white, and her eyes blazing with fury.

"You rotten swine! How dare you touch me!" She rounded on Harry. "It's all your fault! Hit him! Did you see what he was doing to me? Hit him! Make him pay for it!"

Harry regarded her with frank admiration. He liked to see a girl in a rage, and Julie's rage was a real pippin, he thought.

"Keep your hair on, sweetheart," he said with a grin. "You wouldn't want me to hit an old man, now, would you? You come along home with me. He didn't do you any harm."

"I'll teach him to put his dirty paws on me!" Julie screamed, and snatched up a four-pound jar of honey and threw it at Hewart. The jar caught him in the middle of his chest and sent him reeling back. As she turned for another missile, Harry, gasping with laughter, caught hold of her and bundled her out of the room.

"Lock yourself in, Sam!" he shouted. "I can't hold her for long, and she's after your blood!"

The door hastily slammed and the key turned.

Julie, panting with rage, wrenched free and hammered on the door.

"Let me in, you dirty old goat! I haven't finished with you yet. I'll kill you for this!"

"You get out!" Hewart shouted through the door panels. "You're sacked, see? I don't want to see you again. You hop it or I'll call the police."

"I'll give you in charge!" Julie screamed back. "I'll have you up for assault, you — —!! You won't get away with this! Don't you think you will!"

"Come on, Julie," Harry said persuasively, but he kept at a safe distance. "Leave the old geezer alone. You've given him a fright, and he won't try that on again."

She turned on him.

"You've lost me my job!" she exclaimed. "It's all very well for you to stand there grinning. What am I going to do now?"

Harry was thinking, "I said something would turn up, and it has. It couldn't have worked out better."

"What are you going to do about it?" Julie demanded, calming down. She suddenly realized what it would mean not to work at the café again. To find another job worth twelve pounds a week would be impossible. "Oh! Damn you! I wish I'd never seen you. I wish I hadn't helped you."

"Now don't get excited. Come on. We'll talk this over. I have a car outside. I'll take you home."

She went with him because she didn't know what else to do. If she had been alone she would have gone back to Hewart and apologized. But Harry pushed her along, his hand on her elbow. He had got her away from Hewart, and he had no intention of letting her get back again.

"Don't you worry," he said, pausing beside a big Chrysler car, parked under a street light. Julie noticed it had "Hackney Carriage" number plates. "In you get. Where do you live?"

"Is this your car?" she asked, startled.

"Course it is. The plates don't mean anything except I can keep the car on the road without the cops asking me where I get the petrol from."

She looked at the long, glittering bonnet and the big headlights. "If he can afford to run a car like this," she thought, "maybe he has money. He must have. I'll see what I can get out of him."

"Wake up, dreamy. Where do you live?" he asked, and pushed her into the car.

"Fulham Palace Road," she said, settling herself on the broad, comfortable seat.

"What have you got—rooms?" He got in beside her, and trod on the starter.

"It's a self-contained flat."

"Share it with anyone?"

"No. You want to know a lot, don't you?"

"A proper Nosey Parker I am," he returned with a laugh, and drove rapidly through the deserted streets. Neither of them said anything until they stopped outside her flat, then he said, "This it? Right. Let's go in. I could do with a cup of tea."

"You're not coming in and you're not having any tea," Julie snapped. "And if you want those rings back you'll have to pay for them."

He twisted round to look at her. He was smiling, but his eyes had hardened.

"But I want to talk to you. We can't talk here. Now, be nice and invite me in."

"I'm not in the habit of inviting men into my flat at this hour. I want fifty pounds for the rings. You won't get them until you give me the money."

He whistled softly under his breath.

"Have a heart, kid. Fifty quid! Why, the damn things aren't worth that."

"They're worth a thousand, and you know it. Bring the money to-morrow morning or I'll sell them." She jerked open the car door, ran up the steps, opened the door before he could move.

"Hey Julie!" he shouted.

"To-morrow morning or you won't see them again," she said triumphantly, and slammed the door.

IV

Harry waited long enough to see a light flash up in a room on the ground floor then, smiling to himself, he started the car and drove rapidly down the street. He hadn't far to go. He knew the district well, and knew there was an all-night garage close by. He left the car there and walked back to Julie's flat.

For some minutes he stood outside, looking up and down the street. It was after three o'clock in the morning and only a stray cat attracted his attention. Then, moving with confident ease, he swung himself over the iron railings guarding the basement of the house, caught hold of a stack pipe and climbed on to Julie's window-sill. He pushed up the window and stepped into the room and closed the window. He had moved with extraordinary speed and quietness. The whole manoeuvre did not take more than a few seconds.

He pushed aside the curtain. The room in which he found himself was large and shabbily furnished and without much comfort. There was a lamp by the bed that cast a pink glow over the harsh colour of the wallpaper and furnishings.

Across the room was a door that stood half open. The sound of running water told him it was the bathroom. He could hear Julie humming to herself as she prepared for bed, and he grinned to himself. He took off his hat and coat, sat down in an arm-chair and lit a cigarette.

After a few minutes Julie came into the bedroom. She had on a pair of emerald-green pyjamas that set off her figure admirably, and her hair was loose to her shoulders. She came to an abrupt standstill when she saw him sitting there, and turned white, then red.

"Hello, remember me?" he said casually. "Get into bed, Julie. I want to talk to you."

She looked wildly round the room, her eyes went to the dressing-table, and she made a quick dash. But Harry was there first. He picked up the two diamond rings she had half-concealed under her handbag as she reached him.

"Put them down!" she whispered furiously.

Instead he slipped them into his pocket.

"Sorry, kid, they're too important to fool with," he said gently. "I want to talk to you. Don't get angry. Let's be matey, Julie. Get me a cup of tea and let's talk."

"You devil!" she exclaimed furiously. "I did all that for you and now you're not going to pay me. You rotten stinker!"

"Who said I wasn't going to pay you? You want a job, don't you? Well, I've got a damned good one for you. Honest, I'm not fooling."

"What kind of job?"

"Get me some tea and take that scowl off your face," he said. "Go on, Julie, I can't talk until I've had some tea."

"You're the limit, Harry," she said, weakening. "Well, I suppose I'll have to make you tea. I won't be long."

He finished his cigarette while she made the tea.

"It's just the way you handle 'em," he told himself. "I reckon I handled her beautifully. In a little while I'll have her just where I want her."

She returned to the bedroom, set the tray on the table and poured out the tea.

"What about this job?" she demanded, as she handed him a cup. "And don't forget you owe me fifty pounds."

"What did Sam pay you?"

"Twelve pounds a week."

He whistled softly.

"You won't get that again in a hurry unless . . ." He paused, went on: "You wouldn't have to be too fussy what you did, Julie, and there may be risks."

"What do you mean?"

"Just that. How long have you been with Sam?"

"Oh, six months."

"And before that?"

"In a two-penny library."

"And before that?"

"I worked in a factory," Julie said, frowning at the memory.

"So you've only been in the money for six months?"

"Yes, and I'm not going to get out of it if I can help it." Her eyes hardened. "Until now I've never had any fun. Do you think you could find me anything good?"

"I know I can."

He sipped his tea while he studied her.

"I don't believe you have a job for me at all," she said, seeing him hesitate. "You're just leading me up the garden path. If you are . . . you'll be sorry! There's nothing to stop me seeing Dawson and telling him about those rings, is there?"

Harry nearly dropped his cup. A threat like that wasn't funny, even if she were bluffing, and he didn't think she was.

"Now wait a minute, Julie. You be careful what you're saying. There's a word for a girl who squeals to the police and it's an ugly one."

"Words won't hurt me," Julie retorted, tossing her head. "What about this job?"

"One of the big money-making jobs at the moment is being a lady's maid," he began cautiously. "A friend of mine runs a domestic agency. She has a vacancy and could fix you up."

Julie stiffened, and stared at him.

"Are you suggesting I'm to become a servant?" she asked.

"Now, do relax, Julie. You're forever getting on your hind legs. You don't care how you earn money so long as it's big money, do you? What's wrong in being a maid? After all, you worked in a café. You're not all that proud, are you? This is a good job. You'll live in a luxury flat, have time off, good food and money . . ."

"But a maid . . ." She got up and began to pace up and down. Harry watched her pyjama'd figure, aware that his mind was wandering from business. "No, I really can't. Hewart paid me twelve pounds a week. I can't live on less and I'm not going to. A maid doesn't get anything like that."

"This one does," Harry said with a grin. "This one is special. What do you say to fifteen quid a week and a fifty-pound bonus at the end of the job?"

"But no one would pay that," she exclaimed, turning to stare at him.

"Now look, don't be inquisitive." There was a slight edge to his voice. "I want you to make a little easy money and not to know too much about the way you're making it. Are you smart enough to understand that?"

"Oh, I see." She was instantly suspicious. "It's some kind of racket."

"Sort of . . . but if you don't know what it's all about then you won't get into trouble, will you?"

"The same old argument," she thought, a little wearily. "He's right, of course. Hewart used it. See nothing, know nothing and you'll be all right. Well, it's worked up to now."

"All you have to do is to work at a certain place for a month or so," Harry went on. "You'll get three quid a week and all found. I'll arrange for you to get twelve quid in addition, and at the end of the job a fifty-quid bonus. What's more I'll give you a tenner now if you'll close with the deal."

"But, Harry, I'd like to think about it . . ."

"All right, tell me to-morrow. Sleep on it. Fifteen quid a week and a fifty-pound bonus. That's not to be sneezed at."

"You're not pulling my leg, are you?" she asked, suddenly suspicious again. "You could walk out of here and leave me flat. I wasn't born yesterday. I might never see you again. And then what should I do?"

He levered himself out of his chair, went over to sit beside her on the bed.

"I'll tell you a secret," he said, and pulled her to him. Whispering in her ear, he said, "I'm not going to leave you tonight."

She pulled away and jumped to her feet.

"Oh, no! I'm not having any of that. I'm not that easy. No, you get out. I'll chance seeing you again."

He laughed at her.

"You don't know your own mind, do you? First I'm to stay, then I'm to go. Well, I'm going to make up your mind for you."

She made a hasty grab at her dressing-gown, but he caught her in his arms.

"No!" she whispered, struggling. "Stop it, Harry! You mustn't!"

His mouth came down on hers. For a moment she continued to struggle, then her arms went round his neck.

"Damn you!" she said against his mouth, and then, "Hold me tighter."

V

The morning sunlight came through the dowdy chintz curtains. A milkman shouted angrily to his horse and then set down his bottles with a penetrating clatter. Further up the road the postman rapped sharply on a door.

Julie stirred, stretched, yawned. Through the half-open bathroom door came the sound of running water. She moved her legs under the sheet and sighed contentedly.

"Got all you want, Harry?" she called sleepily.

"I'll want some tea in a moment. Aren't you out of bed yet?"

"I'm just getting up," Julie said, turned over and pulled the blanket up to her chin.

"I bet." Harry came to the door. He had a towel round his middle and she thought he looked like a boxer. He was muscular, hard and tanned. "Come on out before I throw you out."

"I'm coming," Julie yawned, threw off the bedclothes. "It's not nine yet."

"I've got a lot to do this morning," Harry said, and disappeared into the bathroom.

She went into the kitchen and put on the kettle.

"It's a funny thing," she thought, "but it seems as if he's always been here; as if this has always been part of my life. But I do wish he wouldn't be so evasive."

They had talked during the night, and Julie had tried to find out something about his everyday life, what he thought, what he did with himself, but she came up against a flippant barrier that turned anything serious into a joke.

Harry was dressed when she returned with the tea.

"Harry . . . those rings. I've been worrying. You can't get away with that kind of thing for long. You know that."

He took the cup of tea she gave him and laughed.

"For goodness' sake don't start worrying about me. You worry about yourself if you have to worry at all."

"But I do worry about you."

"Now look; I have only a few years on this earth—another forty with luck," he said. "What's forty years? Nothing, and then—the worms, the dark and the cold. All right then, I'm going to enjoy myself while I can. I can't do that without money. Money's power; it's fun, food and drink, cigarettes and love. Money's a motor car, petrol, clothes and shoes. It's a night out at the White City dog track; it's a game of poker and a seat at the theatre. It's everything you can think of. I've tried working for a living, but it didn't come off. I've been in the war. I've done my little bit, and now I'm going to have a good time. I don't care how I get hold of money so long as I get it. I help myself. That's all there's to it."

"But what's the good of it all if you spend ten years in jail?" Julie demanded, hoping he could give her a satisfactory answer, since his philosophy matched hers.

"You have to be smart. I've kept out of jail for three years and I'm keeping out of it."

"If it hadn't been for me you would have been in jail by now," she reminded him.

"Don't you believe it. There's always someone around. You'd be surprised. If you hadn't taken those rings I'd've got rid of them some other way. It's happened before."

This annoyed and hurt Julie. She wanted to think she had saved him from prison at a considerable risk to herself.

"And do you always make love to the woman who's helped you? Is that your idea of a reward?" she asked tartly.

"You're a funny kid." He laughed at her. "I'm fussy who I make love to. You'll find that out one of these days."

She had never suffered from jealousy before, but now the thought of any other woman knowing him as intimately as she did tormented her.

"Harry . . . who's that woman, Dana, who rang you?"

"My mother," he said promptly, stretched out his legs. "She's a wonderful old thing: lavender and old lace, or is it arsenic? Anyway, you'd love her."

"I'm not going to be treated like this," Julie exclaimed, stamping her feet. "You've got to stop this silly pose with me. Who is she? I want to know."

He pulled a face, then laughed again.

"Don't bully me, Julie. She's just a girl I know. Nothing to get excited about. She isn't half as pretty as you, and she means nothing to me."

"How did she know the police were looking for you?"

"She's clairvoyant. Saw old Dawson in the tea leaves."

"Are you going to stop playing the fool and tell me or aren't you?" Julie demanded, thoroughly angry now.

"Mind your own business," he said, and smiled at her, but she was quick to see the sudden hard look in his eyes.

There was a long pause while they looked at each other. Julie's eyes were the first to give ground. She could see it was useless to press him and she decided to change her tactics.

"All right, don't tell me if you want to make a mystery of it," she said, trying to sound indifferent. "Have some more tea?"

He handed her his cup, lit another cigarette and yawned.

"I'll have to be off in a moment," he said, glancing at his watch.

She felt uneasy again. He could walk out of her flat and she might never see him again.

"Where do you live, Harry?" she asked, as she poured out the tea.

"Ten Downing Street. I have a little flat on the top floor. It's pretty cosy because I share the Prime Minister's butler."

It was no use, she decided, alarmed and angry. Under his flippant pose was a mercurial character that refused to be pinned down. She mustn't be too possessive. Later, perhaps, when they knew each other better, she might gain his confidence.

She said lightly: "Are you ever serious?"

"What do I want to be serious for? Eat, drink and make money and love for to-morrow the worms will have you. I haven't time to be serious. Having fun is a full-time job."

"So I'm not even to know where you live?"

"The woman's living with him," she thought. "That's why he won't tell me."

"At times you positively shine, Julie."

"All right, be mysterious," she said crossly, and turned away.

"The less you know about me the better," he returned, and picked up his coat. "Well, I'm off. How about that job, Julie?"

"Well, all right," she said reluctantly. "I suppose I'd better do it. All I have to do is to be a maid; nothing else?"

He grinned.

"That's all. Of course, you'll keep your eyes open."

She knew at once then that she was to be the inside plant for a robbery. For a moment she hesitated, and Harry, seeing her hesitate, took out two five-pound notes.

"I promised you something in advance. Here, put those in your pocket."

She hesitated no longer. What she didn't know about she couldn't get into trouble about. She could look after herself. She took the money.

"What do I do?"

"Here." He handed her a card. "Go to this address. Ask for Mrs. French and tell her I sent you. She knows all about it and will tell you what to do. O.K.?"

"And there's no risk? I mean I shan't get into trouble?"

"Not a chance," he returned breezily. "All you have to do is to act like a maid. Simple, isn't it?"

"And keep my eyes open," she said, watching him.

He grinned.

"That's the idea. Well, so long, Julie."

"When am I going to see you again?"

"Soon. I've got a lot of things on at the moment. I'll get in touch with you."

"Just like a man. Get what you want, then cool off," Julie said angrily.

He pulled her to him and kissed her.

"If you want me urgently give Mrs. French a message. I'll be out of Town for a day or so, but she'll know where she can get in touch with me. All right?"

She looked up at him.

"It'll have to be."

He kissed her, gave her a little hug, and left her. She went to the window and watched him walk quickly down the street.

"Planning a robbery," she thought. "And I'm to find out the details. Well, the money's all right. If I don't have anything to do with the actual robbery I can't get into trouble." She locked at the two five-pound notes and smiled. "The money's fine."

VI

Julie found Mrs. French's Domestic Agency was over an antique bookseller's shop in Mayfair Street. She went into the dimly lit lobby. The bookseller's door was on her right, in front of her was a flight of stone stairs, and under the stairs was the lift.

A blonde woman, holding a Pekinese dog under her arm, stood in the doorway. She looked at Julie without interest, then shifted her heavily shaded eyes back to the street. A man paused in his stride, looked at her, saw Julie and continued on his way. The blonde woman didn't care. The man had already twice passed the doorway. Obviously he was the type who took time to make up his mind. He would be back again.

Julie entered the lobby, glanced back at the blonde woman and wrinkled her nose. She would never come to that, she told herself.

As she looked round she became aware of a tall, bony man peering at her through the glass panel of the door leading to the bookseller's shop. He stood very still, his head on one side and surveyed her with intent eyes. He was old and dried up, and his thick, white hair needed a trim. His scrutiny made her feel uncomfortable, and she hurriedly ran up the stairs, knowing he would stare at her legs until she was out of sight.

A door marked *"Mrs. French. Domestic Agency. Enquiries"* faced her at the head of the stairs; she pushed it open, entered a small, well-furnished room, full of flowers and sunshine.

A girl was typing by the window. She was smart, polished and sophisticated. Her auburn hair was done in an elaborate up-sweep with not a hair out of place. Her white linen dress with its smart red buttons and belt fitted her without a wrinkle. She looked as if she had been taken carefully from a box lined with cellophane and placed with equal care on her chair not a moment before. Julie regarded her with envious interest.

The girl glanced up, her scarlet nails still flashing over the typewriter's keys. Seeing Julie, she stopped typing and with an irritable frown pushed back her chair and came over to the counter that divided the room.

She had the easy, graceful carriage of a mannequin and she was tall. She made Julie feel shabby and somehow a little cheap, and that immediately put Julie on the offensive.

"Did you want anything?" the girl asked abruptly and eyed Julie with scarcely concealed contempt. She had a low, husky voice that seemed familiar to Julie.

"Mr. Gleb told me to ask for Mrs. French," she said awkwardly.

"Oh, I see." The girl's mouth tightened. "You're Julie Holland, I suppose? Well, sit down. You'll have to wait. My mother's busy at the moment," and she turned and went back to her typing.

Feeling snubbed and hating the girl, Julie sat down. There followed a long wait. The only sound in the office was the whirr of the typewriter and the sharp ping of the bell at the end of each line. She studied the girl. "They must pay well here," she thought, "that frock has a marvellous cut, and she's wearing nylons, too. I'd like a frock like that. I'd look much nicer than she does."

The girl got up suddenly, swept up a number of papers from her desk, and went into the inner office. After another wait, she came out, jerked her head at Julie.

"Go in. She's free now."

Mrs. French sat at a big desk near the window. She wore unrelieved black and, seeing her, like an unwanted relative at a funeral, Julie was startled. Long jet ear-rings swung backwards and forwards whenever she moved her head. She had none of her daughter's prettiness, but there was a marked resemblance about the determined mouth and chin.

She seemed to know all about Julie and came to the point with startling suddenness.

"Gleb's told me about you. The job's simple enough if you use your brains. You don't look a fool." And as Julie continued to stand before her desk, she waved impatiently to a chair. "Sit down, sit down." Her voice was deep and harsh. "You will go this afternoon to 97, Park Way. Do you know where the Albert Hall is? Well, Park Way is just by it. You can't miss it. It's big and ugly enough. Your new employer will be Mrs. Howard Wesley. You are to be her personal maid. You'll have to look after her things, tidy up when she's finished dressing, answer the door, serve cocktails, arrange flowers and take telephone messages. It's an easy job as far as the work's concerned. The permanent staff of the building does all the rest of the work and the meals are sent up from the restaurant. Mrs. Wesley will pay you three pounds a week and all found. You're to come here every Saturday afternoon for your additional pay. Do you understand all that?"

Julie said, "Yes."

There was something about Mrs. French that made her uneasy: a feeling you have in the dark when you hear a sudden, mysterious sound and you think something horrible is going to jump out on you.

"Your uniform is over there—in that parcel," Mrs. French went on, and touched her ear-rings. They seemed to give her a secret satisfaction for she smiled. "If it doesn't fit you, alter it, but I think it'll be all right. For goodness' sake don't look shoddy. Mrs. Wesley has high standards. And here are your references." She pushed two envelopes across the desk. "Study them. Mrs. Wesley isn't likely to be too particular, but you never know. One of them is from a doctor and the other a clergyman. I've been to a lot of trouble to get them and they cost me money, so don't lose them."

"Thank you," Julie said, bewildered. She put the two envelopes in her bag.

"Well, you know what you have to do," Mrs. French went on. "I'd better tell you something about the Wesleys. You'll find out about them quick enough, but you may as well be on your guard. Howard Wesley, the husband, is the senior partner of Wesley-Benton, the aircraft designers. The factory is near Northolt airfield. Wesley goes there every day. You may have read about him. He's blind: won the V.C. bringing in a burning bomber. He saved the crew or something like that. I forget the details. Anyway, he's enormously rich—and blind." She picked up a pencil and began to draw neat little circles on the blotting paper. "Mrs. Wesley, before her marriage, was Blanche Turrell, the musical comedy actress," she went on, "You've probably seen her. Most people have. She drinks like a camel. That's why she's given up stage work. Wesley's always been crazy about her, but she doesn't give two hoots for anyone but herself. She married Wesley for his money and leads him a hell of a life, so I hear. Her temper's vicious, her nature's mean and she has the morals of an alley cat." She thought for a moment, added, "Oh, yes, she's a first-class bitch as well."

"I see," Julie said, startled.

"You'll have trouble with her," Mrss French went on. "Your work is easy enough, but your dealings with Mrs. Wesley won't be. That's why we're paying you good money. You'll earn it, all right; don't think you're in for a soft job." She stared at Julie, a satisfied expression in her eyes. "As far as I know she hasn't kept a maid longer than three weeks, but it is part of your job to stick it out until I tell you. If you quit before we're ready you'll lose the fifty pounds. Understand?"

"Before you're ready for what?" Julie asked sharply.

"You'll be told when we want you to know," Mrs. French said. "Your immediate job is to get established at Park Way. You're satisfied with the money we're paying you, aren't you?"

"Oh, yes," Julie said. "The money's all right."

"Be satisfied then, and don't ask questions." Mrs. French opened a drawer, took out a cash box and counted out twelve one-pound notes. "Take this. Come in next Saturday and there'll be another twelve pounds for you. You play along with us and we'll look after you, but step out of turn and you'll regret it." She eyed Julie, went on in her rasping voice. "Now get off and take that muck off your face. You're supposed to be a servant, not a movie star."

"Yes," Julie said, hating her. She put the money in her bag.

"And watch your temper. You'll need all your control when Mrs. Wesley starts on you. When she's drunk, she's rotten; remember that. You can't be too careful."

"I see," Julie said.

"Right, get off now, and tell Dana I want her as you go out."

Julie was picking up the parcel containing her uniform when Mrs. French said this and nearly dropped the parcel. Dana! So this was the girl who had telephoned Harry and had warned him the police were looking for him. She remembered what Harry had said about her: *She isn't as pretty as you, so you don't have to worry about her.* Wasn't she? She had everything: poise, prettiness, clothes and immaculate neatness. "How could he lie like that?" she thought, furious and dismayed. "He tried to make out she meant nothing to him. A girl like that . . ."

"What are you waiting for?" Mrs. French demanded. "You know what to do, don't you?"

"Yes," Julie said, and went into the outer office.

Dana was speaking into the telephone, her back turned to Julie.

"She's in there now," she was saying. "Yes, she looks all right as far as she goes—" She looked over her shoulder, saw Julie and stopped speaking.

"Mrs. French wants you," Julie said, aware that her voice was shaky. She went out of the office, closed the door and stood listening.

She heard Dana's voice clearly through the glass panel of the door.

"Just this moment gone," she was saying. "A bit of a slut I'd say, but if she does the job . . . what's that? Well, I'm not so sure. Oh, of course, they all want money. That's all they think about. All right. Let's talk about it to-night."

Who was she talking to? Julie wondered, her face burning, Not Harry. No, she wouldn't believe Harry would stand for her being called a slut. She wanted to rush into the office and slap Dana's face. Then a sudden feeling that she was being watched made her turn. Mrs. French was standing in the doorway that led from her office into the passage. The sunlight coming through the landing window caught the jet ear-rings and made them sparkle. Mrs. French didn't move nor speak. She looked coldly menacing, like a waxwork in the Chamber of Horrors. Julie forgot her anger, backed to the head of the stairs.

"I wasn't listening," she said breathlessly.

Mrs. French continued to regard her with stony eyes. The ear-rings continued to flash in the sunlight.

Julie turned and ran down the stairs. Just round the bend of the staircase she nearly collided with the blonde woman who was coming up the stairs. The man, whom Julie had seen in the street, was following her. He didn't look at Julie, but stared at the stairs, red faced.

In the lobby the thin, bony man stared at her through the glass panel of the bookseller's door. He was still watching her as she ran down the stone steps into the heat and bustle of Mayfair Street.

CHAPTER TWO

I

A blonde woman in a silk wrap over an oyster-coloured nightdress
jerked open the front door of 97 Park Way and demanded furiously:
"What do you want; calling at this hour? Didn't they tell you I haven't
a maid?" Her pretty, doll-like face was puffy with sleep, and she
seemed to have just got out of bed.

"I'm sorry if I have disturbed you," Julie was startled and
embarrassed. The woman made no attempt to conceal her rage. "I
was sent by Mrs. French. I—I understood you were expecting me."

"Then for goodness' sake come in," Blanche Wesley said. "I've been
without anyone for days. It's really monstrous how I'm treated."

She slouched into the hall lounge. Julie closed the front door and
followed her.

"I can't talk to you until I've had some coffee," Blanche went on,
and ran her little claw-like fingers through her blonde curls. "Now
you are here—do make yourself useful. The kitchen's through there.
Just poke around until you find everything. Please don't ask a lot of
silly questions. I have a splitting headache. Just get me some coffee.
I'll be in the end room down the passage." She stared at Julie; "Why,
you're quite pretty. What a pleasant change. I'm so tired of being
surrounded by ugly faces. I can never understand why the working
classes are so hideous. But do run along. You can make coffee, I
suppose, or can't you?"

"Oh, yes," Julie said, and smiled brightly.

Blanche winced.

"That's lovely, but don't grin at me, please. My nerves simply won't
stand it." She frowned down at her quilted satin slippers, went on, "I
think it would be nice if you said 'madam' when you speak to me.
Yes, I think I should like that. It shouldn't be difficult, or do you
think it will?"

"No, madam," Julie said. She turned scarlet, and her smile vanished.

"Are you angry?" The pencilled eyebrows lifted. "Have I said
anything to annoy you? You've turned the colour of a beetroot; so
unbecoming I always think."

"Oh, no, madam," Julie said, and behind her back her fists clenched tightly.

"I probably will, sooner or later," Blanche said, with evident satisfactions "Mr. Wesley tells me I am so tactless with menials. I suppose I am, but I do think if one pays good wages one should be able to say what one thinks."

Julie kept silent. The doll-like face, the enchanting little body, the golden curls that reminded her of a halo, fascinated her.

"Well, do stop gaping at me," Blanche said, frowning. "Of course, I'm used to people staring, but I do think it's a little much when I feel like the wrath of God."

"I'm sorry, madam," Julie tried to look away, but there was something so bizarre about this woman that she couldn't take her eyes off her for more than a few seconds.

"I feel positively ill this morning," Blanche went on. She pressed her fingers to her temples. "And no one cares a damn if I'm dying." Then, with a sudden startling blaze-up of rage, she shouted; "For God's sake get that coffee and stop gaping at me as if I were a blue-bottomed baboon!"

"I'm sorry, madam." Julie backed away. "I'll get it at once."

She went into the kitchen and hurriedly closed the doors.

"Well, I was warned," she said to herself, "but I didn't think she'd be quite like this. Phew! I'll have to watch my step if I'm to keep this job for long."

While she waited for the water to boil, she hurriedly slipped off her frock, opened the parcel containing her uniform and put it on.

"Perhaps she'll be pleased if I wear my uniform," she thought. "At least, it'll show her I know my place," and she giggled.

Blanche's room was ablaze with light when Julie entered carrying a tray. There was a strong smell of brandy and stale perfume in the room and the air was thick and stuffy. Although it was past three in the afternoon the curtains were still drawn, and no windows appeared to be open.

Blanche was wandering about amid overwhelming luxury and confusion. The walls of the room were covered with pale blue quilting. Arm-chairs, a quilted chaise-longue and a blue and white leather pouf were dotted about on the thick, white carpet. The ornate dressing-table was covered with spilt powder, oozing tubes of grease paint, and overturned bottles. Clothes lay about the floor, on the chairs, and over the foot of the bed. Shoes lay in corners where they had been carelessly thrown. A straw hat, almost the size of a sunshade, hung from one of the electric light brackets.

"What a time you've been," Blanche said, crossly. "You'll have to be a little quicker than this if we're to get along together." She peered at Julie, went on, "Oh, you've changed. Why, you look quite nice. What a pretty uniform." She pointed to a bedside table. "Put the tray down and leave me. Perhaps you'd like to tidy the bathroom, then we'll have a talk. It's through there. I'll be ready for you in a minute or so."

The bathroom made Julie envious. There was a shower cabinet, a sunken bath, a dressing-table, a massage machine, a Turkish bath cabinet, and a hair dryer: everything an idle, spoilt woman could wish for. And, like the bedroom, this room was also in confusion. The bath hadn't been emptied. A towel floated on the milky water. Powder was scattered over the floor, and bath salt crystals crunched under Julie's shoes as she moved about, picking up cleansing tissues and hand towels sticky with cold cream.

Working as quickly as she could, she tidied the room, emptied the bath, wrung out the towel and wiped over the floor with it.

Blanche was still pacing up and down when she returned to the bedrooms On the dressing-table, partly concealed by a powder bowl, was a tumbler half-full of brandy.

"There you are," Blanche said, and smiled. She looked brighter now and more amiable. "Did I ask your name? I don't believe I did."

"Julie Holland, madam."

Blanche dropped in an arm-chair, closed her eyes for a moment, then looked up and gave Julie a long, searching stare.

"Did you say Mrs. French sent you? I never seem to remember anything these days."

"Yes, madam."

"Oh, well I suppose you must be all right. You've got references, I suppose?"

Julie handed over the two envelopes.

"That woman's so efficient," Blanche said a little crossly as she ripped open the envelopes. She glanced at the references, tossed them on the dressing-table. "She told you the wages, I suppose?"

"Yes, madam."

"Well, you'd better consider yourself engaged." She leaned forward to peer into the mirror. "We'll see how we get on together. That was very good coffee you made. So long as you keep the place tidy and help me when I want help that's all I shall expect from you. Your room's at the other end of the passage. It's a nice room. I believe in making people comfortable. You can begin at once?"

"Yes, madam."

Blanche picked up a comb and began to run it through her blonde curls.

"I shall be away to-night. I would like you to move in immediately. I don't like the flat left empty if I can help it. Do you think you can manage that, or don't you?"

"Yes, madam." Julie was getting tired of standing before this glamorous little doll.

"And you won't mind being left alone here for the night?"

Julie showed her surprise.

"Oh, no, madam. I don't mind at all."

"How brave of you," Blanche said languidly. "I hate being alone here. Mr. Wesley has been in Paris for the past fortnight and I've been terrified. You never know when someone's going to break in. There are so many burglaries these days and you do hear the oddest noises at night. I sometimes think the place is haunted. But I suppose you don't believe in ghosts?"

"No, madam," Julie said firmly.

"It must be nice to have no imagination," Blanche said, patting her curls. "I'm so sensitive and nervous. There are times when I'm quite positive someone creeps up and down the passage. I suppose it's because I'm highly strung."

"Or tight," Julie thought, wanting to laugh. She said, "Shall I run your bath, madam?"

"I suppose you'd better. And then there's a bag to be packed. I shan't be back until to-morrow evening. I expect Mr. Wesley about the same time. There'll be plenty for you to do. All my things want tidying. I've had absolutely no one for days and everything gets in such a mess. I don't know why. Do be a nice girl and open that cupboard. That's right. You see each of my dresses has a number. It's on the hanger."

The room was fitted with three enormous cupboards with sliding doors. The cupboard that Julie opened contained two long rows of dresses, coats, frocks and evening gowns.

"Each dress has a hat, underwear, gloves and bag to go with it, and, of course, shoes," Blanche explained in a tired little voice. "It's my own system. Everything is numbered and it's simply a matter of keeping the numbers together. Do you think you can manage?"

"Oh, yes, madam."

"There's a safe over there. You can't see it. It's hidden behind the wall. I look after that myself. I keep my furs and jewellery in it. Now I think you'd better run my bath. I simply must catch the five-twenty and time's getting on." She added this as if it were Julie's fault.

While Blanche was in the bathroom Julie did her best to tidy the bedroom, and as she worked she wondered what she was going to do with herself that evening. She hadn't expected an evening to herself so soon. If she could only get hold of Harry they might go to a movie together. But how could she get in touch with him? The only hope was Mrs. French. Harry had said she would pass on a message. It was worth trying.

Getting Blanche off was a maddening and exhausting operation. Twice her suitcase had to be unpacked because she changed her mind about what she intended to take with her: then, when all seemed ready and Julie was about to telephone for a taxi, Blanche became fretful and decided not to go.

"I really don't think I can be bothered," she said, flopping into an arm-chair. Dressed and made up, she was startlingly beautiful: like a painted, irresistibly attractive doll. "It's not as if I like the people. They are too frightful for words. And besides, I don't feel well. I won't go . . . that settles it. You'd better unpack before everything is creased."

At the best of times Julie loathed packing. She had packed, unpacked, repacked and unpacked again and again packed.

Each operation had been supervised by Blanche who had criticized, scolded, and made useless suggestions. Now she was telling her to unpack for the third time. She nearly lost her temper, and longed to throw the suitcase at Blanche, but she managed to control herself and with unsteady hands she once more began to empty the suitcase. When it was nearly unpacked, Blanche suddenly gave an exclamation and beat her hands together.

"What am I thinking about?" she cried in apparent anguish, "My poor Julie. Of course I must go. I was forgetting Buckie would be there. And I simply *must* see *him*. Do hurry and pack again. I'll miss the train if you don't hurry. I can't say how sorry I am to give you all this extra work."

Julie was at boiling point and near tears. She began to slam the various articles back into the suitcase.

"Oh, no, Julie, don't close it yet," Blanche went on as Julie was about to slam the lid shut. "It's not very well packed, is it? There was something . . . of course. I don't think I want that mauve thing. It's somewhere at the bottom. You know the thing I mean. It makes me look like death."

Julie could have strangled her. She snatched the mauve evening gown from the suitcase, disarranging everything as she did so. She looked so distressed and angry that Blanche decided to change her tactics.

"Would you like that gown, Julie?" she asked casually. "I don't want it and it seems a shame not to put it to some use, doesn't it?"

The bottom was knocked out of Julie's fury. She sat back on her heels and stared up at Blanche.

"I beg your pardon, madam?" she said, looked at the gown and touched it with caressing fingers.

"It is nice, isn't it?" Blanche said carelessly. "One of Hartnell's. But, the colour makes me look like hell. I can't imagine why I bought it. Would you like it?"

"Me?" Julie said, her eyes lighting up. "Oh, yes, I would. Thank you, madam."

Blanche smiled. It was a cruel little smile and when Julie saw it her heart sank.

"Well, I'll think about it," Blanche said. "Of course, I couldn't give it to you. It cost a hundred and fifty guineas or something like that. But I might let you have it for twenty pounds."

Sick with disappointment Julie put the gown on the back of the chair, stooped to fasten the suitcase.

"And I don't suppose you have twenty pounds to spend on a gown, or have you?" Blanche went on airily.

"No, madam," Julie said and turned away.

"What a pity. Oh, well, never mind. It would be absurd really for a girl of your class to wear it. You'd only get yourself laughed at. Perhaps I'll advertise in *The Times*. I could do that, couldn't I?"

Julie looked swiftly at her and caught a gleeful expression on Blanche's face. It was gone in a moment, but Julie knew then that she was being deliberately baited.

"All right," she thought, "have your fun, you filthy little cat. But you won't catch me like that again."

"It's no use letting her get under your skin," she told herself when Blanche had gone. "That's what she is trying to do. Thank goodness I'm free of her for the next twenty-four hours. I don't care what Harry does to her now. If I can help him put her rotten nose out of joint I'll do it."

She decided it would take her at least two hours of hard work to put the flat straight. It was now a quarter to five. She could be ready to meet Harry by seven if she could find him.

She didn't want to ring Mrs. French's agency, but there was no other alternative. After some hesitation she put the call through.

Dana answered.

"This is Julie Holland," Julie said, stiffening when she recognized Dana's husky voice. "I want to speak to Mr. Gleb. Can you give me his number?"

"Hold on," Dana said. The telephone was put down with a sharp click. Julie heard her say, "It's the Holland girl. She wants to speak to you."

To Julie's surprise, Harry's voice floated over the line.

"What's up?" he asked sharply.

"Oh, nothing. It's all right. I wanted to see you to-night. Mrs. Wesley has gone away and I've got the evening off. Can we meet about seven?"

"Sorry, kid." He sounded irritable. "I've got a date."

"But, Harry, surely we can meet. I don't know when I'll be free again. I'm all alone here and I've got nothing to do."

"I'm catching a train to Manchester in twenty minutes," he returned. "I'm sorry, but it's something I can't do anything about. I'll see you when I get back. I haven't a minute. So long," and he hung up.

"Damn!" Julie thought. "Oh, damn! Well, you're stuck. You have no one to talk to, no one to go out with and the whole evening on your hands. What rotten luck to have found him so easily and we can't meet. He might have been nicer on the 'phone. After all, we are lovers." Then, anxious to make excuses for him, she thought it must have been difficult for him with the Dana woman listening in.

Sometime later, lying in bed, she forgot her loneliness. Her room delighted her. It was as comfortably furnished as the other rooms in the flat and had a bathroom adjoining, a telephone, and a portable wireless by the bed.

Julie had been to her flat in Fulham Palace Road and had packed her bags and brought them to her new home. In her new luxurious surroundings she no longer felt neglected nor did she wish for company. The room, the hot bath, the wireless and the comfortable bed more than made up for the disappointment of not seeing Harry.

At eleven-thirty she turned off the wireless and settled down in bed. As she reached out to turn off the bedside lamp she heard a sound that made her pause. Somewhere in the flat a door closed softly. She frowned, aware of a sudden uneasiness, and she waited, listening. And while she waited in the silent little room she remembered what Blanche had said: *I hate being alone here. I'm sure it's haunted. There really are the oddest sounds at night.*

"She was trying to frighten me," Julie thought, and she reached once more for the light switch, but paused again as the curtains billowed out. "It's only the wind getting up," she reassured herself, but she continued to listen.

The flat was sound-proofed. She could hear nothing now except the steady ticking of the clock on the mantelpiece and her own rapid heartbeat.

With an impatient shrug she turned off the light. But immediately the room was in darkness it became an object of frightening speculation. Was there someone in the flat? Had someone crept into the room? Was it the wind that moved the curtains or was it . . .?

"This is ridiculous," she thought. "There's nothing in the flat that could possibly frighten me so long as I don't allow myself to be frightened."

And then she distinctly heard footsteps and she turned cold. There was no mistaking the sound: soft, stealthy footsteps that crept towards her door.

She reached for the bedside lamp and succeeded only in knocking it to the floor. It fell with a thud on the carpet and, leaning out of bed, her hair over her eyes, her heart pounding, she scrabbled feverishly for it. Then she became aware that in the darkness her door handle was turning and it flashed through her mind that she hadn't locked the door.

There was a light in the passage and as the door inched open the light crept into the room. She drew back in the bed, crouched down, terrified. A ribbon of light fell across the floor creating menacing shadows. The door ceased to move and she could hear someone in the passage breathing softly.

She waited: too frightened to make a sound, suspended in terror.

Something white and indistinct but moving came round the edge of the door. The scream that had been boiling inside her like a hot, seething ball made a croaking sound through the room. The light went on. Blanche Wesley stood in the doorway. In the shaded light she looked like a mischievous, gleeful little gnome.

Julie screamed again.

"Did I disturb you?" Blanche asked innocently. "I meant to be so quiet and just have a peep at you to see if you were comfortable." The forget-me-not blue eyes never left Julie's panic-stricken face. "I changed my mind and caught the last train home. I'm afraid I frightened you." The gleeful smile widened. "But you did say you weren't nervous, didn't you, or were you boasting?" She turned off the light and said out of the darkness, "Good night, Julie."

The door closed.

II

Julie came to the conclusion that in some odd, perverted way, Blanche was not quite right in the head. She decided the only thing to do was not to get rattled. Oh, yes, she had been badly rattled last night . . . but then who wouldn't have been? And she was still feeling the effects of her fright the following morning. But she had only been rattled because Blanche had taken her by surprise. Next time (and there was sure to be a next time) Julie was determined to be on her guard. The woman was cracked. She drank too much and she liked to bully and frighten. "Very well, then," Julie said to herself. "I know what to watch for and I'll be ready for her." But in spite of trying to adopt a sensible attitude she had a foreboding that she was going to have a bad time with Blanche, and that Blanche had all kinds of beastly little tricks up her sleeve which would succeed no matter how careful Julie was to guard against them. And in this she was right. Not anticipating that Blanche would amuse herself by remote control (as you might say) she fell an easy victim of a practical joke Blanche had prepared for her.

While preparing her breakfast, Julie went to a large store cupboard for some tea and came face to face with the body of a man, lying face downwards on the floor, half-concealed by the shadowy darkness.

For a brief moment she watched herself run out of her body, whirl and run back into it again, and the sunlit kitchen went dark as her senses recoiled from the shock. She found herself half sitting, half lying on the floor, her nerves fluttering, her muscles rigid with fright. It took her several minutes before she could screw up enough courage to look at the body again. A closer examination revealed it to be nothing more frightening than a suit of clothes realistically stuffed with cushions, and she realized that Blanche had scored off her again.

Not quite knowing what she was doing, she removed the cushions, folded the suit and carried it into Howard Wesley's dressing-room. Passing the mirror in the hall she was startled to see how white and drawn she looked and that her eyes were like holes in a sheet.

She returned to the kitchen, made herself a cup of tea and sat down. "If there's going to be much more of this," she thought, seeing how unsteady her hands were, "I'll have to leave. Of course, it was stupid of me to have been so frightened, but who on earth would have thought she'd've taken all that trouble—and the beastly thing did look horribly life-like."

Later, she was putting linen away in a drawer when her hand touched something dry and leathery. Looking down she was petrified to see a gruesome-looking snake coiled up in the bottom of the drawer. Julie had a horror of snakes, and she screamed wildly, dropped the linen and made a mad rush for the door. But when she had recovered from the first paralysing shock, it occurred to her that this might be yet another of Blanche's little pleasantries and she returned to the room to peer fearfully into the drawer. Although stuffed, with eyes made of glass, the thing was, nevertheless, a snake, and with a shudder, Julie threw the linen in on top of it and slammed the drawer shut. She was now completely unnerved and when the front door bell rang sharply she nearly jumped out of her skin.

She had no recollection of leaving the room nor of opening the front door. She suddenly became aware of a tall, well-dressed man towering above her and who regarded her with pale interest.

"I suppose Mrs. Wesley isn't up yet?" he said in a complaining voice and walked into the lounge hall, handed her his hat and stick. He peeled off his gloves and dropped them into his hat which she held vacantly before her, endeavouring as best she could to collect her scattered wits.

She said no, Mrs. Wesley was not up, and wondered who he could be and what he wanted.

"I am Mr. Hugh Benton, Mr. Wesley's partner," he told her. He was thin-faced, clean shaven and pale. Everything about him was pale: his hair was fair and lank, his lips were bloodless and his eyes the colour of amber. He wore an Old Etonian tie and his voice was soft like a man speaking in church. "I suppose you are the new maid," he went on, and looked her over the way a horse dealer examines a new purchase. "Would you tell Mrs. Wesley I am here?"

"She doesn't like to be disturbed so early," Julie said, uncomfortably remembering the reception she had received at three o'clock the previous afternoon.

"How interesting," he said, and smiled, or rather he showed his small, white teeth. You couldn't call this automatic grimace a smile. "I've known Mrs. Wesley a little longer than you and I am well aware of her habits. Tell her I am here, please."

"But I—I don't think—" Julie began, knowing how furious Blanche might be to be disturbed at eleven-thirty in the morning.

"You're not paid to think," Benton said, grimacing at her. "You're paid to do as you're told."

Julie swung on her heel, her face burning, and went quickly down the passage to Blanche's room. She was furious with herself for giving this creature such an opportunity to snub her. She rapped sharply on the door, entered the room.

Blanche was lying in bed, a cigarette hung from her lips and a tumbler of brandy stood on the bedside table within reach.

She looked up; her pale, puffy little face hardened.

"I didn't tell you to barge in here just when you like, did I?" she said, and her eyes began to glitter angrily. "I'll ring for you when I want you. Now get out!"

"I'm sorry to disturb you, madam," Julie said quietly, "but Mr. Benton has called and insists on seeing you. I told him you were resting."

The angry expression vanished and Blanche struggled up in bed.

"Hugh? At this time? I mustn't keep him waiting. Quick, Julie, tidy the room. Give me my make-up box. Oh, come on, stir yourself, don't stand there looking like a stuffed fish." This was a new Blanche: a fluttering, girlish, excited Blanche who was even more hateful, Julie thought, than the cruel, gleeful, sadistic Blanche.

While Blanche worked on her face with expert swiftness, Julie darted around the room clearing up the inevitable confusion.

"Spray some perfume about the place," Blanche commanded as she put colour on her pale cheeks. "I'm sure the room stinks." She put down the rouge puff, swallowed the brandy and put the glass in the cupboard at her side. "And open a window. Do hurry, Julie. You drag yourself about as if your back's broken."

Flushed and breathless Julie did as she was told, cleared away the further mess Blanche had made completing her toilet and bundled the soiled towels into the bathroom.

When she returned, Blanche was lying back on her pillows, her lovely arms above her head: a picture of irresistible seductiveness.

"What that little doll doesn't know about make-up," Julie thought enviously, as she stared at this miraculous transformation from a white-faced little drab to this frail, beautiful creature that now posed before her.

"Let him come in now," Blanche said in a waspish voice, "and stop gaping at me."

Julie found Benton in the lounge. He was smoking and pacing up and down, an irritable, bored expression on his thin face.

"Is she ready?" he asked crossly as Julie came in. "You've been long enough."

"Will you come this way, please?" Julie said, and walking in front of him she had the uncomfortable feeling that he was able to see through her clothes. As she paused outside Blanche's door, his hand touched her thigh: like a spider running down her flesh, and with a shiver she jerked round.

He reluctantly withdrew his hand, stared at her in his pale way, stepped past her and wandered into Blanche's room.

"Ah, Blanche," he said in his thin voice. "How lovely you look, and so early, too." He pushed the door to, but not shut and Julie, her flesh still creeping, heard him say: "I have news. Howard won't he back until Monday. He cabled."

"You opportunist," Blanche exclaimed, and laughed.

"Well, why not?" Benton drawled. "Shall we go? I could get away this afternoon. We could have the whole week-end together."

"Hadn't you better close the door, darling?" Blanche asked archly. "You don't have to shout our misdeeds all over the flat."

Julie moved quickly away. "Ugh! What a pair," she thought. "They're welcome to each other. Did this really mean that Blanche was going away this time for a whole weekend?" She thought immediately of Harry and her heart began to thump with excitement. Would he be back from Manchester by to-morrow? It was no good making plans just yet. Blanche might not go. Harry might still be in Manchester, and she might easily be again stuck in this vast flat all by herself, and this time for a long, lonely week-end.

Later, Benton came out of Blanche's room. Julie, who was in the kitchen, heard him walk down the passage, pause, and then retrace his steps. He came into the kitchen, closed the door gently.

Julie set her back against the table and faced him.

"Is there anything you want?" she asked coldly.

"Want?" he repeated, raised his pale eyebrows. "Yes . . . there was something. I wanted to speak to you."

She waited, hostile and nervous.

Watching her closely, he took out his wallet, dipped into it with finicky fingers and drew out a five-pound note.

"Yes," he said, folding the note into a fine spill, "there was something." He tapped the spill on his knuckles and grimaced at her. "You are Mrs. Wesley's personal maid. You may hear and see things that are no concern of yours. A personal maid doesn't tell tales. Do you understand?"

Julie flushed scarlet.

"I don't need to be told that by you or anyone else!" she blurted out furiously.

Again the pale eyebrows went up.

"Please don't be angry. Mrs. Wesley can be very difficult. It's seldom she keeps a maid longer than a week or so. I find it embarrassing. It is time, I feel, that I should establish a business association with her maid—with you. Do you follow what I am driving at?" He handed the five-pound note to her.

For a moment Julie hesitated. She was in the game for what she could get out of it, wasn't she? If this pale creature wanted to bribe her, why not take it? Five pounds! Perhaps he would give her more later. But she had to steel herself to meet the amber-coloured eyes when she said, "I think so."

"Ah. I thought I hadn't misjudged you. You see, there are certain things I shouldn't like Mr. Wesley to know about." The grimace became strained. "He is blind, and blind people are very sensitive— and suspicious. I wouldn't like to hurt his feelings."

"I understand," Julie said, and felt a little sick.

"So long as you see and hear nothing that goes on in this flat we'll get along well together," Benton continued. "For instance, I haven't been here this morning. Do you understand?"

Julie nodded.

"And I think we'd better keep this little arrangement to ourselves. Mrs. Wesley mightn't like it."

Again Julie nodded.

"Splendid." He stood over her, very tall, smelling of lavender water and cigars. He slipped the note into her hand and patted her arm. It was more of a caress than a pat and his touch made Julie shiver. She tried to draw back, but she was already pressed against the table and he hemmed her in. For a horrible moment she thought he was going to kiss her, but he didn't. He moved away, showed his teeth as he opened the door. "There's more where that came from, Julie. See nothing; hear nothing. It's simple, isn't it?" He went out and as he closed the door Blanche's bell rang.

When Julie entered Blanche's room she noticed immediately that the cupboard that had been hidden by the quilted wall stood open. Inside the steel-lined recess, lit by two powerful electric lights, were several fur coats, hanging in a row. Julie, who loved fur and had spent many hours staring enviously at the fur displays in the West End, longing to own a fur herself, recognized them. There was a chinchilla, a mink, a beaver, a sable, a white fox and an ermine. The other side of the cupboard was given up to a steel chest of drawers in which Julie guessed Blanche kept her jewellery.

Blanche was sitting at her dressing-table, rolling on gossamer-like stockings. She glanced up, saw Julie's staring eyes, followed their direction and smiled.

"That's something every burglar in London is talking about," she said, with an arrogant movement of her head. "No one could ever break in there, Julie. It's the most perfect foolproof safe ever invented. My husband designed it. I believe as many as six burglars—or is it eight?—I can't remember, but a number of them have tried to break into that safe. We've caught every one of them. They don't try anymore. They know it's hopeless. Anyone tampering with it in any way causes a bell to ring in the Kensington police station and along comes the Flying Squad in two minutes."

"So this is what Harry is interested in," Julie thought. "What a lesson it'd be for this little beast if she does lose her furs."

Blanche was saying, "Only Mr. Wesley and myself know the combination and where the locks are concealed."

"Is there anything I can do for you, madam?" Julie said, deliberately changing the subject. She didn't want Blanche to think she was in any way interested in the safe.

"I'm going away for the week-end. Mr. Wesley won't be back until Monday. I want you to pack. Here's a list of things I'll take with me. I've jotted them down for you."

Expecting a repetition of her last packing experience, Julie took the list and began to lay out the clothes Blanche had chosen. Even when she had packed and Blanche showed no inclination to have the suitcases unpacked, she still waited for Blanche to begin her baiting, but she didn't. She seemed occupied with her thoughts and, as she dressed, she hummed under her breath and seemed scarcely aware that Julie was in the room.

Suddenly she said: "What will you do over the week-end, Julie?"

"I—I don't know, madam," Julie returned, not expecting this.

"Well, you mustn't be idle. You'll find plenty of sewing to do and you'd better clean the silver. Do make yourself useful and don't let me have to tell you what to do. There are the flowers, and my shoes want attention and—oh, there's plenty to do if you look around."

"Yes, madam," Julie said.

"You can go out on Sunday, but I don't want this flat left empty at night. You understand that? And for goodness' sake don't bring any strange men in here. I know what you girls are like. The porter knows you are here alone and he'll keep an eye on you."

Julie, flushed and furious, turned away.

"Now don't get into a pet," Blanche said, frowning. "I'm not saying you'd do it, but I want you to know it's something I just won't have. Come here, Julie."

Julie went up to her, her face sullen and rebellious.

"What a pretty figure you have, and what lovely skin." Blanche's fingers, like dry little sticks, touched Julie's cheek and Julie, shuddering, started back. "You mustn't be afraid of me," Blanche said, her eyes lighting up. "You're not, are you?"

"No madam," Julie said uneasily.

"That's right," Blanche laughed. "It's so silly, but some people do seem afraid of me. I try to be kind to everyone. Of course, I do play practical jokes, but that's only my fun." She was now watching Julie closely. "Did the old man in the cupboard frighten you?"

"Not very much," Julie said indifferently.

"Didn't he?" The forget-me-not blue eyes hardened. "The other maid had hysterics. It was too funny. And the snake? Didn't that startle you—" She laughed gleefully. "The snake's my favourite joke. My husband loathes it. I put it in his bed sometimes."

Julie turned away. She didn't want Blanche to see the hatred she felt for her, nor the longing she was sure showed plainly in her face to lay hands on her and shake her.

"Do you like furs, Julie?" Blanche asked abruptly as she put the finishing touches to her make-up.

"You're not going to catch me with that trick again," Julie thought, said, "Yes, madam, I suppose I do."

"Well, look at mine. Touch them, Julie. I want you to like them."

Julie didn't move.

"Thank you, madam, but I'm not interested in other people's furs."

"Oh, nonsense," Blanche said with a gay laugh. "Look at them. There's no woman alive who wouldn't give her eyes to possess them. That mink cost five thousand and the white Arctic fox . . . I wouldn't like to tell you what that cost. Go in and look at them."

Julie drew near the safe, tried to look disinterested, but the beauty of the coats was too much for her.

"Take the mink off the hanger," Blanche said casually. "You can put it on if you like."

Julie stepped into the cupboard, reached for the mink coat. There was a sudden swishing sound and the steel walls slammed to, shutting her in with a soundless rush of air.

For a moment or so she was too surprised to move or think and a tiny spark of panic began to expand inside her, but she quickly controlled herself.

"You asked for it," she thought. "You should have guessed she was up to something. You've got to keep calm. She can't keep you in here for long. She's catching a train. But I wish there was a little more room. These beastly furs make it so hot and there doesn't seem to be much air. I suppose she thinks she'll scare the life out of me. Well, she won't! I'm not going to lose my head. I'll sit down and wait until she lets me out."

Still keeping the threatening panic under control, Julie squatted on the floor. The skirts of the fur coats touched her head and face and worried her.

"But suppose she goes off and leaves me here? Suppose she really is cracked and doesn't care?" she thought suddenly. "I can't last long in here without air. It's getting difficult to breathe now." Then, suddenly, the light went out and hot, choking darkness descended on her.

She heard herself whimper and she struggled to her feet, the soft furs clinging to her. She had always been afraid of confined spaces. This awful breathless darkness made her feel that she was buried alive. She lost her head. Screaming wildly, she hammered on the cold, steel wall; tore, kicked and scratched at the shiny surface like a mad thing. The furs twined round her, impeding her movements suffocating her. Her hands were as useless as rubber hammers as she beat on the door. She felt she was drowning in a sea of choking darkness and fell on her knees, still screaming. Disturbed by her violence one of the fur coats slipped off its hanger and enveloped her.

III

Consciousness returned slowly, like the awakening from a heavy and uneasy sleep, and she found herself lying on her bed, alone. She stared up at the ceiling for a long time and she cried. She had no idea why she cried except perhaps she had been very frightened and she still had no control over her shaken nerves.

Later, when she could cry no more, she wondered who had carried her from the cupboard to her bed, and immediately thought of Hugh Benton. That his hands had touched her filled her with a shivering disgust.

"This settles it," she thought. "I'm not staying. She's mad and dangerous. I might have died."

She got off the bed and walked unsteadily along the passage to Blanche's room. She had a vague idea that Blanche would still be there and she would tell her that she was leaving at once. But Blanche had gone. The big, luxurious room seemed strangely empty without her. The blue-quilted wall once more concealed the doors of the steel-lined cupboard. There was a faint smell of lavender water and cigars in the air, and Julie shuddered. So Benton had been there.

She went to the bedside cupboard and took out a bottle of brandy and a glass. She sat limply on the bed and drank some of the brandy. The silky liquor took instant effect: the unsteady faintness went away.

"But I'm not going to stay," she thought. "I'll pack and get out to-night. There's no point in waiting. It won't matter how careful I am she'll always outwit me. I'll never have a moment's peace from her. No, I'm going. I don't care what Harry says. I've had enough."

It wasn't only Blanche. She pretended it was, but the sight of those expensive fur coats had frightened her, for all her bravado. It was too risky. The police would suspect at once that she had had something to do with the robbery. As soon as they found out (and they would find out) that she had worked for Hewart, they'd know she was the inside plant. No, she wasn't going to have anything more to do with Blanche nor with the fur coats.

She heard a bell ringing somewhere in the flat, and for some seconds she didn't move, then she realized it was the telephone bell and she reached out, picked up the receiver by the bed.

"Julie?"

"Oh, yes," she said. "Where are you, Harry? I was thinking about you. I must see you. I'm so glad you 'phoned. It's extraordinary . . . just when I was thinking of you."

"What's up?" His voice was sharp.

"I must see you," she said hysterically. "I don't care how busy you are. I must see you, Harry."

"All right, all right. Don't get excited. I can see you in an hour. Can you get away?"

"She's gone for the weekend. Oh, Harry, it's good to hear your voice." An idea dropped into her mind. "Come round here. There's nobody here but me. You can see the place. That's what you want, isn't it?"

"Not over the 'phone," he said, raising his voice. "Are you sure no one will come?"

"Oh, no, no one will come. Mr. Wesley won't be back until Monday night." She looked at the bedside clock. It was half-past four. "When will you be here?"

"Six, a little after, perhaps. Say six-fifteen."

"And Harry, be careful when you come in. The porter's watching the flat."

There was a short silence on the line.

"Maybe I'd better not come," he said slowly. "I don't want to box this up after all the trouble I've taken."

"You must come. Take the lift to the top floor and walk down. The owner of the top flat is a Mrs. Gregory. Pretend you're calling on her."

"You're getting smart," he said, and laughed. "All right, I'll be along."

"It'll be wonderful to see you again, Harry."

"You bet."

But as soon as she had hung up she became uneasy, wondering what he would say when she told him she was not going to stay. Then an idea came to her that brought her off the bed and sent her running to Blanche's wardrobe.

"I'll give him the surprise of his life," she thought, delighted with the idea. "I'll make myself look so beautiful he won't be able to resist me."

It took her some time to choose an evening gown from Blanche's vast collection, but at last she was satisfied. The gown she had chosen was the colour of a wild poppy, low cut and with a full sweeping skirt. She dressed her thick, dark hair to her shoulders, and, by a quarter to six, she was ready.

Studying herself critically in the mirror she knew Dana couldn't hold a candle to her as she looked now. She was prettier, younger, less cynical and more seductive. The dress accentuated her beauty as no other dress had ever done. She scarcely recognized herself.

A few minutes after six the front door bell rang, and there was Harry, his grey felt hat at a jaunty angle, his hands thrust into his overcoat pockets. For a moment he didn't recognize her, then he took a quick step forward, a bewildered smile lighting his face.

"Julie! You look wonderful! In borrowed plumes! Well I'll be damned!" he exclaimed, and meant it. He couldn't believe she was the same girl. "She's absolutely terrific," he thought, bowled over. "A real smasher, and I didn't know it." He caught hold of her, but she pushed him away.

"No, don't touch me," she said sharply. "I'm not going to be messed about."

Startled by the hard expression in her eyes, he became awkward and a little embarrassed.

"You're lovely, Julie," he said, still gaping at her. "Cinderella's nothing on you. You're an absolute knock-out. One of her dresses?"

"Of course. You don't suppose I could afford to buy this for myself, do you? But come in. I want to talk to you."

He followed her into the lounge, and for the first time in his life he felt at a disadvantage. Her beauty and her surroundings shook his confidence in himself. He found himself falling in love with her as he stood staring at her. It was something he had never experienced before, and he didn't know how to cope with it.

Julie was quick to see the impression she had made on him, and exploited it. She stood before the big fireplace and looked at him steadily, her face cold and set.

"What's the matter, Julie? Aren't you going to give me a kiss?"

"No, I'm not!" she snapped. "I want to talk to you. I'm leaving here. I can't stand it anymore."

She told him about Blanche.

"You've no idea what she's like," she concluded, her eyes flashing. "She's cracked. I mean it. She's dangerously cracked. She might have killed me. I don't know from one minute to the next what's going to happen. I'm afraid to open a drawer or a cupboard. I'm scared to answer her bell. Well, I'm not going to stand it, and I don't see why I should."

"Now, look, Julie, you're worked up," he said, dismayed by her determined expression. "You'll see it differently tomorrow. You're not going to let a few practical jokes get you down, are you?"

"She frightens me and gets on my nerves. There'll be no peace for me as long as I stay here. It's not worth it. It's no good, Harry, I'm not staying."

He went over to the settee and sat down. This was serious. He decided he'd have to tell her why she was here, to show her it wasn't just something she could chuck up at a moment's notice.

"Look, Julie, you may as well know now as later," he said, as he took out a cigarette with a none too steady hand. "I'm after those furs. You've guessed it by now, haven't you?"

"Do you take me for a fool? Of course I've guessed it. And I don't like it."

"There's nothing for you to worry about. You're safe enough," he assured her hastily. "I want you to find out how that safe operates. It's the toughest job in town. I've made up my mind to crack it and you're the only one who can help me."

"Well, you can't open it," Julie said shortly. "She told me about it. It's wired to the Kensington police station."

"There you are!" he explained, sitting forward. "That's exactly what I wanted to know. What else did she tell you?"

"She said eight burglars have been caught trying to get into it. How do you like that?"

"Four," Harry said. "Not eight. I thought that was how they were caught, but I wasn't sure. Don't you see, kid? You can get me all kinds of useful information if you'll only stick it. Tell me about the furs."

"There's a mink coat. She said it cost five thousand." Julie made a little grimace. She couldn't get the furs out of her mind. Since she had seen them she had been thinking about them, longing to possess them. "And a white Arctic fox. That's a beauty; much too good for that little horror. And there's also a beaver, a chinchilla, a sable and an ermine."

"Seen any jewellery?"

"No, but I know it's kept in a steel cabinet in the safe."

All the time Harry was questioning her he was thinking how he could persuade her to stay. Somehow he had to persuade her to work with him. He had to find a weakness in her and play on it.

"You said the door of the safe shut when you went in. Did it shut fast or slow?"

"Like a mousetrap going off," Julie said with a shiver. "There's no air in there once the doors are closed. You would die if you were trapped in there for long."

"The idea is not to be trapped. Did she close the door or was it automatic?"

"She wasn't near it. I don't really know."

"Well, let's look at it. Take me to her bedroom."

"All right, but you understand I'm not going on with this? You can see if you want to, and you'd better take a good look at it. You won't see it with my help anymore."

He followed her into Blanche's bedroom feeling more dismayed and helpless than ever. Her hard determination defeated him.

She showed him the quilted wall.

"It's behind that. Don't touch it. We don't want the police here."

"You're damned right we don't," he said uneasily, and went over to examine the wall. "No sign of anything. It's a pretty neat job. Did the door open outwards or slide to one side?"

"It slid to one side."

He stood looking at the wall thoughtfully for several minutes, then he shook his head.

"No good. We'll have to find out more about how it works before I tackle it. You'll have to find out for me, Julie."

"I'm not going to," Julie said, aware of his uneasiness. "I've told you. I'm not staying."

He pulled her to him.

"Stick it a little longer and I'll make it a hundred quid instead of fifty. Come on, Julie, be a gutsy kid. You've done fine up to now."

She looked up at him, her full lips near his.

"No, Harry, I've had enough. You see, you've told me what you're up to and that makes me your accomplice. I'm not going to be mixed up with the police, and besides I can't stand any more from that woman. You just don't know how she frightens me."

He had a sudden idea. As soon as it entered his mind he realized to his astonishment how much this girl meant to him now. "All right," he thought, "I may as well face it. She's knocked me. She's what I want. I'm not going to lose her. There's never been anyone like her before. I'm going to have her if I have to marry her, and damn it, that's what I want to do."

"Aren't you getting a little het up, Julie?" he said, taking her hand. "Two or three more days and the job's done. Listen, let's get this job over and we'll get married. How would you like that?" He looked at her eagerly. "I'll have enough money to be on easy street for the rest of my days. We can go to America; live on the fat of the land."

Julie pushed him away and stared at him. This was unexpected, and a little tingle of excitement ran up her spine. "Marry me? Go to the States?"

"Why not? You want fun, don't you?" He was excited now. "I'll give you fun. I'll give you the world on a plate. I love you. Don't you understand, darling? I'm crazy about you."

"If you're lying . . ." she began, her eyes flashing.

"Of course I'm not. I mean it, Julie. Look, suppose you don't go through with this. What'll happen to you? Suppose you break with me? What are you going to do? Go back to Hewart? He won't want you. Earn four quid a week in a factory? You'll love that, won't you? I'm offering you everything you want: clothes, fun, money, and you can have me if you want me. Damn it, I can't be fairer than that, can I? I have friends in the States. We'll have a terrific time together. What do you say?"

She studied him for a moment. It was a triumphant moment for her. He meant it! He was in love with her. She had only to play her cards carefully and she would get anything she wanted from him without risks.

"I love you too, Harry," she said, and slipped her arms round his neck. "But I'm not staying here. I'm not a crook. All right, I admit I've done things I shouldn't have done, but I've kept inside the law. I've never done nor am I ever going to do anything that'd land me in prison. And, please, Harry, don't go through with this. She's too clever. You'll be caught. I know you'll be caught. Then what'll happen to me?"

He held her to him.

"That's torn it," he was thinking. "Now what the hell am I going to do? I'll lose her if I don't look out. I'll have to see Ma French. She'll have to find a way round this. She'll have to find another girl to do the job."

"All right, Julie," he said, and kissed her. "I won't hold you to it if that's the way you feel. It won't make any difference to us. I'm crazy about you, kid. I'll find a way to getting into that tin box. But you quit. I'll see you right."

"Honest, Harry? You really mean that?"

"Of course I do."

"But why go through with it? Let's go to the States now. Don't take the risk, Harry."

"I've got to do the job," he said, a little impatiently. "Where do you think the money's coming from? Listen, Julie, this job's worth eight thousand to me. I've got to do it."

Eight thousand!

For a moment she was tempted to stay and help him, then caution pushed the idea out of her head. Why should she? He could manage. He would find a way. And then he'd spend the money on her and there'd be no risk.

"All right, Harry...." she began.

"What's that?" he broke in, stiffening. "Did you hear anything?"

Julie pushed away from him.

"No . . . what do you mean?"

He went quickly to the door, opened it, closed it immediately.

"Someone's in the flat," he whispered.

Blanche!

Julie nearly fainted. To be caught in Blanche's bedroom in her clothes! She stood paralysed with terror.

Quick steps sounded down the passage, coming towards the room.

"It's Mrs. Wesley!" Julie gasped. "What am I to do?" She made a futile dart to the window. "I must hide . . ."

The door opened. She turned, clenching her fists and stifling a scream. A man came in: a man who wore black-lensed glasses that hid his eyes. He stood in the doorway, the black lenses looked right at her.

"Is there anyone here?" he asked, mildly. "Blanche, are you here?"

And Julie realized with sick relief that this was Howard Wesley who, of course, couldn't see her.

CHAPTER THREE

I

Howard Wesley was not tall, although he gave Julie the impression that he was a big man. He was broad-shouldered and powerfully built, and he carried himself erect. In spite of his disfiguring black-lensed glasses she could see he had excellent features and his determined mouth and chin gave him an air of authority. His broad forehead was capped by dark, unruly hair, turning white at the temples. She was surprised later to hear he was only thirty-eight.

Both Julie and Harry stood staring at him, and as he moved into the room they silently gave ground.

"Is anyone here?" he repeated.

Harry waved at Julie and grimaced. She realized he was trying to tell her that she had to handle this, and she saw he was right.

She said in a husky little voice, "Oh, yes . . . me."

Wesley frowned, continued to look in her direction as if he had known all along she was there.

"And who are you?" he asked. He took from his hip pocket a gold cigarette-case and selected a cigarette.

"I'm Julie Holland, the new maid," she told him, trying to keep her voice steady.

"I see." He patted his pockets and his frown deepened. "I wonder if you could give me a light? I seem to have left my matches in my overcoat pocket."

She looked wildly round the room. Harry took out his lighter and put it on the table. He pointed at it, and jerked his thumb at Wesley. She was surprised to see how calm Harry was. He scarcely moved and was watching Wesley closely, his eyes hard and alert.

In a way his calmness annoyed Julie, who was shaking all over and had difficulty in breathing. She snatched up the lighter and moved towards Wesley. It was a relief to see that he continued to look at the place where she had been standing and did not turn his head as she approached. To her it was proof that he was blind and couldn't see them.

She tried to operate the lighter, but her fingers were so shaky that she nearly dropped it.

"Give it to me," he said, and held out his hand.

She gave him the lighter.

"Where is Mrs. Wesley?" he asked.

"She's away for the week-end, sir," Julie said, looked at Harry who had moved to the door. He shook his head at her, and winked.

"I see." Wesley lit the cigarette, held the lighter out in midair. "Thank you."

Julie took it from him, put it on the table. Harry picked it up.

"Did she say when she was returning?" Wesley went on, thrusting his hands into his trouser pockets.

"She didn't expect you until Monday night. She'll be back by then."

"And you didn't expect me either." He smiled. "I hope I haven't spoilt your evening."

"Oh, no, sir," Julie said hastily, wondering if he suspected anything. "I haven't anything to do. I—I was tidying madam's room."

"Were you? You smell as if you were going to a party." He laughed apologetically. "I didn't mean to be rude, but I have to rely on my nose and ears these days. That's a very nice perfume you are wearing."

Julie flushed scarlet and stepped back. It should be nice. It was Blanche's perfume.

"I—I wasn't going out," she stammered.

"Mr. Gerridge is seeing to the luggage," Wesley went on. "He's my secretary. He should be up in a moment. Can you give us coffee?"

"Yes, sir," she said, thinking. "I must get out of this dress at once."

"Let us have it in the study. I have some work to do." Wesley turned and appeared to look right at Harry who took a quick step back. "I have an odd feeling there's someone else in the room." Wesley went on as he groped for the door handle. "Is there?"

He could have reached out and touched Harry. Julie caught her breath sharply, motioned Harry back.

"Oh, no, sir, of course there isn't."

"I get these feelings," Wesley said, frowning. "All right, let's have the coffee as soon as you can," and he went out.

"Phew!" Harry whispered as soon as the door closed. "That was too damned close. Get out of that dress. This other bloke mustn't see you."

"It wasn't my fault," Julie said, near tears. "I didn't know he was coming."

"Never mind that. Get out of those clothes!" Harry urged. "Go on, hurry!"

She ran to Blanche's cupboard where she had left her uniform and then went into the bathroom. It didn't take her a moment to change.

Harry was listening at the door when she returned.

"Get their coffee," he whispered. "Hurry. I want to get out of here."

"When am I going to see you again?" she asked breathlessly. "I'm not staying here. This settles it."

"I'll see you tomorrow afternoon," he said. "Don't go until then. I'll be right opposite in the Park at three o'clock. Slip out and we'll talk. Now, get off. I want to get out of here."

She hesitated for a moment.

"All right, but it's no use trying to persuade me. I'm not going to stay." She left him, and went quickly to the kitchen.

When she took the coffee into the study, Wesley was sitting in an arm-chair, smoking a cigar. A young man, not much older than herself, whose lean, pleasantly ugly face lit up with a smile when he saw her, was sitting at the desk sorting through a pile of papers. She guessed he was Gerridge, Wesley's secretary. He waved to a table near Wesley and went on with his work.

As she stooped to put the tray on the table, Wesley said: "I suppose you have only just arrived?"

"I came yesterday, sir."

"Well, I hope you will be happy here," Wesley returned, as if he doubted it. "We didn't expect to be back so soon. But don't let us interfere with your week-end plans. You can go out if you want to. We shan't need anything. I think we'll spend the week-end at the factory. We'll only bother you to give us breakfast to-morrow morning. You understand about that? You can order it from the restaurant. We shall be off about nine o'clock. Shall we say breakfast at eight-thirty?"

"Very well, sir."

"How awful for him to be blind," she thought, as she went to Blanche's bedroom. "He's nice and kind. How could he have married that beastly little creature?"

When she had tidied up Blanche's room she went into the kitchen. She didn't know what to do with herself. It was still early, and she would have liked to have gone out but she didn't want to go alone. Instead, she paced up and down and worried about the future.

She thought about Harry. Before Wesley arrived she had been excited at the prospect of going to America with Harry, now she wasn't so sure. She found herself thinking of Wesley and comparing him to Harry. It was like comparing a paste diamond to a real one. She suddenly realized that Harry was characterless and shallow, that his clothes were flashy and vulgar. Wesley was rich. Harry would never be as rich as Wesley. If he did steal the furs, how long would eight thousand pounds last? Not long, if they went to America and spent freely, and then what would happen?

"I might as well face it," she told herself. "Harry's a thief. Dawson warned me against him. Hewart hates him. He's mixed up with that awful Mrs. French. Then there's Dana. What kind of trouble shall I be letting myself in for if I do marry him?"

If she was going to marry, she ought to marry a man like Wesley. She would get what she wanted then: a big house, clothes, servants, a car, everything! But, of course, Wesley wouldn't look at her. Besides, he was already married. But suppose she told him about the robbery? He might be nice to her; do something for her. She pulled herself up, suddenly frightened. She mustn't think like this. It was dangerous. She remembered what Hewart had told her about the girl who had talked. She must get that idea out of her head.

Her thoughts were interrupted by a soft rap on the door and Gerridge came in, carrying the coffee tray.

"Hello," he said with a friendly grin. "I thought I'd bring the tray along. That was cracking good coffee."

"I expect you needed it," she said, pleased, and took the tray.

"I'm Tom Gerridge," he told her, wandering round the kitchen, hands in pockets. "I'm Mr. Wesley's valet and Man Friday. We may as well get to know each other. You'll be seeing a lot of me."

"Shall I?"

"Rather. I told Mr. Wesley I thought you were a stunner."

Julie turned away and began to put the coffee things in the sink.

"I hope you don't mind," he said. "It's true, you know."

She giggled.

"No. I don't mind. But I don't suppose Mr. Wesley was very interested."

"Oh, but he was," Gerridge assured her. "At least he didn't say so, but he pricked up his ears all right."

Julie laughed and began to wash up.

"Mr. Wesley is using the Dictaphone at the moment," Gerridge explained. "That's why I came along to keep you company. You don't mind, do you?"

"No, I don't mind."

"That's fine. How do you like it here?"

"Not very much," Julie said truthfully.

"I suppose Mrs. Wesley has been up to her tricks?"

"She has."

"The usual practical jokes: stuffed snakes, shutting you in the safe?"

Julie stared at him.

"How did you know?"

"Oh, she tries it on everyone. She's tried it on me. I was locked in that damned safe for ten minutes. I thought I was going to die."

"Well, I don't intend to stay here much longer," Julie said firmly. "She dangerous."

"Oh, but you must stay. You won't mind Mrs. Wesley once you get used to her. She leaves you alone after a bit. Never bothers me now. And you'll like Wesley. He's a first-rate chap."

Julie leaned against the sink, quite ready now for a gossip.

"I can't imagine how he could have married her," she said.

"She wasn't always like this, you know," Gerridge said. "When they first met she was the rage of London and she was really marvellous. She swept him off his feet. She knew he had bags of money, and she took advantage of him from the very start. She not only chiselled a fat settlement out of him (she's squandered every penny of that now) but she also persuaded him to agree that if the marriage broke up she was to have another large sum of money. I think he's pretty sick about that settlement now. As far as she's concerned it's heads I win, tails you lose, and she behaves just as she likes."

"But why doesn't he give her the money and get rid of her?"

"He can't afford to. He's working on an invention that'll halve the cost and fitting time of pilotless flying equipment and he's sunk every penny into the research. He just couldn't afford to pay her off, and she knows it."

"I think it's terrible," Julie said, shocked. "And to be blind as well."

"Yes." Gerridge shook his head. "He had a big disappointment this week. A French specialist thought he could operate successfully on his eyes. That's why we went to Paris." He glanced at his watch, whistled, slid off the table. "I must be back. I said I'd only be away five minutes. I'll be seeing you again."

Later, when Julie was in bed, she heard Gerridge call, "Good night," and she started up, thinking he was calling to her.

She liked Gerridge, and smiled to herself when she realized he was speaking to Wesley. She heard the front door close and it occurred to her she was now alone in the flat with Wesley.

"Well, that's nothing to worry about," she thought. "He's safe. If it'd been Benton I should be scared stiff, but Wesley . . ."

She was dropping off to sleep when a sudden crash of breaking glass startled her awake. She listened, then jumped out of bed, slipped on her dressing-gown.

"He must have had an accident," she thought, alarmed and went quickly down the passage to Wesley's room, listened outside the door. She heard movements and she knocked.

"Who's there?" Wesley asked, then, "Oh, come in, Julie." She opened the door. He was standing in the middle of the room, in dressing-gown and pyjamas, and looked helplessly in her direction. He still wore the disfiguring black-lensed glasses, and she found herself wishing he would take them off. At his feet was a smashed tumbler, the contents of which made a dark pool on the carpet.

"Hello, Julie," he said, with a rueful smile. "Come to rescue me?"

"I heard—" she began, stopped short when she saw blood running down his hand. "Oh! You've cut yourself."

"The damn thing slipped out of my hand, and when I tried to clear it up I dug a bit of glass into my finger."

"I'll get a bandage," Julie said, glad to help him. She quickly brought a first-aid outfit from Blanche's bathroom. "If you'll sit down I'll fix it for you."

"Thanks." He groped about, muttered under his breath.

"Where's the chair? I seem to have lost my bearings."

She took his arm and led him to a chair.

"It's sickening to be so helpless," he said as he sat down. "I don't know what I should have done if you hadn't come."

Not knowing quite what to say, and feeling ill at ease, she remained silent. She stopped the bleeding and wound on a bandage. "I'll put a fingerstall on, then you won't have any trouble," she said.

"That's very nice of you. Were you asleep?"

"Oh, no," Julie said, as she slipped a wash-leather fingerstall over the bandage and fastened the tape round his wrist. "Is that comfortable?"

"It's fine." He flexed his fingers. "Have I made an awful mess?"

"It's all right, but I'll clear it up."

She fetched a dustpan and brush, swept up the pieces of glass and wiped the stain with a cloth.

"It's all right now," she said. "Is there anything else I can do for you?"

He startled her asking, "How old are you, Julie?"

"Twenty-one," she told him, wondering why he should ask.

"And pretty?"

She blushed.

"I don't know."

"Gerridge says you are and I believe he is a good judge. It's just occurred to me I shouldn't be here alone with you. I should have thought of it before. Mrs. Wesley wouldn't like it." He fidgeted with his dressing-gown cord. "But I don't feel inclined to get dressed again and go to my club. I suppose I should, but I'm not going to. All the same I think it won be better not to say anything to Mrs. Wesley that I spent the night here. I shall say nothing and I'll be glad if you don't."

"Oh, no," Julie said, realizing at once that Blanche would be utterly filthy if she knew. "I won't say anything."

"Thank you." He was unmoved and not in the least embarrassed. "It's a lot of nonsense really, but—well, there it is. You'd better get off to bed now."

"Are you sure there's nothing else I can do for you?" Julie asked.

"There is one thing you can tell me before you go," he said, and smiled. "Did Mr. Benton come here while I've been away; Mr. Hugh Benton, my partner?"

Julie nearly said yes, but something in the way he was sitting, the way his hands suddenly became still, warned her to be careful. She remembered with a feeling of shame that she had accepted Benton's hush money.

"No," she said, and hated herself for lying. "No one's been here."

"I see." He seemed to relax and sank further back into the arm-chair. "All right. Good night, Julie. Turn off the light, will you, please? I don't need it."

It seemed odd to leave him sitting in the chair in complete darkness: odd and rather sad.

II

Harry Gleb lit a cigarette and threw the match with unnecessary violence into the grate.

"It's no good bawling at me," he said sharply. "She won't play. I've done what I could, but nothing doing. She walks out to-morrow."

Mrs. French eyed him. Her face was set and cold.

"She's got to stay. We'll never get another chance to put a girl in there. I know Blanche Wesley. If she walks out. we're sunk."

Harry shrugged helplessly.

"I've done my best. I can't make the girl stay if she's made up her mind to quit, can I?"

"The trouble with you is you're soft," Mrs. French said harshly. "You ought to have taken the little bitch by the scruff of her neck and given her a damn good hiding. That's what she wants. She'd do what she's told if you handled her right."

Harry scowled at her.

"I'm not beating women up. I don't stand for it. We'll have to think of something else."

"Can't you get into your thick head there is nothing else we can do?" Mrs. French barked. "I'll talk to her."

"You won't!" Harry snapped. "I tell you it's no good. Leave the girl alone."

Mrs. French looked at him intently.

"You're not going soft on her, are you, Harry?"

That was the last thing Harry wanted Mrs. French to suspect. He was scared of her. She knew too much about him for safety. There was Dana, too. Mrs. French was expecting him to marry her daughter. If she thought he was going soft on Julie there would be trouble. He didn't trust her. She might do anything—shop him to the bogies.

"Don't talk wet," he said. "Of course I'm not. She means nothing to me. I just won't stand for violence. You know that."

"It won't come to violence," Mrs. French said. "I'll talk to her. Maybe I'll threaten her, but nothing more. She'll behave after I've talked to her."

Harry didn't like this, but he was scared to protest too strongly.

"All right, but keep your hands off her. I won't stand for it, Ma. I'm warning you."

"You shove off," Mrs. French said curtly. "When I want to see you again, I'll send for you. The job's still on. Our plans stand. She'll do what she's told."

"Okay," Harry said uneasily, and moved to the door. "But don't touch her. I mean it."

Mrs. French didn't reply. When he had gone, she stood thinking. Then she picked up the telephone, dialled a number and waited.

Theo came on the line.

"Who is it?" he asked in his nasal whine.

"Come round here," Mrs. French ordered brusquely. "I've a job for you."

"What's up now? It's late. I was going to bed."

"Harry's gone soft on the Holland girl. She's being difficult. I want you to have a little talk with her."

"That's different," Theo said cheerfully. "That's not a job, that's relaxation. I'll be right over," and he hung up.

III

Theo sat on a park bench, opposite Park Way, his hands in his pockets, his velour hat tilted to the back of his head. A limp cigarette hung from his mouth and the smoke from it curled up into the still air, making him screw up one eye.

It was early; a few minutes to nine o'clock, and Theo was alone in this part of the Park. Except for an occasional bus there was nothing to look at, but Theo was quite happy to sit in the sunshine. Most of his life had been spent doing nothing; standing at street corners, his mind blank, his body resting. He disliked any kind of activity, regarding it only as a means to an end. And when Gerridge came out of Park Way and climbed into the waiting car, Theo sighed. He knew before very long he would have to get busy. Wesley came out some minutes later. The porter at the door guided him to the car, slammed the door and the car drove away.

Theo stubbed out his cigarette, got to his feet. As he entered the vast hall of Park Way, the porter stepped out of his office and eyed him coldly.

"And what do you want?" he demanded suspiciously.

"Going up to see my sister," Theo said. "Maid at 97. Any objection?"

The porter was suspicious. Theo could see that.

"Give her a ring if you don't believe me," Theo went on. "Tell her it's her brother, Harry."

"Don't tell me what to do," the porter snapped. "I don't know if Mrs. Wesley would like this."

"Tell her, too," Theo said, grinning. "Tell everybody. Let the newspapers in on it. Spread yourself, pal, I'm in no hurry. I want you to be happy about this."

The porter turned red. He felt he was making a fool of himself.

"You hop up quick, then," he said. "Go on and see her; and don't stay long. I don't want the likes of you in here."

"Didn't think you would; that's why I came," Theo said. He slouched over to the automatic lift, opened the door, stepped in, slammed the lift door and pressed the button to the fourth floor.

He leaned against the side of the lift as it shot up between the floors, and lit a cigarette.

"I've got to make it snappy," he thought, "or else the old blister might be up to see what's going on."

He rang the bell of 97, and waited.

Julie opened the door.

"Hello, Jane," Theo said. His hand shot out. His open palm fitted under her chin and he gave her a violent shove, sending her reeling into the lobby. He followed her in, closed the door, raised his fist threateningly.

"Don't squawk. I've come from Ma French."

Julie backed away. She saw before her a short, stocky youth (he couldn't have been more than nineteen) with untidy black hair that fell over his ears and on to his greasy coat collar. His round, fat face was pasty and his eyes were close-set and cruel. There was something horribly vicious and spiteful about him.

"Don't get excited, Jane," Theo said, and smiled. His teeth were broken and green. "We're going to have a little talk. Go in there. I want to sit down. I'm tired."

Terrified, Julie backed into the lounge. Theo slouched in after her, looked round and grunted.

"Pretty good, isn't it? Fancy wanting to leave a joint like this." He eyed her speculatively. "You do want to leave, don't you?"

"I'm going," Julie said weakly. "And no one's going to stop me."

"I am," Theo said, and flopped into an arm-chair. "Get the weight off your feet, Jane. Me and you's going to have a little talk."

Julie made a dash for the telephone, but before she could reach it, Theo had left his chair, grabbed hold of her and swung her round. As she opened her mouth to scream, he smacked her face. She staggered back with a thin wail of pain and fear, over-balanced and fell on her hands and knees.

"Next time you'll get my fist," Theo said. He caught hold of her arm, dragged her up and shoved her roughly into a chair. "What's the matter with you? Want to get hurt?"

Julie began to cry weakly. Satisfied she'd give no more trouble,

Theo went back to his arm-chair.

"You're going through with this job or there'll be a load of grief coming your way," he told her. "I don't want any arguments. If you won't play with Harry, you'll play with me."

"I won't!" Julie sobbed. "I'll tell the police! I won't do it!"

Theo laughed.

"That's what you think," he said, and took out a limp wallet from his pocket and produced three grimy photographs. "'Ere, take a look at these. I pinched them from a police photographer. Real life pitchers. They'll interest you."

Julie flinched away.

"I'm not going to look at anything," she said wildly. "If you don't go . . ."

"Do you want me to hit you again, you silly mare?" Theo asked, leaning forward. "Look at 'em or I'll bash you."

He threw the photographs into Julie's lap. She caught a glimpse of disfigured faces and she swept the photographs to the floor with a shudder.

"Pick 'em up and look at them," Theo said, getting to his feet. "I'm not going to tell you again."

Slowly Julie bent down and her fingers touched the photographs, lifted them. She looked at them, her face twisted into a horrible grimace.

"That's vitriol," Theo said. "Smashing pitchers. Proper life-like they are. I knew that bride. Her name's Emmy Parsons. She's a tart. A nigger did that to her. She wasn't a bad-looking bride before she got splashed. 'Ere, keep looking at 'em. I haven't finished yet. That other bride's Edith Lawson. Fooled around with another bride's man, so she got splashed. See that? And this other one. Got a proper basin, didn't she? Slap in the puss. She was a real smasher. Used to work in a café in Leicester Square, but she talked too much. A bloke came in one night, ordered a cuppa coffee, and as she 'anded it to him he splashed 'er. I was there at the time." Theo grinned. "She made a noise like a train going through a tunnel. And listen, Jane. The cops never found out who done it. They wouldn't find out if it happened to you. And it's going to happen if you don't play ball with us."

Julie shivered, dropped the photographs. The sight of the women's disfigured faces filled her with cold dread. No other threat could have been more effective.

Theo tapped her shoulder.

"Look, this is the stuff." He held between finger and thumb a little green bottle. "I carry it around, see? And don't think you can run away and hide. I'm good at finding people. From now on I'm going to watch you. One move out of turn and you'll get it. Keep your mouth shut and do what you're told and you'll be all right. But start something we don't like and you'll kiss your looks good-bye. Understand?"

"Yes," Julie said.

"Right. Well, that's all for this time, Jane. No more nonsense. We want to know how the safe opens by Wednesday. No excuses. Wednesday, or I'll be along and I'll shake you up again. Meet us at the Mayfair Street office at eight o'clock, Wednesday. If you're not there, you'll be sorry. Understand?"

"Yes," Julie said.

"Okay. Now where's the bathroom?"

She didn't know why he should want the bathroom, but she was too dazed and frightened to think clearly. She pointed. "Through there."

"Come on, that's where we're going."

"I don't want to . . ."

"You're going to start a lot of trouble for yourself if you don't get out of that habit, Jane," he said. "Come on."

She stumbled down the passage to the bathroom with him at her heels. She had a presentiment that something horrible was going to happen to her, but there was nothing she could do about it.

"Nice joint," Theo said, closing the bathroom door.

"Everything laid on. Almost a pleasure to keep clean. Okay, Jane, just stand by the bath, will you?"

She cringed away from him.

"Please leave me alone," she implored him. I'll do anything: don't touch me."

"Don't be a silly mare," he said, grinning. "You got me outa bed three hours before my time. You've mucked up my morning. Brides don't do that to me."

"Please . . ."

"And you don't either, you—" The obscenity petrified her.

"See how you like this." He aimed a light blow at her face so she brought up her hands. Then he hit her viciously in the pit of her stomach.

"Didn't want you to sick over any nice carpet," he explained with a cruel little grin, and as she crumpled to the floor and began to retch he sidled out of the bathroom and shut the door.

IV

At three o'clock the same afternoon, Harry sat on the same park bench Theo had occupied in the morning and stared up at the windows of Wesley's flat. He waited impatiently for Julie, but Julie didn't come. At a quarter to four he was angry and slightly alarmed.

"What's happened to her?" he wondered uneasily. "She can't have hooked it without waiting for me."

After waiting another five minutes he got up and walked rapidly to a telephone box not far away. He put through a call to Wesley's flat, but there was no answer.

He began to get seriously worried.

"Where the hell has she got to?" he asked himself as he stood uneasily outside the telephone box and stared up at the blank windows.

It was too risky to go to the flat. For some moments he was undecided what to do, and he was aware of a growing feeling of apprehension. If Ma French had done anything to her! He clenched his fists angrily. It was no good standing here, wondering. He'd have to find out. He waved to a passing taxi, gave an address in Chelsea and sat back, lighting a cigarette with an unsteady hand. If they had done anything to her! He'd make them pay somehow. She was his now. If anyone thought they could touch her, they'd have him to reckon with.

Mrs. French and Dana were having tea in their small service flat when Harry came striding in.

Dana went to him.

"Why, hello, Harry. I wasn't expecting you."

But Harry ignored her, pushing past her and confronting Ma with a look of rage on his face.

"What's happened to Julie?" he demanded roughly. "We were going to meet this afternoon. She hasn't turned up. I've rung the flat and there's no answer. Do you know anything about it?"

Mrs. French met his furious stare calmly.

"You're behaving like a damned fool, as usual, Harry," she said. "Why should you care what's happened to her?"

He pulled himself together with an effort. He mustn't let her suspect he was in love with Julie. There'd be time for that when the job was done and he'd received his cut. If either of these women thought he was going off with Julie they'd stop him. He was sure of that.

"I don't know what you mean," he snapped. "She's working for us. I'm keeping my eye on her. Now she's vanished."

"You said last night she wasn't going to work for us," Mrs. French reminded him. "I think you're making too much fuss of her. It's not fair on Dana, Harry."

Harry glowered at her.

"Does she mean anything to you?" Dana demanded, confronting him.

"No! But I want to know what's happened to her."

"Then that's all right," Mrs. French said and laughed. "I sent Theo to see her this morning. They had a little chat, and she changed her mind about leaving. I expect she's sulking."

"Theo? You sent that stinking rat . . ."

"Why not? You said yourself she was being difficult."

"Theo!" Harry was pale, and restrained his rage with difficulty. "Did he touch her?"

"Why all the interest? I thought you said the girl meant nothing to you?"

Harry stood looking first at Mrs. French and then at Dana. Then he swung on his heel and walked out, slamming the door behind him.

"He'll soon get tired of her," Mrs. French said, as Dana started up to follow him. "If he doesn't, I'll get her out of the way when the job's done. Now, don't be silly about this. There's nothing to worry about."

"Oh, shut up!" Dana exclaimed, and burst into tears.

V

On Monday evening, Blanche Wesley returned to her flat in a waspish mood. The week-end hadn't been a success. Benton had been in a difficult, demanding mood and the hotel had been hell. Of course, Hugh hadn't much money. He gambled recklessly and was up to his ears in debt, but if he thought anything but the best was good enough for her he had better get any further idea of taking her away again for a week-end out of his miserly, pale head. And she hated Brighton anyway. Why it always had to be Brighton she couldn't think. There had been a continuous wind; it had been chilly and it rained. The hotel was unbelievable. They had refused to serve meals in the bedroom and had given her a bit of butter the size of a halfpenny with her toast. When she had complained the waiter had actually been impertinent, and that fool Hugh had told her there was peace on. He seemed to think that was funny. She had wanted a fire in the bedroom, but the management had yammered about the fuel shortage. If it hadn't been for Hugh, who had hustled her away, she would have told the management exactly what she had thought of the hotel. The final blow had been the discovery that the hotel hadn't any brandy, and that was something she just couldn't do without. So she was forced to pub-crawl in the pouring rain, and the muck they offered her wasn't fit even to cook with, and they had the audacity to charge six shillings a glass for it.

And now, as she swept into the spacious entrance lobby of Park Way, she was determined that here, at least, she wasn't going to stand any nonsense. This was her permanent home; if she wanted a fire she would have one; if she wanted service, she would get it; if she wanted a pound of butter with her morning toast the porter would damn well produce it or she'd know the reason why. If there was the slightest indication that the service had deteriorated during her absence, she would have a row; and what a glorious, flaming, hell-raising row it would be.

But the moment the head porter saw her he was out of his cubbyhole, snapping orders to the under-porter and respectfully welcoming her. The taxi was paid off, her luggage was brought in, her mail, neatly tied with string, was presented to her with a flourish. A lighted match appeared as if by magic when she put a cigarette in her pouting lips.

This was better, she thought, much more like it, and she mellowed under the soothing, respectful attention bestowed upon her.

"Well, Harris," she said, drawing off her gloves. "It's nice to be back again. I've had the most damnable week-end. What's been happening at the flat. Any callers?"

The head porter was used to this inquiry. He was well aware that nothing was too petty to escape Blanche's attention. Since he received at least five pounds a week from her in tips it paid him to be servile, although his private opinion of her was startlingly obscene.

"Mr. Wesley and Mr. Gerridge returned to the flat on Saturday night, madam," he told her. "And a person called to see your maid on Sunday morning."

Blanche smiled amiably, flickered her long, spiky eyelashes and revealed her beautiful little teeth.

"Did Mr. Wesley stay the week-end at the flat?" she purred.

"Oh, no, madam, just Saturday night."

"Did Mr. Gerridge stay with him?"

"No, madam."

Blanche tapped ash off her cigarette.

"Of course, my maid was there to help him if he wanted help? She didn't leave the flat?"

"No, madam, she was there."

Blanche nodded, delighted. Here, at least, were the ingredients for a first-class row.

"Going to make something out of this, the little cow," the head porter thought to himself. "Well, let her get on with it. It'll give her something to do for a change."

"And who was this person who came to see my maid?" Blanche asked.

"He told me he was her brother," the head porter said, his fat face darkening, "but I must say I considered him an extremely undesirable young fellow. I didn't like the looks of him at all."

Blanche's smile vanished.

"Then why did you let him up?" she demanded, a rasp in her voice. "Didn't I tell you to keep an eye on that girl? Didn't I leave implicit instructions she was not to have a man in the flat? Surely you know by now that these chits of girls are no better than street walkers? Do you think I want my flat turned into a brothel in my absence?"

The head porter saw too late where his runaway tongue had led him.

"He called at nine o'clock yesterday morning, madam," he said uncomfortably. "He didn't stay more than a few minutes. If he had been longer I would have had him down. I assure you there was no time for any nonsense of that sort."

Blanche gave him a steady stare.

"You can be immoral at nine o'clock on a Sunday morning as easily as at nine o'clock on Saturday night," she said bitingly. "From what I hear it seems that these guttersnipes can misconduct themselves in a few minutes without straining their nervous systems, and as for her having a brother I simply don't believe it. You are a fool, Harris. You have always been a fool and you have every indication of remaining a fool until a grave in some forgotten churchyard claims you."

"Yes madam," the hall porter said, and bowed humbly. Blanche snapped her fingers at the under-porter who was waiting with her luggage and walked to the lift.

The under-porter gathered up the luggage, winked at the head porter who glared at him, and followed Blanche into the lift.

Sweeping into her flat like a miniature tornado, Blanche managed to reach the bell in the lounge and ring it furiously before Julie was aware that she was in the flat.

Blanche looked searchingly at Julie as she came hurrying in. Julie was pale and there were dark rings under her eyes. This was not to be wondered at since she had scarcely slept the previous night.

"Get me some brandy," Blanche ordered, "and hurry. You look thoroughly washed out."

Julie didn't say anything. She had been dreading this moment. She fetched a decanter and glass and set them on the table, then picked up Blanche's suitcase and backed to the door.

"Don't go away," Blanche said sharply. "I want to talk to you. Come here, where I can see you." She poured out the brandy, drank half a tumbler of the liquor neat, refilled her glass and lit a cigarette. "What have you been doing with yourself over the week-end?"

"Oh, nothing really, madam," Julie said, avoiding Blanche's searching eyes, "I—I tidied up. There was a little sewing . . ."

Blanche snapped her fingers impatiently.

"Never mind that," she said. "Did anyone call?"

"Oh, no, madam."

Blanche stared at her.

"You mean to tell me no one except yourself has been in the flat over the week-end?"

Julie hesitated, then said, "Yes, madam, that's right."

"How very odd," Blanche said. "The hall porter tells me your brother called on you yesterday."

"My—my brother?" Julie stammered, realized a little late that Theo probably had difficulty in getting past the head porter and, as an excuse to get upstairs, had made out he was her brother. "Oh, yes, madam. I—I forget. My brother did come to see me. He didn't stay long. I didn't let him into the flat. I hope you don't mind."

Blanche sipped her brandy. She felt that if she wasn't careful the row she was longing to stage might not materialize.

"I think you are lying," she said sharply. "I don't believe you have a brother, and I don't believe for one moment you didn't ask this man into my flat."

"I assure you, madam," Julie said, fear giving her courage, "he didn't come into the flat. He—he's got a job on a ship and only came to say good-bye."

Blanche glowered at her.

"I see," she said.

"There's no point in pursuing that," she thought. "The little slut's slippery, but I've not finished with her yet."

"So, apart from your brother, no one else has been here?" she went on, lifting her eyebrows.

"Had the hall porter told her that Wesley had been back?" Julie wondered. "Had he been off duty?" Wesley had asked her to say nothing. She stood hesitating, not knowing what to say.

"Well, speak up!" Blanche snapped.

Julie decided to risk it.

"No one else, madam."

Blanche smiled.

"Not even, Mr. Wesley, Julie?" she asked gently.

"She knows," Julie thought. "Now, what am I to do?"

But Blanche gave her no opportunity to make excuses. She flared up into a furious rage.

"So that's it, is it?" she stormed, starting out of her chair. "Of course, a blind man can't be too particular. They say all cats are grey in the dark, but I'm surprised he picked on a skivvy!"

Julie felt herself go hot and then cold. But she knew there was nothing she dare do. She had to stay in this flat now until Mrs. French told her she could leave.

"You're making a mistake . . ." she began.

"Mistake?" Blanche's voice rose to a scream. "How dare you lie to me!" She snatched up her glass of brandy and threw it at Julie. The glass whizzed past Julie's head, smashed against the wall; some of the splinters narrowly missed her. "Get out of my sight, you dirty little slut!"

Julie made a bolt for the door as Blanche looked around for something else to throw at her. She nearly collided with Wesley as he came in.

"What's going on here?" he demanded. "Blanche! What's happening?"

"I'll tell you what's happening!" Blanche stormed. "I was just telling your cheap little mistress what I thought of her!"

Julie ran from the room. But she didn't go far. As soon as she was out of sight, she paused to listen.

"You'd better control yourself, Blanche," Wesley said quietly. "You don't know what you're saying."

"I suppose you'll deny you stayed the night here with that chit?"

"I stayed here on Saturday night," Wesley returned. "Does that annoy you?"

"Then why did she say you weren't here if you two haven't been up to something?"

"Because I told her to. Knowing your grubby little mind I foolishly thought it would save a scene. But I was wrong. Now are you satisfied?"

"You cheap cad!" Blanche said furiously, and there came the sound of a blow. There was a sudden crash of breaking glass and a thud as some piece of furniture fell over.

Horrified, Julie peered into the room.

Wesley was standing motionless, his hand to his face. Blanche, livid with fury, faced him. The occasional table lay on its side surrounded by fragments of glass from a smashed vase.

"Now I hope you are satisfied," Wesley said in a strained voice.

"I'm not, you useless fool!" Blanche said, and struck him on the other side of his face with her open hand.

Julie caught her breath sharply, but neither of them heard her.

Wesley stepped back.

"That's enough, Blanche. You're drunk. Go and lie down and sleep it off. You disgust me."

"Oh! I hate you!" Blanche screamed at him. She looked wildly round the room, darted to the fireplace and snatched up the poker. There was a murderous expression in her eyes that chilled Julie. As Blanche rushed towards Wesley, brandishing the poker, Julie cried out, "Mind! She's got a poker!"

But Wesley made no move to avoid Blanche, and Julie darted forward, seized Blanche's wrist as she reached Wesley.

"Don't you dare touch him! How could you, when he's blind?" she cried.

Blanche wrenched her wrist free, gaped at Julie; her rage dying on her. Then, suddenly, she began to laugh. She turned away, dropping into an arm-chair and shook with gleeful mirth.

"Oh, Howard, it's too comic," she gasped. "The little fool actually thought I was going to hit you."

Julie was dumbfounded. She felt herself turn white and then red. She was completely bewildered by Blanche's malicious laughter.

"Oh, run away, Julie," Blanche said, giggling. "You don't have to protect him. I wouldn't hurt him for anything."

Julie gulped, backed away, and as she was leaving the room the front door bell rang.

VI

Hugh Benton handed his hat and gloves to Julie, eyed her thoughtfully.

"Mr. and Mrs. Wesley are at home, I believe," he said raising his pale eyebrows. "I'll find my way in." He entered the lounge, stood in the doorway, surveying the poker, the smashed vase and the pool of water on the carpet. His amber-coloured eyes looked quickly at Blanche.

"Why, hello, Hugh," she said gaily. "How nice of you to come. I've been losing my temper again."

"Ah, I'm sorry to hear that." Benton moved into the room cautiously. "Hello, Howard; glad to see you back. I'm sorry I wasn't in the office to welcome you. I took a long week-end at Brighton."

"They told me at the office," Wesley said stiffly. "I hope you enjoyed yourself."

"Pretty fair, thank you, pretty fair. Weather wasn't what it might have been."

"I do hope you stayed at a good hotel, Hugh, dear," Blanche said sweetly. "Those cheap little places are so horrid, I always think. No fires, no meals in bed, no butter: dreadful."

Benton winced.

"Yes, I know what you mean," he said, wandered further into the room. "Still it's difficult now: difficult times."

"For goodness' sake," Blanche said impatiently. "Where's Julie? Julie! Clear up this mess at once."

Julie came in hurriedly, began to pick up the pieces of glass.

As she worked, she was aware that Benton stared at her with inquisitive, probing eyes.

"Have a drink, Hugh," Wesley said abruptly. "I'm not going out to-night. I have work to do."

"Oh, that's a pity. I was wondering if you two would care to dine at my club," Benton said. "I'll have a whisky I think. Can I persuade you to change your mind?"

"Brandy for me, darling," Blanche said as Wesley made his way to the sideboard. "I'd love to dine at your club, Hugh, my pet. It's such a lovely, dull, stuffy old place. Do let's, Howard."

"I have work to do," Wesley returned quietly.

"Well, I'll go without you then," Blanche said. "I don't see why I should be cooped up here all day."

"Please yourself," Wesley said, brought two glasses to the middle of the room.

Blanche took the drinks from him, and gave the whisky to Benton, who caressed her fingers as she put the glass into his hand.

"Oh, well, perhaps we'll make it some other day," Benton said uneasily.

"But I want to come to your stuffy old club. Howard never goes out anywhere."

"Well, if Howard doesn't mind."

"Why should I mind?" Wesley asked, groped his way to a chair and sat down.

Julie had cleared up the broken pieces by this time and quietly left the room, but stopped abruptly just outside the open door, her heart missing a beat, when she heard Benton say, "Oh, by the way, Blanche, I've never had the opportunity of examining this marvellous safe of yours. I was reading about it in the *Standard* to-night. They say it's the eighth wonder of the world. Won't you stop being mysterious and show it to me? I assure you I'm no burglar."

Julie flattened herself against the wall and listened.

"Why, of course," Blanche said gaily. "I didn't think it would interest you. It is rather fun." She gave a hard little laugh. "I locked Julie in it the other day."

"Why did you do that?" Wesley asked sharply.

"Oh, for fun. I wanted to see how she'd react. The little ninny fainted."

"That wasn't very kind, was it?" Wesley asked. "And rather dangerous, too."

"She didn't complain," Blanche said carelessly. "I must have a little joke sometimes. If she doesn't like it she can always leave."

"I should have thought it was difficult to get maids these days," Benton said mildly. "She struck me as a willing little thing."

"Just because she happens to be pretty in a cheap, sexy way both you and Howard stick up for her," Blanche said, a waspish note in her voice. "Howard's so infatuated with her, he sneaked back last night and spent the night with her alone." There was a sudden silence, and Julie felt her face burn.

"Oh, come, Blanche." Even Benton sounded embarrassed.

"I'm not saying anything happened," Blanche said, and laughed shrilly. "Howard is past chasing girls. But Julie might have tried to chase him."

"Shall we drop this, Blanche?" Wesley's voice was sharp. "I've had quite enough of this nonsense for one day, and I don't think it's at all funny."

"Suppose we get back to the safe," Benton put in quickly, as if he saw a quarrel pending and was anxious to prevent it. "Will you let me see it? I promise not to tell anyone how it works."

"It's up to Blanche," Wesley said coldly. "We had agreed to keep the combination to ourselves."

"Oh well, if it's like that . . ."

"Nonsense," Blanche broke in. "Of course he must see it. We have no secrets from nice old Hugh, have we?"

"Show him if you want to," Wesley said impatiently.

"I feel honoured," Benton said, a tiny sneer in his voice. "May I finish my drink, and then perhaps you'll show it to me."

"We must all go along," Blanche said, and giggled, "The safe's in my bedroom and I must have a chaperon. Besides, Howard can tell you how it works."

Julie waited to hear no more. Here was her chance. She went quickly down the passage to Blanche's room. Where could she hide? She looked around for a likely hiding place. The cupboards were no use. Under the bed? Possible, but dangerous. The window recess? Yes, that was much the best place. Julie pulled back the curtains that screened the big windows, then darted back to the door to turn out the light and groped her way once more to the window, drew the curtains carefully and waited with beating heart.

After a few minutes the bedroom door opened and the light was switched on. By peering cautiously through the chink where the curtains met Julie had a clear view of the room.

Blanche and Benton stood before the quilted wall. Wesley wandered over to an arm-chair, and sat down, away from them.

"Well, this is it," Blanche said. "The safe is hidden behind this wall, which slides back when I touch this spring. It's Howard's idea. He worked the whole thing out himself. He was frightfully clever with his hands before he was blind: now, of course, he's just frightfully clever," and she gave her tinkling little laugh. The sneer made Julie flinch, and she saw Wesley's knuckles turn white. "The spring won't work," she went on, giving Benton a meaning smile, "unless a concealed pointer is set at a certain number. I'll show you the pointer."

"Have you turned off the alarm?" Wesley asked.

"Oh, no. I mustn't forget to do that." She turned to Benton. "If you touch the pointer before turning off the alarm the flat will be full of policemen before you can say Jack Robinson, or whatever it is you're supposed to say." She went over to the bed, fumbled behind the head and Julie heard a sharp click as Blanche turned down a concealed switch.

"Now the alarm is off," she said brightly, came back to where Benton was standing.

"So that's how you caught so many burglars," he said, reached out and pulled her to him. Blanche seemed startled, looked quickly at Wesley who was sitting motionless in his chair, then she smiled and lifted her face for Benton's kiss.

"The beasts!" Julie thought. "How could they when he is in the room with them?"

Blanche pushed Benton away, wagged a warning finger at him, but her face was animated and her eyes showed a naked desire that sickened Julie.

"The pointer is here," she went on, and pulled a square of the quilted wall out of its seating. Julie could just make out a small number dial set in the wall. "I turn the pointer to number three, press the catch with my foot, and the door opens."

The quilted wall had slid back to reveal the shiny steel door Julie had already seen.

"That's pretty neat," Benton said. His hand fumbled at Blanche but she pushed him away, frowning at him.

"There's another alarm fitted to the steel door," she explained. "Would you turn it off, Howard?" She turned back to Benton as Wesley got to his feet. "It's in the bathroom. Actually it looks like one of the electric light switches."

But Benton wasn't listening. He caught hold of Blanche the moment Wesley had groped his way into the bathroom. They strained together, his mouth crushed down on hers.

They stood there, their breath mingling, their eyes closed, swept away by the intenseness of their passion, and neither of them heard

Wesley return. Julie put her hands to her face. It was horrible to see him standing there and to know he was unaware of what was going on. Then Julie felt a shiver run through her as she saw Wesley's fists clench and his mouth harden into a thin line. Could he possibly hear these two, lost in their beastliness?

Suddenly Blanche realized that he had returned, and she pulled away from Benton. She was shaking and had to grip his arms for support. He looked over his shoulder at Wesley and showed his teeth in an angry, frustrated grimace.

"The alarm is off," Wesley said in cold, flat tones.

Blanche was unable to speak for a moment, then with an effort, she said, "Howard had better tell you about the burglar trap, I never could understand how it works."

Benton took out his handkerchief and dabbed his face.

"What's the burglar trap, old boy?" he asked. His voice was unsteady.

"I'll show you," Wesley said and moved towards the safe. "Will you open up, Blanche?"

Julie watched carefully. She saw Blanche turn down a switch by the side of the steel door. There was a sudden hiss of escaping air, the lights in the room flickered and the door slid back.

"Even if a burglar succeeded in getting so far, and none of them have up to now," Wesley said, "he would still be trapped if he entered the safe. There's a concealed beam of light from a lamp on one side of the wall which is projected across the safe so as to fall on a photo-electric cell fixed to the opposite wall."

Benton leaned forward and peered into the safe.

"What happens then?" he asked, looked at Blanche and raised his eyebrows. She shook her head.

"The interruption of the beam by a person walking into the safe causes a decrease in the current through the cell," Wesley went on. "This in its turn causes an increase of the grid voltage applied to a triode valve and brings into operation a series of relays which switch on the thruster for closing the door."

"That's very ingenious," Benton said. "So if I enter the safe, the door shuts and I'd be trapped, is that it?"

"Yes, and if no one let you out, you'd suffocate," Wesley told him.

"I don't think I'll try it then," Benton laughed uneasily, dabbed his face again with his handkerchief. "There's some means of controlling the door I suppose?"

"Of course. You turn out the light that falls on the cell. It's safe then."

"But is all this necessary? It seems so elaborate and must have cost a tidy sum to construct."

"It's more than a toy," Wesley said, and moved away. "I shall get the cost back eventually on the reduced insurance rates. The insurance company was very impressed with it and consequently greatly reduced their rates. The furs alone are insured for thirty thousand and then there's Blanche's jewellery."

"I hadn't thought about the insurance," Benton said. "Yes, I see. It's remarkable, and thanks for showing it to me."

"And now let's go to your stuffy old club," Blanche said. "Do join us, Howard."

"I'm sorry," he said abruptly. "I have a lot of dictation to do. But you go."

"Well, if you're sure," Benton said, exchanged glances with Blanche. "Come as you are, Blanche. You don't need to change."

Blanche took down the mink coat from its hanger, slipped it on.

"Will you close up the safe, Howard?"

"Yes," he said curtly, and waited for them to go.

Julie stepped away from the chink in the curtain and waited too, her heart pounding, terrified that Blanche would suddenly take it into her head to call her. But Blanche was too preoccupied with Benton to think of Julie.

When she heard the front door slam, Julie sighed with relief, and once again peered through the curtains. What she saw rooted her to the floor. Wesley had taken off his black-lensed glasses and was moving about the room, no longer hesitant nor groping. By the brisk way he closed the safe, she realized he wasn't blind at all. She was so startled by this discovery that she gave a half-stifled exclamation. Wesley heard her. He turned quickly, stared at the curtained recess behind which she was hiding.

Without the black-lensed glasses, which she now realised had been as effective as a mask, he was a stranger to her and his odd, glittering eyes frightened her.

"You can come out, Julie," he said quietly.

CHAPTER FOUR

I

Howard Wesley stood before the big brick fireplace in his study. Facing him, in an arm-chair, bewildered and flustered, sat Julie.

She was still dazed by the shock of discovering he could see, and she had followed him into his study, quite incapable of thinking of an excuse to explain why she had been hiding behind the curtains.

Although he appeared at ease, Wesley was strangely pale, and for some minutes neither of them said anything.

"You mustn't think I'm angry with you," Wesley said suddenly. "There's no need to be frightened."

She looked up. His eyes were compelling: dark and glittering as if all his being had come to focus in them.

"It's very important you should say nothing about my sight," he went on quietly. "For the time being no one must know I can see: not even Mrs. Wesley. I can't go into explanations, but I do want you to assure me you'll say nothing. Can I rely on you?"

She was surprised he didn't at once demand to know what she had been doing hiding behind the curtains, and at the same time she felt the return of confidence to know that he was asking her to keep a secret.

"Oh, yes," she said. "I won't say anything."

"Look at me, Julie," he went on, and as she met his eyes he smiled. "You will promise, won't you? It means success or failure in my work. That's as much as I can tell you. It's very important."

"Well, if it is so important perhaps I can make use of it in some way," she thought. "Perhaps that's why he hasn't asked me what I was doing behind the curtain."

"Yes, I promise," she said.

What was a promise anyway? She would see what was going to happen, and act accordingly.

"Thank you." He thrust his hands into his pockets. "Let's talk about you. You're in some trouble, aren't you?"

She looked away, not saying anything.

"Now look, Julie, you'd better be frank. I know more about you than you think. You're here for a purpose, aren't you?"

She felt herself change colour. How did he know that? How much did he know?

"A purpose?" she repeated blankly. "What do you mean?"

"Here, read this. It came yesterday." He took from his wallet a sheet of notepaper and handed it to hers

She stared at the writing and went cold. Hewart! Hewart writing to Wesley. The note was brief and sent the blood from her face:

Dear Sir,
Take warning, Harry Gleb is a fur thief. Julie Holland and
Gleb are friends. If you don't watch out you'll lose your furs.
A Friend.

The old beast had said he would get even. He must have been watching her.

"Is it true you and this chap Gleb are after the furs?" Wesley asked quietly.

She hesitated for a moment, then decided to tell him the truth. He wanted her to keep his secret. It wasn't likely he would do anything to her. After the way that little beast Theo had treated her, she had no compunction for giving them away. It was her only chance to be free of them.

"They made me," she burst out, and taking out her handkerchief she pretended to cry. "You don't know what they're like. They threatened me with vitriol. They hit me. I didn't want to do it."

Wesley sat down.

"Now don't get upset. Let's begin at the beginning. Who wrote this note?"

"Sam Hewart. I—I worked for him," Julie said, still hiding her face with her handkerchief. "He owns a café in Hammersmith. I knew his café was a meeting place for crooks, but I thought I'd be able to keep clear of them. I wanted the money so badly. I've never had any fun. You don't know what it's like to be poor. All my life I've had to go without things I wanted."

There was a long pause, then Wesley said, "You mustn't go on like this, you know. If I can help you, I will, but I must know all the details first. Did you meet this chap Gleb at the café?"

"Yes," Julie said, and poured out the whole sordid tale: how Harry had made love to her, how he had promised to marry her, how he got her the job as Blanche's maid, and how Theo had called at the flat.

She held nothing back.

"I know I shouldn't have come here," she concluded, dabbing her eyes, but keeping her face turned away so Wesley couldn't see she was pretending to cry. "But I swear I didn't know what they were planning to do until I saw the safe. Then when I tried to back out that awful Theo came and hit me. He threatened me with vitriol. He terrified me."

Wesley had listened to her story without interruption, and now when she had finished he lit a cigarette.

"There's nothing to worry about," he said, and smiled. "We'll find a way out of it. Now look, it's getting late. I don't know about you, but I'm hungry. Will you order supper for two to be sent up from the restaurant while I see what can be done? I want a moment of so to think about all this. You run off and get some supper. Then we'll have another talk while we eat." He got up, walked over to the cocktail cabinet. "And you're going to have a drink. There's no need to be miserable. I'm very glad you've told me the whole story. I don't think you're to blame at all." As he mixed the two drinks, he went on, "Was that Gleb who was with you when I first met you?"

Julie flushed scarlet.

"I—I didn't think you could see me," she said. "I'm so ashamed I dressed up like that."

He laughed.

"You looked very beautiful, Julie," he said and handed her the drink. "One of these days you must dress again in something nice, but this time for my benefit."

She stared at him, startled, not expecting anything like this from him.

"It was Gleb?" he went on.

"Yes."

"All right, now run along. Take your drink with you. I want to think this over. Don't be too long about supper, will you?"

Julie's mind was in a whirl as she telephoned down to the restaurant for two suppers. While she was waiting for the trays to come up, she ran to her room and put on a bright red scarf and a red belt to offset her black dress. Looking at herself in the mirror she saw a young, lovely little face that pleased her. So long as she kept her looks, she thought, there was hope for her.

Back in the kitchen she finished the cocktail, which cheered her. Things were going well. Better than she had thought possible. He had seen her looking her best in Blanche's dress and he had remembered her in it.

"One of these days you must dress again in something nice," he had said, "and this time for my benefit."

"He's interested in me," she thought. "If I'm careful and play up to him it might be possible to ask him for anything. There's nothing he couldn't do for me if he wanted to. He has loads of money, and he can get rid of that French woman and Theo. He'll know how to handle them. And there's Harry, too. I'll never forgive him for letting that beast hit me. He must have known. I'll pay him out for that! I don't need him now if I'm careful with Wesley."

When she carried in the two supper trays she found him pacing up and down, his hands clasped behind his back. She still wasn't used to seeing him without the black-lensed glasses and he made her feel nervous.

"All ready?" he said, taking one of the trays from her. "It looks good, doesn't it? You sit there where I can see you."

They sat at the table opposite each other. Under his friendly gaze she began to feel less nervous of him.

"We won't talk business until we've finished," he said. "It's not going to be so difficult as you think, but we'll go into that later. You're not going to be miserable anymore, are you?"

"No," Julie said, not feeling miserable at all. To find out his reactions, she went on. "But I shouldn't really be here. Mrs. Wesley would be furious."

She saw his face harden.

"Mrs. Wesley has no right to complain," he said sharply. "She forfeited that right by her behaviour. You saw what went on?"

"Yes," Julie said. "I thought it was dreadful."

"Then don't let's talk about her," Wesley said. "I'll get you another drink."

There was an awkward silence while he mixed more drinks, but when he came back to the table he seemed to have recovered his calm and he smiled at her.

"I'm glad this has happened, Julie. I lead a lonely life: too lonely I'm discovering. I'm enjoying this. I haven't had supper with a pretty girl for years."

Julie was a little startled; she hadn't expected him to take the initiative so soon.

"I've been thinking about what you were saying," he went on, not appearing to notice her surprise, "about not having any fun. Tell me, Julie, what. exactly is your idea of fun?"

"Being able to do the things you want to," she said promptly.

"And what do you want to do?"

Again without hesitation, she said: "Have money and nice clothes. I want to go dancing, go to the best restaurants, have a car, buy what I like. Things like that."

He laughed.

"My dear Julie, what good are those things to you now? You're living in the past. That kind of fun is over and done with. It's the simple things of life that give fun now; things like good books, a garden, going for a walk, listening to music, things like that."

"That's where you're wrong," Julie thought. To him, she said, "If I had money I'd be able to have a good time. I know I should. I know how to get the things I want."

"Well, we'll see," he said, a little mysteriously, and began to ask her questions about her life at the café, drawing her out and listening with flattering attention to her description of the people who visited the café.

By the time the meal had ended she was thoroughly at ease with him.

"All right, Julie," he said, pushing back his chair. "Let's get rid of these trays and then we'll get down to business." He glanced at the clock on the mantelpiece. "I haven't long to give you. I have a great deal of work to get through before I go to bed."

When she had taken the trays into the kitchen and returned, he motioned her to the arm-chair and stood with his back to the fireplace, looking down at her.

"There's only one thing to do. We'll have to go to the police," he told her quietly.

"Oh, no," she said, alarmed at once. "We mustn't do that."

"Because you're frightened of this gang? I can understand that, Julie, but there's no other way. We must set a trap for them. We must round them all up and then you'll be safe. We can't do that without police aid."

"But suppose they find out?" Julie said with a shiver. "Suppose Theo gets away?"

"We'll take care they don't get away, and they won't find out. See them on Wednesday and tell them how the safe opens. I'll jot down the exact operation so you'll know how it works, and you can copy it.

We must catch them red-handed. I'll see the police to-morrow. If Gleb wants you to help him in the actual robbery, you must do it. He must have no suspicion at all that we're waiting for him. You'll be all right, I'll see to that." He sounded so confident that Julie's courage stiffened.

"But if nothing happens to me they'll know I—I gave them away," she said uneasily.

"It'll be too late then for them to do anything. Now look, Julie, this is the only way to save yourself. You do see that, don't you?"

"Yes," she said reluctantly.

"All right. You carry on as if nothing has happened. See Gleb on Wednesday and try to find out when he intends to rob the safe. That is vitally important. We'll be ready for him. Do you think you'll be able to go through with it?"

"I think so," she said, thinking of Theo. Her voice lacked conviction.

He looked at her for a long moment.

"Are you wondering what's to become of you when all this is over?"

"Well, I don't know. I haven't thought. I don't know what I shall do."

"There's no need to worry," he said quietly. "I intend to do something about that if you will let me. I want to give you an opportunity to find out if your idea of fun is really what you want." He thrust his hands into his pockets and continued to look at her searchingly. "I've been married for six years, Julie. I've had no love nor tenderness during those years. I've been blind for three years. Life has been pretty drab for me, and now I have recovered my sight I'm going to change all that. You're very lovely. I'm tired of leading a life without a woman. I need someone like you. Forgive me if I'm blunt. Do you follow what I'm getting at?"

She could scarcely believe her ears, and stared at him, blood rising in her neck and face.

"I'll never marry again," he went on. "But I could give you security, your own home, and I would settle a thousand a year on you. I wouldn't bother you a great deal and I believe we could make each other happy."

She realized he was serious. A home of her own! A thousand a year! She was quick to realize what this meant. It was his price for her silence. He was offering her this to be sure she wouldn't tell anyone he could see. She was sure of that, but that made no difference to her rising excitement. For this was what she wanted; what she had longed for and hadn't thought possible. She had to control herself not to betray her astonished delight.

"Think it over, Julie," he was saying. "There's plenty of time. We have other things to do first. But I thought I would let you know what's been going on in my mind. Ever since I first saw you I have been thinking of this."

"No, he's lying," she thought. "I don't care. If he wants my silence he can pay for it."

"I—I don't know what to say . . ." she began, but he waved her to silence.

"Then don't say it. Think about it. I'll talk to you again when this is over, but I wanted you to know that if you wished I would look after you. Now run along, Julie, I have work to do."

It was a pity he was so matter-of-fact about it all. If he had only made love to her it would have been so much easier. But he was so calm, distant and cold-blooded that she felt embarrassed. It was as if he knew she knew he was buying her silence, and didn't care.

She was relieved to leave the room.

II

When Julie had recovered from the surprise of Wesley's proposal everything else became of secondary importance. Even Theo drifted into the background of her mind as an unpleasant nightmare not to be thought of—anyway, not for the time being.

Wesley wanted her to be his mistress. He wanted to buy her silence. She was quite prepared to accept the terms. She would have in return for her silence security, money, clothes, a flat of her own, even, perhaps, a car. Wasn't he enormously wealthy? Hadn't he promised to give her a thousand a year? It wasn't as if he was some horrible, fat old man who would paw her about and be jealous of her. He was marvellous. Even before he had made his suggestion she had been attracted to him.

She had to admit he was a little disappointing and undemonstrative. He scarcely spoke to her at breakfast the following morning. When Gerridge had left the room to collect some papers, he did say abruptly, "You're not worrying, are you?"

"Oh no . . . not now," she said and smiled at him, but there was no answering smile. The face, partly hidden by the black-lensed glasses was inscrutable.

"It'll be all right," he said. "I wanted to know you hadn't changed your mind," and he went from the room.

But if his attitude was disappointing there were plenty of nice things to think about. "I wonder where I shall live. He might find me a flat in Mayfair. It's marvellous how everything has turned out. Only seven months ago I was working in a tuppenny library, and now I'm to have a place of my own and a thousand a year!"

Blanche's bell shattered this day-dreaming.

"Well, it won't be much longer now," Julie thought as she went along the passage to Blanche's room. "Then I'll have a maid to wait on *me*."

Blanche was in a poisonous mood. Julie could see that the moment she entered the room.

"Get my bath," Blanche said curtly, "and don't crash about the room like an elephant. I've a splitting headache."

Julie didn't say anything. She went into the bathroom and ran the water. Returning to the bedroom, she found Blanche out of bed and pacing the floor.

"You're to leave at the end of the week," Blanche snapped. "I don't want any arguments. You're to go."

Julie could have laughed. As if she wanted to stay when a new life was waiting for her.

"Yes, madam," she said, so cheerfully that Blanche stared at her in furious astonishment.

"And if you try to make mischief you'll be sorry for it," Blanche said. "Get out of my sight!"

Sometime later, Julie heard Blanche go out and she heaved a sigh of relief. She now had the place to herself, and deciding she wouldn't do any more housework she went into the lounge, settled herself in a comfortable arm-chair, and read the newspaper.

"In a little while," she told herself, "this is going to be my usual routine. I shan't have anything to do except enjoy myself. I may as well get used to it now."

She lit a cigarette, put her feet up on another chair and made herself comfortable.

But after a while she became restless, and finally decidedly bored. She tried to interest herself in a novel she found on the occasional table nearby, but it didn't hold her for long. She put on the wireless, but the boisterous strains of a military band soon irritated her and she turned it off.

She felt lonely. The flat depressed her, and she began to wonder if the new life Wesley was offering her would be such fun after all.

"It'll be different when I have a place of my own," she thought, trying to reassure herself. "I can spend hours trying on clothes and making myself look nice. Then there'll be the shops to look at, and, of course, I needn't get up until late."

But she knew at the back of her mind that there was nothing worth looking at in the shops, and she never really cared for lying in bed once she was properly awake.

By lunch-time she was thoroughly depressed, and for the sake of something to do she settled down to clean the silver.

It was extraordinary then how quickly the time passed, and she was irritated.

"I shouldn't be doing this," she told herself. "I've got to get out of this slavish habit of working to pass the time. It's ridiculous."

Blanche returned a few minutes after five o'clock and sat in the lounge with the novel that Julie had tried to read. Hearing restless movements, Julie guessed Blanche was as bored with herself as Julie had been with herself. The novel apparently didn't hold her either.

"Perhaps I'd be happier in a job," Julie told herself. Then, realizing that this was against all her principles, she went on: "That's ridiculous, of course. I don't want a job. That's what I'm trying to escape from. It's money really. If I had money I could pass the time all right. I could go to the cinema every afternoon. There'd be dances and a musical show now and then. It's being stuck in this flat without money that bores me. I wonder where she's been to-day?"

The sound of an orchestra came floating out of the lounge and then Blanche's impatient, "Oh, damn the thing!" and the wireless was turned off.

Blanche's obvious boredom thoroughly depressed Julie.

"If she doesn't know what to do with herself with all her money," she thought, "will it be the same for me? The trouble is there isn't any fun these days. Howard was right. We do have to find a new standard of life."

She wished Wesley would return. If she could get him alone for a few minutes he might give her some proof that he was fond of her. She felt that at least would be some consolation for a depressing day. She did hope he wasn't going to continue to be so impersonal. He had been so cold-blooded about the whole business. Then there was this extraordinary secrecy about his sight. Why was he pretending that he was blind? She didn't believe that it had to do with his work. She had an uneasy feeling that there was something a little sinister about his pretended blindness and it worried her.

She became aware that Blanche was speaking on the telephone, and because she felt uneasy she went to the door and listened.

Blanche was speaking to Benton.

"I can't to-morrow night, darling," she was saying in her clear, querulous voice. "No, I have to go with Howard to that ghastly dinner at the Everitt's. And I'm so bored I could scream." She paused, then went on: "Absolutely nothing. I went to the cinema this afternoon. No, rotten, but I just didn't know what to do with myself. It's all very well for you. You have your dreary old factory. Now look, Hugh, can't you raise some money? I'm getting sick of this life. I'd get a divorce if you'd only put your beastly money affairs in order. Well, do do something. You don't expect me to go on like this much longer. You don't want to live on my money, do you? I think I'm being very reasonable. It's not as if I'm asking you to keep me; only yourself, darling. If you could do that I'd marry you like a shot." There was another long pause, then she said, "Oh, God! I've been talking with the door wide open. I suppose that little slut's been listening."

Julie quickly closed the kitchen door.

Later she heard Wesley come in, and she hurried down the passage to greet him.

"Julie?" Wesley asked as she came into the lounge. He was sitting in an arm-chair, a half-smoked cigar in his fingers. He didn't look at her and was behaving as if he were blind. This annoyed her. She felt she was entitled to more considerate treatment.

"Yes," she said shortly and came to stand before him.

"It's all right," he said, speaking softly. "The police agree you should go ahead as if nothing has happened. See these people to-morrow as arranged and tell them how the safe opens." He took a sheet of paper from his pocket and handed it to her. "Make a copy of that. It explains the whole thing. We don't want them to become suspicious. The police are anxious to catch them taking the furs away. Try to find out when they're going to break in. There's nothing for you to worry about. The police won't take action against you."

"I see," she said, and waited hopefully. She wasn't interested in the robbery. She was only interested in their future relations together. Why couldn't he talk about that?

"You're not frightened?" he asked sharply, mistaking her silence for hesitation. "You can go through with it?"

"Oh yes, of course I can," she said, then blurted out, "I—I've been thinking about what you said last night—about you and me."

He got quickly to his feet.

"Not now, Julie. Let's get this business over first. And don't say anything to Mrs. Wesley about the burglary. She is not to know. Do you understand?"

"Oh, damn the burglary," Julie thought angrily, said: "I won't tell her."

"That's right. It would be better too if we weren't found talking together. It won't be for long, Julie."

"Mrs. Wesley has told me to leave at the end of the week," she said. "Will something be done before then?"

"If you could suggest Friday to Gleb for the night it would fit in well," Wesley said. "I'll arrange for us to be out that night."

"Can't he think of anything else but this damned burglary?" Julie thought. "He's not thinking of me at all."

"I'll tell them," she said. "But what will happen to me? I'll need somewhere to go when I leave here."

He made an impatient little movement with his hand. "That'll be all right, Julie. I'll see to that. I think you'd better run along now," and he smiled.

"But there's not much time," Julie persisted. If he wasn't going to be more practical, she would have to force him to make plans. "You said I was to have a flat."

"Of course," he said, and she sensed that he was controlling his patience with an effort. "Of course you're to have a flat. We'll have to see about that, won't we?" He thought for a moment, his hands clenching and unclenching. "You have an afternoon off on Thursday? We'll meet somewhere and see what we can arrange. Now run along, Julie. I have things to do before I go out again."

It was unsatisfactory, but there was nothing else she could do. At least she had forced him—unwillingly, she could see that—to consider her for a moment. Well, she'd keep him up to it.

"All right, Howard . . ." she caught her breath, flushed. "I—I may call you Howard, I suppose?"

He had stiffened, and his black-lensed glasses were directed at her.

"Call me what you like," he said, and there was a harsh note in his voice. "Run along, Julie."

She turned at the door and looked at him.

He was motionless, his hands thrust into his trousers pockets, the light from the reading-lamp reflected in the black lenses of his glasses. There was a curious tenseness in his attitude, like a man who hears the whistle of a falling bomb and waits for the explosion.

III

Wednesday.

The morning had seemed interminable and Blanche had been particularly trying. She didn't wish to go with Wesley to the dinner that night and vented her temper on Julie.

Blanche's spite and tantrums and the thought that before long she would have to face Mrs. French made Julie jumpy, and she had a cold, sick feeling that remained with her all day.

It was a relief when Blanche left the flat for lunch. And as Julie was trying to settle down with the newspaper the telephone bell rang.

It was Harry.

"Julie? I've been trying to get you since Sunday. What's happened, kid? Every time I've rung that Wesley woman answered. I've been worried out of my mind, thinking about you. What did Theo do to you?"

Julie felt a wave of fury run through her.

"I don't want to talk to you, you coward!" she cried angrily. "You let that little swine knock me about, and you've done nothing about it. I hate you! I never want to see you again!" and she slammed down the receiver.

A moment or so later the bell began to ring again, but she didn't answer, and after a while it stopped ringing,

She was through with Harry. All right, she had loved him a little when they had first met. But now she had Howard, she wouldn't look at Harry.

She was startled to hear the front door bell ring, and wondered if Harry had come up to see her; or perhaps it was Theo. The bell rang again before she screwed up enough courage to answer the door. But it wasn't Theo; it was Detective Inspector Dawson.

"Afternoon," Dawson said gruffly and tipped his hat. "I want a word with you."

Julie turned red and then white. He was the last person she expected to see. She stood aside and he entered the hall.

"Bit of a change after the Bridge Café, isn't it?" he said, looking round. "Gone up in the world, haven't you?"

"Yes," she said in a small voice.

"Saw her Ladyship go out just now. She won't be back for a bit, will she?"

"No."

"That's all right then. Let's go somewhere where we can talk."

She took him into the lounge and again he looked round, nodding his bullet-shaped head.

"Very nice. No utility stuff here. Well, well, we can't all be so fortunate. You'd better sit down."

Julie sat down. She was glad to. Her legs felt weak.

"Mr. Wesley doesn't want his wife to know about this business. Thinks she'll be nervous. Shouldn't have thought she was the nervous type from the look of her. Is she?"

"No," Julie said. She was suddenly aware that she was twisting and untwisting her fingers, and hurriedly folded her hands in her lap.

"Funny things—husbands," Dawson said shaking his head. "Or does he think she'll take it out of you?"

Julie stared. What was he getting at?

"I—I don't know what you mean."

His cold blue eyes studied her face.

"Never mind," he said a little abruptly. "Now let's have the story. Mr. Wesley told us more or less about you, but I thought I'd like to have it direct. Got friendly with Harry Gleb all of a sudden, haven't you? The last time I asked you about him you didn't know him."

Julie again changed colour.

"I—I only got to know him—after you—" she stopped.

"Did you? All right, we'll let that go. It doesn't matter. I warned you to be careful of him, didn't I? You showed some good sense in telling Wesley. We'd've got them sooner or later and we'd've got you too."

Julie didn't say anything. She was badly scared, realizing the escape she had had.

"Well, let's start from the time you became friendly with Gleb," Dawson went on. "Go on from there. I want all the facts. Don't keep anything back."

It was one thing to tell Wesley but quite something else to talk to the police. Julie hadn't worked at the Bridge Café for over six months for nothing. She knew what happened to squealers.

"It doesn't pay to talk," Hewart had warned her. ". . . they found her in a back alley . . ."

But it was too late now. She would have to go through with it, and reluctantly she told Dawson what she had already told Wesley.

It wasn't easy. Dawson watched her the whole time. He didn't interrupt, but his eyes were coldly unsympathetic, and she felt he was making mental notes and would check up every detail of her story.

When she came to Theo, he thawed a little.

"Now he is a nice lad," he said, with a wintry smile. "We'll have to keep our eye on him. He got six months for bashing a girl a couple of years ago, and we nearly nabbed him for a vitriol job last summer, only his alibi was too good and the fool girl hadn't the pluck to pick him in the parade. Yes, we'll have to watch out for Theo—you watch out, too."

Julie shivered.

"We've had our eye on Ma French, too," Dawson went on. "She's no fool either. That's a smart idea to run a domestic agency. It gives her an in to a lot of rich folks' houses. But this is the first time she's used a plant. You watch her and see you don't slip up. One mistake and she'll smell a rat. You're seeing them to-night?"

Julie nodded.

"All right. I'll have a man outside her place. If there's any trouble throw something through the window: your bag or something," Dawson said. "You're playing with fire, young lady. I don't want to frighten you, but if that mob thought you were selling them out they'd be very nasty."

"I know," Julie said.

"We don't want any mistakes. If we can catch 'em carrying the furs out it'll make a nice clean job of it. Let's have a look at the safe. You can have a dress rehearsal just to make sure you can open it. You can bet your last penny they'll want you to be there when they crack the job."

Julie took him into Blanche's bedroom.

"Wouldn't Mrs. Dawson be tickled to have a room like this," Dawson said, looking round. "How does Wesley get on with his wife?" The question was shot at Julie and she became aware that Dawson was watching her closely.

"He's getting at something," she thought. "I'll have to be careful."

"All right, I suppose," she said. "Perhaps you'd better ask him."

Dawson stroked his long nose.

"Shouldn't think he'd tell me," he said with a dry smile. "He didn't strike me as a friendly individual. Where's the safe?"

Julie showed him.

"Let's see you open it. Don't forget to turn off the alarms. I don't want my people coming over here for nothing."

Julie found the switch behind the head of the bed and turned it off. She went into the bathroom and turned off both switches on the wall. It took her a minute or so to find the square in the quilted wall that hid the dial and pointer. She set the pointer to number three, pressed the catch and opened the first door.

"That's pretty good," Dawson said. "What happens next?"

Julie opened the steel door by pressing the switch, turned off the light that fell on the photo-electric cell and stood back.

"That's how it's done," she said, rather pleased with herself.

Dawson eyed the furs and whistled.

"A beautiful haul," he said. "All right. That's smooth enough. Close up."

Julie shut the safe, turned on the alarms and followed him back to the lounge.

"We want to find out when they'll make the raid," Dawson told her. "If you're careful there'll be nothing to worry about. But keep your eye on Theo. Gleb's a smooth, smart alec, but Theo's dangerous."

"I know," Julie said.

Dawson eyed her thoughtfully.

"And when this little party's over, what are you going to do? Get into more trouble?"

Julie stiffened.

"I'm not," she said coldly.

"That's good." The blue eyes were searching. "Is Mr. Wesley going to do something for you? He seems interested in you."

"I have no idea. I don't have to worry. I can always find myself a job."

"Well, that's something, isn't it? You haven't done so well up to now, but perhaps you've learned sense. Let's hope so. You might not have a rich gentleman to champion you next time, young lady, so watch your step."

He opened the front door and went off down the passage.

IV

"She should be here in a minute," Mrs. French said, with an impatient glance at the clock. "Theo's watching her. I don't think there'll be trouble."

Harry Gleb picked his teeth with a pin. There was a worried look in his eyes although he took pains to appear at ease.

"I don't like Theo," he said. "One of these days you'll be sorry you took him on."

Mrs. French gave an impatient grunt.

"What's the matter with him? You're always on about him. I'm sick and tired of hearing you grouse."

Harry eyed her, put the pin back in his coat lapel, sat forward.

"He's unreliable," he said, tapping the desk with a manicured nail. "He's dangerous. He's like a rat: corner him and he'll bite."

"He's too smart to be cornered."

Harry laughed.

"Theo—smart? Don't make me laugh. His brain is fossilized. All he thinks about is bashing his way out of trouble. One of these days he's going to do murder, and I don't want to be with him when he does it."

"You talk like an old woman," Mrs. French said coldly. "Theo's all right."

"A bloke who throws vitriol is never all right," Harry said. "He did six months for bashing a girl, didn't he? The cops have his fingerprints. If he makes one slip he's had it; and if the cops sweat him he'll squeal. Then what will you and me do?"

"I'm not worrying about him; I'm worrying about that Holland girl. She'll squeal if we don't watch her."

Harry rubbed his face, frowned.

"I'm getting out of this game after this job, Ma," he said. "It's getting too hot. I think I'll slip over to the States and have a look round. Let things cool off here."

"What's the matter with you?" Mrs. French asked sharply. "Getting cold feet or something?"

"Shouldn't be surprised," Harry said frankly. "I've had a good run. I've got a bit salted away and this job isn't going to be for peanuts. Might as well enjoy myself while I can."

"You haven't done the job yet," Mrs. French reminded him.

The office door pushed open and Dana came in.

"Hasn't she come?" she asked, running her slim fingers through Harry's hair. "Hello, Harry, remember me?"

He jerked his head away irritably.

"Cut it out," he said, took out a comb and tidied his hair.

She looked at him, glanced over at her mother who pursed her lips.

"Harry's quitting after this job," Mrs. French said. "Wants to go to America."

"So do I," Dana said. "We'll go together, won't we Harry?"

He gave her a shifty look, smiled.

"It might be an idea," he said, without conviction. "But I haven't made up my mind yet."

A timid tap sounded on the outer door.

"That's her," Dana said, her lips tightening. "I'll go."

She found Julie waiting in the dark passage.

"Come in," Dana said. "You're late, aren't you?"

"Am I?" Julie said curtly, "I don't know." Her heart was hammering and her throat was dry, but she had control of herself and apart from a steadily beating vein in her temple she looked calm and at ease.

"Hello, Jane," said a sneering voice behind her, and she flinched, looked quickly over her shoulder.

Theo materialized out of the darkness.

"Been trailing you all the evening, just in case you changed your mind," he said. His bad, stale breath fanned her face, and she shuddered.

"Come in," Dana said sharply. She disliked Theo, and wished her mother didn't employ him.

She led the way into the inner office. Theo trod on Julie's heels as he followed her.

"I bet you've been dreaming of me, Jane," he said, grinning. "Nice little nightmares that made you sweat."

Harry kicked back his chair and stood up.

"Shut your trap, you half-grown monkey," he said. "Who told you to talk?"

Theo eyed him evilly, slouched to a chair and sat down.

"You'd better tell this bloke to lay off me," he said to Mrs. French. "I'm getting tired of him."

"Hello, Julie," Harry said with a nervous smile. "Come and sit down near me."

Julie gave him a look of contempt and turned her back on him.

Theo sniggered.

"That's pretty good. Give her a kick in the tail," he said.

"Shut up, both of you," Mrs. French snapped. "Here, you," this to Julie, "Sit down. Have you found out how the safe opens?"

Julie faced her.

"Yes," she said.

"Pity," Theo said. "I was looking forward to do you, Jane."

Harry made a move to get up again, but Mrs. French waved impatiently at him.

"All right, sit down and tell us," Mrs. French said.

Julie pulled up a chair away from Harry and sat down.

"I took notes. You'd better read them," she said.

Theo leaned forward.

"They'd better be all right," he said. "You try any tricks, Jane, and you'll be sorry."

Julie recoiled before his vicious scowl.

Harry hit Theo across his mouth with the back of his hand. Theo and his chair went over backwards. For a second or so he lay sprawled on the floor, stunned. Then he began to swear, his face vicious with rage. His hand went to his hip pocket and he dragged out a small automatic pistol. But Harry was ready for that. He kicked the gun out of Theo's hand, picked it up and put it on the table.

"I warned you," he said, glaring down at Theo. "When I say shut up, I mean shut up. And don't try to pull a gun on me again, you cheap little gangster."

Theo got slowly to his feet. There was a look in his eyes that frightened Julie. He touched his nose and mouth with the back of his hand, then slouched over to the settee under the window and stretched out on it. His silence was more chilling than a display of temper.

Mrs. French glanced at him, picked up the gun and put it in her bag.

"How many times have I to tell you not to carry guns?" she demanded. Her bright eyes revealed her rage. "Are you carrying a gun, Harry?"

"Not likely," Harry said, still glaring at Theo. "I'm not a kid like wet-ears over there. I've never carried a gun and I never will. I'm not soft in the head."

Mrs. French grunted.

"I'll talk to you later," she said to Theo.

Theo pursed his lips but said nothing. He stared up at the ceiling, hate in his eyes.

Julie watched all this with fascinated horror. The sight of the gun had turned her cold.

"All right," Mrs. French said. "Let's get down to business. Where's this paper of yours?"

Julie produced a sheet of paper covered with her neat writing and put it on the desk.

Mrs. French read it through and Harry stood behind her, reading over her shoulder.

"Two alarms," Harry said, and whistled. "They're not taking any chances. I said I thought it was a photo-electric cell. This is fine; just what we want."

Mrs. French looked searchingly at Julie. "And you're sure you can open it?"

Julie nodded.

"How did you find out all this?"

"Mrs. Wesley gave a demonstration to a friend of hers. I was hiding in the room," Julie said.

"Good for you," Harry said and smiled at her, but she looked away. She knew he was trying to be friendly, but she hated him and there was nothing he could do now that would change her feelings towards him.

"All right," Mrs. French said, and laid down the paper. "Now we can make a start. To-day's Wednesday. I'll be ready by the week-end. What are they doing on Saturday? Do you know?"

"I'm leaving on Saturday," Julie said. "Mrs. Wesley has given me notice."

They all looked at her; even Theo raised his head and stared with intent concentration at her.

"Why?" Mrs. French demanded.

"She doesn't like me," Julie said. "It wasn't any particular thing I did."

"You've got to be there when we do the job," Mrs. French said. "You're in this up to the neck. Friday, then."

"Why can't you leave me alone?" Julie said, thinking it would be wiser to put on a show of reluctance. "I've told you how the safe opens. I won't do any more."

"You'll do what I tell you. You can't get out of it now, so you may as well make the best of it. We'll take care of you. Harry will tie you up before he leaves. So long as you keep your head they can't pin anything on you. You'll get your share. It'll be worth five hundred to you. When the police question you, tell them three men came to the front door, grabbed you and tied you up. You didn't get a chance to see what they looked like, except they wore dark overcoats and slouch hats. Make up your own description. You're no fool, and stick to your story. Do you understand?"

"Yes," Julie said sullenly.

"All right." Mrs. French turned her attention to Harry. "Your job is to work with Julie, take the furs and put them in the service lift. Theo will be in the basement to receive them. There's room for a car in the back alley. It's only a step from the basement to the alley. As soon as you've sent the furs down, take the jewellery, tie Julie up and take the staff lift to the ground floor. We can go into the details about the exact time later." She shot Julie a hard look. "Think the Wesleys will be out on Friday?"

"I know they will," Julie said. "I heard them talking. They're going to dinner and a theatre."

"All right," Mrs. French said, looked across at Harry. "It's fixed for Friday at eight o'clock."

Harry nodded.

"Suits me," he said, but there was a lurking uneasiness in his eyes.

"Any questions?" Mrs. French asked.

"I don't like leaving Julie in the flat when the job's done," Harry said. "You know what the police are. They'll smell it's an inside job. Think she'll stand up to them?"

"If she keeps her head it'll be all right," Mrs. French said shortly. "There's no other way."

"But if she doesn't?" Harry persisted. "Suppose she loses her nerve and talks. That'll let us out."

Theo suddenly sat up.

"She won't lose her nerve," he said. "That's the last thing she'll lose," and he began to laugh. The high-pitched, cracked laugh was vicious and degenerate.

"Shut up, you fool!" Mrs. French shouted, thumping the table.

Theo stopped laughing and looked across at Julie.

"What's so funny?" Harry demanded, glaring at him.

"You'll see," Theo returned, looked again at Julie.

"Shut up," Mrs. French repeated, turned to Harry. "Don't pay any attention to him. He's stupid to-night. We'll have to take a chance on Julie keeping her head. We can't take her with us. They'll find us through her if we do."

Harry got to his feet.

"All right," he said, but he wasn't happy. "How do you feel about this; Julie? Think you can go through with it?"

"You don't have to worry about me all of a sudden," Julie snapped. "You were quick enough to drag me into this. Why the sudden concern?"

"If that's how you feel," he said, flushing. He turned away. "Anything else?"

"There are other details but we can fix them up between now and Friday. The main thing's settled," Mrs. French said. "Friday at eight o'clock."

"I'll be running along then," Harry said, and moved to the door.

"I'll come with you," Dana said, pushing back her chair.

"I've got to see a man," Harry said, shaking his head. "Sorry. Good night all," and he went out.

Julie felt a little thrill of delight that Harry should have snubbed Dana like this. Not that she cared, she told herself, she was through with a cheap crook like Harry. But it was nice to see Dana put in her place.

She got up.

"I can go now, I suppose?"

Mrs. French nodded.

"And Julie, watch your step. If you try anything smart you'll be sorry. Theo's watching you."

Julie went out of the room without a glance at either Dana or Theo. Her heart was pounding, but she was triumphant. She had found out when they were going to attempt the robbery. Now there was nothing else for her to do but to wait. The responsibility had shifted from her to the police.

She walked quickly along the deserted street, crossed New Bond Street and made her way towards Berkeley Square.

Suddenly she became aware of footsteps behind her and she looked hastily round.

Harry came out of the shadows, took her elbow and moved along at her side. She tried to shake him off, but he retained his grip.

"Now don't be mad with me, kid," he said. "It wasn't my fault. I know that rat Theo had a go at you, but I found out too late to stop him."

She wrenched her arm free, faced him.

"Get away from me!" she said furiously. "I don't want to have anything more to do with you."

He shuffled his feet uncomfortably.

"Don't go on like that, Julie," he said. "I've been thinking about you. Look, kid, let's get this job over and then let's go to the States. I'm sick of this life. I've been thinking a lot recently. Why shouldn't you and me hook up? Come on, give me a smile, and say you'll come with me!"

She eyed him up and down and nearly laughed. The idea of her marrying this cheap spiv, she thought, when she was going to have a West End flat and a thousand a year of her own! She wouldn't marry him now if he were the last man on earth.

"Get away from me!" she repeated. "I hate you. You're nothing but a cheap crook," and she turned on her heel and walked quickly down the street.

He came after her and jerked her round.

"What's the matter, Julie? You love me, don't you? We mean something to each other. I'm sorry, kid. I know I've got you into this mess, but I'll make up for it."

"Leave me alone! How many more times have to tell you I never want to see you again?"

He stared at her, refusing to believe her.

"Don't you want to go to the States?" he asked persuasively. "I'll give you all the fun in the world. Come on, kid, give me a kiss and let's make it up."

He reached for her, and stung to anger by his supreme confidence in himself, Julie slapped his face.

"And now leave me alone!" she cried, and turning, she ran down the dark street.

Harry stood still, his band to his face, a blank, hurt look in his eyes. No woman had ever treated him like this before. It was a shock to him; a shock to his pride. He drew in a deep breath. Well, he wasn't going to take no for an answer. He would do everything in his power to win her back. No other woman he had known had been able to resist him; Julie wasn't going to be the exception. He loved her. When the job was over, and she was away from that flat, she'd be more reasonable, he told himself. It was living in luxurious surroundings that had gone to her head. She'd be all right when she had a place of her own again. She'd want to go to the States with him after a week or so of that.

He shoved his hands deep into his coat pockets and walked quickly away into the darkness.

Theo, who had been watching all this from a shop doorway, leaned forward and spat in the gutter.

CHAPTER FIVE

I

From the moment she had met Wesley in the lobby of the Piccadilly Hotel, Julie had been acutely uncomfortable. And she had been so looking forward to this outing. Up to the moment of meeting him the afternoon had promised well. She was excited and was wearing her smartest outfit. She had had the excitement of making sure Theo wasn't following her; and, dodging from bus to taxi had added spice to what she imagined was going to be a thrilling afternoon. But she had not anticipated how embarrassing it would be to go out with a man who appeared blind. It wouldn't have been so bad if Wesley had been blind, but knowing he was pretending she was embarrassed by the way people looked at him, made way for him and even offered to help him. There had been a long queue for a taxi outside the hotel, but immediately Wesley appeared, his hand on Julie's arm, the commissionaire had insisted he should go to the head of the queue, and no one in the queue had raised an objection.

It seemed to Julie, who was a little superstitious, that it was wicked of Wesley to act in this way. She had an uneasy feeling that God would suddenly rise up in wrath and strike him blind to teach him a lesson.

As the taxi drew away, Wesley seemed to sense her embarrassment, and smiling said: "Poor Julie; I'm afraid you're very uncomfortable. But don't worry, you'll get used to it."

"But must you do it?" she asked angrily. "Isn't it unfair?"

"When you play a part, Julie, you must be thorough," he returned, a sudden sharp note in his voice. "If we are to get along together you must accept me as you find me."

Nothing further was said until the taxi driver drew up outside Fowler & Freebody, Estate Agents, in Duke Street.

Mr. Fowler appeared in person and took them into his office.

Wesley explained what he wanted, and Julie caught Mr. Fowler's startled glance. She saw at once he guessed what was in the wind, and hated him for the shocked expression that jumped into his eyes. But he produced particulars of two flats that he thought might possibly suit. One of them was in Berkeley Square and the other in Vigo Street.

They took a taxi and saw both flats. Julie immediately fell in love with the Vigo Street flat. The bedroom, Julie thought, was too elegant for words. There were silver stars painted on the dark blue ceiling and a pink-tinted mirror covered the whole of one of the long walls.

Wesley stood quietly by the door while Julie examined the room. They were alone and he had taken off his glasses. There was a cynical expression in his eyes as he watched her run excitedly backwards and forwards, through to the bathroom that delighted her and back to the bedroom again.

"I think it's marvellous," she exclaimed. "Much better than that stuffy old place in Berkeley Square."

"So long as you're pleased, Julie. But I think this is cheap and ghastly," Wesley said, shrugging. "It's a tart's place, Julie."

"I don't care!" she snapped, reddening. "I want it."

He studied her for a moment, then shrugged.

"All right, Julie, if you want it, have it."

She was angry with him now. He had taken the gilt off the gingerbread by his criticism. A tart's place! What did he know about tarts! It was lovely. The stars on the ceiling were marvellous. Lying in bed, she could imagine she was looking at the sky. Well, he wasn't going to spoil her pleasure. She had to live in it. If he didn't like it, he could stay away.

"Yes, I want it," she said.

"Then we'll go back to the agents and fix it up."

When they had left the estate agents, Wesley gave her the front door key.

"There you are, Julie. The key to your new home. I hope you will be very happy there."

She took the key without a word of thanks. She was still angry with him.

"Now I suppose I'd better get you some clothes," he told her. "Those days are over for you. No more Bridge Cafés, Harry Glebs or the Black Market for you. You understand that, don't you?"

"I suppose so," she said reluctantly. He was right. She would never again be able to meet any of the old gang. Sooner or later the word would get around that she had talked. They wouldn't want her once they knew that.

He bought her clothes that astonished her. They were severe and plain and beautifully tailored. She didn't like them, wanting something flamboyant, like the lovely clothes Blanche wore, but Wesley didn't even consult her, and she had to admit when she studied herself in the mirror that she looked awfully smart and sophisticated. Wesley's approving nod, when the fitter had gone from the room, pleased her.

But when he bought her a mink coat her rapture knew no bounds, and she immediately forgave him for his criticism of the flat. She wanted to wear it at once, but he gave instructions for the clothes and the coat to be sent on Saturday afternoon to the Vigo Street flat.

"It'll be something for you to look forward to," he said as they left the building. "And now I must get back to the factory, I hope you had a nice afternoon, Julie."

The gift of the mink coat had so thrilled her that she wanted to be nice to him. She was well aware that when a man gave a girl a costly present like that he expected payment, and she was ready to give payment.

"Wouldn't you like to come back to my flat, Howard?" she asked, and gave him an inviting look.

He gave her a quick, startled glance, smiling uneasily and patted her arm.

"Not now, Julie. I must get back to work. Good-bye," and he climbed quickly into the waiting taxi, which drove away, leaving her staring after it.

"The damned stuffed shirt," she thought angrily. "All right, if he doesn't want me, I don't care. I won't be so free next time. When he's in the mood, I won't be."

The plain-clothes detective, who had patiently followed them all the afternoon, was relieved to see Wesley go. The afternoon had been an exhausting one, and he was anxious to return to headquarters and make his report.

"Now I wonder what his little game is," he said to himself as he set off after Julie. "Looks as if he's setting her up in a love nest." He studied Julie's slim legs as she hurried along in front of him and sighed. "Can't say I blame him. For a blind man, he's certainly picked himself a nice piece."

Julie, unaware she was being followed, headed for Piccadilly. The evening was before her. She felt in the mood to celebrate.

II

You could get a drink at the Harlequin Club at any hour of the day or night if you didn't object to paying treble the usual price for it.

Harry Gleb had just come from Mrs. French's office and he felt in need of a drink. The final details of the robbery had been arranged and he had left Mrs. French and Theo together to discuss the type of car to be used. The more Harry thought about the coming robbery the less he liked it.

"I've got cold feet," he thought, as he climbed the stairs that led to the club. "That's what's wrong with me. Well, this is the last job I'll pull; anyway, for some time. I've had about enough of it."

He entered the gaudy little lounge, nodded to the gimlet-eyed doorkeeper and went straight to the bar. At this hour—it was a few minutes past four-thirty—there were in the bar only tarts sitting on stools, sipping whisky, and an elderly man in a corner, reading the evening paper, a plain gin on the table before him.

The barman brightened when he saw Harry. He was bored with talking to the tarts, and hoped Harry would be more entertaining. But Harry wasn't in a talkative mood. He ordered a double whisky, grunted when the barman tried to engage him in conversation, and moved away from the bar to sit in solitude at a table by the window.

He was thinking of Julie. All night he had thought of her, and a sleepless night didn't agree with him. He wanted her; wanted her as he had never wanted any other woman before.

"I was a mug to have mixed her up in this business," he told himself. "If I'd've kept her clear of it there'd've been no trouble with her. And as soon as I'd picked up the dough we could have hopped on a boat and started a nice little honeymoon in the States. Now, I've got my work cut out to win her round. Don't see how I'm going to do it. We're doing the job to-morrow, and I'll have to keep clear of her from then on. The cops'll be watching her night and day." He sipped his whisky and brooded. "All very well for Ma French to say leave her in the flat. But it's cock-eyed, that's what it is; cock-eyed. The thing to do is to take her with me; hide with her somewhere until things cool off a bit, and then slip out of the country." He frowned out of the window.

"But will she come with me? If she doesn't, what's she going to do?" He finished his whisky and was about to order another when he remembered that to-day was Julie's afternoon off. "Now I wonder what she's up to," he thought. "Mooching round the West End looking at the shops, I'll bet a dollar. Maybe I'll run into her if I have a look round." He pushed back his chair and stood up. "That's what I'll do. I'll have a look for her. Maybe I can persuade her to see reason."

Nodding to the barman, he left the club and, reaching Piccadilly, began to walk slowly towards Park Lane. He walked as far as Hyde Park Corner, then retraced his steps. As he was passing the Berkeley Hotel he spotted her across the street, walking towards the Circus.

"That's what I call a real bit of luck," he said to himself. "I knew she'd be around here somewhere. Pretty kid; looks as smart as paint." He grinned to himself, aware of a surge of excitement going through him. "Blimey!" he thought. "I've got it bad. Wouldn't have thought I'd ever chase after a bride like this; shows what love can do to a fella."

He darted across the road as soon as the traffic began to slow down for the traffic lights, and hurried along behind Julie. The plain-clothes detective, who was tiring rapidly of following Julie, recognized Harry and whistled softly.

"Now where did he spring from and what's he want?" he wondered and dropped behind, letting Harry go on ahead of him.

Harry was too intent on pursuing Julie to notice the detective. He overtook Julie as she waited to cross the Circus.

"Hello, kid," he said, raising his hats "I want to talk to you. There's been a change of plan."

Julie started, looked angrily at him.

"Well, I don't want to talk to you," she snapped. "Go away."

"Don't be daft," Harry returned, taking her arm. "This is business. Come on, I've got to talk to you. There's a club round the corner where we won't be disturbed."

Julie hesitated. If Mrs. French had decided to postpone the attempt she would have to warn Wesley.

"Oh, all right then," she said crossly, and went with him along Regent Street.

Neither of them said anything further. Julie didn't want to talk to him. Meeting him had spoilt her plans for the evening. She had decided to go to a cinema and have supper down West before returning to Park Way. She didn't want company. She wanted to dream about her new home and her mink coat.

When they entered the Harlequin Club, which was empty now, Harry asked her what she would like to drink.

"Nothing," she said shortly, and sat down at a corner table. "I don't want anything from you."

He pulled a face, went over to the bar and ordered a double whisky which he brought to the table.

"Julie, you're not still mad with me, are you?" he asked, sitting down opposite her. "I'm sorry this business ever started, but we can't back out now."

She made an impatient movement.

"You said you wanted to talk business. Say what you want to say and let me go."

He studied her and, seeing the cold, unfriendly look in her eyes, realized she didn't love him anymore. The discovery deflated him.

"It's about leaving you at the flat when the job's done," he said uneasily. "I don't like it, kid. It's not safe. I want you to come away with me. We'll hide up somewhere and then hop a boat to the States."

She stared at him as though she thought he were mad.

"I'm not frightened of being left," she said sharply. "And I'm certainly not going with you. I told you last night, I don't want anything more to do with you."

"Now look, Julie," he said, shifting forward on his seat. "I've got you into this mess. I want to get you out of it. I'm crazy about you, kid. Honest; I wouldn't be crawling like this if I wasn't serious. I love you. I'd do anything for you. If I leave you in the flat the cops will be all over you. They'll pin something on you when they know you worked for Hewart. Even if they don't, what are you going to do? You can't live on three quid a week. Come with me and I'll give you a smashing time. Look, I'm sick of this life. I only want a bit more money and I'll be in the clear. After this job, I'm through. I'm going straight and I want you with me. Honest, Julie, I love you so much I can't live without you."

It wasn't what he said, but the way he said it that impressed her; and suddenly she turned sick and cold because she realized something she had refused to realize before. She had once loved him; had given herself to him; and now she was planning to betray him to the police. While she had been frightened it had seemed completely unreal: planning something that wouldn't happen. But now, seeing him before her, hearing him say he loved her and knowing that before long he would be in the hands of the police brought the facts home to her like a blow in the face. For a brief moment she nearly blurted out the truth; nearly told him she had given him away to the police, but the thought of Theo stopped her. There was no turning back. If she admitted that she had told the police, Theo would come after her. There would be no safety for her now until the whole gang was under lock and key.

"No!" she said wildly. "I wouldn't ever go with you. But, Harry, I'm warning you; don't do it. Go away before it's too late. You won't get away with it. I know you won't. Please—please don't go through with it!" And before he could stop her she had jumped to her feet and darted to the door.

Harry stared after her, a cold tingle going up his spine. Then he kicked back his chair and rushed after her. He caught her on the stairs and grabbed hold of her.

"Julie! What do you mean? What do you know?"

She tried to wrench herself free, but he pulled her round so he could look into her eyes.

"You haven't talked, have you?" he demanded, shaking her. "You haven't squealed?"

"Oh, no," she gasped, suddenly frightened of him. "It's just. I—I'm scared. It's too dangerous. I feel it won't come off." Then, as his suspicious eyes searched her face, she exclaimed, "Let go of me! Do you hear? Let me go!"

"Hey, miss, is this fella annoying you?" asked a hard voice from the bottom of the stairs.

They looked into the lobby. A big man in a slouch hat and raincoat was looking up at them. Harry recognized him as a plain-clothes man from Savile Row station and he hurriedly released Julie.

"It's all right," Julie said, scared. She ran down the stairs, passed the detective and on into the street.

"Watch it, fella," the detective said to Harry. "Or you and me'll take a little walk."

Harry said, "I'll watch it," and went back into the club.

III

While Harry was trying to persuade Julie that he loved her, Mrs. French was discussing the last details of the robbery with Theo. She was sitting at her desk by the window. The waning sunlight reflected on her ear-rings, making dancing patterns on her blotter.

Theo sprawled in the arm-chair facing her, his furry hat crushed down over his ears. He never seemed conscious of his looks. It didn't cross his mind that he could improve his appearance if he made an effort. He seemed to go out of his way to make himself look as moronic and hideous as he could. Sitting there, his ears bent down under the hat, a long greasy strand of hair across his eyes, a sullen, hateful expression on his fat, spotty face, he looked like an exaggerated cartoon of a gangster.

Mrs. French had already arranged about what car should be used for the robbery, and now a sudden silence fell between them. Mrs. French brooded out of the window, a cold look in her eyes. Theo picked his nose, twisting his mouth out of shape as he dug a dirty fingernail into his nostril.

"There's nothing else, is there?" Mrs. French asked suddenly without looking round.

Theo grinned to himself.

"There's the girl—Julie Whatshername," he said, and stretched his legs out and regarded his dusty shoes thoughtfully. "Harry's soft on her."

"I wonder if she'll talk." Mrs. French said as if she were thinking aloud. "This is a big job. It'll be worth eight thousand apiece. If she talks . . ."

"You're not going over all that again, are you?" Theo asked sharply. "I said I'd fix her: I will."

Mrs. French watched a car draw away from the kerb opposite. The girl who was driving had a cigarette-holder nearly a foot long clenched between her teeth. Mrs. French thought she looked ridiculous.

"But now Harry's gone soft on her I'll need help," Theo went on.

Mrs. French turned her head, surveyed him with bleak eyes.

"What kind of help?"

"The way I figure it," Theo said, "is like this." As he spoke, he undid his waistcoat, pushed his hand through the opening of his shirt and scratched his ribs viciously. "Harry pulls the job and sends the furs down to me by the service lift. Then he ties the girl up and leaves her. He comes down the front way with the sparklers. I'll put the furs in the car, but Dana must do the driving. It's a three-handed job now, see?"

Mrs. French saw all right, but she made out she didn't.

"I don't want Dana mixed up in this," she said brusquely. "You've always driven before."

Theo stared at her.

"What's the matter with you?" he demanded crossly. "I've got to look after the girl, haven't I?" His nails clawed at his ribs again.

"And just how are you going to look after her?" Mrs. French inquired.

"I'll come up the service lift, wait until Harry gets out, go in there, untie her and shove her in the safe. When they find her they'll think she got trapped like it says in that paper she gave us."

Mrs. French continued to look out of the window. "That's murder, Theo," she said, as if to herself.

Theo picked his nose.

"It'll be an accident," he said after a little thought. "Anyway, that's how it'll look."

"I'm not saying it isn't a good idea," Mrs. French said. "I think it's smart. There isn't any other way we can be sure she won't talk. But I don't stand for murder, Theo."

Theo wasn't impressed. He took off his wreck of a hat, peered into it, found a crumpled packet of Player's Weights inside, selected one that was less greasy than the others, lit it, put his hat on again.

"I want to spend some of that dough," he said, blowing a long stream of smoke down his nostrils. "Like you said, if she talks I won't 'ave a fat lot of time for spending: nor will you or Dana."

"Or Harry," Mrs. French said generously.

"I don't care a lot what happens to Harry," Theo said. "I'd like to get even with that — —"

Mrs. French flinched.

"I won't listen to such language. You ought to be ashamed of yourself."

"Oh, I am," Theo said, and began to scratch himself again. There was another long pause, then Mrs. French said: "He's going to the States, anyway."

Theo sneered.

"Can't you get your mind oft Harry? We're talking about the girl."

Mrs. French shook her head.

"I don't want to know anything about her. I don't stand for murder."

Theo eyed her a little doubtfully. He wasn't quite sure if she were serious or not.

"Don't I keep telling you it'll be an accident?" he persisted, swore under his breath as his skin began to irritate again.

"I don't want to talk about it," Mrs. French said shortly, added after a pause: "You'll have a bigger share than Harry and Dana. Another fifteen hundred."

Theo brightened and grinned to himself.

"Make it two thou while you're about it. It's worth that."

"Fifteen hundred," Mrs. French said obstinately. "I've got to explain to Harry."

"No you 'aven't. We'll make the new split after I've done the job. He can't object then: it'll be too late."

"All right; two thousand," Mrs. French said.

Theo nodded.

"And Dana to drive?"

"I don't see why you can't drive," Mrs. French avoided Theo's eyes. "But if you say you can't I suppose Dana will have to do it."

"What are you going round the point for? We've got no witnesses. You want me to do it, don't you?"

"I said it was a smart idea," Mrs. French said cautiously. "I said it seemed to me it was the only way to stop her talking, but I also said I didn't stand for murder. Let's drop it, Theo."

"I still get the two thousand and Dana drives?"

Mrs. French nodded.

"All right," Theo said, getting to his feet. "You drop it. I'll think about it."

When he had gone, Mrs. French sat for a long time, staring out of the window. Then Dana came in.

"All alone?" she asked. "Theo gone?"

Mrs. French grunted.

"Got it fixed?" Dana went on, looking at her mother with questioning eyes.

"Everything," Mrs. French said abruptly.

"That Holland girl worries me," Dana said, sitting on the edge of her mother's desk. She massaged the red mark where her garter had bitten into her flesh above her knee.

"Don't let her worry you," Mrs. French returned, without turning from the window. "You'll have to drive the car."

Dana's eyebrows shot up.

"Why? Can't Theo drive the car? Isn't that what was arranged?"

Mrs. French got to her feet.

"Theo says he's got something more important to do," she said and ear-rings bobbed in the sunlight. "I don't know what he's got to do and I'm not going to ask and I don't want you to ask either."

Dana stared at her for a moment, then she lost some of her colour.

"Now look, Mother, you don't mean—"

"Shut up!" Mrs. French said, and turned back to the window.

IV

On the following afternoon Detective Inspector Dawson was at work in his office when Wesley was announced. Dawson nodded to the police constable, pushed back his chair as Wesley came in.

"There's a chair just by you, Mr. Wesley," he said, signaled to the constable who pushed the chair against the back of Wesley's knees. Wesley sat down.

"Well, I hope you're ready for them this evening," Wesley said quietly. "I thought I'd look in just to check over any last-minute details."

"It'll be all right, sir," Dawson returned, sat down and stared thoughtfully at Wesley. "Everything arranged. There won't be any trouble."

"Now what in the world is a fellow like this doing fooling around with that Holland girl," he was wondering. "Not as if he could see her and be infatuated by her looks. She's a nice-looking girl; I'll say that for her, but there's nothing else to her. This chap's got a lot of money, plenty of education and culture. They've got absolutely nothing in common. I wonder what the idea is?"

He had been intrigued by the plain-clothes detective's report, but realized that it was no business of his. It had just so happened that in keeping an eye on Julie, Clegg had spotted what was going on between these two. Although it wasn't his business, Dawson couldn't help being puzzled and interested.

"You'll have a clear field," Wesley said after a moment's hesitation. "My wife and I are going to the theatre. I don't usually go to the theatre, but it's the only way I can get my wife away from the flat. I am most anxious she should know nothing of what's happening to-night." He made a quick impatient gesture. "She would insist on being there, and that would make things very difficult." He moved uneasily, went on: "You think no harm will come to Miss Holland?"

"None at all," Dawson returned. "She tells me they plan to leave her tied up when the robbery's over. Anyway, we'll be at hand and she's only got to scream."

"Exactly where will your men be?" Wesley asked.

"We'll have a couple in the hall. Two in the alley at the back, another two on the landing outside the flat, and two more on the roof. As soon as we know they're inside we'll throw a cordon right round the building. We're not taking any chances."

Wesley nodded.

"That sounds all right," he said, and got to his feet. "You won't be able to contact me until after the theatre. We're going to the Hippodrome, but I don't suppose you'll want me. I'll ring you in the interval which I believe is around eight-forty. Will that do?"

"It should do," Dawson said. "But there'll be nothing to worry about."

"Thank you," Wesley said, offered his hand. "Then I won't keep you any longer. I'm sure you have plenty to do."

"Well, I keep pretty busy, sir," Dawson said, shaking hands. "But this little job is a real holiday. It couldn't be better arranged for us. It's not often we get the chance of a tip-off like this, you know."

"Make sure they don't slip through your fingers," Wesley returned quietly.

"No fear of that. We'll have 'em all right."

"I suppose you'll want Miss Holland as a witness?" Wesley asked. "I'd prefer not if you can avoid it. I don't want any publicity about her if I can help it. Is it necessary, do you think?"

"Was this why he's come?" Dawson wondered, said, "I don't think we'll need her. If we nab them with the goods it'll be plain sailing. We'll need you, of course."

"Oh yes, that's quite all right," Wesley said. "You see, the girl has an odd background. But then you know all about that. I'd like her to have a fresh start if I could arrange it. If it gets known it was through her the gang was caught there might be trouble from her old associates."

"There might be," Dawson agreed. "I won't call her unless I have to, sir."

Wesley nodded.

"Good." Still he didn't make a move to go. "Inspector, Miss Holland interests me," he went on after a pause. "You're a man of the world and will know what I mean by that. I'm taking care of her when this business is over. So you see, the least publicity might be embarrassing."

"Well, that's hardly my business," Dawson said, taken aback. It was the last thing he expected.

"Oh, I know." Wesley smiled. "But she has been associating with criminals, hasn't she? I wouldn't want you to be interested in her when this is over. I shall look after her and see she doesn't get into any further trouble. I'll make her my responsibility."

"I wouldn't be interested in her unless she did get into further trouble," Dawson said, a shade coldly. "There was no need to tell me any of this, sir."

"But I wanted you to know. I hope I shall not be followed by a plain-clothes man in the future, Inspector," Wesley said, and his mouth tightened. "It is an experience I can well do without, and if repeated I shall take prompt action."

Dawson grimaced.

"Got me there," he thought. "No wonder he's been so frank. I suppose that blasted girl spotted Clegg."

"That was an accident, sir," he said quietly. "I must apologize. We were giving Miss Holland police protection and happened to run into something that didn't concern us."

"So it seems," Wesley said. "In the future when your man sees Miss Holland and me together, will you instruct him to leave us alone?"

"I hope there won't be any occasion to watch Miss Holland after this evening," Dawson pointed out.

"Of course not," Wesley said, and smiled. "I'll telephone you some time this evening. Could your man kindly show me to my taxi?"

When he had gone, Dawson ran his thick fingers through his hair.

"I wouldn't like to get on the wrong side of that chap," he thought. "His bark is quiet enough, but I bet his bite is hell." He went to the window to watch Wesley's taxi drive away. "Don't exactly blame him. He's a good bloke; lots of guts; V.C. and blind. Well, if he gets a bit of fun out of that girl—good luck to him."

And he settled down once more to his work.

V

Julie was pacing up and down in her room. It was a few minutes to seven o'clock, and in another hour Harry would arrive. The suspense of waiting was becoming unbearable. All the previous night and during the day she had tried to screw up her courage to warn him the police were waiting for him, but every time she moved to the telephone she remembered Theo's threat, and the ghastly photographs of the women he had shown her. If she saved Harry, Theo would come after her, and besides, Wesley wouldn't like it. Now that Harry had told her he loved her some of the old attraction she had had for him returned. If Wesley had been nicer to her she wouldn't have thought of Harry, but it was all too plain that Wesley was bribing her to keep quiet. He wasn't in love with her as Harry was, and a girl needed love, she told herself. Her mind was in an agony of indecision. Even now she was still in two minds as to what to do, although she knew the chance of getting Harry on the telephone was remote. She had left it too late.

A soft tap sounded on the door, making her start. Wesley came in. He was in evening dress, and in spite of the black-lensed glasses Julie thought he looked very handsome.

He closed the door gently, set his back against it and smiled at her.

"Scared, Julie?" he asked. "Heart going like a trip-hammer?"

She nodded miserably.

"It'll soon be over," he assured her, "I wish I could see you through it, but it's the one thing you'll have to do on your own. But it'll be worth it, Julie. Once you're free of these people you can begin your new life and I'll do my best to make it a happy one."

"I—I keep thinking of Harry," she blurted cut. "I saw him yesterday. He wanted me to go to America with him. He—he told me he loved me, and I could see he did."

Wesley's face was expressionless.

"I see," he said slowly. "And you're feeling pretty bad because the police are going to get him, aren't you?" He thrust his hands into his trousers pockets. Although he appeared calm enough. Julie had a feeling that he was inwardly as nervy as herself. "But a fellow like Gleb would never give you any happiness; sooner or later he would get into trouble and then you'd be in trouble, too. You have no alternative really, have you? You must think of yourself."

"I know," Julie said. "But it seems such a rotten trick to play on someone who loves you. I—I wish I could warn him to keep away. If it weren't for Theo . . ."

Wesley didn't say anything for a moment. He studied her as she wandered miserably to the window.

"I have something here for you. See if this'll cheer you up." She turned quickly. He was holding out a cheque-book.

"It's for you. I've opened an account for you. You have two hundred and fifty pounds to spend. Every quarter I'll pay in a similar amount. You can go along to the bank tomorrow and give them your signature. Then you can begin to draw the money."

She had always wanted a bank account and for the moment Harry was forgotten.

"Two hundred and fifty pounds?" she said, staring at him. She took the cheque-book and flicked through the pages. "For me?"

"I said I'd make you an allowance of a thousand a year," he reminded her. "This is the beginning of it."

"I see." She stared at him, then she said, "You don't really care for me, do you? This is because you want to be sure I won't talk. You're not fooling me, you know."

"I didn't suppose I was fooling you, as you put it," he returned quietly. "Your silence is important, Julie. If you want to keep the things I've given you, you must keep my secret. No matter what happens you must say nothing. If you do, the flat and your income won't be yours anymore. And it won't be because I'll take them away. It'll be because I should no longer be in the position to give them to you. You see, Julie, if it got out I could see I'd be ruined. I can't tell you any more than that. I shouldn't perhaps have told you so much. It was chance you found out, and I am going to do everything I can to persuade you from telling anyone. So if you want your flat and this money, if you want clothes and a good time, say nothing."

"I won't," Julie said steadily, and gripped the cheque-book tightly.

"And as far as Harry Gleb is concerned," he went on quietly, "if you show any weakness now you'll regret it later. But I must go now. Don't be frightened, Julie, and good luck. You will go through with it, won't you?"

She had to go through with it, she told herself, and remembered what Harry had once said: "I don't care how I get hold of money so long as I get it. Money is power. I have only a few years on this earth—then the worms, the dark and the cold. I'm going to enjoy myself while I can." That was her philosophy, too. Money was power. She couldn't afford to be squeamish, and she told herself Harry wouldn't have hesitated to do as she was doing if he had been in her place.

"Yes, I'm going through with it," she said.

But the moment Wesley had gone and she heard the front door slam she once more became a prey to her fears. There were another forty minutes yet before Harry arrived and she sat in her room, her fists clenched, sick with apprehension, and her eyes on the clock. As its hands moved slowly towards the hour she became more and more jumpy. Every sound, the creaking of the doors, the ticking of the clock, the soft sound of the passing traffic, and the whine of the lift as it raced between floors, made her nerves tighten.

But she wasn't the only one to be strung up. In the Park, under the dark shadow of the trees, Harry Gleb and Theo were watching the lighted entrance of Park Way.

Harry held a cigarette in his fingers, the glowing end shielded in the palm of his hand. He was also uneasy and nervous, and every now and then he shifted his position restlessly.

Not so Theo. He leaned against a tree, his hands in his pockets, his hat at the back of his head, callously calm. He wasn't going to get excited over a job like this. It took a lot to upset Theo.

"What's the time?" Harry asked suddenly. He took out his handkerchief and wiped his sweating hands.

"Twenty past seven," Theo returned after consulting the luminous face of his wrist-watch. He glanced at Harry, hate in his eyes.

"Time they left," Harry said, dropped the cigarette on the grass and stepped on it. "Think we've missed them?"

Theo scratched his ribs, swore softly under his breath.

"Not a chance. What's your hurry? We can't do anything until eight."

"I don't understand why Ma's dragged Dana into this," Harry muttered. "We two could have handled it."

Theo grinned evilly in the darkness.

"She's right," he returned. "Anyone might spot the car if it remained for long in the alley. It's better this way. I can get round to the back without anyone seeing me, get the furs together, then when Dana arrives all I have to do is throw the furs in and she'll be away. It's a smart idea."

Harry grunted. He distrusted any sudden change of plan.

"There they go," Theo said suddenly and pointed.

They watched Blanche and Wesley get into the waiting taxi. Neither of them said anything but their eyes followed the red tail light until it disappeared.

Harry lit another cigarette.

"Well, that starts it," he said. "I'd like to get in there now. This waiting gives me a pain in the guts."

"What's the matter with you?" Theo sneered. "Got cold feet?"

"Shut up, you ape," Harry snarled.

There was a long silence between them, then Theo again consulted his watch.

"About time I got going," he said. "Give me five minutes and "then come on. See you in prison," and he slouched away into the darkness.

Harry's face tightened. "The little rat has nerves like steel," he thought. "See you in prison! The kind of crack he would come out with on a job like this." Harry crossed his fingers and stood waiting. While he waited he thought of Julie. He was determined to make her leave the flat with him after he had passed the furs to Theo. He didn't care how much she protested. She was going with him.

Deciding that Theo had had time to reach the alley at the back of the building, he turned up his coat collar and walked slowly across the grass out of the Park towards Park Way. His heart was pounding and his throat was dry. He had never before felt like this on a job, and it worried him.

It would have worried him still more if he had known that Detective Inspector Dawson and two plain-clothes men were watching him and moved silently after him as he left the Park.

He entered the vast lobby of Park Way and went up to the porter's office.

"I'm looking for Mrs. Gregory's apartment," he said. "Can you direct me, please?"

He remembered that Julie had told him the top flat was occupied by a Mrs. Gregory. Such information was always useful, and Harry had filed it away in his retentive memory for future use.

"Mrs. Gregory?" the porter repeated, coming out of his office. "Yes, sir. Top floor. Take the lift on your right. I don't know if Mrs. Gregory is in. Would you care for me to find out?"

Harry blew his nose loudly. He had been holding his handkerchief to his face in the hope that the porter wouldn't get a good look at him.

"She's expecting me," he said. "It's all right. Top floor? Thanks." He walked quickly to the lift and pressed the automatic button.

While he waited he had a creepy sensation that he was being watched, but he didn't look round. Sweat began to trickle down the back of his neck and he mopped himself with the handkerchief.

The lift doors opened and he stepped inside. As he pressed the button indicating the top floor he took a quick look round the lobby. It was deserted. The porter had returned to his office.

He drew in a quick breath of relief and leaned against the side of the lift as it shot him to the top floor.

Leaving the lift, he ran down the two flights of stairs that brought him to the landing leading to Wesley's flat. He looked up and down the deserted passage, then walked to the front door and rang the bell.

There was a long, unnerving pause before Julie opened the door. She stared at him, white faced, her eyes wide with fear.

"All right, Julie," he said, trying to sound brisk. "Let's go." He pushed past her into the flat and shut the doors "Come on, kid. Let's make it snappy."

But she could only stare at him. He was wearing a dark overcoat and a slouch hat pulled low over his eyes. A black silk scarf hid his chin. She could see sweat trickling down the side of his face from under his hat and his eyes burned feverishly.

"Harry!" she exclaimed, backing away. "Please don't go through with this!"

He caught hold of her arm and bustled her, protesting weakly, down the passage to Blanche's bedroom.

"Now, take it easy," he said, far from easy himself. "This has got to be quick. In and out, see? Get the safe open, kid, as fast as you can."

She was sick with fright, expecting any moment for the police to appear. She couldn't move, but stared at him with eyes like holes in a sheet.

"Harry! Why did you come! I told you to stay away!" she cried, wringing her hands.

He caught hold of her.

"Come on; for God's sake stop talking and get this damned safe open," he said feverishly, and shook her.

"But Harry . . ." she wailed.

"We'll talk when we get outside." He was controlling himself with difficulty. "Come on, get it open." He shoved her before the quilted wall. "Turn off the alarms. There's one behind the bed, isn't there? Turn it off."

It suddenly occurred to her that if he didn't take the furs the police couldn't do anything to him. She could swear that he had come to see her and then they would have no case against him.

"Harry! Listen, you mustn't take anything. Please go. I'll even come with you if you'll go now."

He rounded on her. His own nerves were at breaking point. He had never before wasted so much time on a job.

"Turn the blasted alarm off!" he shouted at her. "And stop talking!"

"But Harry, you don't understand . . ." she began, but cursing under his breath he caught hold of her arm and gave her a stinging slap across her face.

"Pull yourself together, you little fool!" he exclaimed furiously. "Open that safe."

She stepped back, her hand going to her face. She realized at once that he had struck her because he was frightened, but in spite of that she couldn't forgive him. If he could do that to her after he had told her he loved her, what was his love worth, she thought.

"All right," she said bleakly. "Don't say I didn't warn you."

Harry was now so jittery he nearly struck her again. He had been in the flat for over ten minutes and the safe wasn't opened yet.

"Get on with it," he said frantically. "We've got to get out of here."

She went to the head of the bed, moving like an automaton, and turned off the alarm. Then she went into the bathroom and turned off the second alarm. As she came out of the bathroom he again implored her to hurry.

Without quite knowing what she was doing she opened the safe. Harry gaped at the row of fur coats when the steel doors slid back. As soon as she had turned off the light that operated the photo-electric cell, he jumped forward, scooped up an armful of the furs and rushed from the room. She heard him push up the panel covering the service lift in the kitchen. Suddenly she felt she was going to faint and clutched hold of a chair to steady herself.

Harry came in, grabbed another armful of furs and rushed out again. He worked like lightning, not paying her any attention. There was nothing she could do now, she thought, gripping the back of the chair. In a moment or so the police would burst in and that would be the end of Harry.

Then something happened that rooted her to the floor and sent blood from her heart.

There was a sudden shrill scream that echoed through the flat, immediately followed by the crash of gunfire.

Julie found herself at the door, peering fearfully into the passage.

Harry was standing a yard or so from the front door, which stood open. He was staring down at something at his feet, something his body blocked from Julie's view. Nearby lay an automatic pistol; smoke drifted lazily from its muzzle.

"Harry!" Julie cried, and Harry, suddenly galvanized into life, slammed and bolted the front door. As he moved, Julie caught sight of a little doll-like figure lying on the floor. It was Blanche.

Julie screamed as she saw blood running down the side of Blanche's face, forming a crimson halo round her fair hair.

There came a tremendous crash on the front door, which bulged, creaked, but held.

Harry sprang back, turned and came rushing down the passage towards Julie. His eyes were bolting from his head; his colourless face dreadful to look at.

Julie shrank away from him.

"You shot her!" she gasped, throwing out her hands to keep him off. "Harry! keep away!"

"You know I didn't!" Harry gasped, grabbing hold of her. "I was in the kitchen. I've never carried a gun in my life, Julie! You've got to tell them. I—I didn't do it!"

Then the front door burst open and three police officers came charging down the passage.

Harry flung Julie out of his way, darted into the kitchen, but he hadn't taken a step or two before he was pulled down, his frantic struggles smothered by many hands.

Julie heard him yell, "I didn't do it! I swear I didn't do it. It's not my gun!" and then everything went dark and she seemed to be falling into a bottomless pit.

VI

Theo was hauling himself up in the service lift when he heard the shot and he immediately jammed on the flimsy brake, stopping the lift. He was only a few feet below the service hatch that Harry had left open. The light from the kitchen reflected down the shaft, and by peering through the opening between the shaft and the lift, he could see part of the kitchen ceiling.

He heard Julie's wild scream and the crash as the front door of the flat was forced open, and he cursed, knowing that something had gone badly wrong.

The lift was operated by pulling on a rope from below. It was also possible, but not easy, to operate the lift by pulling on the rope that ran inside the lift. Theo had found it hard work hoisting himself up by hand, but he had kept at it, sweating and swearing, because he knew it was vital to silence Julie. And now this must happen just when he was within a few feet of his destination.

He suddenly heard the sounds of a violent struggle, then Harry's voice, strident with panic, yell: "I didn't do it! I swear I didn't do it!

It's not my gun!"

Theo's face set.

"Someone's got shot," he thought. "This is where I get the hell out of here!"

Over-anxious to get away before anyone spotted him, he released the brake before getting a grip on the rope. Instantly the lift fell like a stone between the floors. Theo made a desperate grab at the brake and slammed it on, but the impetus of the lift was too much for it and it snapped.

Theo gave a howl of terror as the lift plunged down; a howl that was heard by the two plain-clothes detectives who were in the alley.

They saw the lift come down out of the darkness and smash to pieces against its steel bed. They saw a body hurtle out and thud on the damp concrete.

They ran forward, bent over Theo. One of them shone a torch on to his ghastly face. When he touched Theo, Theo screamed, startling both men. They drew back, staring at him.

"All right, son," the taller of the two said. "Just take it easy. We'll get an ambulance for you." He could see by the way Theo was lying that he had broken his back, and turning to his companion, he went on in a lower tone: "Nip up and get the inspector, George. He's had it."

Sweat ran down Theo's face.

"Where's he gone?" he gasped, seeing the other detective run off down the dark passage.

"Gone to get Dawson and the ambulance," he was told.

"Bet old Dawson will raise a cheer," Theo said, his face twisting with pain. "He never liked me." He panted for a moment, trying to get his breath. "Blasted back's broken. Don't touch me. It's all right so long as you don't touch me."

"You take it easy, kid," the detective said, and squatted on his heels beside Theo. "We'll fix you up."

Theo sneered.

"Going to get into the papers at last," he said. "I got a photo of myself in my wallet. Give it to the Press, chum. My old man'll get a kick seeing me in the papers. It'll be front-page stuff, won't it?"

"That's right," the detective said, grimacing.

"Get it now and keep it by you," Theo insisted. "They'll give you a couple of nicker for it. If you don't have it, Dawson will. You know what he's like."

To humour him, the detective took the wallet and found the

photograph.

"This it?" he asked.

Theo peered forward.

"That's it. You give it to the Press." He lay for a minute not saying anything, then he went on: "What was that shooting just now?"

"I don't know," the detective returned. "Gleb wasn't carrying a gun, was he?"

Theo didn't say anything. If he was going to die, and he thought that was what was going to happen to him, he wasn't going to let Harry get away with it. Harry had hit him, and no one hit Theo without paying for it. But Theo wanted to know more about the shooting before he talked.

"I'm not saying anything until Dawson comes," he said. "He'd better hurry. I'm going to croak."

"Not you," the detective said cheerfully. "You'll live to do your ten years."

"They wouldn't give me ten," Theo said. "I'd be unlucky to get three."

Detective Inspector Dawson materialized out of the darkness and knelt by Theo's side.

"Hello," he said, staring down at the white, pain-lined face. "Got yourself into a proper mess this time, haven't you?"

Theo opened his eyes.

"I'm all right so long as you don't move me," he said. "That ambulance coming?"

"Yes," Dawson returned. "Seen this gun before, Theo?" He dangled an automatic pistol before Theo's eyes, turned the beam of his torch on to it.

"Was that Harry shooting?" Theo asked. "Did he kill anyone?"

"We don't know. It depends if this is his gun."

Theo closed his eyes for a moment, then opened them again.

"It's his gun all right. Who did he shoot?"

"Are you sure?" Dawson demanded.

"'Cos I'm sure," Theo lied. "I didn't want him to carry a gun. But he wouldn't listen. He said he'd kill anyone who got in his way."

"Will you sign a statement?" Dawson asked quietly.

Theo nodded. There was a glazed look in his eyes now.

"You'd better hurry," he said. "I ain't going to last long."

Dawson was already scribbling in his notebook. He got Theo to sign the statement after a little difficulty.

Theo was dead by the time the ambulance arrived.

VII

They were bringing Harry Gleb down in the lift as Dawson re-entered the lobby of Park Way. Harry was handcuffed to a burly plain-clothes man. Another detective walked just behind him.

Harry's face was livid. When he saw Dawson, the automatic pistol in his hand, he made a dive towards him, only to be roughly jerked back by his escort.

"I didn't do it, Dawson!" he cried in a cracked, despairing voice. "It's not my gun. I've never had a gun. You know me; I wouldn't do a thing like that. For God's sake, Dawson, don't pin this on me. I didn't do it!"

Dawson's hard blue eyes surveyed Harry up and down.

"Don't give me that stuff, Gleb," he said roughly. "Your little pal, Theo, gave you away. I've got a signed statement from him swearing the gun's yours. You've pulled one job too many, Harry. This is your last little effort."

"He's lying!" Harry shouted. "Bring him here! I'll make the rat speak the truth! Bring him here!"

"He's dead," Dawson said brutally, then, turning to the escort, he went on, "Take him away."

"Dead?" Harry cried, then as the escort began to hustle him to the door he started to struggle like a madman, and it was all the two detectives could do to get him out of the lobby and into the waiting police car.

Newspaper reporters with a battery of cameras were waiting outside and the darkness was split open by the flash-bulbs exploding as they photographed his struggling exit. His wailing, protesting voice could be heard even as the car drove rapidly away.

Garson, Dawson's assistant, came up to Dawson.

"Mr. Wesley's arrived," he said in a low voice. "He's up there now."

Dawson nodded.

"What I want to know is how the devil she got through the cordon?" he said, rubbing his heavy jaw. "And why did she come back on her own like that?"

"I didn't question Mr. Wesley," Garson said. "He's a bit knocked over. I thought I'd give him a moment or so to recover. Will you question him, sir, or shall I?"

"I'll see him," Dawson said grimly. "There's going to be a hell of a row about this, Garson. We had the place surrounded and we knew what Gleb was up to and we calmly let him shoot her. She's a well-known figure, too. Just wait until the papers know what's happened. They're already asking how it is we were on the spot before the robbery. What's happened to the girl, Holland?"

"She's still up there. The M.O.'s having a look at her."

Dawson walked over to the lift. Garson followed him.

"Theo's dead," Dawson said. "Broke his back. The little horror had it coming to him. Jackson's looking after the remains."

They rode up in the lift.

"How did Wesley take it?" Dawson asked abruptly.

"Seemed knocked right out. He came in quietly. I didn't notice him at first. There was a lot going on. The body hadn't been moved and he practically stepped on it. Then he bent down and touched her just as I reached him. It gave him a pretty horrible jolt. I took him along to his study and left him. I thought I'd let him get over it."

"Well, I don't think there was much love lost between those two," Dawson said. "He was planning to make Holland his mistress. From what I've heard Blanche Wesley was a bit of a bitch. But all the same it isn't funny to come home and fall over the dead body of your wife, is it?"

He stepped from the lift and walked in through the front door of Wesley's flat.

Blanche's body still lay where it had fallen. Police photographers were busy taking photographs and fingerprint men were working in the hall.

Dawson didn't stop, but went immediately to Wesley's study.

Wesley was sitting in an arm-chair, his hands folded in his lap, his face white and set. He turned his head as Dawson came in. The black-lensed glasses emphasized his pallor.

"Who is it?" he asked.

"Dawson. Bad business, sir. I can't say how sorry I am."

Wesley nodded.

"Yes." His voice sounded flat. "Couldn't your men have stopped her coming in?"

"They had no instructions to stop anyone entering the building, only to prevent anyone leaving," Dawson reminded him. "None of my men saw Mrs. Wesley come in. If they had and had known who she was they would have stopped her. We had no idea she was in the flat. Why did she return?"

Wesley made a little gesture. It revealed a controlled despair.

"We quarrelled," he said. "To tell the truth, Inspector, we didn't get on well together. In many ways my wife was very difficult to live with. She had no patience with my blindness, and I suppose I'm not particularly easy myself." He hesitated, went on. "She drank a bit, and when she was like that she had a pretty violent temper. She had been drinking rather heavily before we started for the theatre. In the cab we got into one of those interminable arguments that always seem to be cropping up between us. It developed into a heated quarrel, and as I was paying off the driver she left me. I had no idea she had gone until I had got into the theatre. It is very difficult, as you can imagine, for a blind man to be left suddenly high and dry in the middle of a crush of people, all moving to their seats. I left her ticket with the programme seller, thinking she might have gone to the bar or the ladies' room. But after the curtain had gone up, and she hadn't come to claim her seat, I guessed she didn't intend to see the show. I decided to go to my club. Then it occurred to me that she might have returned here and I became alarmed. I had some difficulty in getting a taxi. At last someone took pity on me and stopped one for me. When I arrived here I learned she—she—" He broke off and turned away.

"But how did she get in? No one saw her. Can you explain that?"

"I think so. I suppose she told the taxi driver to drop her at the garage entrance. The garage of this building is below ground and has a separate entrance. You can take the lift from the garage to our flat without entering the hall. She often does that."

"But no taxis were allowed through after Gleb was in the flat."

"Perhaps she walked. I don't know. I'm just making suggestions." Dawson stared at him.

"Oh, yes, I understand that. I didn't know about the garage. I'd better find out if anyone saw her in there. Well, we've got the man who did it. He won't get away with it."

Wesley seemed to turn a shade paler.

"If there's nothing more, inspector, perhaps you wouldn't mind leaving me? This has been a bit of a shock."

"Of course," Dawson returned, suddenly feeling sorry for him. "We'll try not to bother you. Is there anything I can do for you?"

"If you see Gerridge—he's my secretary—tell him to come to me," Wesley said. "He should be in in a little while."

"I'll do that," Dawson said, turned to the door.

"Oh, Inspector, is Miss Holland all right?" Wesley asked guardedly.

"Yes . . . a bit shocked, but she's all right. I'm going to see her now."

"Did she see anything?"

"That's what I'm going to find out."

"I see. Thank you."

Dawson went quietly from the room, closed the door. He stood for a moment or so thinking, then went into the lounge where Garson was waiting.

"Go down to the garage and find out if anyone saw Mrs. Wesley come in that way," he said. "The garage is in the basement and was the one place we didn't guard. Wesley says he thinks that was how she got in."

"Yes, sir," Garson said, made to move off but Dawson stopped him.

"Where's the Holland girl?"

"In her room; end of the passage, sir."

Dawson nodded and went with a heavy tread down the passage. He rapped on the door, pushed it open and went in.

Julie was lying on the bed. Her tear-stained face blanched when she saw who it was.

"Where were you when the shooting took place?" Dawson demanded. He had no intention of wasting any time with Julie.

"In Mrs. Wesley's room."

"What happened?"

"I—I don't know. I—I didn't see any of it."

Dawson surveyed her; his mouth tightening.

"Now look here, young woman, you've been on the fringe of trouble for some time. Now you're mixed up in a murder case. You and Gleb were the only two in the flat. You'd better be a bit more helpful or you'll be getting into trouble."

"But I don't know," Julie cried, struggling up on the bed. "I didn't see anything."

"You heard something, didn't you?"

"I heard Mrs. Wesley scream. Then there was a shot. I ran out. Harry was bending over Mrs. Wesley. He'd just come from the kitchen."

"That's all you saw? You didn't see him shoot her?"

"But he didn't shoot her. He was in the kitchen!" Julie cried, wringing her hands. "He didn't do it. He hadn't a gun. Harry wouldn't do a thing like that."

"It's no use trying to get him out of his trouble. I know you've been in love with him, but it won't do," Dawson said harshly. "If he didn't do it, who did? Did you do it? Only you and Gleb were in the flat."

"Oh, no!" Julie exclaimed, terrified at once. "I—I didn't do it."

Dawson smiled grimly.

"I didn't think you did," he said. "But I wanted to show you lying might make things difficult for you."

"But—but I'm sure Harry didn't do it," Julie said, clenching her fists. "The front door was open. Someone could have shot her through the front door."

"The invisible man? I had a man at either end of the passage. No one could have come up or down the stairs without being seen. As soon as the shot was fired both my men came into the passage. There was no one in sight."

Julie stared at him, going cold.

"Did Gleb have the gun in his hand?" Dawson asked.

"No. It was lying on the floor by Mrs. Wesley; just by the door."

"All right. Well, this lets you out. Theo's dead. Gleb's nabbed and we're roping the Trenches in now. You'd better watch your step from now on." He turned to the door, looked over his shoulder. "You'll be a witness, remember," he reminded her. "This trial is going to cause a lot of noise. Be careful what you do between now and the trial, won't you?"

He ran into Carson as he left Julie's room.

"No one in the garage, sir," Carson reported. "The staff leave at seven."

"You'd better try and trace the taxi that brought her here," Dawson said, frowning. "There's something very odd about the way she sneaked back here. I've got a feeling it'll pay us to put some work in on this angle."

Garson looked a little startled.

"But Gleb shot her, didn't he? There's no doubt about that, is there?"

"There's always a doubt until the trial's over," Dawson said acidly. "I'm not going to have my case shot from under me for the lack of a little hard work. I've wanted to lay my hands on Gleb for a long time. Now I've got him, I don't intend to let him slip through my fingers. Find out what Mrs. Wesley did from the time she left Wesley to the time she was shot."

"Yes, sir."

Neither of them noticed that the door of Wesley's study had opened an inch or so. When Carson hurried away, the door silently closed.

CHAPTER SIX

I

When the police finally left there came over the flat a strange quiet. Julie had hoped that Dawson would have come in and seen her again. She longed for an assurance that Harry would be all right; that they didn't really believe he had killed Blanche, but Dawson didn't come. She heard his deep voice as he stood in the passage outside her door giving instructions to his men, and she had waited, her nails digging into the palms of her hands, hoping he would remember her. But it seemed either she had gone completely from his mind or else he didn't consider her to be of any further use to him, for she heard him say good night to Wesley and go off, his heavy tread resounding through the flat.

Then later she heard Gerridge leave. Even he had apparently forgotten her, and when the final policeman had gone she went quickly to the door and peered into the passage. She looked fearfully for bloodstains but someone had scrubbed the carpet clean. There was still a big damp patch on it, and on the white part of the pattern she could make out a faint brown stain.

Silence hung in the passage like the silence in an empty church. The two passage lights, shaded by green parchment shades, threw an eerie light on the pattern of the carpet.

She was frightened of the passage, feeling that Blanche was still in the flat, that she might suddenly materialize before her, and with a little shudder she closed the door and leaned against it.

She couldn't bear the thought of spending another hour in the flat. Her one thought now was to get away from it as quickly as she could. She had the key to the flat in Vigo Street and she decided to go there. There was no point in staying in this ghastly atmosphere a moment longer, and she immediately set about packing a bag.

Later, she was staring at the contents of the bag, wondering if she had forgotten anything, when a slight sound in the passage made her stiffen and she felt a cold tingle run up her spine.

Blanche?

She told herself not to be ridiculous. Blanche was dead. Then Wesley? Was he coming to her?

She waited and listened, and the sound, no louder than scratching of mice at the wainscoting, was repeated. She crept to the door and opened it by degrees until it was just wide enough for her to peer into the passage.

Wesley was standing by the front door, looking down at the damp patch of carpet. He stood there for several minutes, his pale face expressionless, and then suddenly he passed his foot gently over the patch of damp. He did this several times, and said softly: "She wasn't fit to go on living."

Julie felt suddenly tired and ill, and walked unsteadily to her bed and sat down. She put her head between her hands and closed her eyes. She remained like that for some time, waiting for the feeling of faintness to pass.

She did not hear Wesley come into the room, and when he spoke she started, her body recoiling in a convulsive little leap that seemed to startle him almost as much as he had startled her.

"I didn't mean to frighten you," he said gently. "I should have knocked. I wasn't thinking."

She didn't say anything.

"It's very quiet now, isn't it?" he went on, moving softly about the room, not looking at her. "I didn't come to see you before, because of the police. They told me you were all right. It must have been a horrible shock for you."

Still she could think of nothing to say.

"Dawson was odd. Didn't you think so?" He paused for a moment to look at her, but almost immediately began again his soft pacing to-and-fro. "He seemed suspicious. Why does it matter how Blanche got into the flat? Why does he try to make a mystery of it?"

"I don't know."

"There's no doubt Gleb shot her. I don't understand what Dawson is trying to establish."

"He didn't do it!" Julie exclaimed, starting up. "I know he didn't!"

Wesley turned quickly. Into his eyes came an alert watchfulness that Julie was too strung-up to notice.

"What are you talking about?"

"Harry didn't do it. I know he didn't."

"Why are you so sure?"

"Oh, I know he was bad, but he wouldn't hurt anyone. He didn't carry a gun. Mrs. French once asked him if he had a gun. He said he never carried one and never would. He was speaking the truth then, and he was speaking the truth to-night when he said he didn't shoot her."

"Have you told the police this?" There was the faintest tremor in Wesley's voice.

"Dawson doesn't believe me. He said only Harry and I were in the flat. If he didn't shoot her, then I must have."

"The fool!" Wesley was suddenly angry. "He didn't mean it?"

"No, he was trying to frighten me. But he didn't. I told him the front door was open—"

"What! What do you mean?"

"The front door was open. When Mrs. Wesley came in she forgot to close it."

Wesley suddenly caught hold of Julie's wrist, pulled her to him and stared at her fixedly. "What's the door to do with it? What are you hinting at?"

There was something in the glittering eyes that chilled her.

"Answer me!"

"I only suggested someone in the passage could have shot her," Julie said, trying to free her wrist. "Please let go. You're hurting me."

He continued to stare at her for a long moment, then released her and turned away.

"I'm sorry. And what did Dawson say to that?"

"He said something about the invisible man," Julie sat down. Her legs felt shaky. "He said the police were watching the passage and no one could have come up or down."

"The invisible man! Fancy Dawson saying that." There was a feverish look in Wesley's eyes, but he was smiling, suddenly at ease. "And you meant to be helpful, Julie. But you do see no one could have shot her through the doorway? If the police were there—well, is it likely that anyone could have done that?"

"No," she said, wondering at the change in him. "I suppose not, but I'm sure Harry didn't do it."

"I find your faith in Gleb a little touching. After all, he's a thief. He had no mercy on you. You have no proof at all that he didn't shoot Blanche. You don't love him anymore, do you?"

"No, I don't love him, but that doesn't make any difference. I just feel in my bones he didn't do it."

"It isn't a very convincing argument. I doubt if a jury would be impressed. Well, we'll see."

"Will they hang him?" Julie asked, wide-eyed.

"I don't know. It's better not to think about it. They haven't tried him yet." Wesley fumbled in his pocket for his cigarette-case, lit up, and again began to move about the room. "I don't think I could stand a night here, could you, Julie?"

"No."

"Shall we go to the new flat?"

She flinched from the idea of being with him, of beginning their association so soon after what had happened.

"Could I go there alone?" she said. "I—I'd rather be alone for a little while."

"That's absurd." There was an edge to his voice. "Neither of us should be alone to-night. We must keep each other company. There's nothing to worry about. I shall not bother you if that's what you are thinking. But if you want the use of the flat, Julie, then you must share it with me. Perhaps you have changed your mind? I can't say that I blame you if you have. Perhaps you don't want a bank account or a mink coat or the flat? You have only to say so and you are free to do what you like. And by that I mean you can go from here and forget you ever met me."

Julie stared at him, and her face hardened.

"You seem to forget you're giving me all this because you don't want me to talk," she said sharply. "I'm going to do what I like. I don't want you at the flat."

Wesley smiled.

"Things have changed now, Julie," he said gently. "It doesn't matter if anyone knows I can see. I'm not going into explanations, but my pretended blindness was to do with Blanche. Now she is dead it doesn't matter. Perhaps one of these days I'll tell you about it, but not now. I shall continue to pretend I'm blind for a few more weeks, then I shall regain my sight but it is not important. If you want to be difficult you can talk, but if you do, you won't get anything further from me. If you behave yourself I will continue to give you money and let you keep the flat; but only if you behave yourself."

Julie didn't know if he were bluffing or not. She thought not, but she wasn't sure, and this indecision infuriated her. She wasn't going to give up the flat or her money. She would hold on to that on any terms.

"All right," she said sullenly. "Then you'd better come, I suppose."

"Good." There was a new note in his voice. He looked brighter and less haggard. "Let's get out of here. Let's start a new life together. I'll promise you a good time." He moved to the door. "I'll put some things in a bag and I'll join you in a moment or so. Don't be long, will you?"

She finished her packing and when Wesley returned she couldn't bring herself to look at him. He took her bag.

"Let's go," he said. "I'll get Gerridge to finish the packing to-morrow."

They went down the passage together. Both of them flinched when they had to pass over the brown stain on the carpet. The lift was opposite the front door and Wesley crossed to it and pressed the automatic button.

Neither of them spoke until the lift came to rest and the doors swung open, then Wesley said: "It'll be good to get away from the place. I've always hated it."

As the lift began its descent Julie happened to glance down. In the corner of the lift was something that attracted her attention. Wesley saw it at the same instant. He made a quick dart forward, picked it up, and put it hurriedly into his pocket.

But Julie had recognized it. It was the finger-stall she had put on his finger after he had cut himself on the night of their first meeting.

She was startled that he had concealed it so hurriedly, and saw an odd expression of acute tension on his face as if he were trying to control his feelings and only by the greatest effort had succeeded. She felt sure that behind the black-lensed glasses which he was now wearing his eyes were frightened.

At the time it seemed of no importance to her, just an odd, unexplained incident, but it made an impression on her mind and she was to remember it again later.

II

The West London Court was crowded when Harry Gleb made a five-minute appearance in the dock. Harry was stupefied when he saw the packed court. He had no idea that he was going to be the object of so many intent and curious eyes and he was badly shaken. After one horrified, shrinking glance, he kept his eyes fixed on the wall above the magistrate's head.

A great change had come over Harry since the night of his arrest. The charge of murder against him had knocked all the bombast out of him. He looked older; there was a wild, horrified expression in his eyes, as if he believed he was experiencing a terrifying nightmare and was making desperate efforts to wake up. His face was grey and lined and haggard. His mouth twitched and his hands trembled. If Julie could have seen him she would have been shocked. He was no longer the handsome, blustering swashbuckler she had known. He was a trapped, frightened animal with the smell of death in his nostrils.

Before being remanded for a week he heard Detective Inspector Dawson admit ruefully that Mrs. French and her daughter had slipped through his fingers and were so far still at liberty. He heard the news with mixed feelings; relief and envy. Had he glanced round the court he would have had Dawson's statement confirmed, for Dana was sitting only a few yards from him. It would have considerably cheered him to know that she had risked coming to the court to see him. He felt deserted, experiencing a frustrated rage to think that Theo had escaped all this by death.

Dana wasn't particularly worried about herself. She knew the risk wasn't great. The police had no detailed description of her; she was not known to them, and she had taken the precaution to wear a pair of shell spectacles and to tuck her auburn hair out of sight under a close-fitting little hat.

She thought Harry looked ghastly. He was obviously ill at ease and frightened and she scarcely recognized him. To see the way he gripped the dock rail until his knuckles turned white and to hear his quavering voice when he asked for legal aid sent a pang through her heart; for Dana had been in love with Harry for a long time.

The magistrate seemed to be in a hurry to get rid of Harry. When Dawson asked for a remand he agreed with alacrity. Dawson said he hoped by the end of the week to have made further arrests. As Harry turned to leave the dock he caught sight of Dana who smiled cheerfully at him. He was staggered to see her there, and as the police urged him away he gave her a frightened, haunted look that worried her.

"He's in a bad way," she thought, as she pushed through the crowd to the street. "But they can't hang him. He didn't do it. Theo must have done it. He had the gun. I've got to get Harry out of this mess somehow—but how?"

She wandered along the street deep in thought, but knowing at the back of her mind that there was nothing she could do for him. They had got him. Once they got their claws in you, you were finished.

While she was wrestling with her problem, Inspector Dawson arrived back at his office to find Garson waiting for him.

"Remanded for a week," he said, in answer to Garson's query. "We'll have to catch 'em by then." He sat down at his desk. "Any news?"

"Not of Ma French and Dana. They've hidden up somewhere pretty snug. No sign of them."

Dawson grunted.

"What about the taxi driver who took Mrs. Wesley from the theatre to her flat? Found him?"

"It doesn't look as if she went by taxi. No driver's come forward. And another thing, no driver's come forward about taking Wesley home. That's a bit odd, sir. A driver's not likely to forget a blind man."

"Wesley said he came back by taxi, didn't he?"

"Yes, sir. I have his statement here."

"Leave that for a moment. Find out anything about Mrs. Wesley's movements?"

"Not a great deal, sir. The commissionaire at the theatre saw her get out of the taxi and enter the theatre while Wesley was paying the fare. She's well known at the theatre, of course. She's played there a number of times. She went to the bar. The commissionaire thought it was strange she should leave Wesley to find his way in. He showed Wesley to the entrance of the stalls and told him Mrs. Wesley was in the bar. He says Wesley didn't appear to hear, but went down the gangway, where a programme seller took charge of him."

"I don't see why he shouldn't have heard. He's not deaf. Well, go on."

"Mrs. Wesley went to the bar. The bartender said she seemed in a bad temper and scarcely spoke to her. The woman was disappointed as she looked on Mrs. Wesley's visits as a bit of an occasion. She said Mrs. Wesley drank three brandies and a minute or so before the first bell rang, left the bar. The commissionaire was surprised to see her leave the theatre. She headed towards Piccadilly Circus and no one seems to have seen her again until she arrived at the flat."

"She could have taken the underground. Taxis aren't easy to get these days."

"I think that's what happened, sir. If she caught a train at once she would have arrived about the time she did."

"Let's get back to Wesley. How does his statement compare to the actual facts?"

"All right, sir, with two exceptions. One was the commissionaire told him Mrs. Wesley was in the bar and he says he didn't know where she was. But then, of course, he might not have heard the man. But when he came out of the theatre after the curtain had gone up, the commissionaire offered to get him a taxi, and he refused. That seems a bit odd to me, sir. I have his statement here. He says, 'It occurred to me that she might have returned here and I became alarmed. I had some difficulty in stopping a taxi. At last someone took pity on me and stopped one for me.'"

"Yes, very odd. If the commissionaire offered to get him a taxi and he was alarmed, why didn't he let the man get him one? Why go blundering about the street? He surely would know he couldn't hope to get a cab for himself. I think I'll have another word with him about that. He's not living at Park Way any longer. He's moved into a flat in Vigo Street. He's living with that Holland girl."

Carson showed his surprise.

"That's something that foxes me, Carson." Dawson pushed back his chair, thrust his knee against his desk. "What's the idea of a fellow like Wesley living with that Holland girl?"

Carson grinned.

"She's a pretty nice-looking girl, sir. A fellow doesn't worry too much about what's inside a girl's head these days so long as she's got a good body and a pretty face. At least, not the fellows who want that kind of fun."

"What's a pretty face to a blind man?"

Garson blinked.

"Yes, of course. I wasn't thinking. No, you're right, sir. I wonder what the idea is?"

"I've had a man keeping an eye on them. Wesley's throwing money away on her. They're going everywhere: nightclubs, theatres, bottle parties, dances, restaurants, even riding in the Row. He's not going to the factory anymore. For the past four days they've been everywhere together. I want to know what the idea is."

"Blackmail?"

"I don't think so. If it were blackmail why should she go around with him? A blackmailer likes to keep at a safe distance. And she doesn't strike me as the type."

"Perhaps they're in love, sir."

"Perhaps they are. I don't know. All right, Carson, you concentrate on the Frenches. I want 'em quickly. They're holed up somewhere. Keep after them. I'll have a word with Wesley. And keep after those taxi drivers. There's still a chance one or both'll come forward."

When Garson had gone, Dawson glanced at his watch. It was a few minutes after three o'clock. He'd call on Wesley about five, he told himself. If Wesley wasn't in, he might get a chance to talk to Julie Holland.

III

Benton lived alone in a small but comfortable West End flat on the top floor of an old-fashioned building that contained three bachelor flats and was serviced by a housekeeper and a valet. Breakfast was the only meal provided, and this was served in the small alcove leading off Benton's sitting-room.

At eight o'clock each morning (nine o'clock on Sundays), the meal was set on the table. Benton rose at seven-thirty, bathed and shaved, and then, in pyjamas and dressing gown, had breakfast. He left the flat at nine o'clock for the factory.

His breakfast consisted of cornflakes with watered milk, toast, a scraping of butter and strong coffee: it never varied. When he had finished the meal, he lit a cigarette and unfolded the newspaper that lay in a tight roll on the tray. No matter how important the news, he didn't look at the paper until he moved from the table and sat in an arm-chair.

On the morning following Blanche's death he had bathed, shaved and breakfasted with his usual pale calm. His mind was preoccupied with the two main interests in his life: Blanche and money.

He had met Blanche for the first time at her wedding, although he had seen her several times on the stage and had admired her from a distance. Wesley had given him no warning of his marriage. Wesley and he had been partners for a number of years. Together they had developed the Wesley-Benton Aircraft Factory from a small and experimental idea into four hundred acres of machine shops, runways and hangars. The drive admittedly had come from Wesley, but Benton's contribution had been none the less important. In his quiet, pale way, he had a brilliant flair for organization. He could turn chaos into orderly efficiency with a stroke or two of his pen. He could handle difficult contractors, placate irritable ministers, soothe nervous and suspicious bankers. He undertook all the petty, irritating jobs (vitally important in spite of their pettiness) where Wesley's temperament would have failed. The partnership had been successful, although each man disliked the other intensely, and where Wesley was concerned it had been profitable. Benton was never able to keep money for long. He was a spendthrift and his share of the profits was invariably lost in gambling and unsound undertakings which he could easily be persuaded to finance.

Some six years ago Wesley had wandered into Benton's office and had announced casually that he was getting married. Benton offered his congratulations and was curious to see the bride; curious and inclined to sneer. Who in the world would want to marry a cold fish like Wesley, he wondered. Probably some horsey-looking woman whose only claim to fame was an occasional photograph in the *Tatter* or *Sketch*. Benton loathed that type of woman. But when Wesley introduced him to Blanche he had the shock of his life.

Benton was a profligate. His headmaster had once said before the whole school that he had a mind like a body full of sores. That was when Benton had been involved in a particularly unpleasant scandal and had been publicly expelled. Women were as necessary to him as drugs to an addict. He had admired Blanche when he had seen her on the stage; at close quarters she bowled him over. He hadn't been in her company for long before he was obsessed by her. She had a sensual, animal magnetism that caught him by the throat. This was no passing infatuation; no idle lusting after a pretty woman. It went much deeper than that. It was like a virulent germ in his blood; a craving that tortured him; a suffocating feeling every time he heard her name; a pounding of blood in his ears at the sound of her voice.

When Wesley volunteered for the Royal Air Force, Benton, unfit for any of the Services, did not hesitate to take advantage of his absence. By then Blanche was drinking heavily and Benton willingly became her drinking partner. Drink had no effect on him, but it rotted Blanche mentally and physically.

Somewhat to Benton's surprise his obsession for Blanche showed no signs of waning. He had felt like this before with other women, but once he had become intimate with them the desire for their company wilted. But not so with Blanche. The more he saw her, the more intimate they were, the more he desired her: it was like throwing petrol on a smouldering bonfire. He would have married her if he had had the money. Blanche was willing and kept urging him to put his money affairs in order, refusing to use her own money so long as she could use Wesley's.

From a grimy, erotic beginning, their association developed into an odd but deep-rooted kind of love. Benton led a lonely life. He was not popular and had no friends. There was something about him that other men distrusted, and Blanche was his only companion.

When he unfolded the newspaper and saw Blanche's photograph staring at him from the printed page and read the banner headline that told of her murder, he went deathly pale. He sat motionless, the paper gripped in his long, rather beautiful fingers, his eyes closed.

He remained still for a long time. His mind paralysed by the sense of his loss. When eventually he did move it was to walk with slow, halting steps to the sideboard. He poured himself out a glass of brandy, drank it and refilled his glass. Then he returned to his chair and re-read the account of the murder. And while he read his face went to pieces and he wept.

Later, he telephoned Wesley's flat, but there was no answer. He put through a call to the factory and learned that Wesley hadn't arrived. There was nothing else he could do, and he sat staring at the wall opposite, his teeth chewing on his pale underlip, his hands clenched in his lap.

He was still sitting in the same position an hour later when Wesley telephoned.

Wesley was curt: his voice without feeling. He asked Benton to look after the factory.

"I shan't be coming out for some time. You can get on without me. There's no urgent work. If you want me you can reach me through my club."

Benton was stupefied that Wesley should suddenly shirk his responsibilities. He dared not let him know how stricken he was at the news of Blanche's death. He imagined that Wesley had no idea of his relations with Blanche. Wesley could make things awkward for him if he liked. He was guaranteeing a big overdraft at Benton's bank. If he ever got wind of what Benton and Blanche's relations had been, Benton reasoned, he might easily withdraw the guarantee.

Benton had intended to make some excuse and take a few days off. The thought of going to the factory sickened him. He wished to remain in his flat and mourn for Blanche. He couldn't even bring himself to express sympathy for Wesley's loss. Neither of the men mentioned Blanche, and as soon as Wesley had made sure that Benton would look after the factory he rang off.

Benton had but a vague idea of how he got through the next two days. He took no interest in the affairs of the factory although he was at his desk at his usual time. He looked ghastly; white, drawn and dazed. Fortunately, he had capable assistants who realized he was suffering from a shock of some kind and relieved him of all work except where his signature was essential.

He attended the West London Court when Harry Gleb made his brief appearance and studied Harry with pale revengeful eyes. It gave him some satisfaction to see the fear and suffering on Harry's face.

The same evening he went to Segetti's Restaurant off Jermyn Street. He was known in the grill-room, as Blanche and he went there often when Wesley worked late at the factory. Benton had a sudden nostalgic desire to go there that night, to sit in his usual corner and to commune with Blanche in spirit. But as soon as he entered the crowded grill-room and saw Segetti bearing down on him he realized he had made a mistake. Without Blanche at his side he felt naked in this atmosphere of riches, good food and smart talk. With Blanche, the restaurant had seemed an exciting and friendly place, but now it made him nervous, undermined his confidence. It was a sharp reminder that from now on he was going to be alone. He had no business in a luxury restaurant on his own. He became immediately an oddity: a fish out of water without some richly furred and smartly dressed woman at his side.

Already people were glancing curiously at him as he stood self-consciously in the doorway. Already he knew he had created a problem for Segetti. But it was too late to slink away, and he walked quickly down the red-carpeted aisle towards Segetti, who was coming to greet him.

"My usual table," he said, his pale eyes venomous. "I shall not stay long."

"Of course, Mr. Benton," Segetti said immediately, and as he led the way to a vacant table, he murmured: "Poor madam, we shall miss her sadly. A dreadful, monstrous thing."

Benton sat down.

"She liked coming here," he said, and looked up into the black Italian eyes. "No other place gave her more pleasure."

He would have liked to have taken Segetti into his confidence; to have told him how lonely he was and that the grill-room was full of memories for him. But there was a fatal quality in Benton that made people dislike him. He saw now dislike in Segetti's eyes, and a faint tinge of red rose out of his collar and flooded his face.

"To hell with him!" he thought, furious with himself. "I don't want his pity."

He ordered smoked salmon, which he didn't eat, and a bottle of Blanche's favourite brandy. He sat at the table brooding, unaware now of the curious glances that were shot at him. The brandy in the bottle sank rapidly. He knew he was getting a little drunk, but he didn't care. The brandy released the bitter, hard core in him that stifled him.

Then suddenly he saw Wesley and Julie come in. He recognized Wesley immediately by the black-leased glasses and the queer, half-hesitant walk. Julie he didn't recognize. He saw only a good-looking girl in a flame-coloured evening gown, her glossy dark hair dressed to her shoulders. Round her white throat was a string of glittering diamonds. For a moment or so he paid her no attention. He stared at Wesley, scarcely believing his eyes. How could he do such a thing? he asked himself. How could he come with a woman to a public restaurant not five days after his wife had been brutally murdered? Was this why he hadn't come to the factory? Had he suddenly gone off the rails and was living with this woman? Who was she?

He shifted his bloodshot eyes to stare at Julie. Where had he seen her before? Then suddenly he stiffened, leaned forward, his pale lips tightened. Julie! Blanche's maid! He passed a hot, dry hand across his eyes, then stared again: There could be no doubt about it, although he scarcely knew her in the gown which he now thought he recognized. Blanche had had a gown like that. He remembered it well: the gown she had worn the night she had given herself to him for the first time: a gown that conjured up a complete picture of their association together. Surely it was not the same gown, he thought, sick with horror. And those diamonds! They were Blanche's! Wesley had decked this servant in Blanche's things! To Benton it was an unforgivable blasphemy against Blanche. He felt hot blood rush to his head. The lights of the restaurant seemed to grow dim and a suffocating band encircled his throat. He was on his feet now, a choking, murderous rage consuming him.

He became vaguely aware that someone was holding him by the arm and a soothing voice was asking if he were unwell. He threw off the restraining hand with an ugly oath and walked stiff-legged, his face white and twitching, his eyes burning, to Wesley's table.

A sudden hush fell on the restaurant. People turned in their chairs to look at him. They watched him pause at Wesley's table and point with a quivering finger at Julie.

"Tell that dirty little bitch to take off your wife's dress!" Benton said in a cracked, hysterical voice. "How dare you, you damned housemaid!"

His hand shot out and made a grab at the diamond necklace but Julie struck his hand away and screamed. Wesley jumped to his feet. A young Army officer, dining at the next table, sprang forward and hit Benton savagely across his mouth with the back of his hand, sending him reeling back.

"You drunken swine!" the officer cried excitedly.

Two waiters had come up swiftly. They caught hold of Benton's arms. Segetti, mentally wringing his hands, waved them to take Benton away. They began to drag him to the door.

"Leave me alone!" Benton shouted, struggling furiously. "Take your hands off me!" Then his voice broke and he began to sob: great rasping sobs that sent a chill through those who heard him. He went limply now: muttering and sobbing, supported by the two embarrassed waiters. The glass doors swung behind him.

IV

During the days that followed Blanche's death, Julie achieved an ambition that had tormented her from early childhood. At last she had as much money as she wanted, a flat in the West End and a mink coat. It was unbelievable. If it hadn't been for Wesley she would have been beside herself with joy. But Wesley worried her.

Julie considered all men were alike. They were different only in their approach. As far as she was concerned they wanted only one thing. She found Wesley attractive, and when he insisted on staying with her in the new flat she was prepared to accept him as a lover. But it came as a shock to her pride when Wesley made no attempt nor showed any desire to be intimate with her. He was friendly and kind but impersonal, and it worried her. With other men she had always known where she was and could anticipate each move, but with Wesley she was mystified and frustrated, and as the days passed she began to hate him, suspecting that he could not forget that she was his wife's maid and that was the reason why he was so cold to her.

To punish him she demanded expensive presents, but instead of being annoyed he seemed pleased and urged her to greater extravagance. He took her to Asprey's in New Bond Street and bought her a gold and enamelled toilet set. He bought her a gold cigarette-case and lighter. He took her to the Savoy for lunch, the Berkeley to dinner and to Ciro's to dance. They went riding in the Row. They went to cinemas and theatres. But all the time she was aware of this impersonal barrier between them, and raged against it.

Since the night of the murder she hadn't had a moment to think of Harry Gleb. Wesley saw to that. Her days and nights were fully occupied in reckless spending, visits to night clubs, theatres and cinemas. There was no radio in that flat and no newspapers were delivered. She had no means of learning of Harry's remand or that Mrs. French and Dana hadn't yet been caught. She was kept so busy that she didn't even suspect that to all intents and purposes she was a prisoner. No news of the outside world reached her. No one telephoned nor wrote to her. Wesley never left her for a moment.

She was quick to realize, however, that Wesley was willing to give her anything she wanted, and for some days now she had been hankering after Blanche's wardrobe.

She decided it was time to broach the subject.

Before doing so she took care to make herself look as lovely as she knew how. She was in pyjamas and a polka-spotted red and white silk dressing-gown that Wesley had given her the day before. She looked attractive and she knew it, but Wesley was unmoved. He sat in an arm-chair before the fire and studied her without interest.

"What particular mischief are you up to now?"

She smiled and made to sit on his lap but he pushed her gently away.

"Go and stand by the fire where I can see you."

He was exasperating, she thought, but it was no use letting him see how angry he made her.

"I want some clothes," she began. A cigarette hung from her carefully painted lips and she had her hands in her pockets, drawing the thin silk tight across her small buttocks. She squinted a little as the smoke of the cigarette drifted past her nose and she surveyed Wesley with calculating shrewdness.

"But surely you have enough clothes for the present. Aren't you ever contented, Julie? As soon as you have one thing you want something else."

"I don't like the clothes you've bought me. I've been thinking. There are all those clothes at the flat. They fit me. Why shouldn't I make use of them?"

Wesley stared at her fixedly. She expected opposition and was braced for it.

"They are Blanche's clothes."

"She doesn't need them now; I do."

"I merely mentioned the fact to remind you that she has worn them. I thought perhaps you would feel squeamish to wear the clothes of a dead woman."

She was genuinely astonished.

"But why? Of course, I wouldn't wish to wear the dress she was murdered in—that'd be horrible, but the other clothes, why not? Why should they be wasted?"

"Has it occurred to you that I might dislike to see you in my wife's clothes?"

"Why should you? She had hundreds of dresses. There must be dozens she wore when you were blind. Why should it matter to you if you don't know them?"

He suddenly laughed.

"You have an answer for everything. What a little ghoul you are. All right, Julie, have them by all means. I want you to be happy."

She was quick to seize that opportunity.

"Why?"

He stretched his legs towards the fire and smiled at her.

"Why not? Why shouldn't I try to make someone happy?"

"And what do you get out of it?"

"I have a charming companion, and besides, it interests me to see you emerging from your chrysalis. Why do you look so suspicious? Don't you believe people help others without an ulterior motive?"

"Men don't help me without a motive. You said you wanted me to be your mistress. You have a funny idea of a mistress, haven't you?"

"I don't recollect saying anything of the kind. I have no intention of making you my mistress, as you so crudely put it. I offered you a home, security and a thousand a year. I made no conditions. It is you who are interpreting the terms, and wrongly. I want nothing from you except to know you are happy." He paused to light a cigarette, went on: "Suppose you run along and change? If you want those dresses we'd better go over to the flat and get them."

"You don't have to come. I can get them without bothering you."

"Don't deprive me of your company, Julie; and besides, the hall porter might think you were stealing them."

She felt colour rise in her cheeks.

"Aren't you going to the factory anymore?" she asked, to change the subject. "Should you spend so much time with me?"

"I can manage the factory quite well from here, Julie. Are you anxious that I shall run out of money? There's no need to be worried. I have very able assistants." He was obviously laughing at her. "Will you get changed now? I wouldn't like you to catch cold."

She slammed the door as she left the room. It was the only way in which she could express her feelings.

She didn't notice how pale he was as they rode up in the lift to the flat in Park Way. She was far too excited at the thought of possessing all those lovely clothes even to look at him. She had no misgivings about entering the flat again. Even the faint brown stain on the carpet meant nothing to her. Blanche might never have existed, and Harry was but a vague uneasy stirring of conscience far at the back of her mind.

While she was choosing the dresses Wesley paced up and down, his hands deep in his pockets, his chin on his chest. And when she selected one particular dress and held it up for inspection, he said suddenly with a rasp in his voice: "No! Not that one. Put it back!"

"But I like it," she said, and her mouth set obstinately. "It's just right for my colouring. Why shouldn't I have it?"

"Put it back!"

She saw the lines of pain on his face and the glitter in his eyes and recognized the danger signals. There were plenty of other dresses to choose from and with a little shrug she put the dress back.

"Aren't you nearly ready?" he demanded impatiently. "You'll never wear all those things."

"Oh yes, I will. You don't think I'm going to miss an opportunity like this? All my life I've longed to have masses of clothes: I've got them now."

At last she was ready to leave. She had packed two large suitcases with the clothes she had chosen, but even then she wasn't satisfied. The room, she knew, contained jewellery and furs. She was reluctant to leave without some of them.

"Couldn't I have some jewellery?" she asked, and smiled coaxingly. "Those dresses will look awfully bare without something to set them off."

He stared at her for a long uncomfortable moment. "You're never contented, it seems, Julie. Well, all right. I suppose I'd better find you something."

He turned off the alarms to the safe and opened it, and began to look through the drawers in the steel cabinet. She joined him but he turned quickly, standing between her and the drawers.

"I said I would find you something. Will you please sit over there until I have decided what you shall have?"

"But why can't I choose for myself? I know what I want."

"If you don't sit down, you won't have anything."

She was angry, but again the glitter in his eyes subdued her, and with a sulky shrug she walked to the window. But she needn't have worried: his selection took her breath away, especially the diamond necklace he so carelessly dumped on the table.

"Oh! How beautiful! Can I really have them? Are you giving them to me?"

"I'm lending them to you. Everything you are using is lent, Julie."

She gave him a quick puzzled glance, but she was too excited to bother about terms and conditions. These jewels were for her to wear. She could worry about whether she was to keep them or not later. She wanted to try on the necklace immediately but he wouldn't let her. He seemed suddenly anxious to get away from the flat.

Even when she had the two suitcases full of clothes and the jewellery she still hankered after the furs.

"Couldn't I have one of the fur coats?" she asked as she put the jewellery in her handbag. "I'd love the Arctic fox. Shall we take it with us?"

He closed the safe.

"No! Be content with the mink coat I gave you, and do stop asking for things. You are not having any of the furs. Aren't you ever satisfied?" He picked up the suitcases and made for the door. "It's no use looking sulky. Come on, Julie, don't behave like a child."

She followed him into the lift, inwardly fuming. She wanted the Arctic fox now more than anything in the world, but she knew it wasn't wise at this moment to press for it. Later, she would plan a campaign to get it. She was confident that if she kept on and on at him he would let her have it.

That evening they had gone to Segetti's restaurant because Julie had wished to show off her diamond necklace in the smartest restaurant in London.

Benton had spoilt their evening, and now, in the taxi going home, she sat frozen with rage.

Wesley had remained calm and quiet during the scene and after. She hated him for being so unmoved, feeling he had slighted her by not being angry with Benton. Brooding about this she could no longer keep silent and burst out: "How dare he call me names like that! The beast! You're not going to let him get away with this, are you? He was your wife's lover. You're not going to let him insult me as well?"

Without looking at her he said in a cold, contemptuous voice: "Hold your vulgar little tongue!"

She was so taken aback that she sank against the leather seat of the taxi and lapsed into outraged silence. Neither of them said anything until they were once more inside their flat.

Then Julie rounded on him, her face flushed and her eyes glittered with anger.

"I'm sick of this! I'm not staying with you a moment longer. I don't know why I ever came here. You're always beastly to me."

Wesley wandered across the room and turned on the electric fire. He looked tired and drawn but there was a sparkle of anger in his eyes, too.

"If you want to go, then go. I won't stop you, but you'll take nothing with you. Do you understand? If you leave here you'll go in your own clothes and not the clothes I lent you. Go to your room. I'm tired of you to-night."

She went to her room, white with fury because she now realized that whatever he said or did to her could not be bad enough to make her give up this life of luxury she had discovered. She knew she was in a trap, and she raged against it. She hadn't the strength of character to give up her possessions and go back to the drudgery of the past. It infuriated her to know she hadn't the power over him as she had over other men. After a while she began to calm down, and she sat on the bed and for the first time began to reason out why he should have done so much for her when it was obvious she meant nothing to him. Why was he doing this when he was contemptuous of her; even disliked her? At first it had been because she knew he could see, but then he had made out that it didn't matter if she had talked. If it didn't matter, why was he still pretending to be blind? Suppose he had been bluffing? Suppose he still had a reason for someone to believe he was blind? But why? Who was he afraid of? Someone m the factory? Benton? The police? She jumped up suddenly. The police? Then it came to her in a flash and the shock staggered her. *He had shot Blanche!* It was so obvious she couldn't understand why she hadn't realized it before. It was a perfect alibi. That was it! No one would suspect a blind man. He had hated Blanche. Gerridge had said if they were divorced he would have had to settle a large sum of money on her and he hadn't the means. Blanche was carrying on with Benton. The motive was there. He had pretended the operation on his eyes had been a failure when all the time it had been successful. He must have known sooner or later an opportunity would come, and he could murder Blanche in circumstances that couldn't possibly involve him so long as he kept up the pretence of being blind. And she had given him the opportunity. He had been quick to see how easy it would be to shift the blame on to Harry. That was why he had been so anxious that Blanche shouldn't know about the robbery.

Somehow he had persuaded Blanche to return with him to the flat. But how had he evaded the police? And then Julie remembered the finger-stall he had picked up in the lift and had tried to conceal. She remembered too how agitated he had become when she had told him someone could have shot Blanche from the passage. She was sure now he had come up with Blanche and remained out of sight in the lift while she opened the front door. Then he had shot her as she entered the hall and had thrown the gun in after her. It was simple enough. The police weren't in the passage. All he had to do was to close the lift doors immediately after getting rid of the gun and to wait until the police had broken into the flat. While they were arresting Harry, the lift would take him down to the basement. There, no doubt, he had waited a few minutes then walked in through the main entrances. Who would suspect him?

The discovery filled her with horror. She had known instinctively that Harry hadn't done it. She had known all the time. As she sat there, cold and shaken, not knowing what to do, she heard a step outside and then Wesley came in.

She jumped to her feet and backed away, fear in her eyes.

"It was you!" she exclaimed. "You killed her! That's why you've pretended all this time to be blind!"

He closed the door quietly.

"I thought you would find that out in time," he said, calm and unmoved. "Well, now you know, we'd better talk it over. Sit down, and for goodness' sake don't look so scared. I'm not going to hurt you."

"I don't want to talk to you! Leave me alone! I'm going to the police!"

He pulled up an arm-chair near the bed and sat down.

"It's no use getting excited, Julie. It'll pay you to keep calm and hear what I have to say. Have a cigarette?" He held out his case, but she shrank away, shuddering.

"Julie, will you try not to act like a servant in a melodrama?" The cold edge to his voice aroused her anger, as he intended it should do.

"How dare you! Get out! Get out before I scream for help!"

Wesley lit a cigarette, dropped his case and lighter on the bed.

"Have a cigarette, Julie, and don't be silly. I want to talk to you."

"How can you be so unmoved after what you have done?" she said, staring at him blankly. "You haven't any feeling in you. You're cold-blooded and horrible."

"I assure you I have some feeling in me, Julie, but that's neither here nor there. You are quite right: I did shoot Blanche."

Julie stiffened.

"And you tried to make out Harry did it. You coward! How could you?"

"I haven't the same interest in Harry Gleb as you. He happened to be on the spot and naturally it was assumed he did it. You can scarcely blame me for not coming forward, can you? I think you would have done exactly the same as I did."

She was so surprised by his callousness that she could think of nothing to say.

"After all, Julie, with all respects to your friend Gleb, he isn't of any great value to society, is he? He is a thief, a spiv and from what you tell me a danger to young women. He hasn't anything to commend him as far as I can see. On the other hand I am engaged on work of national importance. My research work on pilotless aircraft which is now coming to fruition will be of immense value to this and the next generation. Putting us both into the scales I feel I have many more claims to life than he has."

"How can you talk like that? He's innocent. You couldn't hide behind him. You couldn't let him hang in your place."

"But I didn't say I was going to let him hang in my place," Wesley returned, and smiled. "Before you get excited, Julie, I'd better explain what has been happening. Now don't interrupt. Just sit down and keep quiet. Please have a cigarette. It'll help to settle your nerves."

Hypnotized by his calm, Julie sat on the bed and took a cigarette.

"That's fine. All right, I'll begin at the beginning. I married Blanche six years ago. I was very much in love; stupidly in love, if you like. I should have known from her reputation what kind of a woman she was; I had enough warnings, but I didn't believe the tales. To me, Blanche was the most attractive and lovely creature out of a fairy tale. In those days I had a lot of money. It seemed only right that I should make her a large settlement. I made her a large settlement. And then she suggested I should also agree to pay two hundred thousand pounds if the marriage broke up. I won't waste time telling you how clever she was about that. She made it sound like a joke. It seemed a joke to me until I had a watertight settlement presented to me for my signature. I refused to sign it, and Blanche promptly refused to go through with the marriage. There were two hundred guests expected, the whole wedding pageant had been arranged and I realized I would either have to sign or lose her and look a fool for the rest of my days. At least, that was how it seemed to me at the time. I behaved like a fool and I'm paying the price now. I was in love with her. I wanted her very badly. I felt the marriage couldn't go wrong. To cut a long story short I submitted to blackmail and signed. To tell it now makes it sound incredible, but I assure you she was very clever about it. She somehow made it seem that I was the one who didn't trust her, that I would be the one to break up the marriage if the marriage was to break up." He shrugged and smiled. "I assure you ninety-nine men out of a hundred would have done the same if they had as much money as I had then.

"The first year of our marriage was happy enough. A little disappointing, perhaps, but nothing that I could actually put my finger on. Blanche was always very bright and sweet; we went everywhere together, did things together, but all the time I didn't feel that she was quite mine. She wasn't, of course; she belonged to a dozen different men, but I only found that out later.

"The factory was developing and I was anxious not to raise capital from public money. I wanted full control as I had certain revolutionary ideas that might or might not succeed. I was gambling, and I preferred to gamble with my own money. The factory expanded. Soon I had practically two-thirds of my money tied up in it. That didn't worry me, as I was sure the gamble would come off. It was then that Blanche began to make trouble. Thinking about it, it is obvious that Benton told her my capital was safely tied up. She didn't wish to give me up, but she did wish to live as she liked. Although I didn't have available capital I did have a good income, and Blanche didn't want to lose that if she could help it. And so she began to drink and have whoever she fancied for a lover and there was nothing I could do about it. I couldn't get rid of her. I couldn't afford it. I was busy at the factory, and after a while I didn't care what she did. By then I was blind and what I didn't see ceased to worry me. We lived like that for a couple of years. Then Benton began pressing her to marry him. It dawned on her that she could get rid of me; she could force me to sell out and give her the settlement. The terms of the settlement were watertight. In court I wouldn't have had a leg to stand on. It came to my knowledge she was going to force the issue and I began to think of a way out. I had nearly completed my work. Another six months would see it through. If she held off until then I could sell out in safety, but she wouldn't." He stubbed out his cigarette and immediately lit another. His hand was steady as he held the flame of the lighter to his cigarette. "Am I boring you, Julie? I'm telling you all this because I want you to know exactly why I had to get rid of Blanche. She was a drunkard by now and a danger. She didn't care whom she corrupted. Any young fellow who amused her was in danger. You have no idea what a beastly little animal she had degenerated into. I was at my wits' end. Then the chance for an operation came along. I had the operation, and while I was waiting for the bandages to be taken off it crossed my mind what an excellent alibi blindness would be if I decided to murder Blanche. It was just a passing thought, but the idea stuck and I thought about it more and more. I decided that if my sight was restored I would kill her.

"The eye surgeon had warned me that the chances of my recovering my sight was a thousand to one. When they took off the bandages I could see nothing. The operation was obviously a failure and was accepted as such. But later in the day I suddenly found that I was seeing a little light, and by the evening I could see fairly well. I said nothing. I pretended that I was still blind.

"When I returned to the flat I was surprised to find you there in Blanche's clothes and with Gleb. I guessed you and he were after the furs and I began to think of a way in which I could use you both to strengthen my alibi. I had every reason to get rid of Blanche. I had no mercy for her. In every conceivable way she was a menace to my activities. There was no alternative. She had to go.

"Well, you know the rest. The plan worked out better than I thought possible. The police are a little worried why Blanche should have returned to the flat, but I don't think that will come to anything. I was very careful. And now, Julie, I have at least three months before I need worry about Blanche's death. In those three months my work will be completed."

"You—you mean you'll tell them? You won't let Harry hang?"

"Of course not. When I've finished what I am working on I shall go to the police and give myself up. It will be at least three months before Gleb will be in any serious danger. I don't care a great deal what happens to me after my work is finished. I wouldn't let such a specimen as Gleb die for something I did. So there's no need to look so tragic, Julie. He's having a bad time now, but he is quite safe. I promise you that. And I can't really bother about him having a bad time: he deserves nothing better."

Julie studied him. Her heart was thumping and her hands felt dry and hot.

"I don't trust you," she said finally. "I don't believe you'll give yourself up. I'm going to tell the police now what you've told me. Why should Harry suffer for you?"

"I took the risk of telling you all this, knowing you might say exactly what you've just said. So let's talk about you for a moment. You realize if you do give me away you'll have nothing except what you can earn? I don't think that will be much. You have had a taste of luxury and you know what it means to spend recklessly. I can't imagine you wanting to give all that up in a hurry. But I may have misjudged you. If so, you are quite at liberty to go to the police, but if I deny what you tell them it may be difficult for them to find enough evidence to release Gleb and arrest me. They may, of course, but it's a gamble, and in the meantime, Julie, you will have talked yourself out of your flat and your clothes and your jewels, all of which seem to give you a great deal of pleasure. But if you'll wait patiently until I have finished my work, then, before I give myself up I'll make you a generous settlement and you can keep the flat and all these other things." He stood up, stretched and yawned. "I'm tired. Let's leave it for to-night. You think it over. If you want to throw away everything you have and go back to your drab little life I won't stop you. You must please yourself. But I assure you Harry will be safe enough." He smiled at her, went to the door. "Good night, Julie."

CHAPTER SEVEN

I

After Wesley had left her, Julie had a pitched battle with her conscience. She hated Blanche and could feel no pity for her. The woman had been a horror and had got only what she deserved. Julie found it impossible to blame Wesley for what he had done, but to shift the crime on to Harry was unforgiveable. And yet, if she agreed to say nothing until Wesley was ready, she would be able to continue to live in her present style. It wasn't as if Harry would hang, she reasoned. Wesley had promised to give himself up when the time came. The work he was doing was important, and she had no difficulty in persuading herself that his request for time was reasonable. Of course, it was rough luck on Harry. But why should she have to give up everything just to save Harry a little suffering? He had made her suffer in the past. Look at the way he had let Theo beat her up. She had suffered then, hadn't she? And besides, although she didn't want to be selfish, if she gave Wesley away now what chance would she have of getting the Arctic fox fur? If she waited Wesley might let her have it as a reward for all she had done for him. And if it didn't occur to him to give it to her she would ask him outright for it.

But suppose Wesley wasn't going to give himself up? Suppose this was a trick to gain time? It was pointless to think like that, she assured herself. All she had to do was to go to the police if he were difficult. It was just a matter of arranging something at the last moment so Wesley should have time to finish his work and she should be sure that Harry wouldn't pay the penalty. And so she argued with herself far into the night until her conscience, battered and bruised, gave up the struggle.

The following morning Wesley asked her what she was going to do. It irritated her that he was so calm and unmoved when she said she was prepared to give him time.

"Well, now that's settled," he said, with an indifferent shrug of his shoulders, "I must get back to the factory. I have a lot to do and time is short."

"He might at least have thanked me," Julie thought. "After all, not many people would have done what I'm doing for him."

"There is one thing," she said awkwardly. "I feel I should—" She broke off and began again. "Those furs. I'd like the Arctic fox. I don't see why I shouldn't have it. I'm doing a lot for you."

"And I've done nothing so far for you, is that it?" Wesley returned, smiling. "When I am in jail I shall be happy to think of you wearing the Arctic fox. But I'm certainly not giving it to you now. Let's be quite frank with each other, Julie. My work and life are in your hands. I have no reason to trust you, and I'd feel a lot safer if I kept something you wanted very badly. It gives me a hold on you. You can see that, can't you? This I promise you: when I have finished my work you'll have not only the Arctic fox but the other furs as well. You won't have to wait long: two months at the outside."

She had to be content with that.

Now that Wesley had nothing to hide from her his attitude towards her underwent a change. He hurt and angered her by his plain speaking. He admitted he had set her up in the flat for no other reason than to ensure her silence. It was unfortunate he still had to live with her. The police would think it odd if he suddenly left her as he wished to do. At this stage he didn't wish the police to think anything he did was odd.

She was free to do what she liked. She had money, clothes and the use of the flat. She could invite her friends here, and he asked nothing of her except her silence.

"The harder I work the quicker your friend Gleb will be free, and the sooner you will have the furs, so don't expect me to take you out as often as you'd like. I simply shall not have the time."

This wasn't at all what Julie had expected, and when Wesley had gone off to the factory she became depressed and lonely. She had no friends. The people she once knew, the people who frequented the Bridge Café, were ruled out. She was afraid to make contact with them again. The morning dragged by and the afternoon spent at a cinema bored her. She was glad when she heard Wesley come in a few minutes after six.

"I hope you had an amusing day, Julie."

"I don't suppose you care," she replied bitterly. "But if you want to know I've had a rotten day."

He went into the sitting-room and she trailed after him.

"I'm sorry to hear that. I have a lot of work to do now, but if you like we can have supper together about nine. If you have something better to do I'll have a tray sent up."

"Oh, no, I'd like to go out to-night." She watched him sit down by the Dictaphone. "What happened to Benton?" she went on. She had been thinking savagely of Benton all day.

Wesley adjusted the Dictaphone, put on a new cylinder before replying.

"I've frozen him out." There was a curt, hard note in his voice. "It was simple enough. He owed money and I had only to withdraw certain guarantees for the bottom to fall out of his financial world. He won't bother me anymore."

"You're hard, aren't you?" Secretly she was delighted.

"I suppose I am. You have to be hard these days, Julie. You're not exactly soft yourself."

She saw he was impatient to begin work and she hated leaving him. She wanted company.

"I suppose I can't help you in your work?" she suggested, hoping he would let her stay with him.

He turned to look at her.

"Help me? You know, Julie, I've never met such an extraordinary young woman. Have you no fear of me? Aren't you horrified, knowing what I have done?"

Julie shrugged.

"Why should I care? She deserved all she got. She wasn't fit to live. Why should I be frightened of you?"

"I envy you your outlook. No, Julie, I don't think you can help me. You should be enjoying yourself. You mustn't waste time, you know. I really didn't expect to find you in at this hour. I thought you would be certain to be out having a good time."

"How can I have a good time alone? I've been bored stiff all day."

"Blanche was always complaining about being bored. You're beginning rather soon, aren't you? Why don't you look up your friends?"

"You know I haven't any friends now. It's all your fault. You're just jeering at me."

"Oh, nonsense." He showed his impatience. "But I've got to get on. We'll go into your troubles at supper. Please run along, Julie, and let me work."

"I'm sure I don't want to stay if I'm not wanted!" she exclaimed, her eyes filling with angry tears, and she went out, slamming the door.

Later she was abruptly jerked out of her slough of self-pity by the ringing of the front door bell. She was startled to find Detective

Inspector Dawson waiting in the passage.

"Is Mr. Wesley in?"

She tried to hide her consternation, aware Dawson was studying her closely.

"Yes, but he's working."

"I'd like a word with him. Tell him I won't keep him long, will you please?"

Julie reluctantly let him into the little hall.

He looked round and whistled softly.

"How do you like it here?"

"It's all right," Julie said sullenly.

"That's a pretty dress you have on. He's looking after you well, isn't he? I wonder why?"

Julie gave him an angry look, but she was scared, wondering what he wanted, and she burst in on Wesley flustered and shaken.

As soon as Wesley saw the frightened expression in her eyes, he said quietly: "Dawson?"

"Yes. He wants to speak to you."

"All right. Has he said anything?"

"Only you seem to be looking after me well and he wonders why." Wesley smiled.

"He's no fool, is he? All right, Julie, show him in. There's nothing to be frightened about. But if he worries you, you'd better tell him the truth."

"You'd look silly if I did."

"But you won't, of course."

"You'd better not be too sure."

"Don't keep him waiting and try not to be melodramatic. It doesn't suit you."

"I'm beginning to hate you," Julie said furiously. "You're always sneering at me."

"Don't be childish."

She went out of the room, her face scarlet, and Dawson was quick to see how angry she was.

"He'll see you," she said, not looking at him. "He's in the end room."

Dawson seemed to be in no hurry.

"I saw your pal Harry Gleb yesterday. He's pretty ill. I told him how you and Wesley had hooked up. When a chap's in prison he likes to hear the latest gossip. But Harry didn't seem to appreciate that item of news. He seemed to think it was your fault he was caught." Dawson shook his head sadly. "Ever think of Harry? I don't expect you have much time for your old friends. You're having a lot of fun, aren't you? Well, Harry isn't. Harry's worried. Between you and me if I were in his shoes I'd be worried too. Off the record, that young fellow's going to hang."

Julie eyed him steadily, but said nothing.

"Perhaps you don't think so? Maybe you've got something up your sleeve that'll save him?"

"I haven't."

"Sure? Anyone withholding evidence in a murder case can get into a whale of a lot of trouble. You still think Harry didn't do it?"

"Did you want me, Inspector?" Wesley asked from the doorway.

Dawson sighed, turned.

Wesley, his eyes hidden by the dark glasses, was standing looking towards Dawson. There was a stillness about him that betrayed his tension,

"I did." Dawson moved slowly across the room. "I was just having a word with Miss Holland. But now you're here—"

"Come into the sitting-room. You'll find it more comfortable. And Julie, you'd better change. When the Inspector has gone we have an appointment, if you remember."

As soon as Dawson and Wesley had gone into the sitting-room Julie fled to her bedroom, thankful Wesley had given her the excuse not to see Dawson again.

Alone, she began to work herself into a panic. Would she get into trouble for not telling the police about Wesley? Was Dawson bluffing? There was such a thing as being accessory to murder, although she had only the vaguest idea what it meant. Could they send you to prison? Should she tell Dawson the truth? If she did perhaps he wouldn't take any action against her. But he might. He didn't like her. He might be glad of the chance to get her into trouble.

She thought of Harry. It was cruel and beastly of Dawson to have told him she was living with Wesley. And it wasn't true. Not in the way Harry would think they were living together. But why was she getting into such a state about Harry? She didn't love him, or did she? Thinking about him she knew she would rather have Harry with her than Wesley. What fun they would have had! She was always thinking about Harry now. Because she couldn't have him, she wanted him, and it wasn't long before she believed she was once again in love with him. She began to make plans. There was no reason why Harry and she shouldn't get together when Wesley had given himself up and the money was hers. With the money Wesley had promised to settle on her, she and Harry could go to America. She supposed they would send Harry to prison for breaking into Blanche's flat, but it couldn't be for long and she would wait for him. Suddenly all the old feeling for him was back. She realized now she had always loved him, and he loved her. He had said so. Hadn't he pleaded with her to join up with him again? And, like a fool, she had turned him down for Wesley.

Dawson's deep voice in the passage outside interrupted her thoughts. She heard him walk to the front doors. A moment or so later Wesley came into her room. He stood just inside the door looking pale and tired.

"He's gone, but it was a near thing, Julie; a very near thing."

She started to her feet.

"Why? What did he want?"

"Asking questions. I wasn't quite as clever as I thought. But he's satisfied now."

"What questions?"

"Checking my statement. I avoided the obvious trap, but if he hadn't been so sure I was blind I might have been in a mess." He ran his fingers through his hair. Julie hadn't ever seen him look so anxious, "I don't feel like doing any more work tonight. This has unsettled me. Let's go somewhere and enjoy ourselves."

But Julie was worrying about herself.

"Dawson said I could get into trouble if I held back any evidence. I want to know what he means. I'm not going to get into trouble for anyone."

"You do worry about yourself, don't you? They can't do anything to you unless you talk. There's nothing to be alarmed about."

"It's all very well for you, but suppose they find out?"

"How can they unless you tell them? For goodness' sake stop worrying about yourself. I have enough worries of my own without having to listen to your selfish little problems. Now get changed and we'll go out."

Julie flared up.

"You don't think of me for a moment! I'm sick of being treated like a servant. You're always sneering and jeering at me."

"You have only yourself to blame," he said quietly. "You don't have to stay here."

"And give up everything? I'm not that much of a fool!"

"I'm afraid you're ruled by greed, Julie. As soon as you have one thing, you want something else. You are never satisfied, and I'm afraid you never will be."

"Are you calling me greedy?" she said furiously. "How dare you! I'm not! I never have been, so there!"

Wesley laughed.

"You're quite hopeless, Julie. Don't be angry. Get changed and let's go out."

"I won't go out with you! I hate you! Get out and leave me alone! I hate you! I hate you!"

She threw herself on her bed and began to cry.

II

There was no happiness for Julie now. Her life with Wesley became a continual conflict: a clash of wills in which she invariably came off second-best.

He was always busy, working late at the factory and when at home working far into the night. She was bored and miserable and haunted with thoughts of Harry. But she could not give up the flat or her possessions. She knew she would be happier if she went back to work, but she hadn't the strength of character to take the plunge.

She had everything that money could buy, except happiness, and her conscience gave her no peace. She began to brood about Blanche's death and the full horror of Wesley's crime slowly dawned on her. Although it was over a week since the murder, the fact that Wesley had killed Blanche only now meant anything to her, and once she began to think of him as a killer she became frightened of him. He had told her she held his life in her hands. If he could get rid of her no one would ever find out he had killed Blanche. She became nervous, and would wake in the night, terrified he was in the room, creeping on her to kill her. She locked herself in; she never turned her back on him; she was always watching to see he didn't have a chance to poison her.

She had an idea that she might sell the jewellery he had lent her and with the proceeds be independent of him, but she calculated that the money wouldn't last her for long and then she would be no better off. He had promised to settle money on her, and even though, as the days went by, she distrusted him more and more, she could not bring herself to lose the chance of being rich at last in her own right.

When Harry came up before the magistrates after the remand she was called as a witness for the prosecution. She was panic-stricken at the thought of publicly admitting she had been a police informer.

She received no sympathy from Wesley.

"You can't have your cake and eat it," he told her. "But please yourself what you say. If it makes you feel any better tell them I did it. I'm not going to influence you one way or the other," and he smiled at her, obviously amused by the furious, frustrated expression on her face.

She raged inwardly that he had so accurately judged her character. He had no misgivings that she would give him away. He was certain he was safe. Again and again, infuriated by his confidence, she was on the point of telephoning the police, but each time she changed her mind at the last moment.

When she stood in the witness-box, stared at by hundreds of eyes, she burned with shame. The sight of Harry sent a pang through her heart. She scarcely recognized him. He had lost weight, his face was lined and drawn, and there was a trapped, terrified look in his eyes. And he wouldn't even look at her. That was the last straw. He stood in the dock, his flashy suit pathetically out of place in the drab, sordid surroundings, his hands clutching on to the dock rail, his head lowered.

The Counsel for the Prosecution led her quickly and kindly through her story. He made things easy for her, drawing for the Court a picture of a terrified, inexperienced young girl caught up in a web of circumstances over which she had no control. Julie thought he overdid it, and wished he would stop harping on her innocence. What could Harry be thinking of her? She glanced across the well of the court, but Harry still wouldn't look at her.

But when the Counsel for the Defence began to question her the friendly atmosphere underwent a swift change. He seemed determined to spoil the good impression the Court had of her and to discredit her as much as he could. He succeeded. He asked her point-blank whether it was a fact she had been intimate with Harry. She hedged, but he kept after her until, red-faced and confused, she admitted it. So much for her innocence! Was it not a fact, he went on, that she had taken the job as Blanche's maid willingly, knowing a robbery had been planned? She denied this so hotly she could see no one believed her. What was she doing now? And he stared down his beaky nose when she said she was looking after Mr. Wesley. As a maid? He wanted to know. As a housekeeper, she floundered.

She left the witness-box knowing she hadn't helped Harry nor herself. The Counsel for the Defence had made her out to be a female Judas. She couldn't bear to stay in court after that, and it was Wesley who told her later that Harry had been committed for trial at the next Old Bailey sessions.

The papers were full of the case, and she read and re-read the accounts, shrinking with shame when she read the veiled insinuations the reporters had made regarding her relations with Wesley. She realized, too, that Harry hadn't a chance. Although no one actually saw him shoot Blanche, when the police had burst in they had seen him trying to escape. Only Julie and he were in the flat. Julie, as a police informer, had no motive for killing Blanche, but Harry had. He was, as the Counsel for the Prosecution had said, a rat in a trap. The whole thing appeared to be a foregone conclusion.

It was then that Julie really began to worry. Harry's white, agonized face haunted her. She kept reassuring herself that he would be all right, that Wesley would give himself up, but when she realized what a hopeless trap Harry was in she began to fear that something might happen to Wesley. Suppose he was run over and killed? Then nothing could save Harry. Tormented by this idea, she went to Wesley.

"Do you think I am utterly heartless?" he said, laying down a sheaf of papers he was studying. "I thought of that weeks ago and there's a signed statement at my bank to be opened after my death. If anything happens to me, he won't suffer."

"How do I know you are speaking the truth?"

"You should try to assess character, Julie. I don't think you believe I'll save Gleb. Do you?"

"If you say so I suppose you will," Julie said sulkily.

One night, a week before the trial, Wesley called her as soon as he entered the flat. She hadn't seen him for two days and she came from her room cautiously.

"What is it?"

She stood just inside the doorway and looked suspiciously at him. He was pacing up and down, a frown on his face, his hands thrust deep into his trousers pockets.

"I've seen Dawson, he tells me Dana French has come forward as a witness for the defence."

"But she will be arrested!" Julie exclaimed, changing colour.

"Apparently she is in love with Gleb."

"What do you mean?" Julie demanded angrily.

"She's sacrificing herself because she thinks she can save him."

"But how?"

Wesley shrugged.

"She's willing to swear the gun belonged to Theo and that it was Theo who shot Blanche. She doesn't realize that her evidence won't save Gleb. But I thought it might interest you. It seems there are still a few people left who are unselfish."

Julie clenched her fists. She was sick with envy and rage. To think that painted creature should have done that for Harry!

"You hate me, don't you?" she exclaimed, facing him.

"No, Julie, I don't hate you. In fact, you interest me. Nothing would please me more than for you to go to the police and tell them the truth. It would prove to me that I was entirely wrong about you."

"I don't know what you mean."

"Yes, you do. Even now, when this girl has set you an example, you won't risk the chance of losing your money."

"You're just trying to be beastly. Harry won't hang. You've promised me. Why should I give up everything for the sake of a few weeks? It's you who are selfish and cruel. You aren't going to let him hang?"

"No, but it's hard for you to believe, isn't it? I'm beginning to think you wouldn't sacrifice anything for him even if I did let him hang."

"I would! You'd better not try any tricks. It's only because I know I can save him that I'm doing this. Why shouldn't I have happiness and money? All my life I've had to do without."

"Happiness? Are you happy, Julie? I doubt it. And when you are on your own and have your money you still won't be happy. A girl like you can never be happy. You're chasing something that doesn't exist."

"I'll see about that. And while we're on the subject just how much money are you leaving me?"

"I was wondering when you were going to ask that. I thought two thousand a year would be enough."

She wouldn't get another chance, she thought, and said, "Two thousand? After all I've done for you? I want more. I want much more. Who else have you to leave your money to? If it hadn't been for me you wouldn't be able to finish your precious work. Isn't that worth more to you? I want five thousand."

"Don't be childish."

"I want it and I mean to have it!"

He looked at her, contempt in his eyes.

"Has it ever crossed your mind, Julie, that I could get rid of you very easily?"

Her anger went like the blowing out of a match flame.

"Frightened?" he went on. "When a man has committed one murder, a second one doesn't increase his punishment. What could be easier and more convenient for me than to wring your wretched little neck?"

She backed away.

"And sometimes, Julie, I feel it would give me such a lot of pleasure. Unfortunately, I don't seem to be a killer by nature. You may not believe it, but I am sorry for what I did to Blanche. She meant nothing to me in the end; she deserved to die, but not at my hands. I shall regret her death as long as I live. The only thing that matters in life, Julie, is peace of mind. That I haven't got; nor have you. And don't look so scared. You're quite safe. I don't want your death on my conscience and, besides, I don't fancy touching you. The more I see of you, Julie, the more I realize what an unpleasant young woman you are."

"We'll see about that," Julie said furiously. "You'll be sorry for that. You see if you aren't."

Wesley laughed at her.

III

Benton sat in the bar of a shabby public house near Charing Cross station. He sipped whisky and stared at the small, wet rings that decorated the wooden top of the table beside which he was sitting. There was a bleak, unhappy expression in his eyes and his thin body was shivering.

He was finished, he told himself. The best way out would be to shoot himself. He had been telling himself this for the past two weeks, but he knew he hadn't the courage either to kill himself or to face his creditors. He was like a man on a high tightrope who has lost his nerve and knows that if he makes a move he will fall. He had made up his mind to keep out of the way and do nothing until something happened that forced him into action. He had left his flat in Dover Street and for the last four or five days he had wandered the streets, sleeping at a different hotel each night. He had thirty-five pounds in his pocket and when that had gone there was nothing.

He owed a lot of money. He wasn't sure how much he did owe, but he thought it might be something like twenty thousand pounds. It might be more and he didn't think it could be less. If they got hold of him they would make him bankrupt. The disgrace of bankruptcy hung over him like a soiled cloak. He would have to give up his club. Ever since his father had made him a member he had never lost the feeling of pride that he had when he entered the dignified portals and had used the big, silent rooms for the first time. He clung fiercely to tradition, knowing there was nothing else to cling to. His school, his club, his flat and the fact his father had been a general were the highlights in his life. They meant more to him than anything else; they and, of course, Blanche. Now he had lost everything and his pale hatred centred on Wesley.

Benton was not a violent man. There was no primitive spark in him that could be flamed to murder. His hatred was spiteful and vindictive but not violent, and as he sat in this dirty little public house he perfected a plan of revenge. It didn't cross his mind to wreak a physical revenge on Wesley. A blind man would be easy to injure or even to murder, but it would only afford a momentary satisfaction. He wanted something more subtle than that. He wanted Wesley to suffer as he was suffering.

He flicked away a speck of dust on his black overcoat. The gesture was unconscious, but revealed he had at last made up his mind. He could now think of something else besides Wesley, and the speck of dust had caught his eyes as his mind was released from its problem. Although he had been living in ratty little hotels with only a change of clothing he still managed to maintain his finicky elegance, and each morning he lowered his shivering body into a cold bath. His misfortunes had not undermined that traditional habit.

He finished his whisky and walked a little unsteadily across the bar to order another. A girl in a red hat and a dirty mackintosh caught his eye and smiled. She was tall, big-hipped and robust, and for a moment Benton's mind wavered and he felt a flicker of desire run through him. Then he noticed her grimy hands and a line of dirt round her neck and a faint sour smell that came from her hair as he stood close to her, and he inwardly shivered to think that such a creature could raise in him even for a moment a feeling of desire.

He returned to his table and sat down again, and drank half the whisky, setting the glass carefully on one of the wet rings. He took a cigarette from his case.

"I'll have one if you can spare it," the girl in the red hat said, coming over to him.

He rose to his feet. A gentleman, his father had told him, behaved like a gentleman even to a whore.

"I'm afraid you are wasting your time," he said in his pale voice. "Please excuse me."

"I'm in no hurry, *cheri*. I'll give you a good time. You can stay an hour if you like."

Again he felt a flicker of desire like pain run through him, and he thought of Blanche. He was alone now; he didn't have to keep faith with anyone except himself. He looked again at the girl, appraising her with his pale, lonely eyes and was again horrified with himself for even contemplating going with her.

"I'm afraid not," he said, still courteous. "You must excuse me."

"You look sort of fed up. I'd make you forget."

"I'm afraid not." His grimacing smile came and went.

"Well, buy me a drink. You wouldn't begrudge me a drink, would you?"

He fingered his loose change in his pocket. He did begrudge her the drink. He needed every penny now, but he felt on him the jeering eyes of three men who were standing at the bar and he was afraid she would make a scene.

"I'm in a hurry. Here, buy one on me. I really must be going."

She looked at the half-crown he held out to her and her full lips curled scornfully.

"You can stick that on the wall. If you didn't want me why did you make faces at me? Oh, hop it, you mean little rat."

He left the bar hurriedly, the jeering laughter of the men following him. It was only when he got into the fresh night air that he realized he was drunk and he had to walk carefully. As it was he lurched against an old woman who was walking towards Charing Cross station. She was very old and bent and shabby and she thudded against the wall from the impact of his shoulder.

He stared at her in stupefied horror, raising his hat and muttering apologies. He had never knocked into a woman in his life. A gentleman, no matter how drunk, didn't fall against a woman. He was crimson with shame.

He saw her old eyes were full of weak rage as she said: "You're drunk, that's wot you are. Tight as a bloody lord."

He was fumbling in his pocket for the half-crown that had already been scorned when the old woman recovered her balance and shuffled on, leaving him to gaze after her, a pale spark of anger flaming up in him like the first twinge of toothache. And as he walked to the Strand he muttered to himself, his head down, his shoulders hunched, a bitter, angry figure to interest the curious eyes of the people who passed him.

Wesley! He wouldn't wait any longer. He couldn't go on like this. First he must settle with Wesley, then his mind could grapple with his own problems; but so long as Wesley occupied his thoughts he would never get himself in hand.

He quickened his pace. In the distance Big Ben struck nine o'clock. The Strand was still crowded. The crowds were coming out of the Tivoli and he could hear their shuffling feet and their cheerful voices behind him. He cut across Trafalgar Square and stopped suddenly by one of the fountains.

There were three watchmen at the factory, he was thinking. He knew their routine well. They had supper together at eleven o'clock. He had once caught them at it. It was against the rules and although they had been warned he knew they continued to meet at eleven. For half an hour the research laboratory was unguarded. He still had the key. It shouldn't be difficult.

His shadow lay across the dark water of the fountain and he stared at it, his mind groping back into the past. He remembered for no reason at all the first time he met Blanche, and recaptured the feeling that had come over him as he looked into her wide, blue eyes. That was something that would never happen again; a precious moment, not valued then, but treasured now. He had nothing to look forward to, only memories to look back on; memories and revenge.

He set off quickly towards Pall Mall, passing his club with a furtive glance at the lighted windows. He would have liked to have gone in for a drink and a last look round, but his courage quailed at the thought of meeting the hall porter, an aged man who knew every member by name, knew what their businesses were and how much money they had. He did pause to look through the window of the smoking-room. The big arm-chairs standing in pairs about the room, the soft lighting, the vast Adam's ceiling, the two fireplaces in which great logs cheerfully blazed, the sedate movements of the old waiter as he carried a tray of drinks to a group of members sitting hunched up in a circle round one of the fires formed a picture that he took away with him: a poisoned barb in his mind.

That room had been a part of his life a week or so ago. Wesley had taken it from him. There was a feverish look in his eyes as he ran into the road, waving his arms at a taxi that had just set down a fare and was pulling slowly away from the kerb.

At first the driver was unwilling to go out as far as Northholt, but when Benton thrust a pound note into his hand he grumblingly agreed.

Benton stared out of the window as the taxi rattled and banged along Bayswater Road. There was a light, airy feeling inside his head and his mouth was dry. He wanted another drink, and as the taxi passed Shepherd's Bush underground he leaned forward and told the driver to stop at the next public house.

He bought the driver a pint of beer while he swallowed greedily two double whiskies. The driver, a thick-set, elderly man, drank the beer grudgingly. Benton could see from his surly expression he had taken a dislike to him. But Benton was used to that. Neither of them said anything except the customary, "Good health," and neither of them meant it.

It was now a few minutes to ten o'clock. Plenty of time, Benton thought, and he paid for the drinks and went back with the driver to the taxi.

As the taxi passed Wood Green underground station, Benton suddenly recollected coming this way to the Kensal Green crematorium for Blanche's funeral. He hadn't gone into the little chapel. Wesley had been the only mourner and he hadn't been able to bring himself to share his grief with Wesley. There had been a big crowd of morbid sightseers and he had mingled with them, nursing his grief as a man nurses a mortal pain. And when everyone had left he had gone to the grave and laid on it a bunch of violets. He had derived a little comfort and happiness to know that his were the only flowers on the wet, raised earth He stopped the taxi a quarter of a mile from the factory and without looking at the driver walked rapidly into the darkness. The broad two-way road was still busy with home-going traffic and he kept to the grass verge, his head bent against the blinding headlights of the oncoming cars.

The gates of the factory were closed and locked, but he had expected that. He knew of a loose plank in the fence further along the road; a secret exit used by some of the workers who slipped out in working hours to buy fruit from the lorries drawn up near the airfield. He pushed the plank aside, stooped and passed his thin body through the opening, then set off quickly towards the research laboratory.

The factory was in darkness. Even the control room and the hangars were shut down for the night. He walked on the grass, his pale eyes alert, his hands deep in his overcoat pockets.

The research laboratory, a one-storey building of brick and tile, was hidden behind the main office block, three or four hundred yards from the main entrance. Coming upon it suddenly, Benton was startled to see a solitary light in one of the windows. The moon, riding high, cast a cold, white light over the building, picking out the mortar between the bricks.

Benton remembered how proud he had been of the building when it had been erected. All his careful organization had gone into it. He remembered the hundreds of forms he had to fill up to obtain the necessary building material, the plaintive bickering of the authorities who had tried to persuade him that prefabricated concrete sheds would do as well. But he had persisted, argued and cajoled, until they had given way in grudging despair.

And now he was going to set fire to the place. It would finish Wesley as Wesley had finished him. All Wesley's money was tied up in the mass of intricate and delicate machinery housed in the building. In a little while it would he an inferno of flames. There was a drum of petrol in one of the outside sheds. He would drag it to the building. A match would do the rest.

He stood looking at the lighted window, wondering if Wesley were still in the building, and as he watched the light went out. He waited, hidden in the shadows, and after a few minutes a man came out of the building. He recognized the limping walk. It was the senior watchman. He was going to supper.

IV

Anyone looking into the room could easily have mistaken the scene to have been one of domestic bliss. Wesley sat in an arm-chair. From time to time he selected a paper from a table by his side and studied it, making neat notes in the margin. Opposite him sat Julie. She was knitting a complicated pattern in blue and white. The two coloured balls of wool rested in her lap and her knitting needles clicked and flashed as she fashioned the pattern with expert speed.

Except for the click of the needles and the rustle of papers silence had hung over the room for a long time. Julie had wanted to go out that evening but Wesley had refused. Rather than go alone she had brought her knitting into his room and, without his permission, had sat by the fire. After one surprised glance he had continued to work, and now she was sure he had forgotten her.

She had been alone all day and yearned for company. Even Wesley's silent company was better than being on her own, and now as she knitted, the warmth of the fire against her legs, she felt herself relaxing, and for the first time for many weeks she experienced an isolated peace of mind.

Then, suddenly, she was startled out of her blank, comfortable mood by the shrill ringing of the telephone. The sharp sound of the urgent bell brought into the quiet room an atmosphere of alarm. Even Wesley started, his mind jerked away from his calculations.

"I sometimes wish telephones had never been invented," he said, laying down his papers. "Would you answer it, Julie? Say I'm busy."

Julie put down her knitting and, with ill grace, went to the telephone. A man's voice asked for Wesley.

"It's very urgent," he said. "I am calling from the factory." There was an excited note in his voice and he spoke loudly.

"It's the factory," she said to Wesley and held out the receiver. He took it from her and their fingers touched. Julie snatched her hand away and moved back to the fire.

She could hear the man shouting; his voice, although loud, was indistinct. She caught the word "fire" and looked quickly at Wesley, sensing immediately that something was wrong. Wesley had stiffened and his face had gone a whitish grey.

"I'll come out."

The man went on shouting.

"All right, all right," Wesley said quietly. "Yes, keep him there until I come. I'm coming now." He set down the receiver and stood for a moment looking at Julie. There was a dead expression in his eyes that frightened her.

"What is it?"

"Benton has set fire to the lab. I've got to go out there at once."

"Benton? But why?"

"Does it matter?" He shook his head and pressed his palms to his temples, like a boxer trying to shake off the effects of a damaging punch.

"Do you want me to come with you?" She made the offer without thinking.

He pulled himself together with an effort.

"I suppose so. I may as well keep up the pretence a little longer, anyway until I see the extent of the damage. It'd look odd if I didn't have someone to lead me about, wouldn't it? Besides, the fire might amuse you. It should be an awe-inspiring sight."

The cold, flat note in his voice sent a shiver through her.

"Is it bad then?"

"It seems so. Come on; with luck we'll find a taxi."

They picked up a taxi in Piccadilly.

For some time Wesley stared through the window in silence as the taxi weaved a way through the last of the evening's traffic, then he said abruptly: "It's strange how things work out, isn't it, Julie? I thought I had been so thorough and nothing could go wrong. The laboratory was, of course, the key to everything, and yet I never gave it a thought. It doesn't look as if your friend Gleb will stand trial now."

Julie stared searchingly at his white face.

"I don't understand."

"If the lab is burned out there's no point in my working anymore. It puts a full stop to everything."

"You mean you wouldn't have the time?"

"Or the money."

Julie recoiled from him as if he had hit her.

"What has money to do with it?"

"To equip the lab I borrowed money. To borrow money I gave securities. If the lab's gone my securities have gone with it."

Julie suddenly felt as if she were going to be sick.

"You mean you won't have any money? Then what's to become of me? You promised to settle money on me!"

"I know. I'm sorry, Julie, but I couldn't foresee this, could I? There won't be anything left of my money. Everything I owned went into the lab. But you'll have the furs and the jewellery. They are worth a good bit. If you're careful you'll be all right."

"You've cheated me!" she cried furiously. "After all I've been through; after all your rotten promises! Damn you! I might have known this would happen. All right, you won't get any more time. I'm going to the police. I'll make you pay for this."

"I'm sorry, Julie. You don't really deserve anything, but a promise is a promise. I would have kept my word. I want you to believe that."

"You talk! That's all you're any good at—talking! You talked me into this! You and your rotten promises!" Tears of rage ran down her face and she sat huddled up in the corner of the taxi, her hands clenched in her lap.

"You'll have the furs. I hope they'll give you some happiness. You're due for a little happiness, but somehow I don't think you'll get it. What will you do, Julie? Will you wait for Gleb to come out of prison? You're in love with him, aren't you?"

"Yes," she said fiercely. "He's worth six of you. I'll wait for him. You can think of us while they're hanging you!"

The taxi rattled past the White City. For a moment or so the inside of the taxi was lit up by the battery of arc lamps that had blazed up for the last race. And in the hard, glaring light they looked at each other.

"Try not to be bitter about it, Julie. I have lost much more than you. But then, I suppose I'm a lot older than you and I've learned to accept disappointments. If I had more time I would begin again, but that is impossible now. It looks as if Blanche has had the last laugh after all. It was a mistake to have killed her. You see, it hasn't done me any good."

Julie didn't say anything; her mind was seething with dismay and fury. After all she had endured from him and now no money!

"I would never have believed Benton had the nerve to do such a thing," Wesley went on. The swiftly passing street lamps lit up his white face. He looked tired and sad. "They say he's badly burned."

"Oh, shut up!" Julie exclaimed, beating her fists together. She was beside herself with disappointment. "That's all you're any good at, talking and making rotten promises." She swung round to face him. "And how do I know you'll give me the furs after all this? How do I know you won't cheat me again?"

"Go to my bank in the morning. They'll have a letter for you. There's a statement, too, for the police. I've put everything in order."

"You go. Why should I run errands for you? It's going to be different now. I'm not going to be ordered about anymore."

"Poor Julie," he said wearily. "I'm very sorry for you."

The taxi began to slow down as the traffic thickened. In the distance they could see a vast red glow in the sky.

"There it is," he went on quietly. "I said it would be an awe-inspiring sight, didn't I?"

She noticed his hands were trembling but she felt no pity for him. At least she would have the furs. She would keep the Arctic fox and sell the others. With the money she raised on the furs and the jewellery and with the money Harry must have put by they should be all right.

As the taxi neared the factory they could see the flames and the spirals of oily, black smoke outlined against the red sky. Lines of cars were parked on either side of the road, and a big crowd was moving towards the fire. The night was full of sounds: excited voices, laughter, the shuffling of feet. Somewhere in the crowd a dog was barking; a sharp sound that blended with the dry crackling of burning timber.

A policeman stopped the taxi.

"You can't get through," he said, with patient good humour. "The hoses are across the road."

"We'll walk," Wesley said, and got out of the car. "Will you wait?" he went on to the driver. "The young lady will be coming back."

Julie followed him along the grass verge and they quickly caught up with the slow-moving crowd. Wesley caught hold of her arm and began to weave his way through the crowd, pulling her up with him. A man jostled him and knocked off his dark glasses. Julie, coming up behind, trod on them. She felt the lenses crunch under her foot. It gave her an odd physical satisfaction. He was finished, she thought. The breaking of the glasses seemed to her to be the final milestone of their association.

"They've broken," she said to him.

"What does it matter? Don't you see, Julie, for me nothing matters now."

They reached the gates of the factory. Now they could hear the hiss of water striking red-hot metal. The roar of the flames sounded near, and the air was hot and dry. Wesley spoke to one of the policemen guarding the gate. He showed him a card and the policeman let him through.

Gerridge came running out of the smoke towards them.

There was a long streak of oily soot across his face and a shocked, scared look in his eyes.

"Is it bad?" Wesley asked, gripping his arm.

Gerridge gulped. For a moment he couldn't say anything. He clung on to Wesley's arm while he tried to get his breath.

"There's nothing left," he burst out. "It's awful. The place is a roaring furnace. They can't save it."

"And Benton?" Wesley spoke quietly.

"He's badly burned, but he's alive." Gerridge was staring at Wesley.

I'LL GET YOU FOR THIS

Chester Cain, professional gambler and gunman, is on vacation. Or so he thinks. The Paradise Palms welcomes him with open arms. They even provide female company, the lovely Claire Wonderly. But that night Cain is set up. The political opponent of Killeano, town bigwig, is found murdered in Cain's hotel room—and Cain's the fall guy. Cain doesn't take well to being framed, and he goes on the run with Miss Wonderly. Soon he finds that the entire city is out for his hide. Killeano's got his sadistic police chief on his tail, with a promise of an unpleasant death if he's caught. But they picked the wrong fall guy. They may be after Cain, but Cain plans to take them down first!

THE PAW IN THE BOTTLE

Julie Holland is convinced that life's dealt her a bad hand. She has to struggle just for a few quid. She wants more from life: money, good times, jewelry and furs. So when she gets a chance to be involved in a robbery she agrees. All she has to do is play maid to a self-centered shrew, figure out how to get into her safe, and share the info with Harry and Mrs. French. But then Julie starts to have second thoughts. So Theo steps in. He's a sadistic little thug who doesn't mind threating a girl with acid in the face if she gets out of line. He convinces Julie to stay the course. If only it didn't involve a betrayal… but it's worth it to get her hands on all that money. Because Julie knows she deserves it.

"Chase somehow manages to be almost insanely readable." —*The Observer*

"His best works sometimes read like a pastiche of a Gold Medal original or noir film…They move fast, and at their best manage to recreate the kind of doomed noirish atmosphere of James M. Cain."
—David L. Vineyard, *Mystery*File*

"You may be horrified by his characters, but your sympathy races along with them."
—*Eastern Daily Press*

"Your eyes, sir. Are they all right? They look all right. Can you see?"

"Yes, I can see. Take me to Benton."

"That's marvellous."

Gerridge seemed bewildered. "But when did it happen? Was it the operation . . .?"

"Take me to Benton," Wesley said curtly.

Gerridge stiffened.

"He's in there, sir. He pointed to a small building near the main block of offices. I must get back. We're shifting our files in case the fire spreads."

"All right. You get off." Wesley turned to Julie. "Come with me."

They had to step over long lines of hose and through big oily puddles of water that swamped the concrete before they reached the building. They found Benton lying on the floor, his head pillowed on an overcoat, a blanket thrown over him. A policeman was sitting on an office chair near him and he stood up when Wesley came in.

"I'm Howard Wesley. May I speak to him?"

"Yes, sir. He's bad. Got burned about the legs. They're moving him as soon as the ambulance arrives."

Julie hung back as Wesley went over to the still figure.

"Hello, Hugh," Wesley said, and knelt down on one knee.

Benton opened his pale eyes.

"Who's that?" he asked feebly. "Wesley?"

"Yes. Are you badly hurt?"

Benton frowned. His big, white teeth bit down on his lip.

It was some moments before he spoke, then the words came out in a desperate little torrent of pain.

"I wish I hadn't done it. I wanted to get even with you, but as soon as the flames started I knew it was wrong. All that work. I tried to put it out but the flames got me in the end. I thought I was finished." He closed his eyes, added, "I wish I was."

"You'll be all right. We all do things we shouldn't do. Regretting them is the worst part. I regret things, too. I know how you feel. We're so sure of ourselves when we're doing wrong, and it's only afterwards we see how stupid we have been."

"Yes; that's right. I'm sorry, Wesley. I really am sorry."

"We had a bit of fun putting the place together, didn't we?" Wesley said and smiled. "It was as much your work as mine."

Benton stared up at the white, tired face.

"I didn't expect ever to hear that from you. It's good of you." A shudder ran through his thin body and he clenched his fists. "It feels as if my legs are still on fire."

"They'll fix you up all right. The ambulance won't be long."

"If it hadn't been for Blanche we might have got on together," Benton said. There was sweat on his face now.

"Yes . . . Blanche." Wesley stood up. "I want to take a last look at the lab. I thought I'd see you first."

"Something's happened to you," Benton said weakly. "I don't know what it is. Is it your eyes?"

"Don't worry about that. Don't worry about anything. So long, Hugh." Wesley leaned forward and held out his hand. "You'll be all right."

Benton gripped his hand.

"I wouldn't have believed it. I thought you would hate me like hell. I've been a fool. I'm sorry. I'm damned sorry."

"So long," Wesley said quietly, and withdrew his hand. He turned to the door. "Julie . . ."

She went to him.

The police officer looked at them curiously.

"Come with me, Julie."

There was a great crash outside as one of the walls of the laboratory collapsed. They stood for a moment in the smoke and the heat, side by side, looking at each other.

"Go back to the flat. The taxi is waiting," Wesley said. "See Dawson to-morrow and give him the statement. That'll get Gleb out of trouble. Be careful how you sell the furs. You should be all right. I hope you'll find happiness, Julie."

She stared at him, bewildered. It was difficult to hear his voice above the roar of the flames.

"What are you going to do?"

"Don't worry about me. Here's Gerridge. Gerridge, will you see Miss Holland to her taxi?"

Then Wesley walked rapidly away.

"Where's he going?" Julie cried, suddenly frightened. "Stop him! You mustn't let him go!"

She began to run after Wesley, but Gerridge pulled her back.

"It isn't safe!"

"Let go of me!" she cried, broke away and ran on.

Wesley had disappeared round the main office block. As she turned the corner of the building the heat hit her like a blow in the face.

Smoke and sparks swirled towards her, reaching out for her, driving her back.

Firemen, sheltered behind a nearby building, were playing water on to the roaring furnace. Suddenly one of them began shouting. He had seen Wesley walking towards the burning building. Two other firemen broke cover and began to run after him. They didn't get far. The scorching heat drove them back. Wesley didn't seem to notice the heat. He walked on, his hands in his trousers pockets, his head up. Julie watched him, her hands shielding her face, and she saw his clothes were smouldering, and suddenly narrow ribbons of flame flickered at his wrists and ankles. She hid her face, screaming.

Gerridge caught a glimpse of Wesley surrounded by flames. There was a great tearing, crunching noise and the blazing mass of wood and metal came down, blotting Wesley from sight. A long, brilliant tongue of flame shot up, marking the place where he had been.

V

With Wesley's letter authorizing her to take the furs and his statement for the police in her possession, Julie knew exactly what she was going to do. Harry's trial was due to begin the following day so it would be a last-minute rescue, the kind of thing you imagine can only happen on the films. Harry, she felt, would never forget that it was she who had saved him from the gallows. But before she rescued Harry she decided to get the furs. Then she would see Dawson. But first it was essential to get the furs. She would feel much more confident if she wore the Arctic fox. Dawson would be impressed and, after the familiar way he had treated her in the past, she was determined he should be impressed. Once he had read the statement he was bound to let her see Harry. She supposed Harry would have to stand his trial for the robbery, but she would tell him she would wait for him. He would be able to face his sentence bravely, she thought, if he knew she would be waiting at the prison gates when he came out. She became quite sentimental about that thought, and even cried a little, picturing Harry coming through the great prison gateway, shivering and cold, the snow (there had to be snow, she decided) powdering his thin overcoat, and she in her furs, snug in a big car, would take him tenderly in her arms.

Wesley had gone completely from her mind. His death meant a new life for her. She had had a bad hour or so after seeing him walk into the fire, but with her mind so much on Harry she quickly forgot him. It wasn't as if he ever liked her, she reasoned to herself. He had used her for his own ends and deserved no pity. It was maddening that she wouldn't have a steady income. She couldn't forgive him for cheating her at the last moment. But at least she had capital. She remembered Mrs. French had said the furs were worth thirty thousand pounds. That was as good as winning the Irish sweepstakes. You could do a lot with thirty thousand pounds. Then there was the jewellery. Diamonds were fetching a good price now. She should make quite a bit out of the jewellery. She decided she wouldn't tell Harry that Wesley had given her the jewellery, but she would tell him about the furs. She would keep the jewellery in a bank just in case something went wrong. She wasn't absolutely sure that Harry and she would hit it off together. A girl had to be careful, she told herself.

Wesley's statement to the police completely cleared Harry. Explaining how he had persuaded Blanche to return to the flat with him, he wrote that he had staged a quarrel about Benton in the taxi, and had hinted that Benton was having an affair with Julie. Blanche had risen to the bait, knowing Benton's weakness. Wesley had told her that Benton intended to see Julie as soon as Blanche and Wesley had left for the theatre. That was enough for Blanche. She stopped only long enough at the theatre for a drink, and then she and Wesley had returned to the flat by underground and had entered the building by the garage entrance. As Blanche was opening the front door, Wesley, remaining in the lift, had shot her and had thrown the gun into the hall. He had closed the lift gate a split second before the police arrived. It had been a near thing, but it had succeeded. The gun, he wrote, belonged to an American soldier, and he gave the man's name and service number. He had bought it from him a couple of years ago and he was sure there would be no difficulty in tracing it.

Julie hugged the envelope containing the statement to her as she walked along Piccadilly. It represented Harry's life. It was more than that: it was her future happiness as well. If she lost it nothing could save Harry. She clutched the envelope tightly, wondering if it wouldn't be safer to take a taxi to the Kensington police station at once, just in case something did happen to it. But the temptation to go to Park Way and put on the Arctic fox to impress Dawson proved too strong. She knew she would look wonderful in the fur: like a film star. So she slipped the envelope into her handbag and looked up and down Piccadilly for a taxi.

As she was being whisked along Park Lane towards Knightsbridge, she continued to build castles in the air. The furs were worth thirty thousand. Of course she wouldn't get quite that amount for them, but if she got twenty thousand, think what she could do with it! If Harry wanted to stay in London it would be marvellous fun to find a flat and furnish it so it would be ready for him when he was released. While she was planning the colour scheme of the bedroom the taxi drew up outside Park Way.

She was a little uneasy about meeting the hall porter, but she needn't have been. The hall porter had gone to lunch and his assistant hadn't yet taken over. She found the entrance hall deserted.

No one saw her as she unlocked the front door of Wesley's flat and entered. For a moment or so she stood just inside the hall, listening. It was odd to be back here, to see the faint brown stain still on the carpet and to smell once again Blanche's perfume that still clung persistently in the air.

She went quickly to Blanche's room, shut the door and snapped off the alarms. Then she opened the safe, turned off the light operating the photo-electric cell and stood for a moment admiring the furs. They were hers now; hers to do what she liked with. It was a moment of triumph. But she wasn't going to forget the jewellery. Up to this moment she hadn't had the chance of seeing Blanche's complete collection, and the thought sent a thrill through her. They, too, would realize a lot of money.

She pushed the furs aside and stepped into the safe, putting her handbag on the top of the steel cabinet containing the jewellery. Then she realized in dismay she had no idea how to open the cabinet. The smooth, highly-polished door of the cabinet had no apparent keyhole, but there was a small black knob set in the centre of the door. She touched it, frowning, then her fingers tightened on it and she pulled.

There was a sudden rush of escaping air and doors of the safe slammed shut.

They found her four days later. It was Dawson who suddenly wondered if she had gone to collect her spoils and had been trapped in the safe. When at last they opened the doors they found her lying on the floor with the white Arctic fox she had coveted so much covering her, and Wesley's statement clutched tightly in her hand.

They were too late to do anything for her but Harry was more fortunate. He got off with eighteen months. Oddly enough it was snowing when he came out, but there was no beautifully dressed young woman to meet him, only a Salvation Army lass who shook a self-denial collection box under his nose.

THE END

JAMES HADLEY CHASE BIBLIOGRAPHY
(1906-1985)

As James Hadley Chase

No Orchids for Miss Blandish
(1939; reprinted as The Villain
and the Virgin, 1948)

He Won't Need it Now (1939; as by
James L. Docherty)

The Dead Stay Dumb (1940;
reprinted as Kiss My Fist!, 1952)

Twelve Chinks and a Woman (1940;
reprinted as 12 Chinamen and a
Woman, 1950, and as The Doll's
Bad News, 1974)

Lady—Here's Your Wreath (1940;
as by Raymond Marshall)

Miss Callaghan Comes to Grief
(1941)

Get a Load of This (1941; stories)

Miss Shumway Waves a Wand
(1944)

Just the Way It Is (1944; as by
Raymond Marshall)

Eve (1945)

Blonde's Requiem (1945; as by
Raymond Marshall)*

More Deadly Than the Male (1946;
as by Ambrose Grant)

Make the Corpse Walk (1946; as by
Raymond Marshall)

No Business of Mine (1947; as by
Raymond Marshall)*

I'll Get You for This (1947)

Last Page (1947; play, filmed as
Man Bait)

The Flesh of the Orchid (1948)

You Never Know With Women
(1948)

Trusted Like a Fox (1948; as by
Raymond Marshall; reprinted as
Ruthless, 1955)

You're Lonely When You're Dead
(1949)

The Paw in the Bottle (1949; as by
Raymond Marshall)

Lay Her Among the Lilies (1950;
reprinted as Too Dangerous to be
Free, 1951)

Figure It Out for Yourself (1950;
reprinted as The Marijuana Mob,
1952)

Mallory (1950; as by Raymond
Marshall)

Strictly for Cash (1951)

In a Vain Shadow (1951; reprinted
as by Raymond Marshall as
Never Trust a Woman, 1957)

But a Short Time to Live (1951; as
by Raymond Marshall; reprinted
as The Pick-Up, 1955)

Why Pick on Me? (1951; as by
Raymond Marshall)

The Double Shuffle (1952)

The Fast Buck (1952)

The Wary Transgressor (1952; as by
Raymond Marshall)

I'll Bury My Dead (1953)

This Way for a Shroud (1953)

The Things Men Do (1953; as by
Raymond Marshall)

Tiger by the Tail (1954)

Safer Dead (1954; reprinted as
Dead Ringer, 1955)

The Sucker Punch (1954; as by
Raymond Marshall)

Mission to Venice (1954; as by
Raymond Marshall)

Mission to Siena (1955; as by
Raymond Marshall)

You've Got it Coming (1955)

There's Always a Price Tag (1956)

You Find Him—I'll Fix Him (1956;
as by Raymond Marshall)

The Guilty are Afraid (1957)

Not Safe to be Free (1958; reprinted
as The Case of the Strangled
Starlet, 1958)
Hit and Run (1958; as by Raymond
Marshal)
Shock Treatment (1959)
The World in My Pocket (1959)
What's Better Than Money (1960)
Come Easy—Go Easy (1960)
A Lotus for Miss Quon (1961)
Just Another Sucker (1961)
I Would Rather Stay Poor (1962)
A Coffin from Hong Kong (1952)
Tell it to the Birds (1963)
One Bright Summer Morning
(1963)
The Soft Centre (1964)
This is for Real (1965)
The Way the Cookie Crumbles
(1965)
You Have Yourself a Deal (1966)
Cade (1966)
Have This One on Me (1967)
Well Now, My Pretty (1967)
An Ear to the Ground (1968)
Believed Violent (1968)
The Whiff of Money (1969)
The Vulture is a Patient Bird (1969)
There's a Hippie on the Highway
(1970)
Like a Hole in the Head (1970)
An Ace Up My Sleeve (1971)
Want to Say Alive? (1971)
You're Dead Without Money (1972)
Just a Matter of Time (1972)
Knock, Knock! Who's There? (1973)
Have a Change of Scene (1973)
So What Happens to Me? (1974)
Goldfish Have No Hiding Place
(1974)
Believe This, You'll Believe
Anything (1975)
The Joker in the Pack (1975)
Do Me a Favour Drop Dead (1976)
My Laugh Comes Last (1977)

I Hold the Four Aces (1977)
Consider Yourself Dead (1978)
Can of Worms (1979)
You Must be Kidding (1979)
Try This One for Size (1980)
You Can Say That Again (1980)
Hand Me a Fig Leaf (1981)
Have a Nice Night (1982)
We'll Share a Double Funeral
(1982)
Not My Thing (1983)
Hit Them Where it Hurts (1984)

Omnibus Editions

Three of Spades (1974; includes The
Double Shuffle, Shock Treatment
and Tell It to the Birds)
Meet Mark Girland (1977; includes
This is for Real, You Have Yourself
a Deal and Have This One on Me)
Meet Helga Rolfe (1984; includes An
Ace Up My Sleeve, A Joker in the
Pack and I Hold Four Aces)

(All titles originally published as by
Raymond Marshall were reprinted
as by Chase except *)

As René Raymond
(reprinted as by Chase)

The Mirror in Room 22 (1946; story,
appeared in Slipstream: A Royal
Airforce Anthology edited by René
Raymond and David Langdon)

For further info on the works of
James Hadley Chase, visit
http://www.hadleychase.co.nr,
compiled by Dr. P. C. Sarkar. This is
the definitive Chase website.